Buried

A Dark High School Romance:
Heavy Hearts Book Three

Sarah Jane Duncan,
Sarah JD

2023 Cover by DAZED Designs

Many thanks to my Beta Readers: Alana, Anoesjka, Jocelyn & Melissa.
Many thanks to my proof reader: Jennifer

DEDICATION

For my husband, Shane.
My high school sweetheart.
My soul mate.
My best friend.
Together, we face this world, hand in
hand.
Forever!

Content Warning

This book contains adult themes and scenes which may cause trigger reactions for some readers, which include, but aren't limited to:
Abusive and sexually abusive situations, non-consensual acts, demeaning acts, emotional and physical blackmail, drug and alcohol use, and foul language.

PLEASE NOTE:
This book is written in Australian English, therefore some words will appear slightly different for my beloved US readers

HEAVY PLAYLIST

https://open.spotify.com/playlist/0M2Jg5lbhIMSh6p6
wzaOyB?si=616afced760641a6

Heavy (feat. Rain Paris) – Fame on Fire, Rain Paris
idontwannabeyouanymore – Billie Eilish
Take the Bullets Away (feat. Lacey Sturm) – We As Human, Lacey Sturm
King of the Clouds – Panic! At The Disco
Dance With The Devil – Breaking Benjamin
Animal I Have Become – Three Days Grace
Courtesy Call – Thousand Foot Krutch
Fire Uo The Night – New Medicine
Failure – Breaking Benjamin
Pain – Three Days Grace
Please – Staind
Comatose – Skillet
Down with the Sickness – Disturbed
lovely (with Khalid) – Billie Eilish, Khalid
Take This – Staind
when the party's over – Billie Eilish
Monster – Skillet
Never Too Late – Three Days Grace
Vermilion, Pt. 2 – Slipknot
So Far Away – Staind
listen before i go – Billie Eilish
Angels Fall – Breaking Benjamin
Without Me – Fame on Fire
Hero – Skillet
I Am Machine – Three Days Grace
Right Here – Staind
Snuff – Slipknot
Until The End – Breaking Benjamin
Awake and Alive – Skillet
Gone Forever – Three Days Grace

One

M y twelve-year-old neighbour looks so tiny on the bed.

Still.

Unmoving.

Frail.

The stark clinical light illuminating the room and the pale blue sheet covering her do nothing but make her look more lifeless.

No. Val.

Hot tears blur my vision as I step closer, and I bat them away, needing to see the evidence of what Mike did to her. I'm torturing myself, I know, but I need to see.

Images flash through my mind. Val tied to the chair. The fear in her eyes. Her near-naked innocent body marred with red marks that would have caused painful bruises.

I flinch, remembering the sickening crack of her skull as it hit the floor.

My gut twists, and I can't control my trembling as I remember how I'd wished death for Valarie so she wouldn't have to experience what Mike had in store for her.

"I hope they are happy tears."

Gasping, my hand flies to my chest as if to hold in my heart. Blinking rapidly through the haze of my tears, I take in Val's face and her drowsy eyes as they sluggishly blink back at me.

"Val," I whisper, and her dry, cracked lips tug up slightly at one corner.

"The one and only." Her voice is husky and sounds like it must feel like razor blades when she speaks.

I stare at her face, into her big dark eyes that are normally full of mischief and adventure. There's none of that now. The eyes that usually dance with life seem dull, almost dead. It's not because of her physical pain, either. I recognise the darkness swimming in her eyes. Whatever sweet innocence Val used to embody has vanished. In its place is a broken, hurting, lifeless shell.

"I-I'm so sorry, Val." Tears spring from my eyes again, and I try fiercely to control them but fail. "I never wanted you to get dragged into my drama. I'm so sorry."

Val shifts her head a little more in my direction, but the rest of her frail body lays still.

"This isn't your fault, Lexi."

I fall to my knees beside her bed and reach for her small hand peeking out of the blanket. Her grip tightens a fraction with my hand in hers, but it's weak.

"He will pay for this." I declare but Val shakes her head slowly.

"No. Please stay away from him, Lexi. He'll kill you if he gets his hands on you again. He'll do all of those horrible things he said he wanted to do." The quiver in her voice almost rips my heart out, and my mind goes back to that terrifying moment when I first found her.

I never imagined Mike would involve anyone else. I never imagined he would use an innocent twelve-year-old girl to lure me to him.

Is he still alive?

There was a gunshot. I heard it. Did someone shoot him? Is he dead?

"Get away from her!" The threatening demand comes from across the other side of the room and I squint, trying to see in the dark corner where someone stands from a chair.

"Mum, it's okay," Val slurs, turning her head in the direction of the voice.

Shen, Valarie's mum, comes into view then, and I swear I've never seen someone look more murderous than she does in this moment.

"I said, get away from her!" Shen's eyes are brimming with thunderous rage as she steps towards the bed, and I flinch back at the utter disgust oozing from her as she glares at me.

"I was just checking in on Val. Making sure she's okay." On shaky legs, I stand from the cold linoleum floor, gently and reluctantly slipping my hand from Val's.

"Okay?!" Shen snarls, "Okay?! Does she look okay?! Get the hell away from her. Now!" Shen bellows, darting to the end of the bed, her face as red as the rage in her eyes.

I glance back at Val, who looks uncomfortable at the confrontation between her mum and me. I don't want to make her feel uncomfortable. I just want to make sure she's okay.

"I'm sorry," I whisper, my voice quivering as tears burn my cheeks.

"This is all your fault! My baby nearly died because of you and your sick family!"

"Mum!" Val cries, trying to sit up, but the action causes her eyes to roll back in her head before she rapidly blinks.

Poor Val.

Is she going to faint?

Shen doesn't notice. She's too distracted with her eyes locked on me. I'm certain if she had magical abilities, her glare alone would snap my head from my neck, and she'd watch with satisfaction as it tumbles to the floor.

"Lexi!" My name floats to me from somewhere distant behind me, but I don't turn to it, not even when I hear a second and third voice calling my name, too. I'm stuck on the spot, my feet unable to move because I can't bring myself to obey Shen and leave Valarie.

"You should never have come home after the first time your brother attacked you! You should have stayed away, you silly girl!" Spittle flies from Shen's mouth, and she storms towards me, her hands balled into fists by her sides. "Get out!"

"Mum, no!" Val cries out when her mum raises her balled fist to me, causing me to stumble backward and trip on the wheeled foot of my IV pole.

"Lexi!"

I don't know if it's because my heart is breaking with each scold Shen dishes out, or if it's because I'm not very well myself and probably shouldn't have left my hospital bed, but when I trip, I can't seem to make my body react in time to help stop my fall.

As if time has slowed, the room tilts while noise and commotion sound around me, and the moment my feet fly out from under my body, I know my head is going to smash into the hard floor.

It's Karma. For getting Val involved in my bullshit. I deserve this. I just know it.

I squeeze my eyes shut when I see the ceiling move further away because I know the floor is about to deliver a blow...

But it never comes.

Instead, something warm and cushioned stops the hard impact, and an "Oomph" sounds as strong arms wrap around me.

"Shit, Lexi!" The deep bellow comes from Marcus before he pops into my line of sight a moment later, standing over me. "Fuck, are you okay?"

I don't answer him because my head feels fuzzy.

Is any of this even real?

"Lex?"

That voice.

My senses instantly stir at the sound of Ayden's voice in my ear, his hot breath feathering over my skin.

"Ayden?" It's a whisper, but I know it's heard when Marcus' face softens, and Ayden's firm body relaxes under me.

We must look ridiculous, me lying face up with Ayden behind me on the floor.

I don't care, though. I need his touch like I need oxygen to breathe.

"Get her out of my daughter's room!" Shen screeches, bringing me back to the present.

Whimpering draws my attention, and I see a very distraught little girl.

Valarie.

I should listen to her mum and leave her alone. She deserves better than this. Better than me.

Marcus shoots Shen a glare before leaning down to help me off Ayden, who somehow threw his body underneath mine to stop my fall. When Marcus pulls me upright, my world spins, and I stagger, nearly falling over. A moment later, I'm swept up in Ayden's arms, his scent wrapping around me like a safety blanket.

"Calm down, woman! We're taking her. There's no need to threaten to hit her! Seriously, what the fuck!" Marcus yells back at Shen as we move to leave Val's hospital room.

"I will do anything to protect my daughter, you animals!" The words of a true mother.

I can't fault Shen for caring about Val. She's like a lioness protecting her cub. You'd be an idiot to mess with her right now.

"Marcus." I need him to hear the plea in my tone. I want him to leave Shen alone. *We* are the intruders in this scenario, and she is just trying to protect her daughter.

Marcus grunts at me, following behind Ayden as he carries me out the door, and I realise a moment later that Marcus must be pushing my IV pole, the annoying squeak of the wheel drawing my attention as I attempt to control my tears.

The murmur of voices floats to me as we put distance between us and my twelve-year-old neighbour.

Rounding the corner, confusion creases my brow because I can't remember walking up this corridor that leads to Val's room. I don't even remember how I got to her room or where I came from in the first place.

Glancing down at my body, which is happily cradled in Ayden's arms, I confirm that I'm wearing a hospital gown the same shade of blue as Valarie was wearing. That's when I notice the cool chill on my back, and I start to squirm.

"What's wrong, beautiful?" Ayden glances down, tightening his grip on me.

My eyes dart to his and momentarily drown in their blue intensity before the cool chill hits me again.

"I think my arse is hanging out," I whisper, hoping he understands.

A slow grin spreads across Ayden's face, one of his dimples caving in slightly as his eyes soften.

"Baby, your arse has been hanging out of that gown for a couple of days. You didn't seem too worried about it when you flashed the nurse a full moon last night." Ayden chuckles.

"What!" I screech, trying to reach under Ayden's hold to pull the gown together.

"Or yesterday morning when you shook your arse at Officer Zimora when he popped in to see you," Marcus adds and joins Ayden, laughing at my expense.

"You're lying." I hiss, and Ayden shakes his head.

"What are they lying about?" Simon's voice draws my attention as we enter a different hospital room, and I glance around to see Simon, Shaun, Jared, and Garrett filling the small space.

"She thinks we're lying about her flashing her arse to the nurse last night." Ayden offers, and they all grin.

"Did you tell her about her arse shake at Officer Zimora? Fuck, that was hilarious." Shaun chuckles, and I pale.

"What the fuck is going on?" I screech, more than confused now.

Why don't I remember?

Leaning down, Ayden places my feet on the ground, and I move swiftly to pull the gown together at the back. I'm not quick enough, though, because Ayden's hand swipes out to give my knicker-covered arse a little slap before I manage to draw the fabric closed.

"Who wants to tell her this time?" Marcus asks the guys, and five smug grins are shared before each of them shrug.

"What do you mean, *who wants to tell me this time*?" I squeak. "Will someone tell me what is going on? And how did I end up in Val's room?"

Ayden gently steers me to the bed, urging me to sit on the side. I let him lead me, happy his hands are on me, and I shuffle my butt onto the mattress a little before swiping at the tears that are yet to dry on my cheeks.

"So, you remember being in Val's room just now?" Ayden asks, standing before me, his face neutral, but his eyes give away his concern.

I nod, confused, and Ayden turns to the others.

"She remembers more now. Maybe it's over?"

"Please. Will someone tell me what's going on? What's over?" I plead, feeling my face burn in frustration.

Swinging back to me, Ayden leans down to take my hands in his. His touch instantly calms me, and my spine relaxes with the warmth that spreads through my body from the simple act.

"What's the last thing you remember before being in Val's room?" he asks, looking nervous.

My brows pull together as I search my mind for my memories. There's a lot of haze in my head, but I think over things for a moment, and my eyes widen when a vivid memory seizes my heart.

"Muz," I whisper as I look at the grim faces of my friends. "And Mike. There was a gunshot. Did Mike get shot?"

"No." Ayden's voice draws my attention back to him.

I stare at him for a moment as another possibility enters my thoughts and my lower lip starts to tremble.

"Muz?"

Offering me a look filled with sympathy, Ayden nods. "Muz got shot. Mike twisted Muz's hold on the gun, and the bullet lodged in Muz's liver."

I freeze. Time slows, and for a moment, all I can hear is the thud of my heart.

When Ayden says nothing else, my stomach sinks.

"I-is Muz alive?"

This time he offers me a sympathetic smile and nods. "For now. But it doesn't look good, Lex. He already has cirrhosis, and there were complications during the surgery to remove the bullet. His liver is failing, and because he's dependent on drugs and alcohol, he isn't a contender for a transplant."

I try to pull my hands from Ayden's grip, but he doesn't let me, holding on tight, knowing me too well.

I'm ready to run.

"Lex. The important thing is that you're okay. Val is okay. The police will catch Mike, eventually. They've increased their search for him. It won't be long until they catch him."

I know Ayden means well, but his words don't set my mind at ease. Mike has somehow evaded the cops so far. He'd been sneaking into my house and stealing my stuff, and still, the police never even had a report of him being seen. It feels like the cops will never catch my brother.

"Val isn't okay, Ayden," I whisper, my bottom lip practically seizing as more tears roll down my cheeks. "She may be alive, but she'll never be the same. All because of me."

"Not because of you." Jared butts in before Ayden responds, and he moves to sit next to me on the bed. "All of this is because of that sick fuck, Mike. You've done nothing wrong." Jared's intensity takes me back to when we were kids. If anyone dared to bully me, he was always getting in their faces and scaring them off.

"Mike may be the one that dished out the trauma, but Val was there because of me." I remind him. "Because she'd tried to protect me. It's my fault. All of it. Val, Muz, they are both suffering now because of me."

Jared sighs and shakes his head giving my knee a squeeze. "You're wrong about this, Six. I know how stubborn you are. I know that trying to convince you otherwise is pointless. So, let's agree to disagree." His blue eyes soften, and he nudges me with his shoulder.

He's right about my stubbornness. He's had to deal with it for a long time. I don't know why he puts up with it.

Nodding, I offer Jared a small smile before returning my eyes to Ayden. He's watching my exchange with Jared closely. There's a bit of jealousy in his eyes, but he says nothing. He just regards me for a moment before speaking again.

"Do you remember everything that happened at Valarie's house with Mike?"

"Yes," I whisper, fighting back tears.

"But nothing afterwards?" Ayden asks, stroking his thumb over the back of my hand.

"No, not until I was standing in Val's hospital room. I thought she was dead when I first walked in there."

"What the fuck happened, Simon?" Jared snaps from beside me. "You were meant to be keeping an eye on Lexi."

I glance at Simon, who screws his face up, his hazel eyes flaring.

"I had to take a piss. How was I meant to know she'd go walkabout?" He spits back, running his hand through his long, ashy hair when it falls over his eyes.

He looks more dishevelled than usual. Actually, all the guys do as I take a moment to study each of them.

Marcus' dark hair is sticking up all over the place like he's had a mad sex session. Shaun's normally slick hair falls flat and lifeless, and while I can't see Garrett's brown waves because they are hidden under a blue cap, I can see his blue-grey eyes, which are framed in dark circles, giving away how tired he is.

"You should have called one of us to come back, Hastings," Jared scolds. "Lexi's been trying to escape this room ever since she woke up."

Simon glares in return looking less like his playful self. "I thought she was fucking asleep!"

"Uh-guys?" I interrupt, hating that they are snapping at each other because of me. "You know I'm sitting right here, right? And what do you mean I've been trying to escape ever since I woke up? How long have I been here? And where is *here*?"

I try to glance around the room, but the movement sends slicing pain through my head, and I rip my hand from Ayden's hold to palm my forehead with a groan.

"You should lie down, Lex." Ayden urges, but I shake my head, adding to the pain even more.

"Answers first." I choke out past the pain, and Ayden slides his hands to my shoulders.

"Lay down, beautiful. I'll answer your questions."

I can't even make myself look up into those ocean eyes I enjoy drowning in because the pain is so bad, so I do as he suggests and lie down. Jared must have moved off the bed because there's suddenly room for me to stretch out, and I instantly feel better, sinking my head into the pillow.

Beside me, the bed dips as Ayden takes a seat, and when I peek around the room, I watch as the guys take seats, which they have clearly been living on for a while.

"Today is Friday. You were rushed here on Wednesday night after the attack," Ayden explains. "And *here* is Melbourne. The Royal Southern Cross Hospital. You have a concussion which has caused short-term memory loss, and for the last day since you woke up, you keep forgetting every time we tell you this information."

I'm quiet for a moment while I take that in and rake my eyes over Ayden's face. His stubble is longer and thicker, and I can't help but wonder what it feels like. Reaching out, I cup his jaw, feeling the tickle of his stubble which somehow sends butterflies dancing around inside me.

Grinning down at me, Ayden places his hand over mine as he tilts his head in my hold.

"Uh... Should we leave? If she's about to take her clothes off again, we should probably bail." Garrett's words cause me to frown.

"I didn't... Did I?" I ask Ayden, who is still staring down into my eyes.

"Once or twice." He grins, and I pull my hand from his smug face to cover my own, the red flush heating my cheeks.

"Speak for yourself, Cole. I quite enjoy seeing Lexi naked." Simon adds, and I peek through my fingers to see Ayden's reaction.

To my surprise, he doesn't react the way I think he will. Apart from the way he bites the inside of his cheek, probably trying to hold back his anger, he turns to look at Simon with amusement.

"Have you forgotten what I said I'd do to you if you try to see her naked again, Hastings?" Ayden reminds Simon, unnerving him.

"Dude. Joking." Simon holds his hands up. "You know I'd never actually look. I already have her body memorised in my spank bank."

Before Simon even finishes his sentence, I knew what he was going to say, so I grip Ayden's shoulders before he can fly across the room to dish out his wrath on Simon.

"Fuck you, Hastings. You'd better keep looking over your shoulder, arsehole!" Ayden spits, and I tighten my hold on him, gaining his attention.

"He's just messing with you." I smile at Ayden. "Ignore his bullshit."

"Hey!" Simon complains, and I poke my tongue out at him, causing male laughter to fill the room. Ayden even laughs, although I can tell he's trying to hold back. He doesn't want Simon to think it's okay to talk that way about me.

While I don't really mind because it's Simon and I'm used to it, if the roles were reversed and some bitch said that about Ayden, I would've gone psycho on her arse.

Unfortunately, laughing causes my head to hurt, reminding me why I'm here in this hospital.

"Is Muz in this hospital too?" I ask, effectively silencing the guys.

Ayden shakes his head. "No. He's across the city at Melbourne Public."

"So… Is he going to live?" My bottom lip quivers again as I speak, and I bite it to make it stop, but it doesn't help. That's when tears start to flow again.

Ayden remains silent, and I think he's not going to answer, but then I see his Adam's apple bob before opening his mouth and shaking his head. "I'm not sure, Lex. It doesn't look good."

Two

After Ayden delivers the news about how serious Muz's condition is, I crumble, drowning in sobs that hurt so deep, I just want someone to reach inside my chest and rip out my heart. The pain is unbearable and something I've endured so much lately that I'm not sure I can handle the infliction anymore.

My first encounter with Muz was, well, terrifying. I still see the barrel of the gun pointed at me as he forced Ayden to snort whatever the white powder was. Thinking about that night makes my insides twist, and sickness rolls my stomach. It wasn't long ago that I wanted to ram that gun down Muz's throat, but somehow, along the way, I've grown a soft spot for him.

He might act tough and threatening, but I see past the armour he wears to keep people at bay and how he manipulates them to follow his commands. He might be a massive prick, but he protected me when I found my dad in my house, and he risked his life to save Valarie and me from Mike. That has to mean there's goodness in him, right?

At some point through all my tears, the guys join Ayden on my bed, surrounding me, so I don't feel so alone. With their eyes fixed on me as I lay in the hospital bed, I squirm under their scrutiny, partially hating their eyes taking in everything I do, and partially thanking a god I don't believe in for bringing them into my life.

"You guys are my family." My voice is soft as I bat away my tears. "I would never have gotten through any of this without each of you by my side."

"We're your family? Like, your brothers?" Simon smirks, his hazel eyes filled with mischief.

"Brothers don't like seeing their sisters naked, Hastings." Marcus spits but then realises what he said, his brown eyes shooting to me in panic.

"It's okay, Marcus. Brothers aren't meant to like seeing their sister naked. Mike is a sick, twisted fuck, and I'll never think of him as my brother. A brother would never do what he did to me. A brother would protect his sister. That's why, to me, you are all my brothers."

Marcus' dark eyes soften in relief, and he offers me a small smile, which I return.

"Except for Ayden. He's not your brother." Simon adds, wagging his brows, and I nod.

"Ayden definitely is *not* my brother." I smile as Ayden lifts my hand to his lips and presses a warm kiss to the back.

As usual, my cheeks flush, and Ayden grins knowingly. Embarrassed that everyone probably saw my reaction to him, my eyes dart to the guys, who are looking everywhere else but at me... except for Jared. His eyes haven't left me. Not once.

"Um, yeah, so that's okay, right? That I call *you* my family?" I say, needing to end the brief awkwardness.

"I already have two sisters. What's another one?" Garrett smiles. "Besides, my sisters love you. They've been bugging me every hour to know if you're okay."

"Really?" I smile, remembering how I'd helped his sisters with their homework when I went to Garrett's for dinner last week.

"Yep. Is it okay if I take a selfie with you and send it to them?" Garrett asks, almost shyly, and I nod before glancing at Ayden.

I don't miss the tick in his jaw. His jealousy is adorable.

Sliding off the end of the bed, Garrett nudges Simon away, who had taken a seat closest to me, to sit opposite Ayden on top of the covers. Surprisingly Simon doesn't complain in typical Simon fashion, instead opting to simply poke his tongue out at Garrett instead.

Shuffling on the bed to get into position, I smile past my cringe at the screen when Garrett holds out his phone in front of us. I quickly tug some of my wavy strands over the side of my face in an attempt to hide some of the bruising, and Garrett snaps the photo before sending it to his sisters' group chat. They instantly respond, and he shows me his screen as it fills with *Yays* and *Hi Lexi's*, and *I'm glad you're okay's*.

Meanwhile, I can't get over what I saw when Garrett took the picture. I look like death itself. Besides the bruising that I've become accustomed to on my face, I look like something off the Walking Dead.

I try not to dwell on it too much or the fact that people actually have to look at me like this, pale as a ghost with red and purple bruising. Is my poor face ever going to catch a break? I'll be lucky if I'm not left with scars.

"I've always wanted a little sister," Shaun butts in, breaking my self-dwelling, and Garrett takes the hint to move back to where he was sitting.

"I'm not your little sister, Shaun. I'm older than you, remember?"

"Semantics." Shaun, the Spanish Casanova of our group, shrugs as his steel-grey eyes dance with humour.

All I can do is shake my head and grin back at him.

"You're definitely *my* little sister then because I'm older than you," Marcus adds, shooting a smug look at Shaun.

"Does this mean I have to call these dickheads my brothers?" Simon asks. "Because if that's the case, I'm not sure I can accept you as my sister Lexi." His words earn him a punch in the arm from Shaun, which just makes them both laugh.

I love these guys.

"How about you, Jared? You happy to think of Lexi as your sister?" Ayden's tone is clipped, and I don't miss the hidden challenge he's throwing Jared, who remains quiet for a moment, his eyes still locked on me.

Then he shrugs. "You know you've always meant more to me than just a friend, Lex. Sister sounds about right." Jared offers me a smile, but it doesn't reach his eyes.

I want to fix whatever is eating at him, but I don't know how, so I deflect and pretend everything is fine.

"Okay, brother Jared." Smirking, I shuffle down under the blankets a little more, tiredness weighing me down with every passing minute.

"Don't call me that. It makes me sound like a monk." Jared complains, the spark in his blue eyes getting a little brighter.

"You're not a monk. You're a man whore." Simon laughs, the action nearly making him tumble off the bed.

"You're the man whore, Hastings." Jared bites back, glaring daggers at Simon's head. "I sure as shit wasn't the one screwing the red-headed nurse, who's old enough to be your mum, out in the parking lot last night."

"What?" I squeak.

"Hey, don't knock it until you've tried it," Simon suggests, and the guys snicker.

"You're kidding, Simon? You didn't do that. Tell me you didn't do that?" In shock, I sit up and let the sheets fall from me a little, sending goosebumps up my arms.

Simon shrugs. "I might have done it. A man has needs you know, Lexi?"

"You're not a man, Simon," Jared says flatly, which causes Simon to shoot daggers his way.

"Weren't you guys leaving?" Ayden pipes up, silencing the banter that I've grown to love.

"Yep, we were." Marcus stands from the bed and steps up to me before leaning down to place a kiss on my forehead. "You should get some rest, Lexi."

I nod as he pulls back, and then one by one, each of the guys gives me a hug or a forehead kiss as they say their goodbyes and leave the small hospital room.

Alone at last, Ayden lays down next to me, and I shuffle over in the bed to make room for him as we come face to face, sharing the same pillow.

"Lex. I know you probably don't want to talk about it, but it's killing me not knowing what happened before I got to you at Valarie's house. Will you tell me?"

I stay silent, taking in his face and the crease between his dark brows as he frowns. Needing to touch him any way I can, I slip my arm out of the blanket and lift my fingers to the crease, slowly gliding the pads of my fingers over it until it relaxes. His eyes fall shut, almost as if my touch has given him some sort of relief, and he sucks in a deep breath.

I totally get it. I feel the same way when he touches me. It's like his touch brings me peace, safety, and security. It's home for me.

Part of me doesn't want to give him the details of what happened at Valarie's house, but another part of me wants him to know all there is about me. I want him to know me like he knows no one else, and I want the same in return.

"I'll make a deal with you." I rasp out, my voice a little scratchy. "I'll tell you what happened at Val's house, if you tell me what happened after you got there and everything else up until today when I stopped being weird."

Ayden chuckles. "You were suffering a severe concussion and short-term memory loss, Lexi. You weren't weird."

My brows shoot up. "I shook my arse at Officer Zimora. I'd call that weird."

Ayden chuckles, linking his fingers with mine before turning serious.

"I was so fucking scared, Lex. I thought I'd lost you after I just got you back. I've never felt fear like that before." A glassy film sheens over Ayden's eyes before he shuts them quickly to hide his reaction.

"Don't hide from me," I whisper, and those stormy ocean eyes slowly open, peering at me through thick, dark lashes.

"I'm sorry. I'm acting like a fucking wuss."

I shake my head. "No, you're not. Don't say that. I want to see all the parts of you, remember? Good and bad. Strong and weak. Happy and sad."

His intense eyes roam my face, and his lips tug up on one side. "I want the same from you, beautiful."

The endearment sends warmth through me, reminding me of how much power he has over my body and my mind. It's not the controlling kind of power like Mike forces on me. It's the addictive power that makes me want to give myself to Ayden. I'm helpless not to lean forward and taste his lips, desperate for the contact. Before our lips connect, my self-conscious mind rears up. Have I even brushed my teeth lately? Mortified, I pull back and slap my hand over my mouth.

Ayden's eyes shoot open, and he frowns. "Lex? What's wrong?"

"When was the last time I brushed my teeth?" I murmur from behind my hand.

Ayden's frown disappears before he chuckles, his smile reaching his dimples.

"This morning. I brought you some toiletries from the supermarket down the road. You've kept up with your daily hygiene, don't worry."

"I have?" I ask, still hiding my mouth behind my hand.

Again, Ayden chuckles and reaches out to draw my hand away. "Yes, you have. There may have been some arse shaking involved, but you've remained clean."

"Smart arse." I feign anger and give Ayden's shoulder a shove before he grabs my hand and re-links our fingers.

"I will always look after you, Lexi. Make no mistake about that." All the humour vanishes from his face, and his eyes do their thing, trying to glimpse into my soul.

I believe his words.

A few weeks ago, I wouldn't have, though. I didn't want to let myself believe I deserved someone like Ayden. Now I know I can't fight the pull we have on each other. This isn't some high school crush. This is real. This is something that will last.

That is, if I can stay alive for long enough.

"I know," I whisper in response, and his straight white teeth make another appearance as he smiles again.

"Good. Now tell me what happened. And don't leave anything out, no matter how I react." Ayden urges, and my nerves kick in.

"Are you sure?" I ask, and when he nods, I take a deep breath before diving into my memories.

"The front door of Val's house was wide open, so I went in. The house was quiet. I remember looking around quickly as I walked to the back of her house. I could hear her crying, and I didn't stop to think about the danger I might be in. I just had to get to her. It's dumb now when I think about it. Why the fuck would I go inside alone?" I shake my head at my stupidity.

"Because you care about Val. You wanted to help her." Ayden's thumb runs up the side of mine as we keep our fingers locked together.

"I guess." I shrug. "I found Val in the kitchen, tied to a chair. She... she only had on a pair of knickers." My lip quivers as I recall her small, innocent body bound naked to the chair. "I ran to her. I pulled the fabric he used to gag her out of her mouth." I squint, trying to remember correctly, and then nod. "Yep. I pulled it free right before Mike ripped me back by my hair."

Ayden's sharp intake of air distracts me from my memory, and I see his struggle to control his emotions.

I haven't even begun to get to the bad stuff yet. Maybe this is a bad idea?

"Keep going," he urges quietly.

My eyes dance between his for a few beats as I consider if I should tell him the rest. I can see how much he wants to know, *needs* to know. So, I continue.

"I think I hit the island bench from the force when he ripped me away from Val. Things get fuzzy after that. I must have hit my head. I can't remember where it hurt. All over, I think. I remember Mike's face, though, and the scratches down his cheek caused by fingernails. Val's fingernails." Tears blur my vision, and nausea rolls through me again. "Fuck, Ayden, I don't know what he did to her before I got there, but I *do* know she fought back, hard. That poor little thing. She must have been terrified."

I can't control the tears now. I can deal with the shit Mike does to me, but not Val. She was a sweet, innocent twelve-year-old girl that wanted to be a spy. Now she has to deal with memories that will likely haunt her forever.

Ayden slips his hands from mine and uses his thumbs to wipe away the tears as they fall before pulling me into the crook of his neck and wrapping me in his arms.

"Shhhh," he whispers. "You got to her, Lexi. You stopped things from getting worse. Val's a strong little girl. She'll get through this."

I want to believe him, but I can't. I saw it myself earlier when I was in her room. The Valarie I used to know is gone. She will never be the same, and she may never get over this.

Knowing Ayden's scent will work its magic and calm me down, I suck in a slow breath and enjoy the instant comfort it brings. It's crazy how a smell can do that.

When I get control of my tears again, I continue.

"Mike told me we had unfinished business, and that Val was there to watch what he does to me, so she knew what was to come for her. Then he said Val and I would swap places, and I would watch him break her in. I kind of went crazy after he said that." My brows pull together, recalling what happened.

"How so?" Ayden asks quietly, pulling me back from the crook of his neck so he can see my face again.

"Well, instead of running from him, I ran at him. I turned into some sort of crazed animal and leapt on him before head-butting him." My eyes widen as the memory induces pain in the front of my skull.

"Holy shit, really?" Ayden's voice rises in pitch.

I nod. "What the fuck was I thinking? I practically knocked the both of us out, and that's when he fell back and knocked Val's chair over, which is when she hit her head and passed out." I gag and close my eyes in an attempt to control my breathing. "The... the sound of her head hitting the floor..." My eyes fly open, and I shift back to meet Ayden's concerned gaze. "I'll never forget that sickening sound."

Tears stream down the side of my face again, coming to rest in a wet patch on the pillow Ayden and I share. "The fight between Mike and me was on after that. He choked me, I clawed at him, and then punched him in the dick." I grin. "That was kind of satisfying."

Ayden smiles. "Good girl." His warm lips kiss my forehead before he pulls back to take me in.

"I managed to get a knife before Mike threw me into the fridge, and when he came at me, I sliced his arm open."

"That must have been why they found his blood at the scene. They said there was a fair bit of his blood. They found it in Val's backyard and on her back fence. They think he fled over it right before the cops got there." Ayden frowns as he puts the pieces together. "What happened after you cut his arm?"

"Well, he got even more pissed and told me he was going to..." I don't want to say the words that I hear as clear as day in my head, and I squeeze my eyes tight. When I feel Ayden's hand stroke my arm, I quickly force the words out. "He said he was going to fuck every hole I have and then use the knife to carve new holes and fuck them until I've been dead for hours, and by the time anyone finds me, they won't recognise me."

I'll never forget those words and how he spoke them with so much conviction.

A growl snaps me out of my memory, and my eyes shoot open to see Ayden's face turning red.

Bright red.

"I'll fucking kill him if he comes anywhere near you ever again."

"No," I whisper. "You stay away from him, Ayden. I don't want him to hurt you."

"I don't want him to hurt *you* either, Lex. I won't hesitate to protect you, even if it kills me."

"That's what I'm afraid of." I choke out. "I can't do this without you, Ayden, so don't you dare put yourself in harm's way. I need you in my life."

With his eyes trained on my lips, he leans forward but abruptly stops before his lips reach mine. He's unsure if he should kiss me, but I need him desperately to touch me with the love he has and remove any hate that has touched my body, so I decide for him and close the distance.

Warm lips crash into mine, and I close my eyes, letting myself feel the full force of Ayden's kiss. Our tongues clash with need, and I reach up, clasping my hands into his hair as he cups my face.

"I need you, too," Ayden whispers against my lips as we kiss. "So much it hurts."

Our kiss deepens like we're starved for each other, and I can't seem to get close enough. This kiss isn't about sex and needing to scratch an itch. This kiss is so much more than that.

It's like Ayden is the blood that pumps through my veins, like the heart that thumps in my chest. It's like we're a part of each other, and we need this connection to live, and together we feed each other life.

Eventually, Ayden pulls back, feathering gentle pecks over my swollen lips before resting his forehead against mine.

"Fuck, Lex. I'm never leaving your side again. I don't know what the olds will think about that, but I don't fucking care. Wherever you go, I'm going too."

I grin. "I mean, a girl needs some alone time sometimes. You know, to pee and stuff."

"You don't remember that either, do you?" Ayden's grin surpasses mine, and I instantly panic.

"What do you mean? Remember what?"

"You wouldn't let the nurses help you to the toilet and shower. You insisted I was your toilet bitch." Ayden chuckles, and my eyes widen in horror.

"You're fucking with me, right?"

He shakes his head. "Nope."

"Oh, my god!" I pull back and hide behind my hand, trying to ignore the sexy gravel of his chuckle. "Please tell me it was just to pee?"

Warm lips kiss my temple. "Yes, beautiful. Only number ones."

"I am not okay with this. That... that... that's too much." I drag my hands from my face and glare at Ayden.

"Don't worry. You made me turn and face the door and whistle while you did the deed. Each time you had me whistle a different song until you decided 'Build Me Up Buttercup' was your go-to peeing song." He shoots me a wicked grin, and I can't help but return it.

"Why are you still here with me? Clearly, I'm loco."

Ayden draws his eyes from mine, glancing up at my hairline before he strokes a blonde wave off my forehead, still grinning.

"Well, Lexi, I like your kind of crazy. I like it a hell of a lot."

"You should've run when you had the chance," I whisper as he strokes a finger down the side of my face to trace over my lips.

"If I'm running, Lexi, rest assured it will be running *to* you, not away from you."

"Good."

When my lips part to speak again, he slides the tip of his finger in my mouth, and I let my tongue briefly taste him before my teeth clamp gently around his finger, and he pulls it free. "Stop distracting me, Ayden. I haven't finished telling you the bad stuff yet, but if you'd rather skip the rest, then I'm down with that."

"Nice try." He grins, settling back. "I'm sorry, I get side-tracked around you. Please continue."

"I don't know if I want to. It will ruin this moment we just shared."

"The moments we share are more powerful than the painful memories we carry. Speaking about those painful memories will help us loosen the grip they have on us."

My brows hitch. "Wow. That's deep."

He grins. "I'm a deep type of guy."

I smile but squint at the same time, shaking my head, causing him to chuckle.

"Okay, I'll admit that the counsellor at rehab said it to me once. It stuck with me, and I didn't really understand it until now."

"So, it's about making new memories, right?" I refer to what we spoke about last week, and Ayden nods.

"Yep, and powerful moments. We can get through this, Lex."

I believe his words. We both carry painful memories, and even though I've been reluctant to open up in the past, when I have, I've felt lighter for it.

Taking a deep breath, I nod before I let myself fall back into the memory of my brother.

"He punched me in the head," I practically whisper. "He hit me so hard that I blacked out. When I woke up, he was...." I suck in another breath, needing to calm my nerves as I remember. "He was pulling my pants off. I pretended I was still unconscious so I could take him by surprise, but when he put his hands on... on..."

I shake my head, unable to hold back my cringe.

"He touched you? Down there?" Ayden whispers slowly. Nervously.

I can't look at him. I don't want to see the pain in his eyes, so I squeeze mine tight and nod. "I gave away that I was awake by making a noise, and he dug his fingers into my skin, so I lurched up and bit into his cheek. It was disgusting, but it worked to get him off me before he threw me across the room, and I landed on the other side of the bench next to Val on the floor. He was on me so fast, spitting in my face and then slamming my head back against the tile floor." My eyes pop open, and my brows draw together as I recall what happened next. "I couldn't speak after that. My body wouldn't obey my mind. That was the moment I thought I was going to die, that I'd never see you again." Tears spring free. "The rest is a bit of a blur. He was strangling me, but then he was gone. I could hear things smashing around me and then someone calling my name. At first, I couldn't place the voice, but then a body fell beside me, and I saw it was Muz. He was fighting Mike and screaming something at me." I close my eyes as the fear I felt engulfs me. "Mike was punching him. There was so much blood." I open my eyes again and look into Ayden's concerned gaze. "Muz was fighting back just as hard, but I couldn't stay awake, and the last thing I remember is hearing a gunshot."

I hadn't realised it until now, but Ayden's body is trembling next to mine.

"I need to see him, Ayden. I need to see Muz and thank him for saving Valarie and me."

Ayden frowns. "I don't know if that's a good idea, Lex. He's in pretty bad shape."

"Please, Ayden. I need to see him."

Ocean eyes dance between my own as he studies me before sighing. "Okay, I'll speak with my dad and see what we can arrange."

It's only then that I feel my body relax. "Thank you," I whisper before I feel a kiss on the top of my head as I snuggle up to Ayden's chest, letting the exhaustion pull me into a deep sleep.

Three

The sound of commotion and yelling pulls me from sleep, and it takes me a moment to figure out where the hell I am. Movement on the bed behind me draws my attention, and I look up to find Ayden climbing off, his dark hair a little messed from sleep.

"What's going on?" I croak, my voice raspy from not being used.

The hospital room is dark, but the shadows of five other bodies slowly come to life, sitting up from the positions on the chairs they must have taken through the night.

Have all the guys been sleeping here every night?

"Is that Rhys?" Marcus stands from the chair he'd occupied and stretches his neck from side to side.

"Bitch, you ain't going in there!"

"Yep, that's her," Jared mumbles, right before Ayden reaches the door and swings it open.

"How about you let Lexi decide if she wants to see me or not?" Abbey hisses back at Rhys, who I can see has her arms and legs spread wide to stop Abbey from entering.

Ayden swings back to me with raised brows.

He's surprised to see Abbey here. Shit, *I'm* surprised to see Abbey here.

"Rhys." I try to call out, but it comes out crackly. It doesn't matter though, Rhys hears and jumps around to face me with Rhys style energy, a smile of surprise on her face.

"Girl! You're back!" Jumping up and down, Rhys claps before bounding into the room like an excited puppy.

"Ah... Yeah. How could you tell?" I'd only said one word to her. Her name. How can she tell from that one word that I'm not still weird Lexi, who shook her arse at everyone?

Throwing her head back, Rhys laughs, holding her middle before turning back to Ayden. "You didn't tell her what she was calling me?"

Ayden grins and shakes his head. "Nah, haven't had a chance to fill her in with all the details yet."

"Oh my god, what was I calling you?"

Rhys spins to face me again. her grin from ear to ear. "My name is, according to you, Georgie Porgie."

I drop my head into my hands. "I am such a loser." I scold myself.

I obviously took Rhys' last name, George, and created Georgie Porgie. How fucking embarrassing.

Laughing, Rhys pops her butt on the side of my bed. "Actually, I thought that's the coolest you've been. Besides the day in the girls' bathroom at school when you shoved wet toilet paper down Tasha's throat. I had such a lady boner for you that day."

Chuckles fill the room, but I ignore the guys, remembering that only moments ago, Rhys was trying to stop Abbey from coming in. Leaning to the side, I glance past Rhys to see my ex-best friend standing awkwardly in the doorway.

Abbey typically wears her white-blonde hair in braids, but today it's all out and the messiest I've ever seen it. Her golden-brown eyes brim with worry as she glances back at me, waiting for me to say something.

"Ah, guys? Can you give Abbey and me a few minutes, please?" I ask without taking my eyes from Abbey's.

The room is silent for a moment with no one moving before Ayden speaks. "Come on, you heard Lex. Everyone out."

Rhys pouts in front of me. "But I just got here."

"I'll give you cuddles soon." I smile at my new best friend, and her dark lips spread wide.

"You'd better. I want better cuddles than you give Ayden. Just because he gives you orgasms doesn't mean he should get better cuddles than me."

My laugh is joined by Ayden's, and I shake my head. "Get out of here, girl."

Sliding off the bed, Rhys rushes forward to kiss my cheek before turning and following the guys out the door. I don't miss how she gets in Abbey's face as she passes her, growling like a feral dog. Meanwhile, Abbey flinches back, looking at Rhys like she has two heads.

Ayden stays behind and raises a brow in silent question, but I shake my head. He doesn't need to be here. Abbey is not a threat to me.

"I'll be right outside the door, okay, beautiful?" Ayden gives me one of his winks as he walks out, and Abbey steps into the room, gently closing the door behind her. She stands by it for a moment, her brown eyes staring at me while her hands clench into fists by her sides, turning her knuckles white. Then she bursts into tears and rushes forward, throwing her arms around my neck.

"I'm so sorry, Lexi," she cries.

I still for a moment, feeling torn about how to react. This is a different version of Abbey from the last time I saw her. But it's still Abbey.

My Abbey.

I relax and wrap my arms around her and she sinks into my embrace, her tears falling faster. It's nearly been three weeks since I found out Abbey was ghosting me, and although she betrayed me in the worst possible way, my love for her is stronger than the anger I have towards her.

Don't get me wrong, I'm pissed. But I still love her, even if I've tried hard not to.

"What's going on, Abbey?"

I've known for a little while now that something strange is going on with her. You can't be best friends with someone for practically your whole life and not notice when something has changed. This girl in my arms right now is not the girl I grew up with.

Besides the fact she looks so thin and generally unwell, Abbey seems almost broken on the inside.

Her crying slowly turns to sobs as she pulls away and extracts a handful of tissues from the bedside table, and attempts to clean up her snotty nose. When her eyes return to me, I see they are red and puffy, trying to hide the immense pain behind them.

"Please tell me what's going on, Abs," I beg, and she nods, sucking in a breath.

"I never wanted to do that stuff to you, Lex. You have to believe that. I love you so damn much, but I had no choice. Or I thought I had no choice. Things are so fucked up." Digging her fingers into her messy hair, Abbey tugs at the roots in frustration.

I say nothing because what am I meant to say? Sure, no worries, Abbey, it's totally fine that you turned against me and stood by while Tasha provoked me and physically fought me? No, it's not okay. And I have no idea why she thinks she had no choice. What does that even mean?

"I'm so sorry Mike hurt you again. I should've been with you to protect you."

I laugh. "Abbey, how the fuck are you going to protect me?"

She shrugs. "I don't know. I just should have been there."

I shake my head. "You're saying sorry to me, but you're not telling me what's going on with you. I can't really accept your apology without knowing the reason you betrayed me."

Abbey nods. "I fucked up, Lex. My parents came home early a few weeks back and caught Daniel and me screwing. As if that wasn't bad enough to be caught naked, my legs in the air while Daniel was pumping into me with my mum screaming at us to stop, but then she stood in my bedroom and watched us struggle to pull free of each other and try to keep ourselves covered so we could get dressed. Then she fucking escorted us to the living room. The next thing I know, my mum is on the phone to Daniel's parents, and they are discussing wedding arrangements."

"What!" I screech.

She nods. "Fucking wedding arrangements, Lexi. Apparently, because Daniel was the one to deflower me, as my mum put it, then he will be the one to marry me. I fucking lost it! I started screaming, and Daniel did nothing but sit quietly like a coward until his parents arrived. He didn't once protest, just nodded and agreed to everything his parents said he would be doing. By the end, and against my will, it was agreed that Daniel and I are now engaged and will marry after we graduate from Uni." She shakes her head in disbelief and she cringes. "But here's the big fucking clause." Abbey takes a breath, her face red in anger. "If I misbehave. If my grades fall. If I associate myself with *you*, Lexi, then my parents will arrange for our marriage to go ahead the day before my eighteenth birthday."

"What!" I practically scream, and the door flies open as Ayden barges in with the others on his heels. "They can't do that!"

Abbey glances at the guys and Rhys filling the room, but she turns back to answer me. "Apparently, they can. It's because of their twisted religious beliefs and protecting the family name, or some shit. I mean, this shit doesn't happen in Australia, right? I've never heard of it happening, but I can tell you right now, it *is* happening. Both families have agreed, and they even put something in writing. I don't know what it says, even though I asked to see it. But they are *dead* serious, Lexi. I'm now Daniel's fiancé, and if they know I've even spoken to you, they will move my wedding forward to August third next year. If not before because they are fucking psychos."

"Wait. Hold up. You're engaged?" Jared asks, coming around the other side of the bed to see Abbey better.

"Yes," Abbey nods, "and not willingly." Tears stream down her face again. "At first, I didn't think it would be so bad, being engaged to Daniel. After all, I thought he loved me. But the moment our parents retreated to the kitchen to write up that damn document, Daniel shoved me into the wall and told me what he really thought."

"And what was that?" Marcus asks this time.

"Besides the fact that he won't get access to his trust fund when he turns twenty-one if he doesn't go along with this, Daniel said that there is no way a lazy lay like me will be the only girl he fucks before he's tied down to me, and that the whole thing is my fault. Apparently, I was a stepping stone on a list he and his mates made earlier in the year. A list of fucks to conquer. The rule is to make a girl fall in love with them and give up the goods within the first month, and then the relationship has to last two to three months before they have to dump that girl and move on to the next one. The prize is five grand." Abbey swipes the tears off her face, anger turning her cheeks red. "Being engaged to me is an inconvenience, so he told me to keep quiet and do as my parents ask, so he doesn't have to marry me sooner. I'm to keep our engagement a secret. I'm to lift my grades. And I'm to stay away from Lexi."

"What the actual fuck." Rhys, who has never been a fan of Abbey, looks furious, like she's ready to go to war for her. "This can't be legal!"

Abbey shrugs. "As far as my parents are concerned, it is." She turns back to me. "That's not all, Lex. I was so upset, I made the mistake of opening up to Tasha, and the next thing I know, she's using it against me. She said I had to do what she says and help her destroy your reputation, or she would tell my mum that I've been talking with you. I didn't know what to do, Lexi. I love you to death. I never wanted to hurt you, but I can't bear the thought of being forced to marry Daniel. He's turned into a monster."

"So, you were happy to let Lexi get physically assaulted, taunted, and harassed by those bitches, all to save your own arse from something that may not even happen?" Garrett's deep growl gives away how pissed he is right now, and when I glance at him, his face is nothing but fury.

"It's not as simple as that," Abbey whispers, tears still falling, her shoulders hunching forward to close herself off to Garrett's attack.

"Abbey?" I say softly, gaining her attention. "Your wrist?"

When I confronted her last week, I grabbed her wrist, which had caused her pain. I can see by the way her face drops and how her other hand instinctively clasps the wrist in question that she knows exactly what I'm talking about.

"Show me," I ask, and she hesitates for a moment before releasing her wrist to tug up the sleeve of her jacket.

My frown is instant when I see the deep purple bruising that spans her wrist, and I hear the moment the others see it too, by the sharp intakes of air that sound throughout the room.

"Who did that?" Ayden asks, but Abbey pulls the sleeve back down, shaking her head.

"It doesn't matter." Her eyes move from Ayden back to me. "I'm taking a huge risk by coming here, but I had to see you while eyes weren't on me at Fox Pines. I'm staying at Gran's for the weekend, and I told her I'd be spending the day in bed because I wasn't feeling well. You know how my Gran is? She hates sick people, so she's not likely to enter that bedroom until I tell her I'm feeling better. I knew it would get her to leave me alone for long enough so I could sneak out and come and see you. But I should probably get back before she finds me missing."

There's more Abbey isn't saying, but I won't push her for now. I'm just glad to know what's been behind her behaviour towards me. Her parents, Daniel, and

Tasha are all the reasons why. They are using her kind heart against her. Manipulating her. Blackmailing her into bending to their will. There is nothing I can do right now other than keep my distance from Abbey in the hopes to prolong her engagement to Daniel. I hate the idea of staying away from her and doing nothing, but reluctantly, I nod up to her, and she leans down to hug me again.

"I'm so sorry, Lexi. I will make this up to you one day. I swear it."

And with that, she pulls away and rushes from the room.

Four

Apparently, today is the day for visitors. After Abbey left and I took a nap, my body still craving downtime to heal, I wake to my pack, plus Rhys crowding the small hospital room with bags upon bags of Maccas for lunch.

For them.

None for me because Dr Rhys George says I have to eat healthy hospital food. I'd hoped Ayden or one of the guys would support me and tell Rhys to back off and let me eat some McDonalds too, but they're all on the same page, standing their ground. So I sulk and pout my way through the not so yummy hospital food while they get to eat the good stuff.

Now Rhys and Marcus have gone for a walk, which I'm sure is code for a fuck, while I lay in Ayden's arms as he watches footy on the small box TV hanging from the ceiling.

I'm feeling a little squashed, though, with Garrett's large frame laying on my other side as he reads a book on his phone, and with Simon sitting on the end of the bed with my feet in his lap, painting my toenails with the new nail polish Rhys brought in.

Purple passion.

In the corner of the room, Shaun snores softly in the armchair where he's been for some time now. Meanwhile, Jared is leaning over Ayden, feeding me a spoonful of red jelly.

That's the moment my mum, who I haven't seen since she screamed at me in her own hospital room over three weeks ago, walks in. My eyes widen when I see her standing just inside the door, right as my mouth closes over the spoon of jelly.

I sit up abruptly, and Jared loses the grip on the spoon before it falls to Ayden's chest with the rest of the red jelly on the spoon spilling over. Garrett nearly tumbles off the bed and reaches out to stay upright, while I must have kicked my legs when I sat up because there's now a smear of Purple Passion on Simon's cheek.

I try to focus on my mum, but I can't, not with the way Simon is looking at me, confusion furrowing his ash-blond brows with the glittery purple smear on his skin. It really isn't his colour, and I'm helpless to hold in my laughter as it rips from me, drawing the guys' attention to Simon.

Moments later, they join in, throwing their heads back, laughing at Simon's expense.

"Dude. I always knew you liked glitter." Jared chuckles, but we all fall silent when my mum clears her throat.

Oh yeah, I forgot she was there.

"Ah, hi, Mum."

It's weird to see her. She looks different from the last time I saw her. Even with the situation she walked in on, she doesn't have the scowl she typically wears. She also looks different physically.

Healthier.

"Alexis. Who are your friends?" Stepping further into the room, my mum glances at each of the guys before they leap off the bed, rushing to stand next to Jared, who doesn't seem too concerned with my mum's presence, meanwhile Shaun, our Spanish Casanova, is still sound asleep in the chair.

"Don't call me that. It's Lexi." I remind her, frowning, and I watch her face soften as she turns back to me.

"Yes, sorry, Lexi." My mum offers a small smile before raising her dark brows expectantly.

Oh yeah, she asked a question.

"Mum, this is Ayden, Simon, Garrett and Jared." I gesture to each of them as I say their names. "You remember Jared, don't you? Jared Crowley? We grew up together."

Frowning, my mum tilts her head to the side as she takes Jared in.

"Hey Ruth... I mean Mrs West. It's great seeing you again." Jared smiles, still looking relaxed with her presence.

"Oh yes. Your parents are Gregory and Janie, right?" Mum asks, and Jared nods. "Oh, my gosh. You don't look like a little boy anymore. You're all grown up."

"Ah, yeah, that's what happens, Mum." I need her to stop looking at Jared because it's just weird, and luckily my comment works, her eyes returning to me, frowning.

"And who's the sleepyhead in the corner?" she asks, swinging her golden-brown hair as she turns her head. It looks the healthiest I've ever seen it. Not just because it looks clean and brushed free of the tangles that are usually present, but I've never seen her strands so shiny.

"That's Shaun." I explain, "The guys have been staying each night with me, so I don't think they're getting much sleep, which is probably why he's passed out right now." After the words are out, I realise how that sounds, and Ruth's deep frown doesn't disappoint.

"*Boys*? These boys have been staying *here*? In *this* room? With *you*, each night?"

I sigh, "Yes, Mum. They have."

"Where's Abbey? And the other girls? That Tasha friend of yours?" Mum asks right as Rhys and Marcus walk back in.

"Trashy Tashy isn't Lexi's friend. That skank is a traitor." Rhys doesn't seem to care that she delivers that information to someone she doesn't know, as she walks past my mum and sits on the end of the bed.

Marcus instantly recognises my mum, and his spine straightens, standing tall as he clears his throat.

"Hey, Mrs West. How are you?"

My mum looks him up and down. "Marcus?" she asks, clearly trying to see the child behind the man.

"Yep." Marcus smiles and nods.

"Oh, my." My mum's hand flies to her chest. "You boys certainly have grown up, haven't you?"

Rhys turns to me then, her face looking regretful, something I've never really seen her wear. "Sorry." She whispers, and my mum turns in her direction.

"And who might you be?"

"Rhys George, ma'am. Lexi's best friend." Black lips spread from ear to ear as Rhys remains seated on the bed with her hand out, waiting for my mum to take it.

I bite back a laugh.

"*Abbey* is Lexi's best friend," my mum says, accepting Rhys' hand for a brief shake.

"Not anymore," Rhys says, pleased, before dropping her hand in her lap. "Abbey and Lexi's old friends have been nasty bitches to Lexi. So, they're all history."

"Is that true?" My mum darts her head in my direction, anger swimming in her brown eyes.

This is new.

"Yeah, but don't worry about it, mum. I don't need those girls. I have Rhys and the guys." I'm hoping my smile is convincing because I kind of want this conversation over with already.

"The guys?" Ruth looks around the room at all the boys again, frowning before stepping up closer to me. "Lexi, are they *all* your boyfriends?"

Soft chuckles float throughout the room as I shake my head.

"No, mum. They are all my *friends*." I look at them now and shake my head. "Wait. No. They are more than my friends." I glance back at my mum. "They are my family."

I swear my mum's brows touch in the middle. "Your family? But *I* am your family, Lexi."

"Actually, *Ruth*," I say, full of attitude as I shuffle to the edge of the bed and swing my legs over the side, "*Family* are there for each other. *Family* protects each other. *Family* cares about each other. Since *you* have *never* done those things, I would probably just call *you* the woman who gave birth to me."

Anger reddens Ruth's face, and her nostrils flare, so I prepare myself for her typical outburst of insults.

But it never comes.

Only tears do.

My mum's tears.

"You're right," she says softly as salty drops stream down her cheeks. "These boys, and this girl... they have been here for you? Protected you?"

I nod. "Yes. Even when I asked them not to, they never gave up on me."

"And they *aren't* your boyfriends?" she asks, and I roll my eyes.

Of course, she is hung up on that. God forbid her daughter acts like a slut.

"Only one, mum," I say, and her brows shoot up in surprise.

Ayden steps around the bed then, offering his hand to Ruth. "Ayden Mitchell. I'm Marcus' cousin and Lexi's boyfriend." He shoots me a grin as Ruth looks at his hand and then up to his face before accepting the handshake.

"Mitchell?" Ruth asks, referring to his last name as she releases his hand. "Is it your parents that have been looking after Lexi? Are you the boy that went in and saved her from that- that- *fucker*?" My mum's growl shocks everyone except Ayden.

"Yes, that's right. Andrea and Peter are my parents, and Marcus and I got Lexi away from Mike the first time."

"So, who is the poor boy that got shot then? You don't look like you got shot." My mum's brown eyes return to me in question.

"That was Muz. He's an... old acquaintance of Ayden's that came to visit."

Nodding, my mum turns her back on us for a moment, pulling one of the chairs closer to the bed and taking a seat.

"This is a lot to take in," Ruth says, massaging her temples, a telltale sign she is getting one of her headaches.

I expect her to open her bag and pop a handful of pills, but she doesn't. She just closes her eyes for a few moments and sucks in slow breaths.

As if my room wasn't full enough, Andrea and Peter walk in, and I squirm, feeling like a caged lion.

"Oh good, Ruth, you found the room okay." Andrea comes in to stand next to my mum, placing her hand on Ruth's shoulder.

What the hell? Andrea and Ruth know each other?

"Hi, Lexi. You're looking much better today," Peter says, coming up to me and giving me a quick hug.

"Have you been here before to see me?" I ask, dread filling my gut.

Peter chuckles. "Sure have."

"Let me guess. I shook my arse at you, didn't I?"

Peter glances at Ayden. "You told her? I thought we were going to keep that a secret to avoid her embarrassment."

Ayden's lips thin. "Well, Dad. So did I, but you just admitted that in front of her. I told her about Officer Zimora, but not you."

My cheeks flame red as Peter shoots an apologetic look back at me, and my eyes retreat to my bare feet as I shake my head. "I'm going to hell."

Andrea laughs. "Nonsense, Lexi. Just forget about all of that."

"If only I could," I whine, looking up at the ceiling and trying to stay calm.

"At least you had knickers on, Lex." Rhys giggles and nudges my shoulder before wrapping her arm across them.

"So, Lexi, the doctors called and said you can be released this afternoon. They are pleased with your recovery." Andrea informs me, and a string of relieved sighs come from the guys. "Your mum has also been released from the hospital she was at, so I agreed to pick her up. We will all stay at Peter's for the night before going back to Fox Pines tomorrow."

"Oh." I look from Andrea to Ruth, who both seem okay with this situation. Then I look at Ayden, hoping he can see the panic I'm trying to hide. He doesn't miss a beat, coming over to me before squatting down and taking my hand.

"You okay?" he asks, and I can feel everyone looking at me, so I avoid words and simply nod.

I can't say what I really think. Not without being rude to my mum. The idea of her in their space unsettles me. Not that she will do anything wrong, but it just feels like she's an intruder.

"Uh, maybe everyone could pop out of the room and let Lexi get changed so we can leave." Andrea insists, and everyone moves, except for Shaun, who is still sound asleep.

Man, he must be stuffed.

"Ruth!" Rhys jumps up from the bed next to me, a ball of energy, as usual. "We have a lot of getting to know each other to do. Let's get started."

Trying to suppress my giggle, I bite on my top lip, sucking it in as Rhys links arms with my mum and escorts her out of the room. Meanwhile, Jared kicks Shaun's foot, causing him to jump up in fear, holding his hand to his chest.

While they banter and the guys follow Peter out of the room, Andrea lays some clothes out for me on the bed while Ayden remains squatting in front of me.

"What's wrong, Lex?"

"It doesn't feel right to have my mum with us," I say quietly, knowing I can be honest in front of Andrea.

"Honey, I know things aren't good between the two of you. Your mum has a lot of making up to do with you, and she really wants to. That's why I brought her here. If I didn't think she was genuine, I wouldn't have offered her a bed with us for the night. I also thought it might be good for her to get to know us as well, and we can be a buffer between the both of you before you return home together."

"Together? You won't be my guardian anymore?" My voice is high pitched, even to my own ears as the thought of not having Andrea as my stand in mum saddens me. I've gotten used to the idea of her looking out for me, and I'm not the least bit prepared to hand over the control to my mum again.

Not that she's looked after me in years.

"I'm not sure if that's a good idea, Mum," Ayden complains. "She didn't look after Lexi last time, and with Mike still on the loose, Ruth can't protect Lexi the way she needs."

"I agree, which is why she is going to spend the night with us and get to know the boys. As much as I don't want any of you in harm's way, Mike kept his distance from Lexi with you boys around. It may be a good idea to continue that for a while." I never thought I'd hear Andrea say that. "And also, Child Services will review Lexi and Ruth's situation. They know I'm happy to keep Lexi on if they feel Ruth isn't up to the job."

"So, I should just ring you when I find her passed out in her own vomit?" I hiss, and Andrea flinches. "Shit. Sorry, Andrea. That was a bitchy thing to say." I shake my head and mentally kick myself for being a fucking ungrateful bitch.

"It's not ideal, Lexi, but yes, if your mum relapses, then you call me."

"I'm not leaving Lexi's side, mum. Just so you know." Ayden stands, causing his grip on my hands to release.

With a warm smile, Andrea approaches Ayden and pats the side of his face gently. "I figured as much. You might have to let one of the boys take over occasionally, though. You still have an agreement to stick to, remember?"

"I guess." Ayden doesn't sound happy, but he nods anyway.

As far as I can tell, the agreement is for him to keep out of trouble and finish high school after he put them through hell the previous year with his drug addiction. There was also an agreement for him not to drive, but Ayden hasn't done a good job of honouring that one.

Standing from the bed, I glance at my clothes and back to the guy that holds my heart and then to his adoring mum.

"Andrea, I'm sorry, but I need to make a stop on the way back to Peter's, please. Or it might be a detour. I'm not sure which it is."

"Lex?" Ayden asks, but I keep my eyes on Andrea.

"I need to see Muz." My words shock Andrea, her brows shooting up in surprise.

"Lex, I'm not sure if that's a good idea," Ayden says, trying to convince me otherwise, so I turn my determined eyes to his.

"I *need* to see him, Ayden. Please understand. This is something I really need to do. If you don't feel like coming, then I'll happily walk or something. Maybe there are buses?"

Andrea laughs. "Don't be silly. I will give Ringo a call now and let him know we will drop by soon."

"Thank you." My smile is genuine as relief washes over me.

"So stubborn," Ayden whispers in my ear before placing a warm kiss on the top of my head.

Five

I t's hard leaving the hospital, knowing I'm leaving Val behind. I hope her mum cools down over time and lets me see Val again, even if it's just as a neighbour across the fence. I owe my little neighbour so much. She's been looking out for me for longer than I realised, and she's become more than just the nosey kid that lives next door. I can't imagine not being able to talk spy business with her anymore.

Thoughts of Val fill my mind as we drive across the city in awkward silence. Peter drove my pack and Rhys back to his apartment in his seven seater SUV while Andrea chauffeurs Ayden, my mum, and me to visit Muz. Melbourne Public Hospital isn't like the one I've been staying in. The exterior looks like it's weathered fifty years, and the interior, although freshly painted, looks much the same.

Meeting Ringo in the hospital foyer, I'm taken back to the night when I called Peter for help with Ayden after Muz forced him to snort the white powder. Peter had called for reinforcements and showed up with three scary-looking bikers with bushy beards and tattoos from head to toe. It turns out that one of them, Ringo, is Muz's brother, and he quickly pulled his little brother back in line on that awful night so Andrea and Peter could get Ayden medical attention.

Now Ringo, still looking as scary as that first night I met him, walks us through the dingy halls of Melbourne Public so I can visit Muz. As I walk hand in hand with Ayden, I avoid my mum's gaze, knowing that she must be about to pee her pants in the presence of Ringo. It's kind of funny, really, and I bet she's realising how much she doesn't even know me. I bet I'll get a lecture later on about the company I keep.

Coming to stop in front of a mint-coloured door, Ringo turns to me, and I'm surprised that I can tell he's smiling behind all of that facial hair.

"I told him you were coming, Lexi. He wanted to speak with you alone, but if you don't feel comfortable in there alone with him, he can eat shit," Ringo mumbles, his deep voice matching his tough exterior.

I shake my head and grin. "I'd rather speak with him alone."

"Lex?" Ayden asks with concern, but I slip my hand from his and look up into his ocean blues.

"I need to speak with him alone. It's okay. He's not a threat to me."

"I know, beautiful, but he's not in a good way. He's pretty sick." Ayden's kind heart almost makes it hard to argue. He cares so much, especially about me.

My eyes instantly glaze over. "I know. I need to do this alone, though." I give his hand a little squeeze. "I'll be okay."

"Uh, excuse me. What do you mean, he's not a threat to you?" My mum's concerned tone gains our attention, and I sigh.

It would be easier if she weren't here. I know I shouldn't think that way. She is my mum, after all, but she hasn't been a very good one, and I've had to learn how to survive without her. Her presence makes me feel like I have to explain my actions all the time, which I'm not used to.

"It's nothing, mum. Can you just sit over there and wait for me, please? I'll try not to be long."

I gesture to the row of chairs down the hall, hoping my tone doesn't sound ungrateful or bitchy.

"Mrs West, let's take a seat." Ringo snags my mum's attention, and I wait for her to flinch or curl her lip at his appearance in disgust, but she doesn't. She surprises us all by linking her arm with his and lets him lead her away down the hall.

"What the fuck is happening right now?" I ask.

"Lexi," Andrea whispers, and I drag my eyes from my mum and Ringo to her. "Language."

"Oh. Sorry." I cringe, and she laughs.

"Take your time, honey." Andrea gives my shoulder a gentle squeeze before following Ringo and Ruth.

"Are you sure you don't want me to come in with you?" Ayden asks, tucking my hair behind my ear before leaning down to kiss my cheek. I nod, wanting nothing more than to turn my head and catch those lips in mine. But there's a time and place, and this sure as shit isn't it.

"I'm sure." I take his hand and give it another squeeze.

"I'll be right here." Not caring where we are, Ayden claims my lips in a kiss that reminds me of how much he craves me, and my body instantly heats.

It's a brief kiss, but it's also a reminder of how much I crave him, too. I shake my head at him and his ability to make me as needy as a crack whore, and I reluctantly break the kiss and turn from him before pushing the door open.

The room is bigger than the one I'd occupied across the city, and along one wall, there's a large window with nurses on the other side monitoring the room.

"Pretty girl." The gravel of Muz's voice shocks me a little. It's filled with ten percent playfulness and ninety percent exhaustion.

Glancing at the bed, I step towards it, taking Muz in.

The hospital gowns are white here, and Muz doesn't look so tough wearing it in the little bed he occupies with tubes and cords running from his body.

I can't speak at first as hot drops roll down my cheeks, but then I read the sign above his bed, and my lips spread into a grin.

"Bobby Musgrove. That's your name?"

His lip lifts on one side, and his dark eyes blink slowly, full of drowsiness.

"You tell anyone that, and I'll smack that fine arse of yours."

I roll my eyes. "I'd like to see you try. You can barely keep your eyes open."

His head moves in a slight nod. "There's that sassy mouth. I'm glad you're okay, pretty girl. You had me worried there for a while."

I can't help it. His words remind me of how dire our situation was and I burst into tears and sob like a little girl that can't control her emotions.

"Come here."

Normally Muz demands things, but his tone is anything but, and I step up to the bed to take the hand he tries to lift to me.

"Thank you for what you did," I whisper.

Slowly, he uses his tongue to wet his cracked lips before he speaks again. "No need to thank me, pretty girl. I didn't get the job done."

My brows shoot up. "You stopped him from finishing what he started. That's enough."

"No. I should have killed him. That would have been enough."

He's kind of right. A dead Mike is a good Mike if you ask me.

"It's okay. He'll get what's coming to him," I say, and he frowns.

"You think?" he slurs.

"Yes," I say with more confidence than I have. "Next time he comes for me, I'll be better prepared. He won't get away with it again."

Muz chuckles slowly. "And how are you going to be better prepared, pretty girl?"

"I was kind of hoping you could give me some pointers?"

"You want me to tell you how to kill your brother?" His voice is a little stronger this time and I notice his dark eyes go a little rounder.

"Well, I just want to stop him, so yes, if that's what it takes to end this, then I need to know how to do that." I nod. "He hurt my little neighbour. He needs to pay for what he did to her. If I'm left with no choice, then I will fucking kill him myself."

The smile that slowly spreads across Muz's face is menacing.

"You're gonna make me hard speaking like that."

"For fuck's sake, Bobby." I tease, and he glares before he grins.

"I think I like hearing you say my real name."

"Dude!" I scold, and he chuckles slowly again.

"Such a firecracker." He lets go of my hand and raises his arm slowly, like it weighs a ton, pointing to a bag on the floor. "In the front pocket of that bag."

It's all he says before his hand flops to the bed in exhaustion, so I go to the bag and open the front pocket, pulling out the only thing in it. It's cold and heavy, and when I turn back to Muz, the dull light reveals that it's a knife of some sort.

"It's a butterfly knife. It's yours." He grunts out before coughing a little.

"What? I can't take this." Even as I say the words, I realise I want the knife. I like the way it feels in my palm. The cold metal is begging for me to hold it tight, and its weight tells me how much damage it can do.

"My gift to you," Muz slurs again.

"How many people have you stabbed with this?" I ask, genuinely curious.

"Too many." It's a simple reply but powerful enough for me not to want to ask more questions.

"Stab up, under the ribs." His hand lifts from the bed, and he tries to show me the stabbing action, but his arm is too tired and heavy. "Or into the side of the neck," he points to his neck, "into the jugular." He moves his hand down his body, which is covered in a thin blanket. "Or the femoral artery near the groin."

I nod, trying to ignore my disbelief that Muz actually knows how to do this. I knew he was dangerous, but I kind of hoped he was all talk and no action.

"Okay."

"Your body can be used as a weapon if you have nothing else to use. Use your fingers. Dig into the eye sockets, throat, anywhere and everywhere. Bite. Your teeth are sharp. Use them."

"Okay," I say again, committing everything he says to memory and remembering that I've already used my teeth to fight off Mike. Basic instinct, perhaps?

Muz chuckles again. "Pretty girl. Maybe just let the cops catch him."

"You don't think I can kill him if I need to?"

"I think it will be a miracle if you can fight him off. I'm a crazy motherfucker, Lexi. But he's a different kind of crazy." Muz coughs again, and a nurse comes in from the side door, so I slip the butterfly knife into my hoodie pocket.

"I should let you rest." I move to step away from the bed, but Muz grabs my wrist.

"Put my number in your phone. We need to talk more about this."

I nod, taking out my phone and saving the number he reels off.

"See you soon, okay?" I insist as I walk back towards the door, taking in the frail sight of the scary gang leader. Fuck, I wish he was all scary right now. What I wouldn't give to have him throwing his weight around like he rules the world.

"Sure thing, firecracker." Muz offers me a weak smile before I quickly turn to leave, hoping he didn't see my welling tears.

When I step out of Muz's room, Ayden is waiting and immediately pulls me to his chest as I let the tears fall. Muz may have done bad shit in his life, and yes, I wanted him dead not long ago for what he did to Ayden, but now, I don't want him to die. I want that smart arse infuriating guy back so I can slap his face and yell at him for getting hurt.

My emotions are shot, and I know that's why Ayden didn't want me to come here and see Muz, but I'm glad I did. I needed to see him. I needed to speak with him and thank him for protecting Val and me.

I stay tucked into Ayden's side in the back seat of Andrea's car as she drives us back to Peter's apartment. My mum and Andrea chat away during the drive, but I'm too consumed by my own thoughts to listen.

I'm pretty sure Muz thinks I'm joking about killing Mike if I have to, but I'm not. At least, I don't think I'm joking. If Mike comes for me again, and the only way I can get free of him and end this madness is to kill him myself, then I will. I'm sure of it. Muz is right, though. Mike is a different kind of crazy. It's almost as if his level of crazy makes him stronger physically. I'm not strong. Not like him, and not like Muz was before he got shot. That's why I need to be smart. I need to outsmart Mike or anyone that tries to hurt me.

"What's this?" Ayden whispers in my ear, pulling the butterfly knife Muz gave me from my hoodie pocket. I'd been so side-tracked in my own thoughts that I didn't even notice his hand slip inside the pocket.

Glancing down at Ayden's hand resting in my lap, I take a better look at the butterfly knife Muz gifted me. It's black, but silver peeks through the few scratches and dents on the handle and blade. It felt heavy in my pocket when we walked out of the hospital, but not heavy enough for anyone else to notice I'd been carrying it. The handle alone must be four or five inches long, so it must be a decent size when it's unfolded.

"Lex, why do you have this?" Ayden whispers again, and I shrug a single shoulder.

"Muz gave it to me."

I look up in time to witness Ayden's brows reach his hairline.

"Why did he give it to you?" His voice isn't a whisper this time, but low enough that only I can hear.

I glance back down at the blade in question, and for a split second, I think about lying to him. I can't do that, though. I need to be honest with Ayden.

"For protection. He told me where to stab Mike if he attacks me again," I admit quietly, peering back at his intense blue gaze.

"Where did he tell you to stab Mike if he attacks you again?"

I can tell Ayden is trying to be patient with me. The flare of his nose and the tick in his jaw tells me he is walking a fine line between staying calm or losing his shit and ranting at me for accepting the knife.

Leaning towards Ayden's ear, I whisper, "Muz said to stab up under Mike's ribs or into the side of his neck. There's a vein there or something."

Ayden nods. "The jugular."

"Yeah, that's it. The jugular. Muz also said there's a vein in the groin area, too." Even though we're speaking in hushed tones, I sneak a glance to the front of the car, making sure Andrea or my mum haven't perked their ears up.

"The femoral artery." Using his other hand, Ayden points to his upper thigh, near his groin. "It's in this area."

I frown. "How do you know about those arteries?" I whisper.

Ayden hesitates a moment before he smirks. "My mum's a nurse, remember?"

Fuck me, Ayden just lied to me.

I don't know how I know that, but I do.

Sure, his mum is a nurse, but that's not how he knows where the arteries are and what they are called. I want to call him out on his bullshit and find out why he just lied to me and how he knows about that stuff. I don't, though, because apparently, I'm too chickenshit.

I offer Ayden a smile, which is fake as fuck, and I'm pretty sure he just picked up on that, but I move on, not ready to face whatever just happened.

"Muz reminded me I can use my body as a weapon, too. I've already used my teeth on Mike."

Ayden's jaw ticks again. His eyes look distant while he clearly falls into thoughts of Mike's latest attack. His hand tightens around the closed handle of the blade, and panic starts to bubble to the surface. Is he going to take it away so I can't use it?

I snatch my hand out and pry his hand open, quickly taking the knife from his grip.

"What just happened?" Ayden asks softly enough that our mums still can't hear.

"It's mine. Muz gave it to me." The weight of it in my hand feels good. Like it belongs there.

"You thought I was going to take it from you?" Ayden asks, and I shrug. "Why would I do that?"

"Because you don't want me to have the knife," I answer honestly, keeping my eyes trained on my hand, clasping the black metal.

"I never said that, Lexi."

"You don't have to say it. I could just tell," I whisper again, and the next second, Ayden's fingers settle under my chin, tilting my head up so I have no choice but to look into his eyes.

"What's happening right now, Lex? I feel like I'm missing something." His eyes are honest and pleading, and I'm helpless not to be honest too.

"I don't know. I'm feeling a little uneasy. Unsettled." I frown, trying to find the right words.

"Insecure?" Ayden asks, and my eyes widen because he's hit the mark.

"Yes."

"Why?" His intense gaze roams my face as if he's desperately trying to find the answers there. I don't know how to accuse him of lying without sounding bitchy, so I avoid his question altogether.

In my lap, I open the knife, trying to close both handles together, but I falter, and the exposed blade tumbles to my lap.

"Be careful, beautiful. This blade is sharp. You'll cut yourself." Picking up the knife, Ayden draws the handles together and flips the latch, locking it in place. "This is how you lock it in if you need to use it. This is the bite handle." Ayden unlatches it and closes the knife. "The bite handle is the part that closes over the sharp edge of the blade to prevent injuries while carrying it." He runs his finger along the bite handle before moving to the other one. "This is the safe handle which closes over the blunt part of the blade. That part of the blade is called the swedge." Ayden opens the knife again, latching it in place and pointing to the blunt side of the blade. "It's basically the blunt spine."

When Ayden looks back at me, his eyes dance in amusement at the fish reenactment I'm doing because WTF! How does he know all this?

"What? How?" I mutter, and he chuckles softly, glancing to the front of the car to make sure our mums are still preoccupied.

"I did an assignment on butterfly knives at my old school." He shrugs like it's nothing, but that just pisses me off because he's just gone and lied to me again.

"Bullshit."

His brows shoot up. "What?"

"You're lying to me. You lied to me before about the arteries, and you're lying to me now about the knife." Heat pools behind my eyes. I feel like I'm balancing on a rope right now. If I fall one way, it means I simply accept his lies and pretend like everything is okay, but if I fall the other way, it means I demand the truth and potentially upset the apple cart, so to speak. I don't want to upset anything, but I can't sit back and accept a lie.

"Shit," Ayden mutters before snaking his hand to the back of my head and pulling me into the crook of his neck. "Lexi, I'm sorry," he whispers next to my ear. "I'm just so used to keeping that stuff hidden from everyone. I didn't even think twice about the lie. I don't want to lie to you, but shit, I fucking hate telling you about who I used to be. I was such a fuckup Lex."

I pull back, catching his eyes with mine. "All of you, Ayden. Remember? I want to know all of you—even your past. I won't judge you. I won't run screaming in the other direction. I just want to know you and what you've been through. How you've changed because I know you have. I know you're not that person anymore, but I also know that time of your life, even if you want to forget it even happened, is really important."

His eyes soften as he regards me before he leans closer to whisper again. "How did I get so lucky to win your heart?"

"I'm the one that got lucky, Ayden. But..."

"But?" Ayden asks, urging me to continue.

"If you lie to me again, I'll dick punch you."

Ayden throws his head back, laughing, this time gaining our mums' attention from the front. I play dumb and shrug at my mum when she turns to look at us in question over her shoulder.

"I'm serious, Ayden," I growl after my mum turns back around, and Ayden sucks in air, trying to calm down.

It takes him a couple of minutes, and all I can do is watch him, amusement dancing across my face.

"Okay. Understood. My jewels are on the line. Got it." He tries not to laugh again.

"So, are you gonna tell me how you know all that stuff?"

That takes the smug look off his face.

"The life I used to live was full of illegal shit, and naturally, that came with violence too," he whispers. "I

70

had to learn how to defend myself and how to protect Dani."

I nod as I process what he says before I lean in close this time, to whisper in his ear. "Have you stabbed someone before?"

Ayden shakes his head. "No. I've come close, though."

"So, when you put that guy in hospital for supplying Dani with the drugs that killed her, that was Muz, right?"

The Adam's apple in Ayden's throat bobs as he swallows, taking a moment to answer. "Yes."

"But you didn't stab him? What did you do to him?" I need to know their history, and I can't remember what Ayden had told me about that. There's still so much I don't know about his past, and I really want to know it all.

Shit, maybe I'm just a nosey bitch that needs to mind my own business?

"I put him in the hospital with my fists, Lex. I beat the shit outta him. I was consumed with blind, out-of-control rage. He didn't stand a chance."

Six

B y the time we arrive at Peter's apartment, Rhys has already taken over the place, walking Peter around to show him, in her opinion, better ways to lay his furniture out. Feng Shui or some shit?

The guys are in the second living room already playing the PlayStation, so Ayden goes to see them while I awkwardly linger, feeling like I have to babysit my mum.

Andrea shows her to their guest room, which has a small ensuite off it, and my mum announces that she's going to rest and have some reflection time to wrap her head around the day's events.

I don't know what the fuck reflection time is, but it's a relief when she says it.

I take a few minutes to use Ayden's bathroom after stashing Muz's butterfly knife in Ayden's dresser drawer before I go in search of Rhys so I can save Peter from her interior design lessons. Once I have my arm linked with hers, I tell the boys that we are going to the rooftop, hoping to get some girl time, but within minutes, they come barging through the rooftop door like a herd of elephants.

Their saving grace is the food and drinks they bring with them.

When I see the cabana loveseat that Ayden and I spent hours loving each other on nearly four weeks ago, my face heats and I want to scream at everyone to get off our roof.

"That was the best night of my life." The familiar voice and warm breath flutters across my neck as Ayden draws my hair back and places a kiss just under my ear, his other hand snaking around my front, pulling me back against him.

I can't hold in my moan, and I'm thankful Rhys has the others occupied with a drinking game she's trying to explain the rules for.

"Mine too," I whisper, turning in Ayden's arms, seeking his lips.

He meets me halfway and lifts me in his arms, my legs instantly wrapping around his hips. A round of annoyed groans come from the guys, but I ignore them as I focus on the soft feel of Ayden's lips moving against mine and the rush of excitement his tongue conjures up. Before I know it, Ayden is lowering me down to the cabana, having manoeuvred us around it while he carried me, taking us out of sight of the others.

"Fuck, I've missed you," Ayden growls as he pulls back, bracing himself above me.

Reaching up, I run my hand over the longer than usual growth on his face and watch how his lust drunk eyes drink me in. I love the way he looks past my bruises, something he has always done.

"You make me feel beautiful," I whisper.

"You *are* beautiful," Ayden responds quickly, no doubt in his tone.

I shrug. "I've never really felt beautiful until you came into my life."

He smiles. "You're beautiful inside and out, Lex. I'm going to spend the rest of my life making sure you know it."

My brows reach my hairline at his admission. "The rest of your life, hey?"

He shrugs. "I won't hold back how I feel because it might be seen as too soon, Lex. I'm never letting you go. You're mine, and I'm yours until the last breath I take. Even after that, too. We will always belong to each other. I can feel it in my bones." He smirks then before leaning in closer. "Can't you feel it?"

I smile. "I can feel it," I agree, captured by the strong magnetic pull that feels impossible to break.

Still hovering above me, I sense that Ayden is holding back, reluctant to touch me fully.

I can't believe we are back in this place, almost as if we are starting again because of what Mike did. His attacks are sexual, which I know is what Ayden is hooked up on, but I don't see it that way.

To me, his attacks are just physical. Just like Tasha's attacks or the ones I dished out to her. It's just a physical action, and I don't focus on the areas I was abused.

My mouth was hurt, my lip split by Mike's fist, yet I still want Ayden to kiss me.

Mike ran his tongue up my cheek, and wrapped his hands around my throat, yet I still want Ayden to touch me and kiss me there.

Just because Mike may have touched me in a place that is meant to be reserved for lovers doesn't mean I can't handle being touched there. It means more that I have Ayden replace any foul touches with his loving ones, even if it's a struggle at first.

"I need you, Ayden," I whisper, and his blue eyes soften even more.

"I need you too."

"No, I mean, I *need* you." I wag my brows, hoping he gets my meaning.

"Lex. There's plenty of time for that stuff later." His tone is soft yet determined but I don't miss the touch of discomfort in his eyes.

I hate seeing it there, but I'm fairly certain the discomfort is more about how he thinks I will feel, rather than his desire for me.

"Later, as in tonight?" I ask, playfully and he rolls his eyes as his lips curve up and he shakes his head.

"Later, as in a few days."

"Like fuck!" I hiss, and my fury just causes him to throw his head back, laughing. "Don't laugh at me." I hiss again, and he sucks his lips in as he regains his control before he responds.

"Lex. You need time to heal."

"I'm healed, Ayden." I fist his hoodie trying to drag him closer. "My body is aching for you."

Still grinning at me, Ayden presses his lips to my forehead before pulling back to stare down at me again.

"It's not just your body that needs to heal, Lex." He places his fingers over my heart. "You need to heal in here," then he moves them to my temple, "and in here."

Dammit.

Why is he so sweet?

Unfortunately, I can't hold back my eye roll.

It looks like I'll have to spell it out for him, and I get it, really I do. He wants to be careful with me. He's worried about pushing me too far, too soon. It's part of what draws me to him—his unwavering care. The thing is, I need more from him. I need to feel normal and fall into the love bubble again.

"I get what you're saying, and I appreciate how much you care, but I need to try and explain myself better before you dismiss this."

"Fine." He sighs, still hovering over me.

"So, you know you've been kissing me?" It's more of a statement than a question, but Ayden nods, unable to hide his smirk..

"Yeah."

"Well, Mike gave me a split lip, twice. He used his fists to do it. I even used my teeth to bite his ugly face," I state.

"I know." Ayden growls, his face contorting in anger as his shoulders bunch in frustration as he holds himself over me.

"Yet you still kiss my lips. You still slip your tongue in my mouth, even though he hurt those places."

Frowning, Ayden goes to pull away from me, but I grab his hoodie again, keeping him in place.

"Lex, I'm sorry. I shouldn't have kissed you."

"Fuck, Ayden, I'm not saying you shouldn't do it." I roll my eyes in frustration. " I'm saying you *have* done it, which *I've wanted* each time more than anything, I might add. So why is that any different from touching or kissing me in other places on my body?"

I wait quietly as a mix of emotions plays over Ayden's face, hoping he understands my weird logic. A moment later, I can tell he needs more convincing.

"Okay, let me try to explain it this way." I loosen my grip on his hoodie, and he doesn't move away. "What happened with Mike *and* with Tasha, to me, is the same thing. They were physical attacks and nothing more. Their intentions may have been different, but to me, they are the same. They wanted to physically hurt me. Does that mean I can't handle you running your hand through my hair, which has been used to launch me across a room or to drag me up a passage? Does that mean I can't handle you wrapping your hand around my neck or kissing me there after Mike did that to me? Does that mean I can't handle you touching my breasts, which Mike and Muz have both groped?"

"Lexi, stop," Ayden growls.

"No, Ayden. Please try to understand. I *need* you to see the difference here. They were all just physical actions on my body." I reach up and press my hand to his chest. "You, your touch, is *more* than physical to me. It's done with care, with passion, with the need to make me feel good. With the need to bring us closer together to feed our souls. Don't you understand?" I plead, hoping like hell that he finally gets it. "I *need* to have you close. I *need* to touch you as much as *I need you* to touch me. It's not just about orgasms and scratching an itch for me." I fist his hoodie again, pulling him so close I can feel his breath fan across my face. "Fuck, I feel like I need to crawl under your skin just so I can breathe."

My lower lip quivers as my emotions buzz like crazy through me. I don't know how else to explain this to him, and I'm scared he's not going to understand.

"Lex," he whispers, his eyes glassy as he hovers his fingers over my lips.

"Touch them," I beg, and his ocean eyes flick to my lips before he does what I ask and lowers his fingers gently to my lips.

A sob escapes my throat when his fingers feather over them, and through my blurred vision, I see the internal battle he's fighting before his face morphs into something else.

Something primal.

Ever so slowly, Ayden glides his fingers to my cheek, running the soft pads over my skin still marked from Mike, before he lowers his lips to kiss me there.

"Do you understand?" I whisper, scared that if he doesn't, I might break.

"I think so." Lifting his head back, Ayden's blue gaze takes me in as his fingers travel down the side of my neck and across the front, tracing over the bruising left by my brother's choking hold. Then, ever so slowly, he gently spreads his fingers out to wrap around my throat, his eyes darting to mine.

"Yes," I whisper, my sight no longer glassy and instead now filled with nothing but the desire I feel.

Lowering his weight on me more, Ayden's hips press down on mine, pushing me gently into the cushioning of the cabana loveseat. The sensations that ripple through me inject heat into all the places I yearn for him to touch, and I can't hold in my moan.

Moving his hand from my neck, Ayden strokes my wayward hair off my face and leans in to kiss me again. As soon as our lips meet, my hips grind up to meet his hardness, and this time we both moan.

"You guys better not be fucking over there!" Simon calls out, and we break apart in shock, completely forgetting we aren't alone on this rooftop.

"Fuck. I need to get rid of them." Ayden hisses quietly, and I giggle.

"Maybe if we just fuck, it will scare them away," I suggest, wagging my brows and at my comment, Ayden growls, grinding his hard length against me again.

A gasp slips past my lips as I drop my head back, my need building.

"I fucking love it when you speak like that." Ayden nips at my ear and rolls his hips again while my aching, needy core wishes my damn clothes would disappear already.

"In that case, I need you to know," I pant as Ayden nibbles down my neck, "that I really need to feel your cock inside me, Ayden."

"Fuck, Lexi,." he rasps, shifting back to see my face. "Are you sure? You've been through so much."

"Look at me, Ayden. You can see how much I want to have you as close as two people can be. Look at my face. Look how flushed my skin is. I can feel the burn of my skin, so I know you can see it." I give my hips a roll this time. "You can feel the heat between my legs. You must be able to. I'm on fire for you."

"Fuck it." Ayden hisses, rearing back a little. "Marcus!"

My eyes widen. "What are you doing?"

"What?" Marcus calls back.

"Come here," Ayden barks, and I squirm, trying to push him off.

The cheeky fucker grins at me, though, leaning forward to place his fingers over my mouth to shoosh me when he sees I'm about to complain.

"What?" Marcus' voice is closer now, and I strain my head back, trying to see him.

It's no use. I can't see him from where I lay.

Ayden can, though.

"I need you to take the others down to the studio. You remember the code to get in, right?" Ayden asks, his cheeks flushed, and fuck I love that he's just as affected as I am.

"Really?" Marcus sighs. "So you can get laid?"

"Hey!" I snap, and Ayden chuckles, flashing amused eyes my way briefly before talking to Marcus again.

"No. Not so I can get laid," Ayden says in all seriousness. "So I can give my girl what she needs. Are we going to have a problem?" Ayden lifts unimpressed brows at his cousin, wherever the hell he is behind me.

Meanwhile, my face is burning up with embarrassment. Did he just basically admit to Marcus that he's about to fuck me?

Oh. My. God.

"Fuck. Okay, give me a minute to round up the others and get them out of here."

Dragging his gaze from his cousin, Ayden grinds against my aching core then, and I'm helpless to hold back my moan. It slips past my lips, long and loud.

"Make it quick," Ayden demands before returning his eyes to mine and repeating the grinding motion.

I'm losing my control, the fever building inside me. Hell, just the fact that Marcus knows what we are doing makes me turn into even more of a horn dog.

What the fuck is wrong with me?

"Don't hold back, Lexi," Ayden demands again, and I open my eyes.

When did I shut them?

I can't even respond as his hand travels down my front to slip under the band of my trackies. My core is hungry for his touch, and my hips lift, seeking his fingers.

The moment they touch my sensitive clit, I'm lost.

"Fuck... Ayden." I pant, "I want you so bad."

His lips crash against mine then, his tongue demanding entry. Nothing about this is gentle, and I fucking love it, needing to feel the ferocity of our love for each other so it can burn away all the other unwanted touches that others have inflicted.

What's happening right now between us is more than lust. It's more than need.

It's undeniable, irrevocable love.

I feel like I will die without it. Without him.

"You have me, beautiful." Ayden declares as he sinks two fingers inside me.

I have no idea if the others are still on this rooftop, and I really hope they aren't because the moment Ayden's fingers stretch me, I'm sure my moan sounds more like a feral animal's mating call or something.

"Fuck yes, baby. Ride my hand." Ayden growls into my ear, so I do as he demands and grind my pussy against him, building the pleasure.

With each thrust of his fingers, I respond with a thrust of my hips, and when Ayden adds his thumb to circle over my clit, I explode.

Moisture rushes out of me as Ayden curls his fingers up, pressing on my inner wall, prolonging my climax until I see stars.

Cold air meets my skin as Ayden yanks down my pants, knickers and all, and then slides my hoodie up over my head.

The goosebumps that pebble my flesh are forgotten the moment I open my eyes to see Ayden stand and grab his shirt from behind his neck, pulling it off.

"Damn, that's hot." I admit, my voice husky as Ayden's eyes heat.

"What's hot is *you* right now," he growls, quickly flicking the button on his jeans and tugging the fabric free.

I don't think I'll ever get used to the sight of him standing before me, hard. My mouth actually waters, desperate to have him in my mouth, but then he rips open a condom wrapper with his teeth, and I know all he wants is to bury himself inside me.

Shit. I want that too.

So damn bad!

As he rolls the protection down over his cock, I spread my legs apart more, opening myself to him. I'm fully exposed right now, but I love the way he drinks me in and makes me feel worshipped by his eyes alone.

That is, until his ocean blues stop their travels, and his lust-filled gaze twists into a frown.

Confused, I look down to see what has caught his attention.

Bruising, in the shape of fingerprints, stands out like a beacon on my pale skin. I'd forgotten the angry marks were there on my pubic bone.

Shit.

"Ayden." I need to get his attention back, but he doesn't look away from the bruises at hearing my voice, his mind elsewhere. "Ayden, don't fucking ignore me," I snap.

That gets his attention, his gaze flicking to meet mine, a growl in the back of his throat.

I hate that my bruises hurt him. I need him to know I'm okay, not just for me, but for him. I feel like it's slowly killing him inside.

Deciding to distract him, I run my hand down the front of my body and watch his frown morph into desire as I reach my aching bud, circling my finger and showing him what I want.

"New memories, Ayden, remember? I need you inside me. Please."

His breathing is deep, but he keeps his eyes fixed on me as his tongue darts out to lick his bottom lip before his teeth show, biting into it.

"Are you sure?" he growls.

"Yes. Ayden, please. I don't want to go through this every time..."

"There won't be a next time, Lexi!" Ayden roars.

His yell doesn't scare me, but makes me more determined even though I want to tell him there *will* be a next time. Because Mike won't stop. Not until one of us is dead.

I don't tell Ayden that though. Bringing up my crude brother has no place in our thoughts right now.

"Stop, Ayden, please. Stop thinking about that and think about *me*. Think about *us*. Think about how much *I need* to have you fill me right now."

His face softens. "I'm sorry." He shakes his head as if he can shake off his thoughts. "I just love you so fucking much, Lexi."

My frustration falls away as Ayden's words register.

Tears spring to my eyes as I realise he just said he loved me.

"You do?" I whisper.

"Fuck yes, I do," he admits with no fear. Just unbridled honesty.

I fight back my tears, taking a moment to let his admission sink in. I already thought he felt that way, or maybe it was just hope. The way he cares for me feels like love, and I'll admit I like hearing him say it too—a whole damn lot, which only adds to the ache between my legs.

"I'm yours, Ayden. Show me how much you love me." I drop my legs apart and run my fingers through my slit as he falls to his knees, watching how I pleasure myself.

"My tongue or my cock?" he asks, his stormy ocean eyes flicking up to meet mine.

"Your cock. Nice and deep."

His nostrils flare before he crawls up over my body, claiming my lips in a searing kiss.

Our tongues clash, and we both moan as the head of his cock slides over my heat. Too eager to wait any longer, I lift my hips and meet his next glide, my insides igniting as he slowly sinks inside.

The stretch from his hard cock is more intense than his fingers, but my pussy craves it, gripping him as he slides out and then back in.

"Fuck, Lexi. I want to stay inside you forever."

"Yes." I moan as he moves faster.

Holding himself up, Ayden uses his hands to brace himself as he delivers each thrust. I fix my eyes on him as he works his body against mine, loving the way his face contorts, almost as if he's in pain.

"Stop," he growls.

"What?" I pant, rolling my hips to build the pleasure.

"Stop looking at me."

"I want to see your face as you fuck me." I smirk.

He pumps into me, moaning loud, my words affecting him the way I knew they would.

"You are," he pants, "too in control right now." He pants again, still thrusting. "Doesn't this feel good?"

"Hell yes, it does." I moan when he pumps into me hard, sinking as far as he can go.

"It's not good enough," he pants, "if you're too busy watching me."

As he continues to piston inside me, he slips his middle finger into my mouth.

"Suck. Cover my finger in your spit," he growls, and I do as he says, confused but also turned on by the act.

Still plunging inside me, Ayden slides his finger out of my mouth and moves to spread my legs wider, raising them in the air.

I probably look ridiculous, but the change in position feels amazing, and I can't help but close my eyes. That is, until I feel something at the entrance of my arse, and my lids fly open just as Ayden sinks his middle finger in.

"Wha…" I can't even finish the word as pleasure ignites my body with Ayden's finger inside my back passage while thrusting his cock deep inside my pussy.

The sounds of the city fall away, and I lose my hearing as I reach new heights, my body greedily taking everything Ayden has to give. There is nothing but feeling now, and Ayden rips another orgasm from me as I scream something incoherent, and a moment later, he follows me over.

If I died right now, I'd die happy.

The way Ayden makes me feel is more than I can comprehend or explain. I'd never realised such blissful happiness even existed, and now that I know it does, I'm never giving it up.

"Are you okay?" His gravelly voice whispers in my ear, right before he nibbles on my lobe.

I nod.

I think.

I can't really feel anything right now.

Ayden chuckles. "Can you speak?"

I shake my head but contradict the action by speaking, "What. The. Fuck."

It's a whisper holding no menace, and it causes Ayden to draw back and look at me.

"What?" he asks.

"Ayden… that-that's a no-go zone."

His whole face lights up in amusement, and he throws his head back, laughing, but quickly tries to compose himself.

"A no-go zone, hey?"

I nod.

"Well, your no-go zone fucking loved swallowing my finger, Lexi."

My face heats at the dirtiness of this conversation.

"Didn't it?" he asks, leaning down, nose to nose with me, waiting for my answer, before he draws back. "You don't even need to answer. I can tell how much your body loved the invasion. Like I said the other day, I'm going to have fun finding out what you enjoy. A good spanking and some arse play are on the list."

I should be more embarrassed than I am, but I'm not because I still feel greedy, and I want more.

Seven

The drums and I are a thing. I love tapping out a beat on them and building it until I turn into some sort of drum-crazed animal. Do drummers say tap out a beat? Shit, I need to find me some drummer friends so I can get the lingo down.

After Ayden convinced me to get dressed, we came down from the rooftop to the studios in search of the others. Some sort of sound coming out of the Live Studio led us to them, but I wouldn't call it music. Even the scene we witness as we walk in is comical.

Simon is bashing the drums while head-banging. Shaun is trying to do some sort of spin on his back while playing an electric guitar. Garrett and Jared are trying to figure out the keys on the piano with a YouTube video instructing them. And Marcus and Rhys try to strum guitars while singing 'Life is a Highway' into the mics.

I can't hold back my laughter as Ayden looks on, mortified.

A little mortified myself at what Simon is doing to the drums, I storm to the back of the room and kick Simon off, ignoring his whining as I re-adjust the throne. A moment later, Simon finds some sort of cowbell thing to *ding* in time with what I start playing.

My eyes search for Ayden, always needing to have him in my sights, and I grin as I watch him approach the others, trying to show them the basics of what they were trying to do. He's probably wasting his time, but I can see he enjoys helping them, so I leave him to it and focus on tapping the hi-hats.

"We could totally have our own band," Rhys announces through the mic, making everyone chuckle.

"Let me guess. You'd be the lead singer?" Shaun raises his dark brows at Rhys, but she shrugs.

"Of course. It's not like you douchecanoes can sing."

"I hate to tell you this, George." Using Rhys' last name, Shaun puts the guitar down and strides over to her. "But you can't sing either." He snatches the mic off her and starts trying to beatbox, and then Rhys leaps on his back, sending them both to the floor.

"Your friend is weird." Simon's voice startles me. I hadn't seen him pull up a seat next to me.

Shaking my head, I turn to Simon and smile. "Maybe. But you like her."

"I never said I didn't like her. She's actually kind of cool, in a weird kind of way. You know what I mean?" Simon keeps his eyes on Rhys and Shaun as Marcus and Ayden step in to end their wrestle over the mic.

I giggle, "Actually, I do."

"So, Lexi. My new sister." Simon turns his attention to me, playfulness dancing in his hazel eyes. "As your brother, I should probably have a bit of a *birds and bees* chat with you now that you have a serious boyfriend."

"Nice try, but no, we aren't having *that* talk, Simon." I lay the sticks to rest on the drum and swivel the throne, stretching as I stand, my body still aching from Mike's attack four days ago.

"Fine, but tell me one thing, please?" Simon's tone turns from class clown to serious, so I spin back and take in his straight face.

When I nod, he continues, "Does Ayden treat you right?"

Frowning, I nod and step up to Simon. "Yes, he does. He makes me very happy."

Simon smirks. "Good, because if he wasn't, then I'd have to fight him, and I'm pretty sure he'd kick my arse, but I'd still give it a go... for you."

"Thanks, Simon." I smile and reach up, wrapping my arms around his neck in a hug.

Simon hugs me back, but it's a short-lived hug because Rhys crashes into us where we linger at the rear of the studio screaming "group hug," and then we're engulfed by the others joining in.

Ayden stays back laughing. "Where do you get all of your energy, Rhys?"

Wiggling around in the group hug, Rhys dislodges us before answering Ayden.

"Sex."

I nearly choke on my own saliva, and Ayden's brows shoot to his hairline while the other guys coo and pat

Marcus on the shoulder like he's done a stellar job since she's a ball of energy.

"Sex?" Ayden asks, leaning a shoulder against the red fabric wall of the studio.

Grinning, Rhys throws her arm over my shoulder and nods. "That's correctamundo. Doesn't sex have that effect on you?"

Her giggle tells me she knows sex doesn't have that effect on any of us.

"It makes me tired," I say, trying not to blush like the vanilla girl I am. Well, in front of everyone else, I'm vanilla. I'll have to ask Ayden if he thinks I'm vanilla in the bedroom.

"Yeah, a good fuck knocks me out for hours." Shaun pipes up from across the room, where he pops the top on a beer bottle.

"Not me." Flashing her white teeth, Rhys walks over to Shaun and steals his beer, chugging it down.

"Hey!" He protests while we laugh and watch her down the whole thing.

"Uh... maybe you drinking isn't such a good idea," Simon warns, heading across the room to Rhys while Ayden makes his way back to me. My body instantly relaxes when he nears, and it's like we both can't handle being apart for long.

Pulling the beer bottle away from her mouth, Rhys gulps a few times and then lets out the most obnoxious burp I have ever heard a human do. Instantly the guys are in fits of laughter because burping and farts are that funny, apparently. I try my hardest not to laugh and end up biting my lip when a grin slips free.

"Me drinking is a brilliant idea. Especially if you want me to *not* be so energetic. A few drinks will keep me nice and calm." Rhys strides up to Marcus and cups his junk in front of everyone.

"If you don't want me to fuck you right here in front of everyone, then you should probably remove your hand from my cock," Marcus growls, his dark eyes smouldering at Rhys, who just grins wider.

"Who says I wouldn't like that? I love a good audience."

The guys, except for Ayden and Marcus, hoot, and it's apparent quite quickly that Marcus is pissed about Rhys' comment. His dark brows draw together, and I can tell he's biting the inside of his cheek to stop himself from responding.

"Since no one wants to see that, why don't we head back to my dad's apartment and order pizza for dinner? Maybe watch a few movies?" Ayden suggests.

Marcus doesn't even answer, but pushes Rhys off him and storms out of the room, leaving us all a little stunned. Not seeming to care, Rhys skips through the studio, picking up discarded hoodies and phones, while Jared, Shaun and Garrett pack up the food and drinks. Simon doesn't help, though. He's too busy trying to play Twinkle Twinkle Little Star on the piano.

"Is everything okay with Marcus?" I ask Rhys as we make our way out of the studio.

Shrugging, she gives me a small smile. "He'll be okay. He's been a bit off after a conversation we had this morning."

Part of me doesn't want to push for more information because I honestly don't want to make Rhys feel like she has to tell me everything. It's not that I don't want to know stuff. Because I do. It's just that I have a feeling she has some dark demons that would rival mine, and I'm fairly certain she wants to keep them buried.

The thing is, Marcus is also my friend, and I know how much he wears his heart on his sleeve. I have a bad feeling he's going to get hurt by Rhys.

"What conversation did you have this morning?" My question scores an odd look from Rhys as we step inside the elevator, moving to the back so the others can pile in too. Marcus is nowhere in sight.

The lift starts climbing, and I sneak a glance at Rhys to find her already looking at me.

"Later." She mouths, and I nod. This is a conversation she doesn't want the others to hear.

The smell of something delicious cooking causes a wave of mouth-watering moans from the guys as we step inside Peter's apartment and find Peter, Andrea and my mum chatting away as they cook. All three of them.

I'm instantly on edge, and I think I'd briefly forgotten that my mum was here. Ayden's hands and mouth have a way of doing that to me, it seems.

Looking up, Andrea smiles. "Dinner will be ready soon."

"I guess we don't need to worry about ordering pizza," Ayden mumbles, and offers me a smile when I glance at him.

Fuck, I can hardly handle not touching him, like, every fucking minute.

"Mrs Mitchell, you look radiant this evening." Shaun turns on his Casanova charm as he slides onto a barstool and drops his chin in his hands, watching Andrea.

"Bossi, you'd better not be hitting on my mum!" Ayden hisses, causing the others to chuckle and Andrea to turn red.

"Don't be ridiculous, Ayden." Andrea scolds.

"He's not being ridiculous, Mrs Mitchell. I'd totally hit on you if your husband wasn't here," Shaun says with conviction.

The sound of Shaun getting pushed off the barstool by Ayden is all I hear as I turn to leave the kitchen and drag Rhys by the hand behind me.

"Oooh, where are we going?" Rhys whisper-yells behind me. I don't answer because a moment later, we pass a brooding Marcus lying on the couch in the second living area before I pull her into Ayden's bedroom and shut the door.

"Okay. What's going on with you and Marcus?" I take a seat on the end of Ayden's bed, hoping Rhys doesn't notice how tired I am. I actually feel a little lightheaded.

"Wow, Ayden's room is nice here, hey? His dad must be rich or something."

"Rhys?" I urge because she is totally deflecting.

Sighing, she drags her eyes away from her surroundings to focus on me. "You're being a party pooper."

"Yes, I know I am, but if we can take a minute to be boringly serious, I'll let you get back to having your fun in no time. I promise." My sober tone causes Rhys to pout before she huffs and shrugs, coming to sit next to me on the bed.

"I told him, from the beginning, that I don't do relationships. I don't do clingy, and I don't do exclusive. I told him he can see other people, that what we are doing is just a bit of fun to blow off some steam, and he totally agreed to it." Rhys sighs and drops her chin dramatically to her chest. "Now I've gone and hurt his feelings by reminding him about that. Ugh! I'm such an idiot. I usually stay away from high school boys. I usually try to stick with Uni students, but there was just something about Marcus that drew me in, and I fucking caved. Now look at what's happened. He's gone all clingy and shit, and I hate having to let him down like this, but I never once said this was anything more than some good fucking."

I'm taken aback by Rhys' admission. I've heard guys from school talk about sex like this, but never a girl. Not that there's anything wrong with that. She can do what she wants with whoever she wants, but when it comes to Marcus, to any of the guys, I can't help but feel defensive.

Rhys isn't usually so serious. She is always joking around or a ball of energy, excited about something. There have only been a couple of times where she's shown me she is more than the wild, crazy girl she wants the world to see. This is one of those times, and I can tell with the way her eyes seem almost nervous that the situation with Marcus is a concern to her.

"So that's what the conversation was about this morning? Did you like, break up with him or something?" I ask, and Rhys nods, but then shakes her head.

"Yeah-nah, no breakup because we weren't even together. It's just been hooking up, Lexi. That's all I'm into, and Marcus was hoping it would be more."

"So there's no part of you that wants more with Marcus?" When she frowns at me, I add, "I'm not trying to be pushy. I'm just trying to understand because if you ask me, Rhys, you *are* into Marcus. I don't understand how you can say you aren't when I've seen it with my own eyes. It's not just about sex."

"Fuck." Rhys grits out, flinging herself back on the bed and staring at the ceiling. "That's why it's time to cut and run, Lexi. I don't do relationships. I can't let myself fall harder for him."

"Can I ask why you don't do relationships?" My question earns a glare from Rhys.

"Are you judging me, Lexi?"

"What? No," I squeak, pulling my legs up on the bed to face her better. "I just don't want Marcus to get hurt, and believe it or not. I don't want you to get hurt, either. The thing is, I feel like you're just causing yourself pain by doing this. You two really do have a good thing going."

She frowns, studying my face. I don't take my gaze off her dark eyes.

"You don't have to answer my question. I'm just struggling to understand how you can say you don't want a relationship when I can see you really want that." I shrug.

Studying me a beat longer, Rhys sighs, turning her head on the bed to look at her hand before she starts biting at the Purple Passion polish on her nails.

"I learnt pretty quickly that committed relationships aren't for me, Lexi." Rhys says quietly, "I'm a cheater. I can't do monogamous, which is why I need to end things with Marcus now. In the end, he's going to get hurt worse." She shrugs like that means nothing. "I've never been able to be with just one person. I can do it for like a week or two, but then I wander, and it turns out that guys don't like to share. Weird, I know." Rhys gives me an exaggerated, exasperated look.

"Is there some reason in particular that makes you wander? Like, are you always looking for a guy's faults or something?"

"You mean am I self-sabotaging? I guess in a way it's like that, but then again, it isn't. I can't really find the words to describe it, Lexi, but I just can't stick to one dude or chick. I love the different sexual encounters I get from remaining single, and they even get old quickly for me. So, I move on to a new encounter. That's the only way I can explain it. When I tried to explain it to Marcus, he started coming up with different sexual scenarios we could try." Rhys shrugs again. "I mean, we could try them, Lexi, but it will only get us through a couple more weeks before we've done everything a couple can do together. Then we'll be back where we are now. He was the one that brought up fucking me in front of everyone, which, I'll be honest, turned me on so bad my panties are soaked through."

"Oh my god, Rhys! I don't want to know that." I cover my ears with my hands, and Rhys throws her head back laughing before sitting up and prying my hands away.

"Don't tell me you wouldn't have sat back and watched Marcus make me come, Lexi. You totally would have."

Shoving away, Rhys' hands drop mine as she grins wickedly.

"Rhys, I've already practically witnessed you and Marcus going at it, and I can tell you now, I did not want to see that."

Rhys sighs, and her smile falls. "It doesn't matter anyway, Lex. Marcus got pissed off when I told him I like an audience. He's not actually into the shit that might keep me interested for a bit longer. He's a fierce lover, don't get me wrong. Lots of heat and passion, but I don't always need that. Sometimes I need to be dominated, sometimes I need to be the one to dominate, and sometimes I need a weird kink that most high school guys have never thought of." Rhys shakes her head. "That's why I tend to stick with older guys. They're only interested in the hookup, and that's it. They are experienced, and most have done or have knowledge of things that are more than a dick in a hole. I know chicks aren't meant to think the way I do, but I've never been one to succumb to the social norms."

I can't help but smile. Rhys definitely doesn't do normal, which is what drew me to her. She has this freedom about her. She doesn't care what others think. She just walks this fucked up world being who she wants to be.

"Hopefully Marcus will get over it." My words catch Rhys off guard, and her face slowly contorts into a black-lipped grin.

"So, you still love me?"

"Of course I do, but be kind to Marcus. I love him too." Smiling, I move forward and hug Rhys, which she returns before pulling me down on the bed and screaming.

"Yes! Lexi! Oh yes! Right there!"

As I struggle through laughter and tears to try and pry her off me, the bedroom door flies open, and a murderous Ayden and Marcus barge in with the other guys on their heels.

Sitting up abruptly, Rhys grins ear to ear, throwing her hands up in surrender while I'm still in a fit of laughter rolling around on Ayden's bed.

"I couldn't control her. She's like a sex-crazed animal." Rhys teases, and I can't even find it in me to protest because I'm so consumed with laughter.

The room suddenly sounds with seven different message alert tones, and everyone pulls out their phones as I lay on my back, gripping my middle to catch my breath.

"What the fuck?" Marcus hisses, and I pop my head up to look at him.

"Who the fuck is this from?" Rhys asks, and my attention is drawn to everyone in the room. They're all frowning down at their phones before looking back at me.

"What? What is it?"

"It's a message from you." Confusion laces Simon's tone.

I sit up. "What?"

"No. It's not from Lexi. It's from her old number," Ayden growls, his nostrils flaring as he glances up at me.

I lean over to Rhys. "Show me?"

"No!" Ayden hisses and starts towards us, but I grab Rhys' phone and quickly read the screen.

> *Being Lexi's friend is a fucking bad idea.*
> *Look what happened to poor innocent Valarie. Not so innocent anymore, is she?*
> *You have two options, arseholes!*
> *Ditch the bitch and leave her to her fate, OR stay and join her knowing she'll watch me*

fuck each of you up the arse before killing
you until there's no one left to protect her.
Her pussy isn't worth your life. Make good
choices!

"Lex." Ayden squats down in front of me where I'm perched on his bed, his ocean eyes swimming with a mix of emotions. His expression blurs as hot tears fill my eyes, and anger that has been dormant since waking from my concussion breaches the surface as I leap off the side of the bed and scream.

"NO!"

"Lex. Ignore the message. He's just trying to get a reaction," Jared says from somewhere behind me. I can't look at them. Not when I'm like this. Not when I know I could easily kill Mike if he were in this room right now.

"Lex." Ayden's hand lands gently on my shoulder, but the touch sears me, and I shrug his hand away as I turn to look at him.

"Don't touch me right now." I've never felt more on edge than I do in this moment.

With Rhys' phone still clutched in my hand, I look at the screen again and re-read it. Then, I tap on the number, *my* old number, and press call.

"Lexi, no," Ayden begs, but I shake my head and take a few steps back from him, waiting for the call to be answered.

A moment later, the call connects, but the line is quiet.

"Fuck you, Mike!" I hiss, my voice filled with venom.

"Ali. So nice of you to call me. Did your friends like my message?"

"You stay the fuck away from them!" My body is burning up as if flames are dancing just beneath my skin. I can't even see anyone else in the room. My blinding rage has given me tunnel vision, and all I can see is my fucked up half brother.

Mike snickers. "That would be boring. I'm having way too much fun, so my answer is *no*. I'm going to turn each one of them into my bitch, Ali. And you're going to watch me break them until they are begging to kill you themselves."

"I fucking hate you. I'm going to kill you!"

Mike snickers again, and I scream as the phone is snatched out of my hand, and my rage unleashes as I swing out at whoever stole it from me. My hands connect with anything in my path, and voices sound around me, but can't make anything out as the rush of blood fills my ears. Arms. A lot of arms wrap around me. I struggle against them, screaming as I'm pulled down.

My screams won't relent, my struggles won't give in, my rage has turned me into a monster. I scream, and I scream until my throat is raw, and no more sound will come out. Then my body falls limp as I quietly sob. It's guttural, heart-wrenching, soul-crushing pain that flows from my body as I'm cocooned, wrapped in arms. So many arms.

I should feel like I'm suffocating, but instead, my body accepts the warmth from each embrace and the care that flows from each body. I'm buried in love right now. Love that I did not ask for, yet it found its way to me.

Mike thinks he can hurt my friends, but I won't let that happen. That fucker has to get through me first.

Eight

Last night turned into a shit show. My memory is vague from the point I relinquished control to the beast inside me, my mind a red haze of snapshots. I remember soft whispers and feeling safe wrapped in an embrace. I could be wrong or could have dreamed it, but I could have sworn there was more than one set of arms wrapped around me and more than one voice whispering to me tenderly.

Whatever it was, it helped me fight the monster that took over, and to tame the blinding rage until sleep dragged me under.

Now, in the early light of morning, I lay silently listening to the quiet snores that fill the room, as well as my rumbling tummy.

Damn, I didn't get to eat dinner last night.

As my stomach growls in protest, I pry my sore eyes open, lifting my head a little to spot Rhys on the floor next to my side of Ayden's bed.

She's wrapped in Marcus' arms, looking content, snuggled up with him. I guess she's as confused as I am because yesterday, she told me she doesn't want a relationship with him. Why is she laying in his arms like that if she feels that way?

I'm pretty sure she's trying to fight something that deep down, she really wants, but is too scared to accept. The problem with that is poor Marcus' heart is getting dragged through the mud while she figures her shit out.

Maybe I should have another chat with her.

"You okay, beautiful?" Ayden's voice wraps around me like invisible energy making my heart skip a beat before taking off in a sprint.

I'll never get sick of hearing his voice or hearing him call me beautiful.

Snaking his arm over my side, he pulls me back to his front, his warm lips pressing gently to my temple. It's hard to hold back my moan, loving the feel of every place his body contours with mine. I instantly relax in his embrace, my body needy for his touch, even though I sure as shit don't deserve it.

Not after my meltdown last night.

Fuck. How humiliating.

They all saw it. They all saw me switch into the monster that runs through my veins.

"Did I hit you?" I ask in a whisper, my skin heating with self-loathing. "I remember my hands connecting with someone. Was it you?"

Tugging me closer, Ayden's breath dances over my hair. "Don't worry about any of that, Lex."

He really should know me better by now. As if I won't worry about it. How can I not be concerned about lashing out at him? Hitting him? The thought alone makes my stomach roll.

Shuffling in his arms, Ayden loosens his hold, giving me the space to roll over and settle on my side to look at him.

Big mistake.

Guilt burns like a bitch as I take in his face, and even in the dim light of the room, I can still see the shadow of a red mark on his left cheek.

Shit. I did that.

I inhale sharply, my eyes burning and my gut twisting with regret.

"I'm so sorry, Ayden." I whisper past my quivering lip, "Fuck. How many times did I hit you?" Shame feels like an elephant on my chest. It's crushing.

Those ocean eyes that call to my soul soften as they roam my face, my expression.

Lifting his hand, Ayden strokes back some of my wayward hair. "Lexi, it's fine. You only got the one hit in. I moved away pretty fast after that with the phone."

How can he be okay with how I acted?

The red mark on his cheek has to hurt. I did that to him. He should be pissed at me.

"One hit?" I ask, frowning, trying to reach inside my mind to retrieve the memories. They are too fuzzy, though. "I remember hitting someone more than once. Who was it?"

Ayden grins, and it's smug as fuck. "That would be Jared, Marcus and Garrett."

I bolt upright, my mouth in an O of horror as I glance around the room, panicked, until I spot Jared and Garrett on the floor at the end of the bed in sleeping bags.

Ayden sits up next to me, chuckling, and before I can say anything like, *dude this isn't funny*, he weaves his fingers with mine.

"They're tough, Lex. No need to worry about them, either. We all just wanted to protect you and keep you safe."

Keep *me* safe?

Dragging my gaze away from the guys on the floor, I glance at Ayden. "Keep me safe from myself, you mean?"

Ayden tilts his head, his lips thin as he shrugs one shoulder. "It was a fucked up situation. The best thing we could do was stop you from hurting yourself. I'm sorry you had to be restrained."

My gaze drops to where Ayden's strong hand is entwined with my dainty one.

"Jesus, I'm messed up. Do you think I should see a therapist or something? What I did... losing control like that... it's not normal."

Lifting our linked hands to his lips, Ayden presses a warm kiss on the back of my hand, his lips soft and comforting.

"What's happened to you isn't normal, Lexi, but your reactions to it *are* normal. In saying that, a therapist may be good at helping you work through your feelings."

I nod, knowing he's right. I should talk to someone other than Mr Matthews, the school counsellor. I hate talking about my feelings, though. I'd much prefer to push that shit down and bury it. Doing that won't help me, though. I'm sane enough to know that.

"Did you speak to Mike when you took the phone from me?" The idea of my brother speaking with Ayden unsettles me. I don't want Mike getting his claws into Ayden. He's too good of a person to deserve to have such vileness taint him.

Before Ayden answers my question, he releases my hand and pulls the blankets back off his thighs. Before I can ask him what he's doing, he reaches over and lifts me like I weigh nothing, positioning me on his lap to straddle him.

"I may have had a chat with him." He smirks at me, brushing back my blonde waves so he can see my face better in the dim light, before tugging the blankets up to wrap over my shoulders.

My brows rise in curiosity. "What did you say to him?"

Ayden settles his arms around my middle and strokes his hands up and down my back. Oooh, that feels good. A girl could get used to this.

"I might've told him he can make all the threats he wants, but none of us will ever stop protecting you. And then I hung up before he could say anything."

Oh man, I bet that pissed Mike off. I would've loved to see the sick fucker's face.

Even though I hate the idea of Ayden talking with Mike, it's sweet that he declared they will never stop protecting me. They can't possibly live up to it, but it's sweet that he thinks that. I know deep in my bones that Mike's not going to stop. Not until either he's dead, or I am.

"What's that look?" Ayden whispers, examining my expression before brushing warm lips across the tip of my nose.

Shit. Why am I so easy to read?

"What look?" I try to straighten my face, hoping he didn't see the fear in my eyes.

Even though I don't believe he and the guys can protect me from Mike, I don't want him to know that I doubt him. It's not that I doubt his abilities and desire to protect me. It's that Mike is another level of fucked up, and I know he'll do whatever it takes to bring me down.

"I'm not sure how to explain it." Ayden responds, his ocean blues dancing between mine. "There was fear, but there was also something else? Acceptance maybe? What were you thinking about?"

Bringing his hands out from the blankets, Ayden cups my face, his eyes doing that thing they do when they try to peer into my soul.

I shrug. "I don't know what you're talking about." I lie.

Did I just accept that this will only end with mine or Mike's death?

"Maybe that was her lust look." Rhys' voice floats up from beside the bed, and she props her chin on the mattress, looking up at us with puppy dog eyes.

Ayden chuckles. "Nope. That definitely wasn't her lust look."

"You two look cosy. Were you about to fuck?" Rhys wags her brows.

"Rhys!" I whisper-yell, and she grins cheekily.

"Maybe we already have." Ayden taunts, and I dart my head back to him with my mouth open.

"Ayden." I hiss.

"What?" He shrugs, and Rhys giggles quietly.

"Nah, I would've heard the sex noises. There's no way I'd sleep through that." Rhys teases, and I throw my hands up. This chick is infuriating. Funny but still infuriating. Especially when it comes to embarrassing me, and damn it, Ayden has jumped on board too.

The cheeky shit.

"Maybe we were really quiet." Ayden teases, sliding his warm palm up the side of my neck to tilt my head back so I have no choice but to look at him, and then he shoots me a wink.

And now my pussy is hungry too.

Great.

"No way. Lexi is a screamer. The entire city heard her from the rooftop." Rhys giggles, and my head darts in Rhys' direction.

"You heard us?"

She shoots me a *well duh* look. "Only once I made Simon stay quiet so we could hear properly. That was until party pooper Marcus made us leave. Such a drag."

A loud slap dances off the walls in Ayden's room, and Rhys' eyes roll back in her head.

"Oooh yeah, baby. Do it again."

"Come back down here and leave Lexi alone," Marcus croaks, his voice husky from sleep.

Rhys rolls her eyes but focuses on me again. Jesus, she totally enjoyed that slap. Hell, I'd probably enjoy that slap.

Not from Marcus, though. That would just be weird.

Ayden, though? Hell yes.

"Lexi, before I get side-tracked," Rhys mutters, trying to keep her attention on me which makes me wonder what exactly Marcus is doing to her that I can't see. "I should tell you that while you were the juicy filling in a fucking hot sub sandwich last night, your mum kinda got upset after she witnessed you go Cujo."

"My mum saw that?"

Crap. I keep forgetting she's even here. What the fuck is wrong with me?

"Uh, yeah." Ayden speaks this time, drawing my attention to his kissable lips, "After I hung up on Mike, my parents came in with your mum. I filled them in, and dad called Officer Reynolds. My mum wanted to check on you, but the guys wouldn't leave you. The fuckers wouldn't even let me get to you until you fell asleep."

"Really?"

I'm surprised punches weren't thrown. Ayden gets a little jealous of the guys. I mean, I don't blame him. I'd lose my shit if he had close friends that were girls who showed him the affection the guys do to me.

Crap, maybe I should have a word with the guys and ask them to dial it back a bit.

"The way your pack cared for you was kind of sweet."
Rhys shrugs. "I was jealous, let me tell you. What I
would have done to be the filling in between all that
hard muscle." Rhys licks her lips seductively, and Ayden
chuckles, "I swear I thought Ayden was going to go
caveman on them. The way Jared, Marcus and Garrett
had you in their arms, and the way Shaun was stroking
your hair. Who would have thought Casanova would
be so sensitive? Oh," Rhys laughs, "and Simon. He had
your feet covered, giving you a foot massage. I swear
that guy has a foot fetish."

I shudder at the thought, and I feel the rumble of *my*
man's chuckle against my chest.

"Your mum really was pretty upset, though." Rhys
turns serious.

"She was?" I frown. The concept of my mum being
upset about me is foreign.

"Yeah, she mumbled something about wishing she
had run away with you when you were little. I asked her
what she meant, but that woman closed up tighter than
a clamshell. She walked out crying after that. I went and
sat with her for a bit, but she didn't want to talk."

I wouldn't be surprised if all this heavy crap sends
mum to drink again, which will lead her back to the
pill-popping. She's not used to feeling, well, anything.
She's barely been out of rehab, and she has to take on
all this bullshit because of Mike.

Marcus sits up abruptly, snaking his arms around
Rhys' mid-section, and drags her back down to the
floor. I expect my goth girlfriend to squeal, but the

horny bitch moans and I have the overwhelming urge to cover my ears.

Exhaustion hits me hard then, wrapping itself around me like a vise. As if sensing it, Ayden pulls me to his chest, laying back with me on his chest, and my eyes flutter closed, desperate for sleep.

I can't stop thinking about Mike's text message to the guys and Rhys. He's got a lot of nerve doing that. He obviously doesn't care anymore if people know what he's up to. The message had been sent from my old phone, the one he swiped when he ran off after his first attack on me. The thing is, I wasn't friends with Rhys back then, so how did he get her number if it wasn't already in my phone?

"Stop thinking, beautiful. Try to get some more sleep." Ayden's whisper is a caress against my ear, and I bury my head into the crook of his neck, inhaling his spicy scent.

I've said it before, and I'll say it again. I need to put his scent in a bottle and spray it everywhere. Smelling him everywhere would make me happy *all* the time then.

And horny.

I'd definitely be horny, too.

The smell that is Ayden Mitchell works its magic, and I somehow manage to stop thinking about everything and slowly fall into a peaceful sleep.

Nine

Peter's apartment buzzes with energy the next morning as everyone washes, eats, talks shit, and prepares to head back to Fox Pines. Slowly nibbling on a piece of toast, I try my best to drag out our stay for as long as possible. I'm dreading going home. I'd much prefer to hide away here in Peter's apartment and pretend like my sibling isn't threatening my friends and trying to kill me.

Sitting quietly at the kitchen table, I watch the guys banter while they repeatedly try to drag Peter into it, all the while I sense my mum's eyes on me. I can feel her stare burning into the side of my head, almost like she wants to say something to me, but she's holding back. We haven't really spoken again, but her eyes take me in differently, as if she's studying me. Seeing me for the first time.

Hell, maybe she is. For so much of my life, she's been wearing substance goggles. Ruth probably has no idea who I really am, just like I have no idea who she really is as a sober person.

The idea of going back home with her is unnerving. It's not just about going back to the house that holds my nightmares, although that's playing a good part in my stalling. Having my mum back there with me makes me feel uncomfortable, especially since I've gotten used to having the guys around me all the time.

How's Ruth going to handle that? Is she going to try to be all parent-like and tell me they can't sleep over?

We will definitely have problems if she does that shit.

Even though I'm not a fan of the lilac room at Marcus' house, it feels less scary than being alone in my house with my mum right now.

On the drive back to Fox Pines, Andrea fills my mum in on the events since she's been gone. My mum listens quietly as Andrea explains how things have gone missing from our house, and the lack of progress in the hunt for Mike and my dad. Taking in all the information, my mum's expression is strained, showing how hard her brain is working to commit it all to memory.

The buzz of my phone in my pocket draws my attention away from my mum in the front of the car, and I slip it from my hoodie pocket to see a message from Ayden. A grin tilts up my lips, and I turn to him, sitting right next to me in the back seat.

Why is he messaging me when I'm sitting right here?

He flashes white teeth at me, his grin broad as he gestures with his head towards my lap where I'm holding my phone.

Silently sighing, I look down and open his message.

Ayden Mitchell
Are you okay?

Turning my blue eyes back to his, I raise my brows, and he grins again before keying in something on his phone, and a moment later, a second message comes through.

Ayden Mitchell
You look worried, Lex. Let's talk about it.
It's just you and me in this conversation.

I'm helpless to hide my smile.
This guy.
He is so in tune with my emotions, always knowing when things aren't right with me. It's something I love about him.

Lexi West
I'm feeling a bit off about going back home with my mum.

Looking back up at Ayden, I watch his face and the nod he gives as he reads my message before typing in a response.

Ayden Mitchell

That's understandable. You both have a lot to talk about, I guess.

Lexi West

We've never really talked. I doubt she's going to start now.

Ayden Mitchell

She's sober now. It may change your relationship for the better.

Lexi West

Maybe. It's hard to imagine it being any different than it's always been. I'm not sure she even deserves to have a relationship with me.

Ayden Mitchell

I guess that's something you have to decide, eventually. Maybe just take each day as it comes.

Nodding, I glance back at Ayden and smile, which he returns before leaning over and pressing warm lips to my forehead. I close my eyes at the contact as I savour his touch, wishing we were alone so I could have his lips on mine.

Slowly pulling back, Ayden leans down and strokes my blonde waves, hooking them behind my ear before his warm breath flutters over the skin there.

"I'm not leaving you, Lexi. You won't be alone in the house with your mum."

It's really hard to focus on his words when he is so close like this, his scent turning my brain into mush.

My heart flutters like it's grown wings, and I take only a moment of indulgence before pulling back and typing out a message.

Lexi West
As much as I like the idea, you can't stay with me all the time, Ayden.

Ayden Mitchell
If I can't be with you, then one or two of the guys will be.
We're not risking anything until this thing with Mike and your dad is over.

Lexi West

So, you guys will still stay with me? Even with my mum there?

Ayden Mitchell

Yes, Lex. Nothing against your mum, but she can't protect you.

Lexi West

But who's going to protect you? Mike's message isn't just an idle threat, Ayden. Look what he did to Val. I don't want any of you to get hurt because of me.

Ayden Mitchell

Don't you worry about us, beautiful. We have it covered.

I don't know what he means by that, so I glance back up at him and frown, but he just offers me a smile and sends me another message.

Ayden Mitchell

I forgot to tell you. My dad spoke to Officer Zimora this morning, and apparently, on his day off, Jason went to your house and installed a full security system. Cameras, alarms and all.

Lexi West

Um, who's Jason?

Ayden Mitchell

Officer Zimora.
He's more than just a man in uniform for you to drool over, Lexi!

My mouth drops open, and I slap Ayden's shoulder, and the cheeky shit chuckles, drawing the attention of Andrea and my mum.

"I hope you're behaving yourself, Ayden." Andrea's tone is laced with humour while she eyes us in the rearview mirror as she drives along the highway.

"Always." Ayden flashes his mum a cheesy grin.

"Hmmm." The hum comes from Andrea before she withdraws her attention, and I take the opportunity to type out a new message.

Lexi West

So, Jason Zimora, the copper, installed a security system at my house?

That's not part of his job. Why has he done this now? I could have used a security system before. Not that I'm ungrateful or anything, but what's changed? Do you think he knows something more about Mike and isn't telling us?

Ayden Mitchell

I'd like to think he'd keep you updated if there's any news on Mike, but who knows? I was curious about why he installed the security system too, so I asked my dad if he knew why. It doesn't really seem like part of a cop's job, but my dad thinks Jason feels guilty or something. Apparently, he mentioned something about wishing the department had the resources to do more. I guess he took it into his own hands.

Lexi West

But that must have cost a fortune.

Ayden Mitchell

Yeah, that stuff isn't cheap, but it turns out his brother is in the security business, so he got everything at cost. Don't worry about that, though, Lex. The important thing is that you have extra protection now. Dad said the police will also do regular drive-bys at your place and all of ours too, plus the school. If Mike's lurking around, they will catch him.

I'm about to respond to Ayden when a SnapChat notification pops up on my screen from the boys' chat. My eyes drift to Ayden's phone in his hand, and I see that he's switching over to check the message, so I do the same.

Rhys-George

Lexi!! It's official!! I'm part of your pack now! Shaun added me.

Jared-Crowley

She actually squealed. I can't hear shit now.

Shaun-Bossier

I deserve a kiss for adding you, George. Pucker up.

Marcus-Grady

Put that filthy mouth anywhere near her, and I'll fuck you up, Bossi!

Rhys-George

Boys. Let's not fight. There's plenty of me to go around.

"Should I warn my dad that there's about to be a bloodbath in his car?" Ayden whispers in my ear, and I grin up at him. Poor Peter. He really drew the short straw in who he is driving back to Fox Pines.

Lexi-West

Welcome to the pack, Rhys. First rule of the pack is not to cause drama.

Rhys-George

Oh well, you guys are fucked. Simon is all about the drama! How is he still part of the pack?

Simon-Hastings

Hey! I'm only a little dramatic.

Jared-Crowley

We should vote him out.

"Oh, no!" Andrea cries.

Ayden and I dart our eyes out the front window to see Peter's SUV swerve on the road before straightening up again.

Ayden-Mitchell

WTF just happened?

Marcus-Grady

Hastings threw a punch into Crowley's leg and bumped your dad's seat from behind.

Simon-Hastings

He fucking deserved it! He should be the one to be voted out!

Marcus-Grady
FFS Hastings! No one is voting anyone out.

Rhys-George
All this drama is making me horny!

Jesus Christ. I can just imagine all the guys groaning at Rhys' comment. Maybe I should've made her travel in Andrea's car with us.

Garrett-Cole
Hey Lex, are you coming back to school tomorrow?

I'm about to type out an answer when Ayden answers for me.

Ayden-Mitchell
No. Since it's the last week of term, she'll stay home and recover. She'll go back in term four.

"Excuse me?" My head darts to Ayden, and his lips thin as he turns those ocean blues on me.

"You know it's the safest option, Lex," he responds, trying to look all sympathetic and shit, which just pisses me off.

"What's the safest option?" My mum pipes up then, butting into our conversation.

Ayden mouths a "sorry" before responding to my mum.

"I was just saying that maybe Lexi shouldn't return to school until next term, since this is the last week of term three. It will give her time to heal, and it'll be safer for her to lie low until they catch Mike."

My mum nods. "Yes, I agree. Ayden is right, Lexi. You'll stay home until this situation is over."

What the actual fuck.

My face burns as anger courses through me. Not only do I hate being told what to do by anyone, but I especially hate being told what to do by my mum. A mum that hasn't shown an interest in my life for years now. I especially hate feeling ganged up on, and even though I'll probably look back at this later and cringe about how much I've overreacted, I can't help the way I feel in this moment.

"Actually," I say, my voice oozing bitch, "*I* will do what *I* want to do when *I* want to do it, *Ruth*." I deliberately use her name to piss her off. "If *I* don't go to school this week, it's because *I* decide not to."

I'm being petty and immature and all the things a bratty teenager is. I can't bring myself to pull my attitude into line, though. My mum doesn't just get to pop back into my life and pretend she gives a shit and order me around. Not when she chose drugs and alcohol over me for so many years. Not when she lied to the Ambo's and told them that an intruder broke into our house when really Mike assaulted her. Not when I went to visit her in the hospital in Melbourne because I was worried about her, only to have her scream at me and blame my dad's and Mike's behaviour on *me*.

I may have had short term memory loss from the concussion only a couple of days ago, but my memory sure as shit hasn't forgotten what sort of mother she was before she turned up sober yesterday.

"Lexi!" My mum's voice rises in anger from the front of the car, but Andrea jumps in to diffuse it.

"Perhaps Lexi can just take each day as it comes. Maybe making decisions like this should be put on hold. There's no rush for Lexi to return to school, but maybe going to school will be a good distraction if she needs it."

I relax as Andrea speaks. That is, until Ayden opens his mouth.

"Mum, it's too dangerous. She's not going back."

"What the fuck, Ayden," I snap.

When did he become so fucking controlling?

My glare would kill if it had the ability to throw blades in his direction, but Mr fucking hot and panty-melting sexy just glares back at me with as much bravado as me.

"This isn't open for discussion, Lexi. It's too dangerous."

"Don't tell me what to do, Ayden!" My yell is loud in the confined space of the car, and Andrea swerves off the road, pulling the car over.

Taking advantage of the opportunity, I click off my seat belt and throw the car door open, ignoring Ayden as he calls out for me.

Red rims my vision as the anger simmers at the surface.

Fuck, I need to punch something!

When did I become so aggressive?

Oh yeah, that's right, when my brother tried to rape me!

"Lexi!" Andrea calls at the same time Ayden does, and I hear another car pull over as I stomp through the scrub on the side of the road that leads into a pine plantation.

They are everywhere around Timber Valley, which means we mustn't be too far from Fox Pines.

The slight breeze that weaves through the trees instantly cools my heated skin, and for a moment, I feel my anger subside. That is, until heavy feet pound the forest floor a moment before strong arms wrap around me from behind.

"Lex," Ayden whispers as I let him pull me back against his chest. "Please don't run from me."

I sigh and turn in his arms. "Don't try to control me then."

"See, I told you she'd be pissed." Rhys' voice comes from behind Ayden, and I peer over his shoulder to find her with Jared and Marcus.

Great. A fucking audience.

"No one disagreed with you about that, Rhys. We just said she wouldn't smack him in the face in front of his mum." Jared's voice is filled with amusement.

"You guys wanna give us a minute?" Ayden calls over his shoulder, sounding pissed.

"Nope," Jared responds. "We're here to watch Lexi hand you your arse. What the fuck are you thinking, telling her what to do?"

Ayden lets go of me, spinning to face Jared in anger. "What the fuck is your problem!"

"You are!" Jared hisses, stepping up to butt chests with Ayden. "Don't fucking tell Six what to do!"

"Stop calling her that!" Ayden growls, standing taller to meet Jared's height.

"Hey! Why don't you both tuck your dicks back in? I'm not interested in seeing you swing them around."

My words gain their attention and cause Rhys and Marcus to snicker. Meanwhile, I glance back at the roadside and see Andrea consoling my mum as she... cries.

What the fuck?

Stepping back from Ayden, Jared sneers. "I will never stop calling her Six, so get fucking used to it!"

Sighing, I drop my chin to my chest and close my eyes, hoping for calm.

"Lex." Ayden's voice is close, and a moment later, his warm hand reaches for mine.

I let him take it because I'm hopelessly addicted to him. The feel of his skin against mine calms me, and I instantly feel an apology on the tip of my tongue.

Glancing up into his concerned eyes, I watch his dark brows dip as he visibly chews on the inside of his cheek.

"You can boss me around all you like in the bedroom, Ayden, but that's it. I need to be in control of how I live my life. I really need you to understand that."

"He'd better not fucking boss you around in the bedroom!" Jared hisses, coming to stand beside us. "You fucking hurt her, and I'll kill you myself!"

"Jar!" I hiss, shooting him a glare.

"What? You like being thrown around when you fuck?" he growls, and Ayden growls back, making a move to face Jared again.

Shooting my arm out, I hold Ayden back and face my lifelong friend. "Jar, it's not like that, and it's also none of your business."

"But... how can you like that after what your brother did?" The pain swimming in Jared's blue gaze instantly slices my heart open.

"I'm not having this conversation with you or anyone else. That is my private business." My quiet words only cause him more pain, but as always, Rhys has perfect timing and adds her thoughts.

"I can answer your question, Jared," she says, and we all look at her, wondering what she will come up with this time. Her dark hair is parted in the middle with her typical twisted bun style on each side, and her dark lips are drawn into a straight line as she darts her eyes to each of us. "My therapist once told me that victims of abuse often like to be treated a certain way or even re-enact certain situations that happened to them, so they get to feel in control."

"But..." Jared's brows dip. "Lexi said Ayden can boss her around in the bedroom. That sounds like *he* has all the control."

Jared is genuinely concerned, and my chest hurts for him.

The things inflicted on me haven't just affected me, they have affected everyone close to me, too. Including Jared, who I know has been having a hard time coming to terms with my relationship with Ayden. He hasn't said the words outright, but I know he has feelings for me that surpass friendship or family. I don't want to hurt him, but I can't help how I feel about Ayden.

"Is Ayden really in control, though?" Rhys asks. "The moment Lexi uses a safe word or tells him to stop, I bet he does, or he would. During an assault, a victim's plea to stop is always ignored. I doubt very much that Ayden would ignore Lexi if she asked him to stop."

"That makes sense." Marcus speaks for the first time, and Rhys grins at him, although it doesn't reach her normally playful eyes.

"My therapist also said victims like it that way because they are taking a bad situation that happened to them and replacing the memories with good ones. It's all about control and trust."

A single tear pops free and rolls down my cheek as I take in Rhys' words and the fact that I think I just learnt something new about her.

She has been a victim in the worst possible way. The therapist told her those things because she, too, has endured her power being taken from her.

I'm hopeless to stop myself, and I step up to her, throwing my arms around her neck.

"I love you, Rhys," I whisper, and she instantly hugs me back.

"I'm a keeper, right?" she asks jokingly, although it really is *no* joke. She acts carefree, and she loves a good time, but she carries her own burdens, which I think have everything to do with why she can't commit to a relationship.

I nod my head. "Yes. I'm keeping you for as long as you'll let me."

Rhys takes that moment to smack a kiss on my lips, and I hear a round of curses before I push her back, laughing.

"Girl, stop fucking around." I laugh, and she just bares her teeth and growls at me before snickering. She's such a fucking troublemaker.

"Right. Now that everyone has calmed down, why don't you two," Rhys points to Marcus and Jared, "escort your new pack member back to the cars, so these two can fuck and make up? Whoops, I mean kiss and make up."

I don't know if Rhys meant to diffuse the situation like she did when she came over here with Marcus and Jared in tow, but it's entirely possible that's exactly what her plan was. She drew the attention to her, even if it made her look insensitive or vulnerable. She offered insight, and then she changed the vibe by shocking us all into laughter.

Jesus, I think it was actually deliberate.

A little unorthodox, maybe, but it did the trick because Marcus and Jared are walking in the other direction, leaving me with Ayden, and I no longer feel like killing anyone.

That girl is a genius.

"Lex." Ayden's smooth voice beckons me, and I turn to him, now able to see the pain in his beautiful eyes that I couldn't see before when I was angry.

"I'm sorry, Ayden. I'm so fucking hot-headed these days. You didn't deserve my outburst." My hands twist and fidget together as I stand a couple of feet from him, not sure what to do with myself.

Those piercing eyes roam my face as he contemplates a response.

Shit, it makes me nervous.

Has my anger pushed him away?

Is he rethinking his feelings for me?

"I can't lose you, Lexi." His eyes fall to the ground at our feet before he throws his head back in frustration, growling like an animal up into the pine trees. A panting moment later, he returns his stormy gaze to me. "I don't want to be *that* guy who tells you what you can and can't do. I don't want to control you." He exhales, his brow twisting in a frown that looks agonising. "But if that's what it takes to keep you safe, Lexi, then it's something we will both have to get used to."

Well, fuck me. I wasn't expecting him to say that, and I also wasn't expecting to feel my body betray me and react like I want to pounce on him and dry hump his face.

Holy shit, why is his bossiness such a fucking turn on?

I need to calm down. I need to focus on what we were talking about.

Shit! What were we talking about again?

A primal growl is the only warning I get before Ayden drags me against his chest and slams his lips to mine. Moans slip from both of us as our tongues clash and fight for dominance.

A moment later, the rough bark of a tree trunk digs into my back as Ayden's body presses deliciously against mine. My body is on fire, need coursing through me. That is, until a car horn blares in the distance.

"Fuck." Ayden hisses, pulling back from me to peer around the tree to the roadside.

"Holy shit," I whisper, leaning my head back against the tree, sucking in the cool air, hoping it will douse the flames dancing over my skin.

Ayden pulls back to look at me, but he doesn't let go.

"I don't want to fight with you, Lex, but if it makes you look at me the way you did a minute ago, then be prepared to fight all the fucking time."

My laughter bursts free, and Ayden grins back at me.

God, I'm so in love with this guy.

"Seriously, though. I don't want to fight with you," Ayden whispers, sobering me up.

"I don't want to fight with you either."

"So where are we with this dilemma, Lex? Will you stay home from school until next term?"

I still feel defiant about this. "I get that you want to keep me safe, Ayden. I really do. But I can't accept being told what to do and have the decision taken away from me."

His eyes dance between mine, his hand smoothing back my blonde waves as he thinks. "Shit, Lex. It's just a week. Can't you just take it off?"

"Sure, I can take it off, Ayden, if *I* want to." I can't help myself. I run my hands up his firm chest, needing to feel him under my touch.

"Do you *want* to?" His voice is strained, like it's hard for him to ask that.

"I don't know. I don't want to go back to school tomorrow," I shrug, "but I don't know how I'll feel on Tuesday, or Wednesday, or each day after that."

An audible sigh slips past Ayden's lips, and he presses his forehead against mine. "So, can we agree to take it each day, then?"

It's hard having him this close. My need to lean forward and taste his lips is almost overpowering. "Are we going to have an argument about this if I say one night this week that I want to go to school the next day?"

"Probably." Ayden's lips quirk, and my tongue sneaks out to brush over my bottom lip, desperate to kiss him. His ocean eyes heat when he catches the movement.

"I don't like fighting with you," I whisper as he leans closer.

"Let's not fight then. Let's promise to hear each other out before jumping to conclusions or blowing up at each other." Ayden's lips hover over mine, and our breathing deepens as we hold back from closing the space between us.

"I'm a bit of a hothead, Ayden. I'll try not to go crazy again, but my emotions are ruling me lately. I'm scared I'll fly off the handle and push you away." The honesty leaves me easily, which surprises me. I've held things close to my heart for so long that I thought it would be harder to admit that to him.

"Lexi, no matter what you do, you will *never* push me away. My heart is yours. You own me."

I close the distance, no longer able to hold back, my lips brushing his until he pulls back slightly.

"Do we have a deal? We'll take each day as it comes and talk things out?"

If someone were to walk up, they would think we were kissing with how close we are. Our faces hover so close that I can see the dark blue flecks in Ayden's eyes.

"Yes, we have a deal." I agree against his mouth, before his rigid body relaxes against me and our lips collide again while the car horn blares in the distance.

Ten

Being back inside my house isn't as bad as I thought it would be. What's hard, though, is knowing that just next door a few days ago, Valarie's life changed forever. Just thinking about it sends me into a dark spiral of anger, so I'm grateful to have a boxing bag to punch again instead of the people I love.

Officer Zimora was waiting to greet us when we arrived home, as well as Marcus' parents, who brought my bags of clothes back from their house. I bet they are happy as shit to have me out of their space after all the drama I caused. At least Tony can go to sleep without having to worry about me waking them with my screams in the dead of night, and his white arse can stay tucked up in bed.

Although my mum stays quiet for the rest of the drive home, once we pull into the driveway, her mood perks up, and she bails Officer Zimora up, asking questions about how the security system works. Jason, whose name I will never get used to, is patient with my mum and takes both Mum and me through the setup, walking us around the outside of the house to show us where the cameras are.

It's a pretty cool system, actually. It must have cost a ton, even at cost price. Jason even converted the little cupboard under the staircase into the security closet, with a small desk and two monitors to watch the outside of our house. Jason tried to show my mum how to review the footage should we need to check back over anything, but it all went over her head, and she ambled off, leaving me to learn the ins and outs of it.

The footage gets stored in *'the cloud'* for three months before it's written over with new footage or we wipe it. Jason said we'd only need to review the footage if we need to check on something and that the cameras are more of a deterrent to intruders. It all sounds pretty good to me since we've had nothing like it before.

Hopefully, if Mike sees the cameras, he'll back off.

Val would love to see this. It's right up her alley. Not that she'll get a chance. Her mum seemed pretty adamant that I won't be seeing her. Maybe Shen will cool down over time, and I'll get to see my little spy again. For now, I'll have to wait to catch a glimpse of her once she comes home from hospital.

Officer Zimora has truly gone above and beyond his duties, not only installing a security system but replacing all the door locks and having window locks installed. He even purchased new doors and put them on upstairs, even on Mike's room, which he completely cleaned out. Where the carpet was, there's nothing but ply boards and a few holes in the walls from my outburst when I smashed up the room with the baseball bat.

After everyone goes their own ways, leaving Ayden, Shaun and Simon to stay the night at my house, my mum retreats to her room, mumbling that she's going to bed early, and she leaves her credit card on the bench so we can order pizza for dinner.

Besides our interactions with Andrea and Officer Zimora, my mum has barely spoken to me. She probably took one look at my outburst last night and lobbed me into the crazy category with my dad and Mike. Maybe I should have tried to talk to her and explain why I lost control like that.

The day has been long, and we all crash earlier than we usually do. Now, I grin as Ayden snores quietly next to me on the living room floor. His face relaxed and peaceful. I roll over for the hundredth time, wishing I could find that sort of peace as I try to chase sleep.

Simon and Shaun have taken up the two couches, their own snores adding to Ayden's. They are all exhausted after spending days and nights with me at the hospital, and I naturally feel guilty for uprooting them like that. I tried to convince the guys that I didn't need the three of them to stay over, but once again, they wouldn't listen to me.

Sleep evades me as my brain turns over all the events that have happened over the last month. Rhys' words this afternoon were a bit of a shock, too. I now know she has suffered through something terrible at some point in her seventeen years.

Abbey is in my thoughts as well. I wish I could reach out to her without it causing her any issues. She must feel so alone right now. The situation with Daniel and her parents is fucked up. They can't really force her to be engaged to marry him, can they? Surely that can't be legal. Not here in Australia.

Asking Officer Zimora comes to mind, but what if that backfires? What if he tries to get involved, and it makes things worse for Abbey?

Mike's message to my friends is unsettling me the most right now. I've never felt so much hate for one person. The police know about his message and are going to keep an extra eye on my house and my friends, but dread sits heavy in my gut, knowing that won't stop Mike. If he really wants to, he'll get to each of them, and I'll be helpless to stop it.

When I screamed at him on the phone last night, I'd told Mike I was going to kill him. At the time, I meant it, and if I could have reached through that phone, I would have.

Unfortunately, in order to kill him, I have to come face-to-face with him, and while the angry part of me is rearing for that fight, the happy part of me that is in love with Ayden, is terrified to risk being torn away from him.

That's how I know I *will* kill Mike if we come face-to-face again. The only way I will ever be safe, and the only way my friends will be safe, is if Mike is dead.

A noise from the back of the house snaps me out of my thoughts, and I lift my head off the pillow, straining to hear.

Is my mum up?

I hear the faint noise again, so I slip out from under the blanket and leave Ayden, Simon, and Shaun sleeping soundly in the living room.

The house is dark with shadows as I walk silently through it, my bare feet feeling the chill of the tiles as I approach the back section of the house. I don't go into the kitchen living area, instead, I stay in the doorway listening for any noise, keeping an eye on my mum's door as if that will help me hear better.

A scraping sound comes from my right, and I freeze, realising that it's not coming from my mum's room, but just outside the patio door.

Holy shit.

With my heart pounding in my ears as my fear spikes, I will myself to calm down so I can hear past the beating.

The house is locked up like a fortress. I know because the guys and I checked it three times before going to bed, so I glance back to the door that sits below the staircase, knowing the security monitors will pick up whatever is happening outside my house. With any luck, it's a possum or a stray cat.

Making my way quickly to the closet, I quietly open the door and slip into the small space, sitting at the desk. The two monitors are split up into four sections, each showing the different areas surrounding the house. Finding the patio camera, I lean in close to the screen but see nothing there. I glance at the other sections, finding nothing until movement catches my attention back to the first monitor.

At first, I think I imagine the shadow, but then it moves closer to where the camera is, and I can see clearly that there is a man just outside the laundry door trying to unlock it.

My breath hitches, getting stuck in my throat, my lungs constricting as air fails to get in.

Fuck, Lexi, now isn't the time for a panic attack!

I try like hell to suck some air in, counting to four as I do, before slowly blowing the air out and counting to four again. I do this a couple more times before standing on shaky legs and forcing myself to leave the small closet.

I should wake Ayden and alert him, but then I hesitate.

If it *is* Mike, then he might hurt Ayden. He might even kill him. That thought alone brings tears to my eyes and sends my heart into a panic.

I can't risk that.

I can't risk the safety of the guy who owns my heart.

With my stomach practically in my throat, I tiptoe into the kitchen area and pass by the knife block, quietly pulling out the large butcher's knife before going around the corner to the laundry. The internal door is ajar, so I ease it open, glancing in at the blind, which is drawn down over the window.

Hearing the same scraping noise I heard earlier, I step inside the room, approaching the back door with my sight trained on the lock. If that lock turns, I will only have a few seconds to act before the alarm squeals and wakes the house.

If Mike hears the alarm, will it scare him off, or will he ignore it and come inside?

Fuck, if he comes inside, I need to be prepared to use this knife and hope like hell that I'm successful.

When the scraping noise stops, and I hear the word "fuck" come from behind the door, my heart sinks, recognising the unmistakable voice of my half brother.

I can make out his vile voice anywhere.

After all, it's the voice that haunts my dreams.

I get the strange urge to dart forward and pull the door open. He wouldn't expect that. I'd probably startle him, the thought tugging at my lips.

Shit. I am as fucked up as he is, aren't I?

My ears strain, but I can't hear any more noise, so I tiptoe out of the room and back to the security closet to see if Mike is trying to find another way inside.

With the knife still clutched in my hand, I study each screen, searching for any signs of movement, only it never comes. I stare at the screens, almost hoping for Mike to show his face so I know where he is, but after another ten minutes of staring, I know he's gone, and I quietly leave the closet.

Stepping out in the hall, the tall shadow of a male moves in my peripheral and I startle with a strangled cry, raising the knife, ready to kill.

"Hi, Lexi." Shaun's familiar voice stops me in my tracks, and I suck in a breath as I watch his shadowed form drag lazy feet across the tiles in front of me.

"Lex!" Ayden whisper-yells, coming down the hall, shouldering Shaun out of the way to get to me. "What are you doing?"

Light fills the passage as Simon pokes his head around the corner, taking in the scene, and I watch with concern as Shaun blinks a few times, looking around as if he has no idea what is happening.

"Shit, Shaun. I'm so sorry." My lip wobbles as my emotions take over, realising that I nearly fucking stabbed my friend.

I will not cry. I will not cry.

"Why do you have a knife, Lex?" he asks before the squeak of my mum's bedroom door opens behind me off the living area.

"Is everything okay out here?" My mum's voice is filled with concern I'm not used to hearing.

My eyes nearly bug out as I look from Shaun to Ayden and to where Simon is still peeking his head around the corner up the other end of the hall.

Trying to seem unaffected, I spin to face my mum, hiding the butcher's knife behind my back.

"Uh, yeah. All good here. I couldn't sleep and went for a walk through the house. I didn't mean to worry everyone." The lie rolls off my tongue so easily, and I can feel Ayden's eyes boring into the back of my head.

"Oh. Okay. Maybe try some warm milk if you can't sleep." My mum offers, her brown hair pulled back in a low ponytail that disappears underneath her yellow dressing gown.

"Okay. Thanks, Mum." I'm acting way too sweet right now. Surely, she can tell I've just lied to her?

"Night." Mum offers a smile to the guys behind me, and they say good night to her, not for the first time tonight.

Once her bedroom door closes, my shoulders relax right before Ayden speaks behind me.

"I'm just gonna take this." His warm hand slides over the one I have behind my back, and he takes hold of the knife, slipping it out of my grip.

When it's free, he steps around me, blocking my view of my mum's door.

"Are you okay?" The concern swimming in his gaze is intense, and I worry my lip.

"I heard a noise. I thought I was being paranoid."

"Understandably," he whispers, leaning down to press his lips on my cheek before turning and walking into the kitchen to return the knife.

"I guess I was kind of lucky I didn't get stabbed, hey?" Shaun grins as Simon approaches, clapping him on the shoulder.

"Dude, what were you doing up?"

Shaun shrugs, "I don't remember."

"Shit. Were you sleepwalking again?" Simon asks, and I frown.

"You sleepwalk?"

"Who sleepwalks?" Ayden asks, joining us back in the passage.

"Bossi does. Well, he used to years ago." Simon offers before turning to Shaun. "That's happening again?"

Shaun shrugs, looking out of sorts. "I'm going to take a piss." He turns away from us and heads upstairs to use the toilet.

"He okay?" Ayden asks, and Simon shrugs, his ashy hair shaggy and dishevelled from sleep.

"Fucked if I know." Simon has never had a good poker face, and his hazel eyes reveal his worry. I'll need to remember to check on Shaun tomorrow. See if he wants to talk. I know little about him other than he's a decent guy who gets all the girls chasing him, but Simon's obvious concern worries me. What if he's going through something, and my crap is just another thing he has to worry about?

"Maybe we should watch a movie since we're all awake." Ayden places his hand on the small of my back, urging me to walk, but I dig my heels in, and he turns back to me, frowning. "Lex?"

"Mike was here."

"What?" Ayden and Simon say in unison, both of their heads tilting as if they didn't quite hear me.

"The noise I heard. It wasn't just paranoia. Mike was outside, trying to get in."

"What the fuck, Lexi. We need to call the cops." Ayden growls, charging towards the living area, probably to grab his phone.

"He's gone, Ayden," I whisper-yell after him, not wanting to coax my mum out of her room again.

"What do you mean, he's gone?" Simon asks on my heels.

Two sets of eyes land on me, waiting for an explanation, and I suddenly feel like I'm about to get into trouble.

"Who's gone?" Shaun asks, coming back into the living room, his sleepy dark eyes bouncing between each of us.

"When he couldn't get in through the laundry door, he left. I sat at the monitors for like, ten minutes, and he didn't show up again." I shrug, trying to play it off as no big deal, even though I know this is a really big fucking deal.

"Shit, Lexi. Why didn't you wake us or call the police?" Ayden hisses, and my wall of anger instantly slams back into place.

Ayden's right, of course, but I'm fucked if I can control how I'm reacting to his reaction.

"Obviously, I didn't see the need to wake you. What would you have done, Ayden? Gone out there," I point to the window, "and got yourself killed. Not. Fucking. Happening."

"I wouldn't have gone out there, Lexi. I would have called the police, which is exactly what you should have done as your first instinct. But no, once again, your first instinct is to try to handle it yourself." Ayden growls and digs his hands into his hair. "What are we even doing here with you if you won't let us fucking help you?"

Hot, angry tears burst from my eyes as I suck in shallow breaths, veering on the edge of losing all of my control.

"I'm still playing catch up here," Shaun says, gaining our attention. "Are you saying your psycho brother was trying to break in while we were sleeping, and instead of calling the cops, you watched him on the security monitors?"

I bite into my lip, trying to hold back the rush of tears fighting to burst free.

"Why'd you have the knife, Lex?" Simon asks this time, and my blurred vision darts to him.

When I don't answer, he raises his ashy brows at me and puts his hands on his hips. Not only am I in trouble with Ayden, but I'm in trouble with Simon and Shaun, too.

I feel like I'm being ganged up on again, but the slight resemblance of rationality that I still possess reminds me I'm the one that fucked up. Once again, I let my emotions control me, and while I was thinking I was protecting Ayden, I have actually put us in more danger because if I had called the cops, Mike could be on his way to the lock-up right now.

"I'm sorry." The tears spill free, and I look at each of them.

"Why did you have the knife, Lexi?" Ayden asks Simon's question again, his tone still pissed.

"When I thought he was going to get through the laundry door, I was waiting in there to stab him," I admit quietly as I keep my eyes trained on the floor, too ashamed to see any more disappointment on their faces.

A round of curses fills the room, and Ayden growls again.

I don't look up. Instead, I turn on my heel to leave the room, needing to flee.

I don't get far before a hand darts out and takes mine. At first, I think it's Ayden, but when I'm tugged around, I'm met with the concerned face of our class clown before Simon pulls me into a hug.

"I'm sorry," I whisper again, past my tears into Simon's chest, before I hear Shaun at my ear.

"It's okay, Lex. We know you're just trying to protect us."

Simon scoffs, "She's trying to protect lover boy over there."

"Well, he *is* kind of pretty. I don't think any of us wanna see that face get messed up." Shaun teases, and I realise he's trying to lighten the mood, which is working when I feel Simon's chuckle rumble against my ear.

"Shut up, Bossi." Ayden hisses, his voice still coming from the other side of the room.

Shit, he really is pissed at me.

Why do I keep fucking up like this?

"If you were man enough to put your fucking anger aside and look after your woman, then maybe Hastings and I wouldn't have to be over here doing your job for you." Shaun pushes and Ayden bites.

"Fuck you, prick! Maybe if you fuckers would back the fuck off her and stop acting like you have a claim on her heart, I could get a damn minute to help her."

"Dude. We are her brothers. It sickens me that you would suggest such preposterous things," Simon says, exasperated, and I try really fucking hard not to laugh. These clowns are going to get black eyes soon.

Pushing back from Simon, I meet his gaze and he shoots me a mischievous wink, knowing all too well that he's stirring Ayden to breaking point.

"We were going to watch a movie, weren't we?" Simon asks, stepping back from me and glancing over his shoulder to Ayden, whose face is red in anger.

When no one says anything, Shaun sighs and flops down on the couch with the TV remote in hand, flicking Pay TV on and finding the footy channel.

Simon eyes Ayden and me for a moment longer before moving across the room to take up the other couch and slipping under the blanket.

I feel empty, like there's this big divide between Ayden and me, but when I flick a glance at him, he gestures to our bed of blankets on the floor, and I slowly step forward and sink to our makeshift bed.

Ayden doesn't immediately join me, leaving the room for a few minutes and turning the lights off when he comes back in. I'm still sitting awkwardly, feeling like I don't belong, until Ayden sinks down in front of me and pulls me to straddle his lap. I don't care that Simon and Shaun are probably watching us instead of the TV, and my arms snake around his neck while my legs wrap around his waist.

"I love you, beautiful." His whisper instantly breaks me, his words filling the emptiness I felt minutes ago. "I'm sorry for acting like an arsehole. The idea of something happening to you again makes me crazy."

"I don't deserve you," I whisper into the crook of his neck, not wanting Simon and Shaun to hear.

"More like I don't deserve you," he whispers back, pressing a kiss to my temple.

"I should've woken you up earlier. I'm sorry, Ayden."

He strokes his hand over my hair before combing his fingers into the locks and cupping the side of my head.

"I'm glad we at least woke when we did, otherwise I have a feeling Bossi would have woken the whole house. I'm pretty sure he was sleepwalking to your mum's room."

I giggle. "I bet that's totally where his dream brain was taking him."

Ayden falls quiet for a few minutes then, his fingers still combing through my hair before he speaks again.

"Please let us help keep you safe, beautiful. Please don't do anything to put yourself in harm's way anymore." Pulling back, he locks his eyes with mine, the light from the TV dancing off one side of his face. "Please, Lexi. Fucking promise me you won't keep putting yourself in danger. If you don't want to ask me or the guys for help, then please call the police."

I nod, "okay."

Ayden visibly relaxes and releases a breath. "Good. I'm sorry for being a prick. Forgive me?"

Shooting me puppy dog eyes, I'm helpless to refuse him and give him a nod right before his gaze falls to my lips. The simple shift of his eyes sends butterflies through me, so I tilt my head and close the distance, desperate to taste him again.

As usual, his kiss ignites fire beneath my skin as our bodies mould together like a perfect puzzle piece.

"If you two are going to fuck, give me a heads up so I can get some popcorn." Simon snickers, and Shaun joins him.

Breaking the kiss, Ayden gives me an apologetic look.

"Excuse me," he says before twisting with a cushion in his hand and tossing it hard across the room to smack Simon in the face.

Eleven

When I wake to find the living room empty on Monday morning, panic seizes my heart. Shit, did I oversleep? Has Ayden left already? I search through the blankets for my phone but calm when I hear the deep hushed voices of the guys coming from down the hall.

Shit.

I hate the idea of Ayden leaving and not saying goodbye.

I find Ayden, Simon, and Shaun crammed in the security closet, watching the camera footage of last night on the monitors. When I tug the door open a little wider, three sets of eyes land on me and offer me smiles. Well, maybe not all three smile. The tug at Ayden's lips looks more like frustration more than anything.

"What are you doing?" I watch as Ayden slips a USB drive from the computer port.

"Backed up the footage of Mike trying to break in. I've already emailed Jason the file." Ayden doesn't look at me as he speaks, and I get the feeling he's pissed at me again.

What have I done now?

"Oh. Right." I step back as Shaun and Simon try to squeeze past to come back out into the hall.

"You sleep okay, Lexi?" Shaun asks, and I nod, offering him a small smile.

I did sleep well after having a good make-out session with Ayden on the floor of my living room.

"How about you guys? Did you get back to sleep okay?"

"I didn't sleep that great. I was too paranoid that Bossi was going to sleepwalk again and try to hump my leg or something." Simon's face is deadly serious, but his words hold humour like they always do.

I expect Shaun to throw a punch into Simon's arm or something, but he just grins and wags his dark brows. "You'd like that, huh?"

The frown that twists Simon's face is laughable, yet I can't make mine present itself as Ayden brushes past me to unfold himself out of the closet, his eyes looking everywhere but at me.

My heart sinks, and dread pokes at me, knowing that something is up with him.

As Shaun and Simon head to the kitchen chatting away about footy, I follow Ayden back to the living room and watch as he sits on the edge of the couch and slips his school shoes on. He's already dressed for school. In fact, it looks like he's been up for hours.

"Ayden."

"What?" He doesn't look up from tying his laces.

"What's wrong?"

Angry eyes look up at me then, and on instinct, I take a step back.

Those normally crystal blue ocean eyes are a dark, raging storm.

Fuck me, as fiercely hot as it makes him look, I'm pretty sure this is a side of him I don't want to come across often.

He goes to speak but then snaps his mouth shut and sucks in a deep breath, shaking his head.

"Ayden?" I speak softly, like I'm trying to calm a beast. By all rights, I think I am.

"He was here for long enough that we could have called the cops, and they would have gotten here in time to catch him." Ayden's growl is deep and laced with anger.

"You're angry at *me* about this? *Again*?" My tone has its own anger laced with it. Didn't we already go over this last night?

"I'm not angry at you. I'm just angry in general." He hisses, standing from the couch and picking up his school blazer.

Not believing him, I cross my arms over my chest and pop my hip. "Ayden. You can't even look at me without looking like you want to kill me. I'm pretty fucking certain you're angry at me."

Diving his arms into his blazer and shrugging it on, Ayden meets my gaze with heat before he stalks towards me.

"You're right. I'm angry at you. You should have woken me as soon as you heard a noise so we could investigate together."

Ayden comes to stand a foot in front of me, and I crane my head back to keep my eyes locked on his as my brows lift.

"Didn't we go over this last night?"

A rumble sounds in his throat as his frustration gets harder to control. "We did. But then I watched the footage and saw *that* fucker trying to break into *my* girl's house so he can fucking try to rape her. You'll excuse me if my anger at you trying to take things into your hands has resurfaced!"

Okay.

So he has a point.

I get where he's coming from, but it doesn't mean I have to like it. I guess I should avoid making things worse, though, by letting my anger run my mouth. Besides, Ayden's reaction reminds me of how much he cares and how much the things that have happened have also affected him.

Jutting my chin up so Ayden can see that I'm not just saying this with emotions ruling me, I drop my arms from my chest and rest my hand over my heart.

"I really am sorry, Ayden. I'm still getting used to asking for help and having people I can trust. I know you're here for me. I know the guys are here for me. I'll try hard to remember that and think before I react." I sigh as the flames behind his eyes die down a little. "I'm sorry that I haven't considered what all this has been like for you. I'm *not* sorry for what I'm about to say, though." Ayden's brows hitch at that part, and I fold my arms back over my chest. "If you're the type of person who struggles to move on from things, and like, brings shit up in arguments later, then we are going to have a real fucking problem."

I don't expect the brief quirk to his lips before he steps forward and pulls me to his chest.

"I should spank your arse for what you did."

And there he is.

The guy who owns my soul.

"You say that like it's a punishment." I quirk a single brow, and he grins mischievously.

"It will be when I don't let you come." He moves back and steps around me towards the hallway.

"You wouldn't?" I hiss, spinning to track his movement.

The cheeky fucker grins over his shoulder in a challenge. "Wouldn't I?" He walks out of the room.

"Ayden Mitchell, get back here!" I demand, and I'm met with silence.

Fuck me. What the hell just happened?

Sighing, I'm about to flop back on the couch when Ayden rounds the corner, stalking me like I'm his prey. My body heats, and moisture pools between my legs barely a moment before his hands grip my arse, lifting me as he claims my mouth.

My legs wrap around him, and my hands claw into his hair as he lays us down on the couch. His weight on me ignites fire to my core, and I moan when the hard length of his cock rubs against my needy bud through our clothes.

A throat clears, and Ayden pulls back, looking down at me with a smirk, while I turn my head to see Shaun and Simon standing in the doorway with their bags.

"We need to leave now if we want to make it in time for the English Assessment," Simon says, smirking and tilting his head from side to side as he takes in my provocative position.

My eyes dart back to Ayden's to see he's still smirking.

That's when I realise he knew damn well he had to leave, and he deliberately got me worked up to prove his point.

Not letting me come is my punishment.

Son of a bitch!

Peeling my legs from around his waist, Ayden stands and rights his clothes before leaning down to my ear.

"You look really pissed right now, but just remember that I love you." And he slaps a kiss on my lips before moving away quickly.

I growl in frustration and launch cushions at him and the others, which they duck, laughing as they walk out. As soon as Simon and Shaun are out the front door, and Ayden is about to step out with them, I call to him, and he takes a step back to glance at me.

"Two can play that game," I say and when he frowns, in confusion, I slide my hand to the waist of my shorts and slip it inside. "I don't need *you* in the room to make me come."

The taste of victory is sweet, and his eyes widen and darken at the same time. His frustrated growl is all I hear before he storms out to head to school, and even though he thinks I've won, I haven't. I pull my hand back out of my shorts, knowing too fucking well I won't go through with it. I'd much prefer him in the room with me.

Although Ayden promised one of the guys would be with me all the time, he kind of forgot that he and the others need to go to school because the end of term assessments are on. That leaves me alone in the house with my mum for the first time in over four weeks.

I eventually drag myself out of the living room to find my mum in the kitchen, cooking some toast. I figure she's cooking it for herself, so I go to make my own when she tells me to sit at the table because she's making my breaky.

This is another new thing.

I don't argue, though, and sit patiently while she finishes.

We eat in awkward silence together before my mum informs me that Ayden let her know Mike paid us a visit last night. I wait for her to have a dig at me for not calling the police, but it never comes. If she had a problem with my decision, she doesn't voice it.

After we eat, I ask her if it's okay for me to use her shower. Her confusion quickly turns to mortification when she realises *why* I want to use her shower and not the one upstairs. I'm not sure who filled my mum in on the details of Mike's attacks, but it's clear someone has with the way she pales.

Stepping out of my mum's room a little later as I towel dry my blonde waves, I freeze when the eyes of Principal Rogan and Mr Matthews turn to me.

"Uh. Hi?" My greeting sounds more like a question as I take in my principal and school counsellor sitting at the kitchen table with my mum.

"Lexi," Cynthia, the principal, who is also Rhys' foster mum, stands from the chair and approaches me with a warm smile. "It's so good to see you. We were so worried."

Had this been my old principal, I would have called him out on his bullshit, but Cynthia has genuinely been rooting for me since she took over the role a few weeks back, so I give her a small smile as she reaches out and awkwardly rubs the top of my arm.

"Hey Cin." I glance over her shoulder, giving Mr Matthews the same smile. "Hey, Mr M."

"Lexi, please call your teachers by their correct names." My mum tries to be all mum like and shit. It's cute. Really.

Mr Matthews chuckles. "It's okay. We don't mind her cheek. It builds character."

"Oh." My mum looks confused, and I can't help but laugh, which scores me a glare from her.

"I didn't realise teachers do home visits." I stay standing by the table after following Cynthia, watching as she takes a seat again, smiling up at me.

"Well, Lexi, given the circumstances, we wanted to reach out and offer our support. Claudia from Child Services notified us of your return home with your mum." Cynthia turns and smiles warmly at my mum before continuing. "So I reached out to your mum so we could pop in and see you today. And lucky for you, Stephen's morning is free, so you two can have a session."

My brows dart up, and I shoot Cynthia a *'really'* glare, and she offers a smug smile in return.

"Aren't you lucky?" Mr Matthews chuckles and stands from his chair. "Where can we chat?"

I drop my chin to my chest in defeat and mumble, "In the front living room, I guess."

"Great, lead the way." Mr M's tone is full of humour. The prick knows this is torture for me.

"I'm just going to stay here and chat with your mum, Lexi," Cynthia says as I drag my feet past the table and nod, acting like the immature teenager I am.

My mum starts chatting away with Cynthia when we leave the room, and I can't help but feel weird about it. She has never been much of a chatter, so this is another new thing. Cynthia is pretty good at getting people to talk, which may not necessarily be good. Maybe I should go back and stop it.

"This room is cosy. Have you been sleeping in here?" Mr M asks when we enter the room.

Both couches have a mess of blankets on them, and the floor still has the makeshift bed Ayden and I slept on last night.

I can't help myself. I plop myself down on the blankets we shared and pull Ayden's pillow to my chest, his scent instantly dancing before my nose.

I keep my eyes on Mr Matthews as he glances around the room and then pushes aside the blankets on the side couch to take a seat.

"Who slept here?" he asks, his blue eyes finding mine.

"Simon. I'm pretty sure he didn't jack off on it. I can't be sure, though."

Mr M's face twists into a cringe, and I throw my head back and laugh.

"Oh, man. Your face." It's way too much fun stirring Mr M.

"Hilarious, Lexi." His smirk tells me he's not angry, which is why he's good at his job. It can't be easy getting people to open up to you. You'd need to have an open mind and a shit ton of patience.

"I was thinking about becoming a comedian. What do you think?" I grin, still clutching Ayden's pillow to my chest.

"As funny as you are, Lexi, I think you have a lot more to offer the world." His face is serious, and I know joke time is over. "How are you feeling today?"

"I feel like being a comedian today."

"Come on, Lexi. We made good progress last week." Sitting forward, Mr Matthews leans his elbows on his legs, not taking his intense gaze off me.

"That was before my brother ruined an innocent girl's life in order to get to me." I hiss, feeling the pain slice through my heart as I think about poor Valarie.

I wonder if she will come back home today?

"Is the anger you've been feeling lately worse now, after what happened?"

I take a moment to think about his question.

"My anger feels different. Like it's there, but it doesn't feel so out of control. Well, except for when Mike sent messages to my friends, and I rang him to tell him what I thought. I had no control then." I shrug. "I've been pretty on edge, though. It doesn't take much to piss me off."

Mr Matthews straightens his spine in surprise. "You spoke to your brother?"

"I wouldn't say I spoke with him. More like I screamed at him, which only amused him."

"What did the messages say that he sent your friends?"

"He threatened them. Basically, if they don't ditch me, then he will come after them first."

Mr Matthews frowns. "Have the authorities been notified?"

"Yep," I sigh. I'm so sick of Mike consuming my life. "Ayden's parents spoke to the cops. Can we talk about something else?"

"Uh, sure. Like what?" he asks, and I shrug.

"How's Miss Dice going? You and her sealed the deal yet?"

Mr M lets out a sigh and sits back on the couch, taking a moment to stare out the front window.

"She was so terrified, you know?" His eyes find mine again. "Amy was distraught when we heard what had happened. I've never seen her so unhinged." A small smile tugs at his lip. "She really does have a soft spot for you, Lexi."

Well, fuck.

"She's my favourite teacher. Besides you, of course." I smile when he grins.

"Oh, of course. But I'm not a teacher. I'm your counsellor, and honestly, Lexi, I don't know how to help you if you don't want the help."

My bottom lip instantly quivers, like it's having a fucking seizure.

"I *do* want help... I'm just not good at asking for it or accepting it." My words are a whisper and warm tears roll down my cheeks as I remember how angry Ayden was with me.

"Admitting it is a good start." Mr Matthews leans forward again, tilting his bald head as he looks at me. "Since you've had a lot of heavy stuff happening, why don't we talk about something that makes you happy?"

I can't hide my smile as my mind instantly thinks of Ayden.

"Oh, would you look at that smile? Where is your happy place right now?" Mr M asks.

"Ayden."

He nods. "Of course. I should have known after our last chat."

I snicker, remembering how I word vomited everything to him about Ayden and me.

"So, he's a good support for you?"

"Yes." I nod. "He somehow knows when something is wrong with me or worrying me. I don't have to tell him. He just knows. He also knows how to calm me. Well, most of the time. Things don't seem so dark when Ayden's around."

"That's good to hear." Mr M leans back on the couch again. "You guys have any issues? Like, does he have really hairy toes, and you're struggling to get past it?"

A burst of laughter jumps out of my throat, and I drop Ayden's pillow onto the floor in front of me.

"Ew, that's kinda gross. But no, his toes are nice. Just the right amount of hair…"

Mr Matthews doesn't miss my hesitation, "but? Is there something else, Lexi?"

"We had a bit of a blow up yesterday, and last night, and this morning." Shit, maybe things aren't as good as I thought they were.

"Tell me what happened yesterday," Mr Matthews asks, lounging back on the couch.

I sigh. I hate talking about this shit. I know I need to, though. Maybe it will help me stop flying off the handle so much.

"When we were driving back home from the city yesterday, Ayden declared that I wasn't returning to school until next term or until Mike is caught. It wasn't a suggestion. He was telling me that's how it is."

"I'm guessing that didn't go down too well with you."

I scoff, "Fuck no. I lost my shit and screamed, and then his mum pulled the car over, and I jumped out and ran off into the trees." I sigh. "We had it out in the middle of some pine plantation with our friends butting in. We eventually came to the agreement to take each day as it comes, but if I tell Ayden I want to go back to school tomorrow, it's going to start another argument."

"Why do you think he's trying to tell you what to do?"

My shoulders drop. "Because he cares. Because he fears something happening to me. I get that and all, but I really hate being told what to do." Looking down, I see my hands clutched tightly onto Ayden's pillow. I didn't even realise I was doing it. Needing the calm Ayden brings, I pull the pillow to my chest again and let his scent work its magic.

"Do you understand where he is coming from? I'm not saying what he did is okay, but it's important to try to see where the other person's emotions are coming from. He's obviously terrified of something happening to you again. It's probably the only way he knows how to control his fear."

I nod and stay silent, and when Mr M realises I'm not going to say anything, he continues.

"So, what happened last night and this morning?"

"Mike tried to break in, and instead of waking Ayden or calling the cops, I just watched him on the monitors until he went away." There's no way I'm going to tell him I had a knife and was preparing to stab the fucker if he got through the door.

Mr Matthews frowns, the lines in his forehead reaching his bald scalp. "I'm confused. Why didn't you get help?"

"In my defence, my fear and emotions took over, and I couldn't comprehend a scenario where Ayden gets hurt or worse. So I kept it to myself until Mike left, and then everyone got real fucking angry at me, and I felt like everyone was against me, but I know it's just because they didn't understand my logic." I drop Ayden's pillow again and let a sigh slip past my lips. "I know it makes no sense to anyone else, but I just can't stand the thought of Mike hurting anyone else but me."

"But you? You would rather be the one getting hurt?" Mr M sits forward again, his blue eyes trained on my face.

"If it means that everyone else is safe, then yes. I don't want to get hurt, but you need to understand, my heart can't take it if he hurts another innocent person." I drag my eyes away from his because I can't handle their intensity.

"You're an innocent person, Lexi. You don't deserve to be hurt, either."

"I know," I whisper.

"You *do* know that the way you feel is the same way Ayden feels?"

I nod again.

"He told me he loved me," I whisper loud enough for Mr M to hear.

"Wow. That's big. Did you say it back?"

I shake my head. "Honestly, I'm too scared that the moment I admit how much he means to me, something bad will happen, and I'll lose him forever. I can deal with having the shit beat outta me. I can deal with bullies.

But *I can't* deal with the idea of not having Ayden in my life."

Mr M nods. "Love is hard. It means we have something to lose."

"Yeah." Resting my head on the pillow, I close my eyes, trying to will myself not to think of all the scenarios that Mike could do to take Ayden away from me.

Voices float up the hall, snapping me out of my thoughts, and Mr Matthews stands looking down at me. "I'll pop in and see you again, but in the meantime, try to do one or two things each day that you enjoy. You need to have happiness in your life even when things aren't going so well."

I smirk. "Does sex count?"

He shakes his head, trying not to grin at me. "See you next time, Lexi."

My mum and the principal come into view then as they make their way to the front door.

Last week, I'd decided to tell Mrs Rogan about my part in the school vandalism, but then Mike came along and put a big hurdle in my path that I had to detour around. I hadn't changed my mind about it and now seems like as good a time as any.

"Um, Mrs Rogan, I need to tell you something." I stand from my safe place on the floor and drop the pillow, knowing I can't hide behind it for this.

"Yes, Lexi. What is it?" Cynthia asks, stepping into the room. She looks out of place in my shabby house with her pristine skirt suit and perfectly straight hair.

"I was going to tell you this last week, but then... things happened." I take a deep breath, hoping that telling the truth is the right thing. "The school vandalism last month. That was me."

"What?" Cynthia frowns, and my mum's head pops out from behind Cynthia. "The police caught the culprit. He does community service for the school every afternoon."

"Yes. Travis Watson. I was with him that night."

I glance to the side, to where Mr Matthews is leaning against the wall by the doorway. I expect to see disappointment in his eyes, but instead, I see pride.

"You were with Travis Watson the night he broke into the school and vandalised it?" Cynthia's calm exterior hasn't faltered as she asks for confirmation. Shouldn't she be looking mad by now?

"Yes. We were at a party, and I got a little too stoned. I don't remember much, but we ended up on the school grounds, and I punched one of the Art room windows, and then we threw chairs through them. I didn't wreck the artwork. That was Travis, but I *am* as much to blame as he is."

"What the fuck, Lexi!" My mum's angry growl takes Cynthia by surprise.

Be careful, mother dearest. You're starting to show your stripes.

"Where were you, Mum?" I snap, getting defensive. "Oh wait, I remember. You were too busy popping pills and downing bottles of wine." I hiss, poking my face out in anger. "Don't start trying to be my mum now!"

"Now, wait just a minute!" Ruth growls, stepping in front of me, her cheeks red in anger.

"Let's all just take a breather here." Mr Matthews steps in, coming to my side.

"Yes, I agree. Let's just take a moment to compose ourselves." Cynthia suggests, and to my surprise, my mum nods her head and steps back away from me, sucking in deep breaths.

I sigh. "Look, it's no excuse, but things were escalating with Mike at the time. I became reckless and did some really stupid shit that I will forever regret." I turn to Cynthia. "I'm sorry it's taken this long for me to grow a pair of balls and own up to what I did. I understand you will need to notify the police. I also understand that I'm probably not welcome back at Fox Pines Catholic. But I need you to know that I really am sorry."

Unfortunately, the weight of what I did still sits heavily on my chest. Admitting it hasn't relieved me like I thought it would. If only I could turn back time, I would do so many things differently.

"Thank you for your honesty, Lexi." Cynthia smiles. "It takes a big person to own up to their mistakes. I won't get the police involved, and I expect you to return to school once you are feeling up to it, but I also expect you to be there at 3:45 every school day to help Travis with the community service."

"Hang on a minute." My mum butts in. "Lexi can't just do that without protection. Not while her brother is still on the loose."

"Yes. You're right. We have already added extra security staff to the college and new security protocols to protect students, even from their parents. I can make sure we have security monitoring Lexi during her community service, too, and I'm happy for her friends to linger nearby if it helps to make her feel safe."

My mum looks at me in silent question, and when I nod, she turns back to Cynthia.

"We would appreciate that. Thank you."

"Good, well, in that case, you can start tomorrow afternoon. We have a lot of fun jobs for you."

And that's why I respect this woman so much.

She isn't a pushover.

She is fair.

In my case, probably a little too fair, but she won't let people get away with their transgressions.

Nodding, I accept my fate. It's time to take back control of my life.

Twelve

E xhaustion hits me after Cynthia and Mr M leave, but the moment I lay down to have a rest and inhale more of Ayden's pillow scent, we get another visitor, followed by another.

First, Claudia from Child Services pops in to see how I am and to question my mum while she looks through our house. She advises my mum that her visit is to assess if she is fit to care for me, even though I'm seventeen. Where was this woman when I was twelve? I guess my mum really did a good job at hiding her addiction all these years.

Once Claudia is happy with the information she gathers, we get a visit from Officer Reynolds and Officer Zimora. I'll admit, it's nice to see Jason again in his uniformed glory. It always is. What isn't nice to see is my mum flirting with Officer Reynolds.

Ew!

No one wants to see their mum flirting.

Thank fuck Jason distracts me.

Besides being nice to look at, he's actually a pretty decent guy, and he let slip that his boyfriend helped him hang the doors upstairs. Jason is gay. I feel a little embarrassed because while I've been drooling over him, he's probably been drooling over Ayden.

It's nice to have a conversation with Jason that doesn't involve my dad or Mike. I find out that he became a cop because he witnessed his stepdad beating up his mum when he was little. He hated how his mum was too scared to call the police or how when the police got involved, his stepdad would lie, and the police did nothing. Jason wanted to make a difference, and for a moment, I consider if it's something I could do. I know I want to help people, especially those who are powerless, but I'm not sure if I want to put myself in the line of danger.

It isn't until after lunch that I'm able to get some quiet time to rest. I can't sleep, of course, because each time I do, all I can see is Mike's face as he tried to choke the life out of me. I've been lucky for the most part that these brief flickers of memory haven't haunted me more often but today they seem to be plaguing me.

Maybe it's because Mike was so close last night. My nerves are a little shot.

When I accept that I'm not going to get any shuteye, I get up and go in search of my mum, finding her in her room sitting amongst old photos spread across her bed.

"What are you doing?" I ask, gaining her attention.

She smiles, holding up a picture of a chubby-cheeked blonde toddler with chocolate cake batter all over her face.

Me.

"Have a look at you. Gosh, you were just the most adorable thing ever." My mum's eyes are glassy as she speaks, and I smile back at her but dart my eyes around her room when she looks away.

Has she taken something? Has she been drinking? Is that why her eyes are glassy?

"What do you mean, 'were'? I'm *still* adorable." I flutter my lashes at her when she turns her brown eyes on me before rolling them.

"You have too much attitude to be adorable," Mum says, and this time her eyes look clear. Maybe she's just... happy?

"Probably." I laugh, and Mum looks up at me again, smiling.

"Come sit." She pats the bed next to her, clearing away some of the photos.

Taking a seat next to her, I get sucked into our past when our lives looked normal. Things looked happy. I see the photo from my fifth birthday and giggle, noticing Abbey, Jared and Marcus in the picture. Man, they were dorks. But they were *my* dorks.

"Do you remember this?" Mum asks, holding out a photo of me clinging to her leg for dear life.

I shake my head. "No. What was I doing?"

Mum giggles, "It's cute. There was a thunderstorm rolling in, and you were scared. Your dad tried to console you, but you wouldn't go to him. You stayed clung to my leg until I picked you up and took you inside the house."

"I don't remember that," I say honestly. I can hardly remember a time my mum was like a mum to me, yet this picture makes it look like those times existed once.

She sighs. "You were only three. Things were simpler back then." She glances up from the picture, her eyes scanning the room. "I think that was one of the last times this house seemed like a happy home." She shakes her head then. "I hate this house now. I think I've always hated it, but I was too wasted all the time to think about it."

Shit. That's the first time I've heard her come close to admitting she's a substance abuser.

"I know you're getting older and will probably move on with your own life soon," my mum drops the pictures to her lap and turns to me on the bed with her legs crossed. "But before you do that, I'd really like to live in a happy home with you. One where there aren't any old memories when we walk in a room."

"How do we do that?" I ask.

Strangely enough, I like the idea of what she is saying. I never thought I'd want that with my mum, but I also never thought she would be sober enough to care.

"We get a new house, I guess." She shrugs, turning to grin at me.

"But how?" I frown.

She *does* realise she needs money, or a job to get a mortgage, doesn't she?

"Leave it with me. I'll figure it out." Her face turns sombre then. "I'm sorry that you have to come back here where all the awful stuff happened. You deserve better than that."

If I didn't already know what my mum was like when she's under the influence, I would think she'd taken something with the way she's speaking right now. This woman talking with me now definitely isn't my drunk or high mum. She is someone else entirely.

Shaking her head, my mum takes me in with tear-filled eyes. "I should have taken you away when you were little. I should have packed a bag and ran. I'm so sorry, Lexi. This is all my fault."

"Mum..."

"No, Lexi. I don't want you to *ever* forgive me for being the weak human I was. A mother is meant to protect her daughter, no matter the cost."

"What happened? What changed our house from a happy home?" I ask the question I've asked myself over and over, but have no memory of anything other than her spaced out all the time.

She sighs, drawing in a deep breath before reaching out and taking my hand in hers.

Just another thing I'm not used to her doing.

"I feel so ashamed to be admitting this to you, but you deserve the truth, Lexi." She shakes her head, her chocolate messy bun flopping around from the action, and her brown eyes turn distant like she is somewhere else.

"Your dad has always been a cruel man. I didn't see it when we first met. I was blind to his flaws, just so happy that someone like him would give me the time of day. He was successful and older and sucked me in with ideas of the white picket fence and a big family with a dog and a cat and the nicest cars on the street. He made me think we would be a power couple together, and foolishly, I believed every word.

He hooked me in fast, and before I knew what was happening, he proposed, and we were married a couple of weeks later. We moved into this house, and I could see our future just how he had said." She sighs again, her shoulders dropping in defeat as she releases her hold of my hands. "It wasn't until I fell pregnant with you that he told me he had a son. It was too late for me by that point. I was already trapped, and all of a sudden, I was six months pregnant with you and meeting my new stepson. It was an instant family."

Her eyes fall to her lap then, her fingers picking at the corner of one of the pictures as she continues.

"At first, it hurt me that Max didn't tell me about Mike, but then I thought it could work. I wanted it to work. I would be a mum to this boy, too, and we would continue to grow our family." Shaking her head, her eyes lift to meet mine again. "Mike seemed a little odd when we first met. He misbehaved a lot and would break things around the house and blame me for it. It sounds ridiculous when I say that out loud." She scoffs, her voice rising in pitch. "He was only a seven-year-old boy, for god's sake. But he had the devil in him, and I came to learn Max did too." She glances down at the photos again before tossing them onto the mattress next to her. "It was after Mike's second school holiday visit that Max started getting more aggressive in the..." She clears her throat. "Bedroom."

What the fuck!

Closing her eyes, my mum shakes her head. "I don't think I can tell you. I've never told anyone, but I shouldn't be telling my daughter."

"Mum." I reach out and squeeze her hand, gaining her attention. "The reason why things got so bad for *me* is because I was too ashamed to tell anyone. I thought I'd die if people found out, but you know what? I'm stronger for it." I offer her a sympathetic smile as I look into her pain-filled eyes. "I want to know, but you don't have to tell me if you don't want to. I think you should tell someone, though. It's time to take your power back."

"I knew from the moment you were born that you'd be a force to be reckoned with, Lexi." She smiles. "I may be your mum, but honestly, I look up to you. If I can be half the amazing woman you are becoming, then I'd be happy."

A rogue tear slips from my eye. I never imagined having a conversation like this with my mum. This is an Andrea and Ayden type of conversation. Not a Lexi and Ruth one.

"I will tell you the gist of it, Lexi. Not the finer details, though. That is something a daughter should never have to hear about her parents."

"Okay. Whatever you're comfortable with," I say with a small smile, hoping it covers my sinking feeling of dread.

What has my mum been through?

Taking a moment, my mum seems stuck in her own thoughts before continuing, keeping her eyes cast down at her lap.

"It all started in the bedroom. He wanted me to do... weird stuff. I did it at first, just wanting to make him happy, but then it got weirder, so I said no. I learnt really fast that I should never say no to Maxwell. He doesn't understand the word, and he'd do what he wanted, no matter how much I protested." Her eyes flick up to meet mine. "The twisted part was that during the day, outside the bedroom, he treated me like a queen. So I started accepting that was the way it was." She shakes her head and scoffs at herself. "This went on for a couple of years before Max stepped it up."

Taking a moment to sit taller, my mum blows out a breath as she struggles with her emotions. It makes me nervous for what I'm about to hear, but nerves aside, I think I need to hear it and I think she needs to tell it.

"One night, he had a colleague over for dinner, and after I put you down for bed, I served them dessert." Ruth shakes her head, her nostrils flaring. "They didn't eat the dessert I served them, though. They wanted..." She clears her throat, her eyes dropping to her lap again in shame. "They wanted *me* for dessert." Her eyes dart back to mine, this time with more fire in them. "I said no, but as usual, Max ignored me and watched his mate..."

She shakes her head, unable to continue, and I give her hand a squeeze.

"Watched his mate, what?" I ask, even though I'm not sure if I want to know, but with my encouragement, she whispers the words.

"Maxwell watched his mate rape me before he joined in."

Everything inside me is screaming while I sit frozen in place.

Did I really just hear those words right?

Did she say my dad watched his mate rape his wife and then join in?

What. The. Actual. FUCK!

"Oh my god," I whisper in response, shaking my head frantically.

This can't be true. This can't be real. Why would my dad do that?

A sob escapes me as tears sear a path down my cheeks and an overwhelming feeling of rage bubbles in my gut.

Even though I don't want to believe what my mum is saying, I know it's true. The man I'd looked up to for most of my life is a monster. How could he treat my mother that way?

"It's not the worst part, Lexi." My mum sobs too, our eyes locking as her expression morphs into regret. "I'm so sorry. I should have known how all of this would end."

"What do you mean?" I ask through my tears, swiping at them with one hand, the other still clutched tight in my mum's hand.

"Not long after that night with Max and his colleague, Mike came to visit. He was only nine years old. Just a child. An innocent child, but that didn't matter to your father." She shakes her head and her lip curls in disgust. "That's the first time it happened."

"What happened?" I can't even imagine what happened.

Jesus, do I even want to know what happened?

My mum goes to speak, but at first, she can't seem to make her voice work. She clears her throat and swipes at her tears, sucking in a shuddering breath before she is finally able to reveal what happened next.

"Max started bringing Mike into the bedroom with us."

"What!" I jerk back as if someone just slapped me and my breath catches as my lungs start to burn.

Did she really just say that?

Oh my god.

What the hell!

This can't be real!

"At first, he would force Mike to watch. And I'm not talking about just sitting in a chair in the corner of the room." She shudders as her eyes fall distant. "He would make Mike get really close next to us on the bed and watch all the...." My mum hesitates, sucking in another deep breath. "Mike would watch all the positions and actions." My mum's hands fly to her mouth as she gags and then she starts sucking in deep breaths while she counts out loud, trying to shake off the panic and revolution.

I want to help her, but I don't know how.

"It's so sick." She growls then, her hands in tight fists as they thump to her lap. "I won't say more than that except that the last time before Mike stopped coming for visits, Max forced him to interact with us."

"What the fuck! I can't even... I... what?" I leap off the bed, my hands twisting in my hair as I try to breathe past the nausea rolling inside me.

No!

This can't be real!

Why would he do that?

Why would *anyone* do that?

Oh my god, I'm going to be sick.

"Lexi, I'm sorry. I shouldn't have told you." My mum drags herself to the side of the bed, looking panicked.

I'm about to tell her it's okay, but then I look past her, and I realise that this bed is where those crude things happened.

How has she lived through this?

As soon as I think it, I know the answer. Drugs and alcohol.

"Is there more?" I ask, my lip quivering and my rage reeling inside me. I start pacing at the foot of the bed, trying to maintain some sort of level of calm.

"Yes, but it's best if you don't know."

I stop pacing and face my mum. "Actually, I do need to know. I need to understand why Mike did those things to me and why Dad changed from my hero to my nightmare in one night."

"That's how your dad has always been, only he was always nice to you, Lexi. I was thankful for that. But the change you saw in him is what he's been like with me since I was six months pregnant with you."

"Tell me the rest." I pace again because I need to keep moving, or I'm going to explode.

"Your dad kept up with the weird stuff, and every time he invited a mate over for dinner, I knew what was to come, so I would get ridiculously drunk or high. Sometimes I woke up the following day with no memory of what they had done. I ignored my aching body. The grazes and bruises. Instead I went in search of more drugs.

When he took the job in the city, I was relieved. Having him gone for a few nights a week gave me a break, but I was already an addict by that time. I got really depressed, and I missed him, the *nice* side of him. When he came home, I became more willing to give him what he wanted, but he found my willingness boring. He liked me fighting him and saying no. He enjoyed raping me."

My mum slides off the end of the bed, coming to rest on the floor, brushing back her brown flyaways.

"When Mike moved in a few months back, things got really bad. Max wouldn't come home because he was having too much fun fucking his assistants, so he told Mike to take care of me, how he saw fit, and to make sure the drugs were accessible for me." She shudders as she shakes her head like she is trying to shake the memory from her brain. "So, Mike did exactly what Max asked of him. He started coming to my room each night and doing the same things Max did to me all those years ago when Mike was forced to watch. I didn't know what to do. I thought if I kicked up a fuss, then Mike would do those things to you. I saw the way he looked at you, Lexi." My mum glances up at me, her voice raspy from crying. "I realised I had to keep him occupied, keep him happy in order to keep him distracted from you. But it wasn't enough, was it? When he got so pissed about you having a lock on your door, I knew he must have been doing something already or planning something. That's why he attacked me that day. He said when you got home from school, he was going to tie you down and make me watch what he does to you. I couldn't let that happen, so I fought back. When I went to call triple zero, I only managed to hit speed dial one, which called you."

My mum stands then, still sobbing but with fierceness in her eyes. "Shen must have heard the racket and called for help, and the sirens scared Mike away since he's on parole and doesn't want to go back to prison."

"Fuck. Mum," I say, completely in shock with what she's just told me, but it all makes sense. It all falls into place.

We stare at each other for a moment, both victims of the same men, and then I pull her into a hug, and we fall apart in each other's arms.

How the fuck has this become our life?

I understand now why Mike is so fucked up. Not that it excuses the things he's done.

Why is my dad like that, though? Did that stuff happen to him when he was younger, too? Or is he just a twisted sicko?

The scary part is that my dad is really fucking good at hiding what he's really like from everyone. How do you reason with a man like that?

I can't even comprehend how my mum has felt all these years.

Alone.

She must have felt like the loneliest person on this earth.

I hate the thought of her feeling that way. Shit, I've been bitching about her being a bad mum, all the while she's been trying to protect me.

Fucking hell. She let Mike do sick stuff to her in the hopes he would stay away from me. She let her body be used for.... I don't even want to consider what. All to keep me from enduring it.

I used to think my mum was weak. Not anymore. She's the strongest person I know. She's a fucking superhero in my eyes.

God, it hurts like hell knowing she went through all that.

Eventually, our sobs ease, and mum's able to talk again.

"The file," she says, and my brows shoot up as I pull back to look at my hero's face.

"The file? That Dad wants?"

She nods. "It doesn't exist. Well, not anymore, anyway. It was an old paper file with documents he got me to sign back when we were first married. Of course, I didn't know what I was signing and didn't care. I stupidly trusted him. But basically, it was for an offshore bank account. He used it to test out his first embezzling attempts. I guess it worked because it had a couple of million dollars in it."

"What?" My pitch is high, and Mum grins past her tear-stained cheeks.

"I reacted the same way when I found out. I came across the file when he first started travelling to the city for his new job. I was bored and nosey, and when I found it, I reached out to my sister—your aunt. We weren't that close because Max scared her off after we got married, but a sister's bond can't be broken, and she helped me find out what the file was."

Reaching out, my mum smooths away the tears lingering on my cheeks as she looks at me like I'm everything. "We were both shocked when we put all the pieces together, and then my sister realised that because the account was in my name, I could withdraw money from it. At the time, we weren't sure how much access Maxwell had to it, so with Beth's help, we started taking small amounts of money from it to buy investments in your name, and we used Beth's post office box as the address." This time, she runs her fingers through my wayward hair, her eyes following its length. "It turns out Max opened another offshore account to avoid suspicion several years before that, so the money in the account with my name was small potatoes. Beth helped me get all but fifty dollars out of the offshore account in my name, and we purchased investments in my name as well as hers, too. Beth didn't touch her investments. She left half of them to me and the other half to you when she died."

"Holy shit," I whisper and she giggles.

"Yeah, we have a lot of money that no one knows about, but because Max is now under investigation, we have to keep it quiet. There's a chance it could be found if the investigators do their jobs properly, and if that's the case, it's been set up to look like Max did it."

"And if they don't find it?" I ask, dumbfounded.

"Then, we'll be able to buy that house I was talking about." Mum winks, and I throw my head back, laughing.

"Why did you buy the investments in the first place if you never intended to leave Dad?" I say after I get air back into my lungs.

"It was all Beth. She knew things weren't good with Max. She saw the bruises, so she said that doing this was my backup plan. It was a stupid plan, given I've been too much of a coward to try to get clean until I was forced to. But Lexi, I am clean, and I don't intend on living my life like that ever again."

My lips wobble again as tears fill my eyes, and I want more than anything to believe her. I could never have imagined all that she's been through. Never in a million years would I have thought my dad capable of doing such sick things.

"So why does Dad still think there's a file? And why does he want it after all this time?"

"I've let him believe the file still exists and have tried to steer him away from any idea that I took the money. He only wants it now because his other accounts have already been seized."

Everything makes sense now, and while I'm glad I finally understand what has been going on, the vileness of it all twists my gut.

I've endured a lot from Mike mostly, but a little from my dad. Even though he didn't do unspeakable acts to me himself, he knew what his son intended. After all, he trained him to do it.

I hate that I'm only now finding out. I hate that I've despised my mum all these years, thinking of her as a weak addict who didn't care about me. Even though she was too fucked up to show me how she felt about me, deep down, she has always been trying her best to protect me. I can't even begin to imagine what she's been put through at the hands of my dad, but one thing is for certain. My dad and Mike are going to pay for what they have done.

I'll make sure of it. Even if it kills me.

Thirteen

My emotions are shot. Like, dangling my heart in front of a firing squad holding machine guns, type of shot. Shot to fucking bits. Even though my mum was the victim, I feel traumatised at finding out the truth.

This house really is a house of horrors.

Hiding my feelings from Ayden is impossible, and he calls me during his lunch break when he notices I haven't responded to or joined in with any of the banter in the group chat that has flowed steadily through the day. I give him a rundown of the morning's visitors and my admission to Principal Rogan, and then I tell him that my mum told me what has been going on right under my nose since I was a baby. I don't give him any details, but tell him I need to process it all before I speak the words aloud to anyone.

Instead of paying anyone attention at school, Ayden chats with me for his whole hour break. He's pretty happy with his English Assessment but isn't feeling great about his Psychology one later this week. Then he tells me about a song he's found that he'll add to my Heavy playlist tonight. I beg him to tell me what it is, but he holds strong, and our call ends when the bell rings.

Talking with him helps boost my mood slightly, and I spend the next hour taking out my aggression on the boxing bag in the garage. At first, my punches are prissy because my mind wanders to last week when Muz dropped by Ayden's for a surprise visit. Even though we were enemies at the time, he'd offered me boxing advice. That was after he held a gun to my head, and I'd shocked him by stepping forward to press the barrel to my forehead.

Shit, maybe I really *do* need to see a therapist. That isn't normal.

As soon as school is over, Ayden jogs to my house, with Rhys and Marcus not far behind. Ayden greets me with a heart-stopping kiss that takes my mind to places involving us being naked, but as soon as I think it, my mind shoots to my mum's trauma.

Since Ayden, Marcus and Rhys need to study for their Maths Assessment tomorrow, we get comfy in the front living room, where they help each other revise while I sit awkwardly, not having anything to do.

Is it weird that I feel left out?

I don't like Maths, nor am I good at it, but I kinda hate sitting on the outside like this.

"Are you sure you're okay?" Ayden asks for the fifth time since arriving earlier, and I nod for the fifth time, hoping he can't see through my fake smile.

I'm really *not* okay. My mind keeps conjuring up images that have no right to be flashing through my mind. I haven't been witness to any of it, yet my mind's eye sees my dad restraining my mum, hitting her, and raping her. I even see Mike as a kid, his eyes wide with curiosity as he watches his father rape his step mum.

It's sick. It's all too much, and I really need to switch my mind off.

Ayden sets aside his laptop and takes my phone, sitting on the floor next to me. When I arch a brow at him, he shoots me one of his fucking sexy winks and focuses on my phone.

"Here." He holds out his earbuds, and I take each bud as he plugs them into my phone. "Have a listen to the song I found."

My grin is real this time as my eyes stay locked on Ayden's face as he uses my phone. My heart feels full as I watch the way he bites his upper lips as he concentrates. It's like I fall more and more for him with each moment we share.

In a love-struck puppy haze, I pop the buds in my ears and wait for the music to start, and when those ocean blues flick back to mine, music fills my ears.

I immediately fall into the music, closing my eyes and giving in to the way it grabs my soul and drags me in. It doesn't take me long to realise why Ayden shared this song with me, and by the time it's finished, my eyes burn with unshed tears.

Leaning forward, Ayden pulls the earbuds free. "You like it?"

"It's perfect," I whisper, my smile widening at the song he found for me.

It's called Heavy.

"The original was by Linkin Park, but when I heard this cover of it, I knew you would love it." Ayden hands me my phone, and I look at the Spotify screen.

"Fame on Fire?" I ask, and he nods.

"Yep, Fame on Fire, featuring Rain Paris. It's good, hey?"

"Yeah, it is." I've just found my new favourite song. Well, technically, Ayden found it, which makes it even more special.

"I've added it to your Heavy playlist." He grins, and I leap at him, crashing my lips into his as we tumble backwards to the floor.

"Wait. So all I have to do is find a sick song, and Lexi will kiss me like that?" Rhys' voice floats to us, and Ayden and I chuckle into each other's mouths.

"Sorry to burst your bubble, but I'm pretty sure you have to be Ayden to get that sort of reaction from Lexi." Marcus chuckles nearby, so Ayden and I reluctantly break apart and glance over to where Marcus and Rhys are huddled close together.

Has she decided to try a relationship with Marcus now?

"I can do everything that Ayden can do." Rhys whines, and Marcus scoffs.

"Is that so?" He teases, and she pokes her tongue out at him.

"Rhys, I'm sorry to tell you this, but you don't have a pretty cock like Ayden." I tease her this time, and she drops her dark lips open, exasperated at me.

Ayden takes that moment to slap his hand against my arse, and I bite my lip when a moan nearly escapes.

Leaning in, Ayden's breath fans against my ear. "Stop saying the word cock." Then he nips at my lobe with his teeth.

"Unless I'm missing something, Rhys doesn't have a cock at all." Marcus taunts, and we all laugh.

"Do I have to prove you wrong and bring out my strap-on?" Rhys asks, deadly serious, and Marcus freezes, his eyes widening.

"Jesus," Ayden chuckles under his breath before putting his lips against my ear again, "Your friend is kinda scary."

I hum under my breath in agreement and drag my eyes away from the frown twisting Marcus' face as they have a hushed argument.

I'm still lying on top of Ayden on the floor of the living room, and I wish more than anything that we were alone right now. I could really use some Ayden time to drown in him.

Eventually, Marcus and Rhys stop arguing and turn back to their studies, and I leave Ayden to finish his revision as I go in search of my mum. If what she told me today has affected me so much, then surely, it's affected her, too.

When I find her in her room, she has the radio playing while she moves her hips as she rips my dad's clothes from the wardrobe.

"Please tell me you're going to burn them." Leaning against the door frame, I grin at my mum when she looks over her shoulder at me.

"Sure am." Her grin is wide and so unfamiliar. It suits her. I'd love to see her smile like that more often.

"Do you need any help?"

My mum turns back to me, looking hopeful. "Yes, if you feel like helping me burn your father's clothes."

"Hell yes."

I step into her room and join her at the closet to pull out the last pieces my dad left behind before moving to the city for work. It's not like he's needed these clothes for a long time now, but my mum needs to do this, and I don't want her to feel alone in this.

Together, we gather up the clothes and make our way out the patio door. Once we have the clothes piled in the fire pit that has only ever been used once, I go to the garage to find some metho and matches and return to Mum.

Ayden, Marcus and Rhys come to see what my mum and I are up to right as the clothes whoosh up in flames. They hang back as I stand with my mum, our arms linked as we watch the flames dance and sizzle, reducing the clothing to a charred mess.

Given what my relationship was like with my mum only yesterday, I'm sure my friends are curious as to what has changed. I have a lot of getting to know my mum to do, and she the same with me. We have a lot of darkness to get past, and I'm almost certain we will in time.

When there's only smouldering ash left in the fire pit, my mum declares that she is making us toasties for dinner, and we all join her in the kitchen to prepare them.

It's nice.

Like really fucking nice.

So nice that I know it will kill me if she relapses and the old version of her comes back. I don't think I can bear to lose this version of my mum. I've felt so alone for so long, and even though Ayden and my friends have helped to fill a void, I know that more than anything, the void will only vanish if my mum is in my life completely.

After dinner, we all wash up together, and my mum turns in for another early night, letting me know I can come and use her bathroom whenever I need to.

Settling in for the night, we retreat to the front living area after changing into comfier clothes. Marcus and Rhys huddle together on the couch as Marcus plays a new fighting game on the PlayStation. I'm not sure how he focuses on the game with Rhys poking his ribs, trying to throw him off his game, though.

Ayden and I sit back on the floor where we were earlier, and his intense blue gaze locks on to mine as he lifts his hand to stroke my hair back. Something I've realised he enjoys doing.

"You and your mum seem to be getting along well."

I shrug. "Yeah, things have... changed."

"How so?" Ayden takes my hand and presses a kiss to the back.

"I understand more now after she told me some stuff today." When my mind flitters to think about what she told me, I shake my head in an attempt to scare away the memory.

"Do you want to tell me what she told you?" Ayden asks, leaning close as he whispers, his hand travelling from my hair to run his fingers down my cheek and under my chin.

"It's not really something I can say here. Can I have a bit more time to process it before I tell you?" I ask quietly, my eyes flutter closed as his finger slides down my neck and back up again.

That feels so good.

Soothing.

Ayden shifts next to me before his whisper warms my ear. "Okay."

The action causes me to forget to breathe for a moment before my heart does a little flip inside my chest.

I wonder if he realises how much he affects me.

"Ayden," I whisper back, completely lost to the sensation of his touch and his nearness.

"Yes?" His warm lips nip my lobe, and I have to fight to hold in my moan.

"I missed you today."

"Fuck baby, I missed you too." It's a low growl in my ear this time as his other hand slides up around my neck to cup the back of my head under my hair. Still, with his lips near my ear, Ayden whispers again, "Sorry about this morning. I was a prick."

I try to pull back to look into his eyes, but he holds me in place, so I whisper back.

"That was kind of mean working me up and walking out without finishing the job."

"Not what I was apologising for, Lex." Ayden growls, nipping at my ear. "Anyway, weren't you finishing the job when I walked out?"

I grin into his neck at the reminder. "I couldn't go through with it. Not without you in the room."

Ayden growls again, and even with my eyes closed, my lips find his, desperate for the contact. Our tongues clash with hunger, and I clutch at Ayden's school shirt, pulling him closer, desperately needing to fall into his trance and forget what I learnt today.

"Uh, guys?" Rhys' voice in close proximity makes us freeze, and my eyes pop open to find her kneeling right beside us.

Frowning, I release my lip-lock with Ayden.

"What?" I snap, and she grins.

"I'm all for PDA, but you two are on another level where I'm pretty sure one day soon you're gonna forget there are other people in the room with you. I'm totally down for a show, don't get me wrong, but I get the feeling the vanilla in you would be mortified, Lex."

"Vanilla? You think Lexi is vanilla?" Ayden draws back to look at Rhys.

"Not the point, but yes," Rhys states, and I giggle.

"I'll dial it down, Rhys. Thanks for the heads up." I snap, but my tone doesn't faze her.

"She's not vanilla. She's just learning the ropes. That's all." Ayden teases, and I push him off me, standing to weave past Rhys.

"Who wants a drink?" I ask, getting a round of nos.

I take that opportunity to leave the living room and head to the kitchen to get a breather from my addiction to Ayden. I do another check of the doors to make sure they are locked, even though I've already done it twice. When I return to the kitchen, Ayden is leaning against the kitchen counter, waiting for me.

"I was thinking, maybe you and I can stay up in your bedroom tonight. Rhys and Marcus will be fine in the living room, and I kinda don't want to be there when they start fucking."

I giggle at the cringe that morphs Ayden's face.

"We don't have to do anything." He adds. "Just sleep. I know it's still hard for you to do that, but sleeping on the living room floor can't be helping, either."

Aw, look at that.

He's nervous.

How utterly adorable.

He probably wants to demand that we sleep upstairs tonight, so I get a better sleep, but he's trying not to be controlling. It's cute.

Smirking, I step up to Ayden and lay my hand on his chest as I rise on my toes and hover my lips over his. "There's no way we are going to my room for the night *just* to sleep."

A low growl comes from the back of Ayden's throat before he closes the distance, claiming my lips. The kiss is hot and heavy, a promise of what's to come, and when I pull back, I witness Ayden's lust drunk gaze, and it's all I can do not to run like a horny bitch up the stairs while stripping my clothes off.

"Come on," I whisper and reluctantly draw myself back from him, snagging his hand to drag him behind me.

I need to be alone with him.

Like, now!

Fourteen

After saying good night to Rhys and Marcus, who are already grinding on each other in the living room, we make our way upstairs. As usual, I've avoided coming up here. I've practically turned the living room into my bedroom with my bags of clothes shoved in the corner.

Upstairs, Ayden leads the way, opening my new bedroom door thanks to Jason, and flicks the light on.

Standing in the doorway, I wait for the usual rush of memories from the night Mike attacked me the first time, but they don't come. Instead, I just remember the night Ayden slept with me in the bed when I friend-zoned him. It was the night of the party in Redfield, and we'd come up here to find that my bedroom door had been removed and stolen while we were out.

"You okay?" Ayden asks, and my shoulders relax in relief.

"I am."

Stepping into the room, I move to the side of my bed to plug my charger into the wall to charge my phone while Ayden closes my door and kicks off his school shoes.

He's quiet as he looks around my room, probably remembering the night he snuck in here to save me, but when I study him, I realise he's actually checking out my stuff.

I don't have much. I've never been a *things* type of person and find more importance with the few essentials I carry daily rather than other mundane objects.

Standing at my dresser, Ayden lifts the lid of a little music box and looks inside.

"It's empty," I confirm what his eyes are seeing. Absolutely nothing inside.

"Has it always been empty?" He turns to me, watching as I slip my hoodie off.

"Yep. I've never had jewellery or much of anything like that. Abbey and I had those corny best friend necklaces years ago, but we both lost them somewhere. They were just cheap stuff, anyway."

Ayden approaches me then, his ocean blues never leaving mine.

"You deserve boxes of jewellery." Reaching me, he tangles his hand in my hair.

I giggle. "I'll take boxes of chocolates."

"You can have that too." He smirks as he leans down to claim my lips.

I melt at his touch, need surging between my thighs as our tongues clash. I slide my hands around to his back as he pulls me closer, a primal rumble coming from his chest. Stepping forward, he backs me up against the bed, and the moment my calves hit the end of the mattress, the terrible things that happened to my mum engulf my mind.

How could I have slept up here all those nights, unaware, while my dad, and more recently Mike, had been raping my mum and doing vile things to her?

"Hey." Ayden pulls back, looking down at me with concerned blue eyes. "What's wrong?"

I must have stopped kissing him or something, so I shake my head, trying to clear it of the sickening thoughts and reach up on my toes to resume our kiss.

At first, Ayden's lips are slow and unsure, but when I slip my tongue between his lips, he relaxes back into our kiss, deepening it as he guides me back onto the bed.

The moment my back touches the mattress, my mind is back to my mum.

Ayden stops kissing me again and pulls back, the silver chain around his neck dangling.

"Where's my girl at right now?" His words are calm yet concerned and hold no anger or frustration. "Talk to me, beautiful."

Huffing, I throw my arms back and punch the mattress next to me. In an effort not to scream, I squeeze my eyes shut and suck in deep breaths.

What the fuck is wrong with me?

This amazing, caring, generous, and utterly lick-able guy of mine is here giving me all of his attention, and I can't get out of my fucking head.

Seriously, fuck my life!

Prying my lids open, I find him still hovering over me, waiting patiently for me to speak. He really is a good guy. I don't know what my life would be like if he never moved here.

"I'm sorry." I say softly, "It's the shit my mum told me. I can't seem to switch my brain off."

"We don't have to do this, Lex. We can just cuddle and talk." The honesty in his tone matches the honesty in his eyes. He really would ignore his hard-on and snuggle with me, if that's what I wanted.

The thing is, I *do* want that, but *after* I have him inside me because I *need* him close. So close that I won't be able to tell where I end, and he starts.

"No. I want to do this. Let's try again." My eyes are practically begging, which coerces that sexy grin of his and the caving in of one of his dimples.

"I have an idea. Do you have a scarf?" Ayden rises above me, moving off the bed, and I instantly miss his nearness.

"Why?" I ask curiously as I prop myself up on my elbows.

"Do you trust me?" he asks in all seriousness, his smirk falling away.

"Of course. You know I do."

"Good. Scarf?" His dark brows rise like he's annoyed that he had to ask again.

All it does is turn me on even more.

"There's a few hanging on the hook inside my wardrobe door." I nod my head towards my wardrobe, and he winks before turning.

Finding what he needs, Ayden lays a black scarf on the bed next to me and then reaches inside his blazer pocket to pull out his phone and earbuds, sitting them on top of the scarf.

"What are you doing?" I'm curious as hell, but he doesn't answer me as he eases off his blazer, laying it on the floor next to his shoes before he works on the buttons of his shirt.

"Aren't you going to tell me?" I glare at him then, even though I'm not actually angry at him. I'm just impatient and want to know what he's up to.

He slides his shirt off, giving me a good eyeful of his solid, bare chest. "Stand up."

When his shirt hits the floor, I sit up and shuffle to the edge of the bed, eagerly taking the hand he offers to help me up.

"Let's take these off." Finding the bottom of my hoodie, Ayden eases it up over my head. Then he moves to the hem of my t-shirt, and we repeat the same process. This time, the cool chill in the air sends goosebumps over my bare skin. "So beautiful," he whispers before claiming my lips in a short, searing kiss. Hooking his fingers in the band of my trackies, he slowly eases them down over my hips and arse before they fall the rest of the way down my legs.

Kicking them off, happy to be free of the material, I now stand with only my white bra and cotton knickers on. Not at all sexy, and I mentally punch myself for not thinking ahead and finding something less plain Jane to wear.

Ayden doesn't seem to mind, though, and with gentle fingers, he glides them down my neck and over the lace edge of my bra before coming to a stop just near my belly button. His face contorts as if he's in pain right before he drops his hand from my skin and bends to the side to pick up the scarf.

"You need to remember that you trust me and that I won't do anything to hurt you." His eyes lock with mine, dancing between them like he's assessing my reaction. "I'm asking you to give up your control and allow me to worship you. Let me do it my way and I promise I'll get you out of your head."

With my heart dancing like it's on crack, I manage to nod past the thrill rippling through me as I slowly take in the scarf Ayden is running over his palm.

"Okay, but," I say, dragging my gaze from the scarf to his face again, "I need you to tell me *how* you're planning on doing that."

He grins. "Can't you just trust me?"

"I do trust you... I just..." Shit. My eyes fall to his bare chest for a moment before flicking back to his smoldering gaze. Why is it so hard for me to just relinquish control? "Can you tell me a little, at least?"

His intense blue eyes roam my face before he nods and holds up the scarf.

"This will go over your eyes so you can't see."

"What? But what if I want to see?" I'm all annoyingly whiney, which is not attractive, but a girl has needs, and looking at Ayden Mitchell in all his naked glory is fucking essential.

"Too bad, beautiful. Sight is another distraction. If you can't see, then it will allow you to focus more on the *feel* of every place I touch you."

"Oh."

His grin is sinful. And fuck me, I want to go to hell with him.

Lifting the black scarf, he steps behind me, bringing it to rest over my eyes before securing it at the back of my head. My world plunges into darkness, something I'm not all that fond of, but the moment his warm hand falls to my shoulder and runs down my arm, I forget all of my worries.

"Lay on the bed." The heat of his words dance over my ear, sending a shiver up my spine. I'm about to remind him I can't see where I'm going when his hands gently grip my shoulders, and he helps me move back onto the mattress.

Laying back, I shuffle a little to get comfy and then the bed dips to my left before Ayden's fingers glide up my arm.

"I'm going to put my earbuds in your ears so you can't hear anything but cello music."

"Cello music?" I'm confused. Why would I want to listen to cello music?

"Trust me, Lex. Cello music is very therapeutic and is perfect to help you focus on the task at hand."

"The task at hand?" I giggle.

"Yes, the task of letting me worship you." Warm lips nibble at my lobe then, inducing my moan.

"I love that sound, Lexi." Ayden shifts on the bed next to me again. "I'm putting the earbuds in now. Just relax and focus on the *feel* of where I touch you."

I'm about to say okay, but my words falter when the earbuds slide in one ear and then the other, and my head fills with the most beautiful music I've ever heard. It's captivating and haunting and relaxes me at the same time as uplifting me.

I'm not sure how long I lay there with my world in darkness and filled with the music of angels before I feel Ayden's fingers touch my feet.

Like a feather, his fingers glide up the outside of my left leg, the sensation so much more than just a simple touch. Sliding over the thin fabric at the side of my knickers, Ayden's fingers continue their path up the side of my stomach, which instantly causes me to pull away, giggling. He doesn't stop, though, his fingers grazing the swell of my breast, my nipple instantly pebbling under the white cotton of my bra. I expect his fingers to keep travelling up to my neck, but they don't. Instead, he hooks his fingers under the cup of my bra to pull it down and the chill of the air is brief before hot moist lips close over my nipple.

My back arches off the bed, and I feel my moan vibrate through my chest.

Shit. I hope that wasn't too loud.

I forget what I'm thinking of because, holy hell, this feels so good. Ayden feels so good, and I don't want him to stop.

When his tongue sweeps over my nipple, my hands reach up, seeking his head, the need to hold him in place too consuming. Wet heat pools between my legs each time his tongue lashes my pebbled skin, and I become fevered for more.

He must be able to feel how desperate I am because he releases my nipple and starts pressing searing kisses down to my navel and toward the ache between my legs.

I'm panting.

I think.

I can't really tell because I'm so engrossed.

I still can't see a thing, and all I can hear is the deep tenor of the cello, while the sensation of Ayden's touch sends me into a frenzy.

The moment his warm mouth kisses over my fabric covered mound, I nearly lose it.

I think I say yes. Who the fuck knows, but Ayden gets the hint, and a moment later, the fabric glides quickly down my legs and vanishes into thin air.

I don't even get shy when I feel him spread my legs apart. Wide apart. Baring me completely to him.

When his finger circles my clit, my arse lifts off the bed as pure pleasure builds inside me, and a moment later, the hot silk of his tongue glides between my folds while he slips a couple of fingers deep into my heat.

That's all it takes. He's barely even gotten started when my insides start spasming, and mind-numbing pleasure crashes through me. A hand slaps over my mouth as my climax bursts free of my lips, but Ayden doesn't stop. His fingers curl up, kneading at my upper inside wall, dragging my orgasm out.

His touch becomes too intense, and I grab at his hair, pulling it, not too hard, to get him to stop. He gets the hint, and a moment later, my mouth is released of his hand, and I feel his weight shift off the bed.

I'm panting like I've run a marathon and go to pull the earbuds out, but his hand quickly seizes mine, stopping me. With my hand still in his, he places it on his hot skin, and the firm ridges of his abs ripple under my touch.

I smile, my lips stretching wide.

I love the feel of his body, and I especially love the place he's directing my hand as he guides it down over the coarse hair that leads south.

The moment his hard length touches my hand, I moan and glide my hand to the tip, spreading the pre-cum over the taught skin with my fingers. Instinctively, I lick my lips, desperate for a taste, and Ayden doesn't keep me waiting as he moves next to me on the mattress before nudging his cock at my lips. Opening with eagerness, I lift my head a little as Ayden slides his hardness into my mouth.

Instinctively, I look up, wanting to see his face and how I affect him, but the barrier of the blindfold is still in place. It's one thing for me to lie back and have him worship me, but it's another to deny me a view of his face as he comes apart.

Gripping the base of his shaft with one hand, I continue to work him in my mouth while I use the other to quickly remove my blindfold. With the cello still filling my head, my eyes adjust to the light in the room as I eagerly take in Ayden, holding himself up with one hand on the mattress well above my head and the other off to the side of my head. His face is a mixture of pleasure and concentration as he pumps his hips forward in sync with me as I devour his hard cock with my mouth.

When his eyes meet mine, he frowns, his lips moving as he says something that I can't hear. He doesn't stop his thrusts, though, not even when he moves one of his hands off the mattress to tug out one of the earbuds.

"Why'd you take the blindfold off?" he pants, still thrusting. It's so hot to have him basically on top of me like this, thrusting into me, taking control. I know if I try to push him off or make a sound of distress that he'd stop, but pushing the limit like this, where I know that if he gets any more worked up, his thrusts will be more forceful, is a rush. I'm fucking yearning for him to push me further.

Since he's deep in my mouth, I can't answer him, so instead, I release his shaft with my hand and slide both my hands over the hot skin of his hips until the globes of his arse are under my touch. I squeeze and tug him closer until his length makes me gag.

"Fuck, Lex." Ayden hisses, which I only just hear over the cello music still playing in one ear. "Stop, baby." He pulls back, using one of his hands to break my grip on his arse, and with a pop, his engorged cock slips from my mouth.

"What are you doing?" I whine, already missing the feel of him inside my mouth.

Shaking his head with a grin, Ayden tugs out the other earbud and pulls me up to sit.

"I don't want to do that." Standing from the bed, Ayden snatches up a condom packet off the bed, which he must have put there after he blindfolded me, and bites the end, tearing it open.

Fuck me.

He looks so good.

Hot.

Sexy.

Fuckable.

Ridable.

Jesus, I'm starting to think like Rhys.

"What don't you want to do?" I'm quickly forgetting what we are even talking about as I watch him hold the condom to his tip and roll it down his hard length. "Fuck, that's hot."

Ayden's soft chuckle floats to my ears.

"I don't want to choke you with my cock, Lex, even when you beg me with those greedy eyes."

"Greedy?" My brows shoot up, but then I smirk. "I guess I am greedy. How could I not be? You make me want to do things I've never thought of doing before."

"Really? That's interesting." He shoots me a smug smirk. "We will do it all, beautiful, I promise." With his hard cock pointing in my direction, Ayden steps up to the bed, lifting my chin with gentle fingers. "But tonight, I have other plans." He steps back, releasing my chin. "Stand up."

I don't hesitate. No fucking way am I going to make either of us wait. I shuffle to the edge of the bed and stand in front of him, eagerly awaiting further instructions. Leaning down, Ayden claims my lips in a searing kiss, and I taste myself on his tongue, which shoots pleasure straight to my core. His warm skin caresses mine where our fronts meet as his hand slides up my neck to cup the back of my head, deepening the kiss. I'm melting in his embrace, under his touch. I'm helpless to resist anything he offers me.

Breaking our kiss, I keep my eyes closed as Ayden peppers kisses down my neck while he moves around my body to sit on the bed behind me. I automatically go to turn around, but his hands land on my hips, halting me before his grip tugs me backwards.

"Legs apart, beautiful. Straddle me."

At first, I'm confused and try to turn again, but again he stops me.

"Stay facing that way, just move back, baby." Ayden leads me backwards with gentle hands, and I find myself standing over the top of his legs with my butt pressed to his chest. Sliding his hand up over my hip, it travels north until his fingers brush over each of my pebbled nipples a few times until they become intensely tight.

"Ayden," I whisper and sigh, letting my head fall back as I close my eyes.

"You feel like heaven, Lex." Warm lips press to my back as Ayden's other hand finds the aching, wet heat between my legs. "Sit on my cock, beautiful."

Ayden shifts his hands to my hips, tugging me down gently, and I finally understand what he wants, so I lower myself down, feeling the firm tip of his cock nudge my entrance.

"Like this?" I whisper, the ache more urgent, deep inside me.

"Yes, fuck yes." Ayden tugs me down with his own urgency and he slides inside.

Our moans are loud, filling my small bedroom. For a fleeting moment, I worry that we'll be heard, so I make a mental note to try to stay quiet.

One of Ayden's arms wraps around me from behind, his hand cupping my breast, and the fingers from his other hand dig into my hips as we start to move together. The angle of his thrusts hit places inside me that instantly ignite. Each time I rise and fall over him, I think I'm about to come undone, but the intense pleasure keeps building higher and higher.

"Fuck, baby, I'm not going to last," Ayden growls in my ear, his lips nipping at my lobe. All I can do is moan. Words fail me as the sensations reach new heights, and releasing my breast, Ayden slides his hand down my stomach.

"Give me your hand," he demands, and I obey, still matching his thrusts.

With my hand finding his, Ayden takes control, gliding our hands south, and I moan when he guides my hand between my legs. With his hand over mine, Ayden wraps our hands around the base of his cock where our bodies join.

"Feel that, Lex?" He pants. "Feel how we fit perfectly together?"

"Yes." I pant, and he growls in satisfaction.

"Let's make you come." Ayden's husky sex voice increases my need, and he unwraps our hands from where he is impaling me to slide over the bud of my clit.

Then, with his fingers guiding mine, we work together applying gentle circles which is like flipping a switch, and seconds later, I shove my wrist in my mouth, biting down to stop the guttural scream that wants to rip from me as I explode.

White lights flash across my vision, and I haven't even finished pulsing around Ayden's cock when my convulsing walls milk an orgasm from him.

Fifteen

There are just some conversations you don't want to have with your mum, and my need to flee makes me edgy.

How do I get out of this?

Maybe if I pretend to faint?

No, that will involve fussing.

Perhaps if I had earphones, I could sneak them in, but I don't have them with me right now.

"Are you sexually active, Lexi?" My mum repeats herself because I ignored her the first time. Maybe if I keep ignoring her, she'll go away.

"Shall I just ask Ayden if you two are having sex?"

"No!" I squeak, darting my head to her in mortification.

My mum cocks a brown brow. "Now that I have your attention, do you mind answering my first question?"

My shoulders drop as I realise she tricked me into paying her attention.

"I don't really want to talk about this with you," I admit, drawing my knees to my chest as I sit back deeper into the couch. I was quite happy reading an e-book in the front living room before my mum invaded my space a few minutes ago.

"Oh, come on, Lexi. Why? I thought we would be past that sort of awkwardness after what I revealed to you yesterday." Sitting forward on the other couch, my mum keeps her eyes fixed on me, her brown hair popping free from where she tucked it behind her ear.

"It's not the same thing," I mumble, trying not to let my thoughts go back to the terrible things she told me yesterday.

"No, you're right, it's not, but I'd still like to know."

"Why?" I whine as my eyes find hers.

"Well, I guess I'd like to make sure you're being safe, and he's treating you right."

Last night flashes through my head, and heat rises over my body.

I wonder if she would think the things Ayden did to me last night are considered as *treating me right*?

It feels right. It feels perfect. Last night was yet another experience with him that I'll never forget. I'd been so sated afterwards that I passed out and slept all night in his arms. I didn't even hear when Mike tried to break in again. No one did, but he tried. Ayden and Marcus checked the security footage from last night before leaving for school and saw that he turned up about 3am again, trying the same doors as the night before. Or perhaps I should say the morning before.

"Ayden treats me like a queen," I whisper, and I see my mum straighten on the couch in my peripheral vision. "We are safe."

"Oh. Right. Okay, so you are sexually active?" she asks, and I shoot her a *"really"* glare, feeling my face heat in embarrassment.

"Mum, please. I don't want to talk about this stuff. Just know that I'm being treated right, and we are safe, and I'm even on the pill. Now, can we talk about something else?" *Or better yet, leave me alone to finish reading the juicy sex scene I was ripped away from when she entered the room.*

I'm trying so hard to not be a bitch, but it's hard to speak like this with her. Besides the fact that she's had no interest in my personal life until recently, this isn't the sort of stuff you want to talk about with your mum.

Well, at least I don't think it is. I guess I don't really know, given I've never experienced mum talks until Andrea came into my life, but even so, the Wests have never been *those* people. My mum and I have never been *those* people. Even when I got my first period, she was more concerned about the inconvenience of having to take me to buy sanitary products rather than talking about what was happening to my body and teaching me how to manage it.

She's always avoided these sorts of conversations, and I've gotten used to that. Now she wants to know things I'd prefer to keep to myself.

Slowly, my mum nods. "I can see he makes you happy, Lexi. I can also see how smitten he is with you. I'm glad you have him in your life."

My brows dart up. "Smitten? Really?"

My mum laughs. "Yes, smitten."

I'm saved by any further interrogation when Mr Matthews knocks at the front door for another session. It's good to see him, and not just because he's saving me from the sex talk with my mum. He's become a safe, familiar, dependable person in my life, and I'm lucky Principal Rogan has approved the home visits.

"How are you today, Lexi?" he asks, taking the same seat that my mum occupied a minute ago. She hurried off to her bedroom to leave Mr M and me in peace.

"Okay, I guess. I had a good sleep last night." I admit sparking his interest, his blue eyes brightening under his bushy black brows.

"That's good. Sleeping well will help you handle things better. Did you do something differently before you went to bed? Hot milk? Read?"

I bite back a laugh because he's going to hate it if I answer truthfully. "You don't really want to know the answer to that."

"Of course I do, Lexi. Every bit of information can help." He looks so oblivious to what I'm about to say.

"Well, if you absolutely must know, Ayden fucked me until I couldn't walk, and all I could do was sleep."

"Christ." Mr M shakes his head and looks up at the ceiling. "Why did I think working with teenagers was a good idea?"

"Because despite our attitude and smart-arse bullshit, we need your help."

Mr Matthews drops his eyes to mine at my honest response and grins slightly, but doesn't speak for a minute, raking a hand over his shiny bald head.

"Mum just asked me if I was sexually active. That was an awkward conversation." My admission refocuses Mr M, and he settles back on the couch.

"Were you honest with her?" he asks, and I shrug.

"I was vague, but she understood."

Again, he nods. "Your mum has been pretty vacant in your life up until now. It's only natural to not want to open up to her."

"I don't open up to anyone about that stuff. It's private." Drawing my knees away from my chest, I stretch out my legs.

"You don't seem to care about telling me about your sex life, Lexi."

I frown at his words and realise he is right, but then I laugh. "I think I enjoy shocking you, to be honest."

"Maybe, but you also trust me because we've built a relationship where you feel comfortable telling me stuff, even if it is to shock me. You haven't had enough time with the sober version of your mum to do that yet." Mr Matthews tilts his head. "Do you think you will give your mum that chance? Will you give her time to build a relationship with you?"

I instantly think of what she told me yesterday and how she must have been so scared and lonely every time my dad did those horrible things to her. I never used to think she deserved anything from me, but now I feel differently. Now I wish I could have stopped those things from happening to her.

"Yes."

"That's good." His eyes widen in surprise. "You've changed your tune."

Nodding, I debate what I want to tell him. I don't think I can tell him about my mum's past with my dad and Mike. I'm not ready for people to realise how far back the depravity goes.

"We had a little chat yesterday. I understand a few things better now. As long as she stays sober, then I'm willing to work on our relationship."

He nods. "That's fantastic, Lexi. I'm so pleased that things are improving."

While certain things are getting better for me, other things are no better or even worse.

This stuff with my dad is truly sick. I can't even let myself think about it without feeling blinding rage. How could he have done those things to my mum, yet treated me like a princess? At least that's what he did until he worked away. Then he basically forgot about me. That's a good thing, I guess, because he could have taken more of an interest in me like my mum feared he might, or he could have forced me to watch like he did to Mike.

Fuck, that's so sick. No wonder Mike is so screwed up. My dad raised him to be the monster he is.

"How's Amy?" It's time to steer this conversation in another direction, so I smirk when Mr M shoots me an unimpressed glare.

"If you would like to know how Miss Dice is, you will have to wait until you return to school."

"Well, that's boring." Crossing my arms over my chest, I jut out my bottom lip in a pout.

"How are you feeling about doing community service at the school this afternoon?" Mr Matthews effectively steers the conversation back to me, and I shrug.

"I don't hate the idea. I'm pretty bored staying locked up in this house at the moment, so I'm actually looking forward to having some time outside."

"That's really great. It took a lot of courage to own up to what you did." Mr M smiles at me, and I offer a slight tug of my lips, "Was your involvement in the vandalism what you were referencing when you asked me what I'm obligated to report a couple of weeks back?"

Sighing, I blow out a breath and nod. "Yep. I was a coward back then."

Mr Matthews nods, "I wouldn't say, coward. I would say you were trying to figure things out. You've had a lot on your plate. The important thing is that you knew you did something wrong, and you came forward to carry your share of the blame."

"I guess," I mumble, still feeling guilty about the whole thing.

We spend the next twenty minutes talking about the night I broke into the school with Travis. It's nice to know I have nothing more to hide from Mr Matthews now that the cat is out of the bag. Before he leaves, my mum comes back into the living room to see us, and I'm a little stunned, my brows shooting up as I look at her.

"Mum. What are you wearing?"

"What?" she asks in confusion, her brown eyes darting between Mr M and me. "Oh, this. It's a Fox Pines Foxes Jersey." My mum looks down, holding out the old orange and black football jersey from the bottom hem as if it will give us a better view.

"I can see that. Why are you wearing it?"

"Well, I've reconnected with Tina. You remember Tina, my old friend that used to live down the road? She invited me to come to the footy grand final this weekend. Everyone will be there, so it's a great place for me to find some new friends." My mum is excited. Her eyes are wide, and they have a glint to them I haven't seen before.

"Oh. I guess that makes sense then," I mutter, taking my mum in.

"Okay, Lexi. I have to head off now, but I'll check in again tomorrow." Mr M draws my attention away from my mum.

"Are these daily visits really necessary?" I whine, which earns me a glare from my mum.

"Let's just take it one day at a time, okay?" Mr Matthews suggests and inclines his head to my mum. "See you tomorrow."

My mum smiles and shows him out while I flop back on the couch and unlock my phone to see a new message from Ayden.

Ayden Mitchell

I can't stop thinking about you.
And last night.
I never got a chance to say this last night
because you passed out straight away.
But thank you for trusting me.
Also, I'll be spending my lunch break on the
phone with you again, so keep it close. xx

My heart does a little flip as I read over Ayden's message. He's such a sweetie, yet he isn't. He's so strong, and manly, and demanding, and wild, yet so lovingly sweet. I don't think I'll ever get enough of him.

Like ever!

I have a little while to wait until he has his lunch break, so I go out to the garage and pull on the gloves, needing to punch out some of this bored energy. I give the bag a few light taps before sadness sweeps over me.

Muz.

Hitting the bag still reminds me of Muz, and without second-guessing myself, I tug off the gloves and reach for my phone in my back pocket, bringing up his number before hesitating a moment.

What if he doesn't want to speak to me? What if he's too sick today?

I guess I'll never know if I don't try, so I hit his number and listen to it ring.

"Pretty girl, to what do I owe this pleasure?" Even though he's trying to sound confident, it's hard to believe with the weakness evident in his voice. Shit, he doesn't sound good at all.

"Sorry, I can call back a different time." I offer, feeling awful. Maybe I woke him from a nap?

"Don't be silly. I always have time to speak to you, pretty girl." He coughs harshly then, and tears well in my eyes.

It's my fault he's so sick.

"Are you sure? I was just checking in. I wanted to make sure you weren't harassing the nurses." I let a little humour sound in my voice, even though I feel anything but.

"More like they are harassing me. Do you know how many sponge baths I've had? These chicks are hungry for a bit of Muz meat."

I burst out laughing. "Muz meat? Oh my god, don't say that ever again."

He chuckles slowly and weakly. "You bet that pretty arse of yours, I'll say that again. Muz meat." He coughs a little again and clears his throat. "How's things with you? Any sign of danger?"

He's talking about Mike. He knows how dangerous my half brother is. He knows Mike won't stop until he gets what he wants.

"Yes, actually. He's been lurking around each night, trying to find a way in. The locks have been changed, and we now have a state-of-the-art security system, so he can't get in without alerting everyone close by, but I've seen him on the security footage. It's only a matter of time before he figures out how to get past it."

"You still have my knife?" Muz asks in a low voice, obviously not wanting to be overheard on his end.

"I do." I grin, knowing it's safe under my pillow on my bed.

"Good. And don't forget, other things can be used as weapons. Just look around you. Look at the things inside and outside your house. A chair can provide a barrier, be an obstacle, be a throwing or hitting weapon. A vase can be thrown or smashed for a sharp shard. A rock can be used to throw or hit."

"Oh, I already know all about what rocks can do." I'm a smug bitch as I say it, remembering back to how I'd used a rock to smash the window of Muz's car to get mine and Ayden's phones out of the glove box to call for help.

"Oh, that's fucking right. Little bitch, you owe me a window repair."

I giggle because Muz doesn't sound pissed, despite his words.

"Yeah-nah…. Not going to happen." I respond and enjoy the sound of his chuckle down the line before he turns serious again.

"Start preparing, pretty girl. Know your surroundings wherever you go. Make yourself familiar with all the objects that are around you. They are potential weapons. If Mike manages to get through the security in place, he'll be coming for you hard. You may be small and physically weaker, but you can outsmart him, pretty girl. I have no doubt about that."

"Muz?" Tears pool in my eyes again.

"Yeah?"

"You're going to be okay, right?" Hot drops roll from my eyes and down both cheeks, but I keep my voice steady.

"Don't you worry about me. I'm tough." Muz sounds confident now, but his words do nothing to make me feel better because I'm pretty sure he's lying to me.

My mood is flat after speaking with Muz. Even though he tried to make our conversation light, he couldn't hide how unwell he is, so when my phone rings a little later, and Ayden's name flashes across the screen, I'm eager to hear his voice.

He spends his whole lunch break talking with me again. He gives me a play-by-play of Shaun and Simon's argument over what the best position on the footy field is, and even though I don't know what they are talking about, it's still amusing and works wonders for my mood. Ayden also lets me know that Marcus' mum, Barb, will swing by just after school has ended to drive me to my first community service shift.

I hadn't even thought about how I was going to get there this arvo, yet Ayden is busy at school doing assessments and trying to focus and still manages to take care of me.

There's a part of me, a stubborn part, that wants to tell him I don't need Marcus' mum to pick me up, that I can just walk. Why? The thing that bothers me is that I don't want to put anyone out. My mum sold her car when I was thirteen, and ever since then, I've had to fend for myself if I wanted to go anywhere. Part of me is still that girl who has to look out for herself because no one else will, but I'm not that girl anymore, and just like Ayden keeps reminding me, he and the guys are here to help.

So, when Barbara toots the horn just after 3:30pm, my mum escorts me out to the car, looking around frantically as if she's preparing for an attack in broad daylight. Mike would have to be stupid to try that, but who knows how unhinged he is.

Just as Principal Rogan said, there are two security guards close by, watching over Travis and me as we work. It's strange to see them here on the school grounds. It makes me feel guilty. The only reason they are here is because of me and what's happening with my family.

Fox Pines schools haven't needed security guards before this and it makes me wonder how the student body feels about it?

It's probably just another thing that won't work in my favour. I can just imagine how much Tasha is going to carry on.

Besides the two security guards, Garrett and Ayden are close by, sitting under one of the oak trees while I work with Travis, pulling out weeds from the garden bed framing the Administration building.

"I think your boyfriend wants to kick my arse," Travis grumbles, glancing up through his light lashes to where Ayden sits.

"Probably." I chuckle, keeping my eyes focused on this damn weed that won't come out. I keep trying to get a grip on it, but it slips free each time I try to tug it out.

"Here." Travis leans over and digs the dirt out around the weed with his gloved fingers before getting a better grip on the stem and tugs it free.

"You made that look easy," I complain, sitting back on my haunches to meet Travis' brown eyes.

"What can I say? I'm a talented guy." Travis shoots me a cheeky smirk, and I can't help but grin at him.

He's a year younger than me and goes to Fox Pines High, but he's a regular at the FP Catholic parties. Probably to sell drugs or something. I really don't know, but he knows of my brother and was the one to tell me that Mike was still in the area before his last attack.

"Have you seen Mike lately?" I ignore the weeds and keep my eyes fixed on Travis. I want to see if his expression gives away anything.

"Nah, I haven't. But a mate of mine heard some interesting tea about him."

"What? You have info on my brother and haven't passed it on?" I'm pissed, and my raised tone captures Ayden's attention. He sits a little straighter against the tree, putting his book down on the ground beside him.

"Hey, don't shoot the messenger, Sexy Lexi. My source isn't exactly reliable. He's a fucking meth head. He could have hallucinated that shit for all I know." Travis holds his gloved hands up in surrender, a stringy weed dangling from one.

He looks ridiculous in the purple gloves.

"Tell me what you know." I point the small hand spade at him and realise I'm not coming across as intimidating at all. Not with the shit-eating grin that spreads across his face.

"Down, girl. I'll tell you." Travis chuckles, and I lower the spade, glancing at Ayden again. He's standing up now but hasn't made a move to come over to me. It's a relief, actually. I need to do this stuff myself, and he knows that's how I feel. I know he wants to sweep in and save me, but I'm no damsel. Well, I try not to be, anyway.

"Rumour has it that Mike has shacked up with some chick who is keeping him in hiding. And before you ask, no, I don't know who it is. If I did, then I would tell you. I've been trying to find out, but Mike has been a ghost."

"Shacked up… like living with a girlfriend or something?" What the fuck is wrong with that girl? Surely, she would have seen the news? Surely, she knows who he is?

"Yep. Exactly like that." Travis nods, his sandy hair bobbing with the motion.

"I need to find out who the girl is," I say more to myself, but Travis responds.

"I'll keep looking into it for you, Lexi. I got your back." He smiles proudly, the freckles across his nose scrunching together.

I nod and mutter a *"thanks",* glancing down at the garden bed we are sitting in, pretending to work hard but not really doing much at all.

"So, why'd you dob yourself in? I had it covered." Travis pulls me out of my thoughts, and I look back at his curious expression.

"I'm trying to make up for the bad shit I've done, I guess. It wasn't right that you take the fall for me, and the guilt over what I did was eating at me. I guess I'm just not as badass as you thought." I shoot him a grin, and he throws his head back, laughing.

"Actually," he says between chuckles. "I think you're not as sweet and innocent as you think."

Poking my tongue out, I grab a handful of dirt and toss it at him, but he's too fast and does a weird army roll to get out of the way, crushing the pretty yellow flowers as he goes.

It feels great to laugh and to be sitting outside in the warm spring sun. When I sneak a glance at Ayden and Garrett, Ayden is sitting down again, and he and Garrett are watching my exchange with Travis, wearing their own grins.

For another hour I have to listen to Travis harp on about who's screwing who at Fox Pines High. I don't care, but it's nice to not think about my bullshit for a while.

The moment it's time to pack the spades and gloves away, my mind is back on what Travis said about Mike.

Somewhere in this town, Mike is shacking up with a chick, and either she knows he's a monster and doesn't care, or she is yet to meet that part of him. Either scenario isn't good for her.

Sixteen

We take our time walking back to my house. At first, I think it's just because it's a nice day and we are all enjoying the sun, and while that may be the case for Garrett, it's not for Ayden.

"My mum sucks," he whispers, pulling me into his arms after Travis walks off.

"Why?" I ask as I pull back, and we start walking, my hand linked with his as Garrett joins us, walking on my other side.

"She said I have to stay at home tonight and have a family dinner. It's not a family dinner if my dad isn't there." It's funny hearing Ayden whine. He's normally so much more mature than the rest of us, yet right now, he reminds me that he's not that much older than me.

"You should do that. She must miss you, since you spend so much time with me." I sneak a glance at him as we step outside the school grounds, and he catches my eye and pouts.

"But I want Lexi time."

Garrett chuckles next to me. "That's what you're calling it. Sex is Lexi time?"

I giggle, too, because it sounds ridiculous, even though I know Ayden didn't mean *that* exactly. I'm sure it's part of it, but it's not all of it.

"Cole, I was beginning to like you. Don't make me change my mind." Ayden snaps, shooting Garrett a glare, but it just makes Garrett laugh harder. "Every fucking moment I get to spend with Lexi, no matter what we are doing, is Lexi time, dickhead."

Garrett tries to stop laughing. "Okay. Okay. Chill." He puts his hands up in a show of surrender, and Ayden shoots him one last glare before looking ahead.

"So, who's staying over tonight, then?" I ask, trying to lighten Ayden's mood, but it doesn't work. He's genuinely bummed about not getting to spend the night with me again. I'm kinda bummed too. Last night was something else entirely. Each new moment we spend together hooks me deeper into my addiction to him.

"Shauno and me," Garrett answers, smiling down at me, and I smile back. I really am so lucky to have these guys in my life. I wish Abbey was still around, though. I really miss her despite her betrayal.

"No sharing beds on the living room floor." Ayden snaps, and I bite my lip in an attempt not to laugh.

"We'll see," Garrett mumbles grumpily, and I risk a glance at him and nearly come undone when I see him trying hard not to laugh as well.

I really shouldn't laugh at Ayden's caveman attitude, but it's hard not to. He's all sorts of adorable with the broody look he's wearing, but when Ayden darts his head in Garrett's direction, I know I need to tame the beast.

"He's only stirring you, Ayden. It's fine. I won't be sleeping on the floor with anyone but you, okay?"

Dragging his glare from Garrett, heated blue eyes meet mine. "You won't be sleeping next to anyone but me on any surface."

Smiling wide, I tug on his hand and pull Ayden closer to my side as we walk. "Yes, Ayden." I flutter my lashes at him and know I've broken through his grumpy mask when his lips quirk up at the corners.

"So, Travis told me something interesting." When I see both Garrett's and Ayden's heads turn to me in my peripheral, I continue. "His source isn't reliable, but if what he said is true, then Mike is staying with a chick here in Fox Pines. A girlfriend who is helping to keep him hidden."

"Shit." Ayden hisses at the same time that Garrett growls, "What the fuck."

"What else did Travis say?" Ayden asks, still keeping our pace slow.

"Nothing really. That's all he knows. He's trying to find out who the girl is, but that's all he's been able to find out. He said he'll keep trying."

"And we trust this Travis guy?" Ayden asks. "How do you know he's telling the truth?"

"Travis doesn't have any reason to lie. And he was the one that told me Mike was still in town last week. He may be into some pretty shady shit, but I trust him."

"I gotta agree with Lexi here. Travis *is* into some bad shit, *but* that also gives him access to people we wouldn't normally associate with. Besides liking to smoke his product a little too much and hanging on the wrong side of the tracks, he's a reliable source." Garrett's acknowledgement about Travis warms my heart.

Just because people do some shady stuff doesn't make them bad. It's because of where he lives and goes to school that he was introduced to that world. Even so, and despite his smart mouth, he's a decent guy. I think so anyway.

Ayden stops walking then, his blue eyes dancing to Garrett before returning to me.

"We need to tell the cops about this."

He's right, I know, but I don't like the idea of them questioning Travis about it. What if that pisses Trav off, and he stops sharing information with me?

"Can we wait? I'd like to speak with Travis about it before we tell the police. If it brings heat to him, then I'd prefer to leave him out of it, but he might be happy to help the cops. Unlikely, but you never know."

"And if he doesn't want to get involved?" Ayden tugs me along to walk again, and Garrett follows.

"Then we say there's a rumour going around or something."

Ayden nods, happy with that, and leans over, pressing warm lips to the top of my head as we walk.

When we reach my house, Ayden orders Garrett inside while he says goodbye to me.

"I haven't had a big enough hit of Lexi yet. I don't wanna go," Ayden growls as he presses his body into mine, backing me against the brick wall next to my front door before nibbling at my lips.

I instantly melt, weaving my hands into the short hair at his nape. When his tongue darts out, I open for him. Our lips dance together, fuelled by desperate need. My blood turns to lava, and without even thinking, I rub my core against his leg.

"Fuck, Lex. I want you so bad," Ayden rasps as he pulls back to look at me.

His lips are already a little puffy, and the way his eyes drink me in makes me want to strip out of my clothes right here on my front porch.

"Can you come in for a bit?" I let my vagina speak for me because she is the one in control right now, and she's hungry.

An apologetic smile tilts up those kissable lips, and Ayden shakes his head right as a car horn sounds from the street behind him.

"Mum's here now." He gestures his head back to the street, and I nearly cry.

I don't want to be away from him tonight.

It's pathetic, I know.

I actually think I do have an addiction, for real, because I consider duelling Andrea over this preposterous idea of him going home for the night.

Preposterous? Really? I think Simon is rubbing off on me.

I don't know what story my face tells, but Ayden's warm palm cups my face as he presses his forehead against mine.

"It's just one night. I'll be here for breaky in the morning. I'll even see if I can get Mum to let me drive tomorrow so I can pick you up for community service and maybe go for a drive afterwards."

I pout but nod against his forehead. "Call me later?" I sound as sad as I feel. Maybe it's just my vagina talking because she needs an ice bath right now.

"Absolutely. After dinner." The kiss he leaves me with is long and searing, like a brand I will feel for hours after we part ways.

Mum has discovered that cookie dough is a thing. She had a heap of groceries delivered while I was out, and while Garrett and I hang in the front living room, she cooks up a batch filling the house with that freshly baked cookie smell.

When she enters the living room carrying a plate, she looks proud as shit, and it makes me grin. She looks so happy, for once. Not because she is on a bender, but because she is getting joy from the simple things in life.

It's just after 6pm when Shaun arrives at my house, all smelly and muddy from football training. While he showers upstairs in the bathroom I pretend doesn't exist, my mum orders us pizza for dinner, which we devour before settling in for an hour-long of scrolling Netflix where not one of us can agree on what to watch.

Ayden saves me from the argument when he calls, and I quickly retreat up to my room so we can have some privacy.

"Why is Bossi texting me, asking me to convince you to watch an Anime TV show?"

"Ugh! He's annoying. It's all he wants to watch tonight. And Garrett wants to watch Brooklyn Nine-Nine," I whine, and Ayden's deep chuckle comes down the line.

"And what does my girl want to watch?"

"Besides you getting naked in front of me?" I tease, and a low primal growl vibrates the speaker at my ear.

"Please tell me you didn't just say that in front of Bossi and Cole?"

"Hmmm. Maybe I did." I wish I could see his face right now. I bet he'd have that sinful expression on his face.

As if he read my mind, my phone beeps with a FaceTime call, and I accept it, desperate to see his face.

"What room are you in?" Ayden's voice is demanding as it fills my room, and his face comes into view.

I giggle. "You are so gullible. I'm in my bedroom."

Ayden's face morphs from caveman to serious. "You okay in your room alone?"

"I'm not alone. You're here with me." I offer him a confident smile, and I get a wide dimpled grin.

"I wish I was really there with you. I need to touch you." He speaks in a caring way that says, I miss you, and I want to hold you. But since my vagina is awake, and I have no filter when she's in control, I completely keep my head in the gutter when I speak.

"Where do you want to touch me?"

"Lexi," he growls. His ocean eyes darkening on my screen. "You're not playing fair."

"I'm sorry. I blame you entirely." I shrug, not at all sorry.

"Me? Why?"

"You created this sex beast inside me. Now she's hungry all the fucking time." Fluttering my lashes, I try to appear innocent, but Ayden's deep laughter explodes from my phone.

"Lexi West. I'm going to smack that perfect arse of yours in the morning."

"Promise?"

"Yes," he growls, and it's so primal that moisture makes itself known between my legs.

Holy shit, this guy has so much power over me, and it's power I'm willing to hand over to him on a platter.

"Now that you've got my dick hard, I need a new line of conversation to take it away." He mutters and I lift a brow.

"Do you, though?" I tease, "you could just show me."

This time Ayden's growl is low and deep, his blue eyes piercing through the screen.

"And then what? You gonna rub that juicy little pussy for me while I stroke my cock, Lex?"

My core clenches, and my face heats, but Ayden's determined eyes don't waver from the screen. He's analysing me to see how far I'm willing to take this.

Am I willing to take this further?

Do I want to have phone sex with Ayden?

While I'm pretty sure I want to have every version of sex with him, I'm not ready for phone sex because even though my vagina is trying to take control, I need more than an orgasm. I need him. I need to feel his arms around me. Feel his lips against mine. Feel his breath against my ear as he tells me how much he loves me.

Ayden must see my internal battle written all over my face because his voice softens when he speaks. "I miss you too, beautiful. I wish I could be there and hold you in my arms."

I shake my head with the reminder that he reads me like a book. "I'm sorry for teasing. If anything, I've just gone and worked myself up. Ugh!" I let my head fall back and bang it against the wall above my bedhead.

"New conversation?" he asks, and I sigh and nod, looking back at the screen. "What do you want to do with your life when you finish school?"

Oh. He went with a serious conversation.

Okay.

I want to say, besides being with you, but I don't because it's too soon to speak like that, right?

Ayden and I are new. Yes, we've been through a lot, and have probably gotten closer faster because of that, but I can't tell him all I want to do is to be by his side and one day have his babies. I know he's spoken of forever before, but I haven't even told him I love him yet.

"I'm not sure exactly. I think I'd like to help people." I shrug. "I dunno. How about you?"

"I'd like to learn the ropes of MitchWave Studios. I learnt a bit when I was, you know, recovering. It's a fun industry to work in." Ayden has pride as he speaks. For his dad. For the studio. I can totally see him working there with his dad. They make a great team, and Ayden already knows so much about music.

"I think you would be amazing at that job, Ayden. Remember me when you become a famous music executive."

"I won't need to remember you. You'll be right by my side."

And... I blush.

Shocking, I know.

My tell causes Ayden to chuckle, and I'm helpless not to grin back.

"You think I've got what it takes to be a music executive's arm candy?" I flutter my lashes and laugh along with Ayden.

"You're fucking stunning Lexi West and way too fierce and smart to be just arm candy. You could rule the world if you wanted to."

Well, fuck me. He has a way with words, and I'm swooning at the compliment.

While I'm doubtful about the *ruling the world* part, it's nice to know that he thinks I'm more than the blonde hair, blue-eyed Aussie beach chick that I resemble.

"Ayden Mitchell. I think we will rule this world together."

"Fucking oath we will, baby." Ayden's tone brims with a determination that tells me he believes it.

And fuck. I think I do, too.

After an hour of chatting with Ayden and learning more about each other, I get changed and join Shaun and Garrett back in the living room to watch yet another footy talk show they are engrossed in. I don't complain and figure I might learn something about the sport if I pay attention.

I don't.

I'm still none the wiser.

I'm surprised I'm able to fall asleep so easily with Ayden not here. Maybe it's because my mind is so occupied going over all the stuff I learnt about Ayden tonight, or it could be the string of text messages he sent a little later, some of which I should probably delete in case someone snoops on my phone.

Those messages are only for me and Ayden.

It's a little after 2am when I wake to a noise. My first instinct is to go searching for the source alone, but then I remember what Ayden said the other night.

They are here to help me, so I don't have to do this alone.

Slipping off the couch, I tiptoe quietly over to Garrett, who's sleeping on the other couch, and give his shoulder a shake.

I'm caught off guard when he suddenly grabs me and flips me under him, slapping his hand over my mouth with his other fist raised in the air, ready to strike me.

My eyes widen as I brace for the impact of his punch, but it never comes. Instead, Garrett's eyes widen to match mine, and he leaps off me like I've scolded him.

"Fuck, I'm so sorry, Lexi," he whisper-yells, and I leap up too, putting my finger in front of my lips to shoosh him.

"It's okay," I whisper. "I didn't mean to scare you."

Sighing softly, Garrett rakes his hand through his brown waves, and I can tell he's mentally beating himself up over his reaction to me touching him when he was asleep.

The noise that woke me sounds again, and Garrett hears it, both of us darting our heads toward the front door.

Garrett gently grasps my arm and pulls me up. "Is that why you woke me?" he whispers in my ear, and I nod.

With a quick nod back, Garrett releases my arm and kneels to the floor where Shaun is snoring softly, and he nudges his shoulder.

"Dad, I closed up the barn earlier," Shaun mutters, his eyes filled with sleep and ready to fall shut again.

"Bossi. Wake up, man." Garrett's quiet voice awakens Shaun from his dream state, and his eyes widen. "I think Lexi's brother is at the front door trying to get in."

Garrett shifts back quickly when Shaun bolts upright, looking around the room, probably trying to remember where he is before Garrett offers him a hand, tugging Shaun to stand as the noise sounds again.

My heart races knowing Mike is so close, and he's getting gamer. Tonight, he's at the front door, where there's a higher risk of getting sprung by the neighbours or someone driving by.

Garrett whispers something to Shaun that I can't hear, and with a nod, Shaun comes to me, taking my hand and quietly leads me out of the living room, past the front door, and up the hall to the security closet.

We slip inside, and before I pull the door closed, I see Garrett standing around the corner from the front door with his phone out, texting someone.

"There he is." Shaun's voice drags my attention to the monitors.

There, in the bottom corner of the monitor, is Mike trying to get through the front door. He's only there for a minute before moving away, and we watch as he leaves that part of the screen to enter a new one.

He really is getting more desperate to get in because he's climbing onto the roof, the same way I do when I'm sneaking back in.

Mike's not going to stop until he gets in.

I just hope tonight isn't that night.

The closet door opens, and I nearly squeal because I'm so fucking scared, and Garrett mouths a *"sorry"* as he joins us in the closet and looks at the monitors.

"What window is that?" Shaun whispers, sitting forward to get a better look at the monitor.

"My bedroom," I whisper, trying to ignore the dread settling in my gut.

"Cops will be here as soon as they can. Ayden said there's an incident across town that the night shift cops are dealing with, but they are calling others in now. Should we wake your mum?" Garrett asks, but I shake my head.

"Not yet. If we can hold off until the last minute, I'd prefer not to fill her with fear. She's suffered enough."

Garrett and Shaun shoot me a confused look, but I ignore them as I watch Mike trying to bust the lock on my bedroom window. If he's desperate enough, he'll smash his way in. Hopefully, he's not at that stage yet.

My heart is in my throat, pulsing so fast and hard that I think I might choke on the sensation. What if he breaks the lock and gets in? Then what? My mind flicks to what Muz said over the phone. I need the butterfly knife he gave me, and I need to use any objects around me as weapons.

My butterfly knife is in the living room under my pillow on the couch. If he gets in, I'm running for that.

I'm about to send myself into a spiral when I see Mike's figure shift away from my window and then climb back down off the roof.

"Where'd he go?" Garrett asks what we are all wondering as we look at the monitors to try to locate him.

At first, we can't see Mike anywhere on the monitors, but then a shadow moves on the screen that shows the backyard. We watch him moving through the backyard towards the back fence. I remember then what Ayden told me about the day he attacked Val and me.

The police had found evidence that he escaped over Val's back fence.

Maybe that's why no one has seen him. He's been climbing over the back fence.

Not wanting to lose sight of him, I rush out of the closet.

"What are you doing?" Garrett whisper-yells on my heels as I run into the laundry that looks over the backyard. When I shift the blind back, I see Mike reach the back fence.

"I need to follow him."

"What? No!" Garrett hisses as Shaun joins us.

"He's getting away. The cops won't make it here on time. If I follow him, I can find out where he's staying. He won't be expecting me to do that." I make my plea as Garrett and Shaun look at me like I've grown two heads.

I spin again and pull the blind back just as Mike disappears over the fence.

"Shit. He just jumped over the fence." I hiss and feel someone press against my back, trying to look out the small window too.

"I saw," Shaun says quietly by my ear, and I look over my shoulder as he looks at Garrett. "I'll go. I'm the fastest one here. I can outrun him if I need to."

"I can't ask you to do that," I tell him, letting all of my fear be heard.

Shaun and Garrett have some sort of silent conversation with their eyes before Garrett nods, and Shaun faces me and slaps a kiss on my cheek.

"I'll take video evidence and stay in touch. Be back soon."

I'm about to protest when he moves past me and keys in the PIN to disarm the security system and then quietly opens the back door, moving silently out into the night.

Seventeen

Sitting still is impossible. I have to fight the urge to chase after Shaun and beg him to come back. What if he gets hurt? I don't want anything to happen to him. He's my brother, my family. I need him, damn it!

"Ayden will be here soon." Garrett's hand lands on my jiggling knee to stop it.

"We shouldn't have let him go. It's too dangerous. What if Mike sees him?"

"Shaun was right when he said he could outrun Mike. He's a fast little prick. Don't worry." Garrett grins, and his confident demeanour eases my nerves a fraction.

"He doesn't even have shoes on," I complain, and Garrett just smiles that confident smile again.

"He can be more stealthy with bare feet."

"What if he cuts his feet? He has the footy grand final on Saturday. What if he can't play because of me?" My body is thrumming with fear, and I can't figure out how to ease it.

"Firstly, stop blaming yourself. He chose to go. Secondly, nothing will stop Bossi from getting on that footy field on Saturday. Please stop worrying." Garrett pleads right before we hear a car pull up out front. "That will be lover boy."

I roll my eyes at Garrett but still can't keep from fidgeting until Garrett opens the front door and lets my man in. I know it's only been a matter of hours since I've seen him, yet I can't stop myself from running to him and leaping into his arms, wrapping my legs around his waist.

"I'm here, beautiful." His soothing voice works like a hit of morphine, and I relax into him as he carries me across the living room to sit on the couch with me still wrapped around him.

"Shit, he's already up near Spring Lane. They are moving fast." Garrett's eyes read over something on his phone as I lean back from Ayden to look over my shoulder.

"That in the group chat?" Ayden asks, and Garrett nods.

I give Ayden room so he can use his phone, but when I go to move off his lap, his firm hand grips my hip, silently telling me to stay put.

I don't complain. I'd be happy to straddle his lap for the rest of my life.

Holding his phone up so we can both see it, we get new messages every now and then from Shaun, telling us where he is at that moment, but when his messages go quiet for about ten minutes, I begin to freak out.

"Something's happened to him."

"He's fine. Just busy stalking bad guys." Garrett insists, but I can't help but think he's wrong. If Mike catches Shaun, he's as good as dead.

Garrett's phone rings then, and I just about jump out of Ayden's lap from the buzzing noise. My nerves are shot.

Jesus, this was a bad idea. I should have kept my mouth shut. I should never have said anything about following Mike.

"It's okay, beautiful." Ayden soothes, running his hands up and down my back.

"You okay, man?" Garrett says into the phone. "Hang on. I'll put you on speaker." Garrett puts the speaker on his phone, and we listen. A moment later, Shaun's voice fills the room.

"You there, Lex?" Shaun asks, and I have to clear the lump in my throat before I can speak.

"Yep."

"Well, I found out where he's been hiding. You're not going to believe it."

"What? Where?" I leap from Ayden's lap and look at the phone as if I'll be able to see Shaun in it.

"I'm sending a video through now. I'll be back soon." Shaun pants down the line like he's jogging.

"You want me to come and pick you up, Bossi?" Ayden asks, but Shaun just grunts.

"Nah, all good, man. This is a good workout. The chicks love an athletic body."

Garrett rolls his eyes at Shaun's comment while Ayden chuckles.

"Okay, see you soon." Ayden shakes his head at Shaun as Garrett ends the call, and we wait for the video Shaun took to come through.

It takes a minute, and when it loads in the group chat, the three of us sit on the couch, Ayden and Garrett on either side of me as I hit play.

Even though it's dark, familiarity has me moving closer to the screen as the video zooms in on Mike as he approaches a house I know all too fucking well.

All my questions are answered like a cold slap in the face as I watch my half brother walk across the tree-lined street, up the front path and into the open arms of Tasha fucking Pritchard.

"No way," Garrett whispers next to me as the video ends, and I hit play again, needing to confirm what my eyes just saw.

When it gets to the part where he approaches Tasha, just before they hug, I hit pause and take a screenshot.

Where my body thrummed with fear only minutes ago, it's now replaced with violent rage.

That bitch!

That fucking fuck face of a fucking bitch!

I fly off the couch, my hands balled into fists as I pace the small living room.

"I'm going to fucking kill her!"

"Not if I get to her first!" Garrett hisses, and I drag my eyes to his to see the same rage.

He may seem quiet to some people, and he may read romance books on his phone—yes I've seen them—but Garrett Cole has a dark, feral beast inside him that he works really hard to keep hidden. If I were Tasha, I'd be scared.

"I knew her vendetta against you seemed misplaced. This entire time she's been doing Mike's dirty work for him." Garrett hisses, his blue-grey eyes wild with rage.

Ayden's phone starts buzzing with an incoming call, and he darts his eyes to me when he sees the screen. "It's Jason. You want to tell him where Mike is, or you want me to?"

I shake my head. "Don't tell him. Not yet."

"What?" Both Ayden and Garrett say at the same time as the call stops.

"Tell him that Mike tried to get in again, but not that we know where he went. I know he went to Tasha's, but he can't be staying there. Her parents wouldn't allow that. It makes no sense. He probably called in for a booty call. By the time the cops get there, he could be long gone, and then he'll know that we are on to him and won't go back. Then we'll be back to square one." I throw up my hands. "We need to figure out if he's staying with her. If we send the cops in, then I need to know that he's one hundred percent there. I can't deal with him evading them again."

"Maybe the cops can do surveillance or something?" Garrett asks, but I shake my head.

"Mike is paranoid as hell. He'll be keeping an eye out for that stuff. I'm surprised he didn't spot Shaun following him."

"He was too busy talking on his phone." Shaun's voice draws our attention as he closes the front door behind him and enters the living room.

Taking three steps to get to him, I throw my arms around his neck. I'm so glad he's back. It makes me sick to my stomach that he could have been hurt.

Shaun hugs me back and whispers in my ear, "Your boyfriend really doesn't like us touching you, does he?"

I snicker into his shoulder and pull back, turning to Ayden, who is glaring daggers at him.

"Dude, she's my sister." Shaun taunts, and I roll my eyes at how Ayden's eyes darken with more menace.

"Any idea who Mike was talking to on the phone?" Garrett draws us back to the important topic.

"If I had to guess. I'd say Tasha." Shaun offers before sitting on the couch and lifts his foot to massage it.

"Shit, Shaun, can I get you anything?" I ask. His feet must be in so much pain right now. They look a little red on the bottom.

"All good, sister from another mister." Shaun grins at me and chuckles when I roll my eyes.

Ayden's phone starts buzzing again. "So, I'm *not* telling Jason about Tasha's?"

"Give it a day or two until I can figure out if he's just calling by her house for a quickie."

Ayden nods and answers the phone, moving out into the hall to speak. I flop back on the couch, mixed emotions swarming through me.

I don't know if keeping this information about Mike going into Tasha's from the police is a good idea. I also know having the police turn up there and walk out empty-handed will be worse, so maybe it's the best idea for the current situation. I guess time will tell if I've made another fucked up decision.

"Ah, what's going on?" My mum's voice draws my attention to the doorway as Ayden comes to stand behind her, shooting me an apologetic look. "Why am I waking up to," my mum waves her hands around, "whatever this is?"

I stand from the couch, about to approach my mum, when there's a tap at the front door, and I nearly jump out of my skin. One look at my reaction and my mum's eyes widen as Ayden steps up to the front door and pulls it open to reveal Simon and Jared.

"How long was Mike here for?" Simon askes as he shuffles in behind Jared, his cheeks rosy from the chill in the night air. They must have walked here.

"Mike was here?" Mum asks, turning back to me, her pitch high, revealing her fear. Shit, I don't want her to be scared.

"He tried to get in again. We called the cops, but he left before they could get here," I explain, stepping up to my mum and taking her hand in mine in the hope to reassure her that everything is okay.

"Why didn't you wake me?" My mum's brows knit together, her brown eyes searching mine for answers.

I shrug. "I didn't want to scare you. If we didn't have things handled, then I would have woken you."

"Lexi. I'm the adult here—your mum. I'm the one who's meant to protect you, not the other way around.

You should have woken me as soon as you knew something was going on."

I want to tell my mum that she can't protect me from Mike, that she wasn't able to protect me before. I don't, though, because she's not stupid. She knows better than anyone in this room how dangerous Mike is. How vile and brutal he can be. She knows that in order to protect me, she will likely suffer, which is exactly why I didn't wake her.

She's suffered enough, and even though she's the adult in this situation, I refuse to allow her to be the one to take on that role. No one has been there to protect her for all these years. She's been alone in her suffering, and even though I was only alone for a short time in my own suffering, I can't imagine how hard it must have been for my mum to do that all day, every day for all of those years. Maybe if she had someone looking out for her, she wouldn't have turned to drugs and alcohol. Perhaps she would have run from my dad and taken me with her years ago.

She has me now. And my pack. So yes, by all rights, she's the adult, but I won't stand by and let her be the one to suffer for me anymore.

"Mum," I whisper, holding her gaze and hoping she can read the hidden meaning behind my words. "It's my turn to protect you."

I keep my voice low because the guys don't know what my mum has gone through, and I'm yet to fill Ayden in because I can hardly bear to think about the brutality she suffered. I know the guys can hear me, though, and I'm sure they will have questions, but for now, all I need is for my mum to understand.

"Lexi." Tears pop free from my mum's eyes, leaving a wet trail down her cheeks before they roll under her jawline and down her neck. Reaching up to cup my face, my mum strokes my cheek with her thumb. "One day, when you're a mother, you'll understand that there is nothing you won't do for your child. There's no pain that will ever be harsh enough to stop a mother from doing what she has to in order to protect her child." She wipes away my tear a moment after it escapes. "I love that you want to protect me, Lexi. It's a feeling I'm not used to, yet a feeling I want to hold on to as it means that there's a chance you may want me to stay in your life, but even if you don't want that, I will never, ever stop trying to protect you. I just need you to let me. Don't take this on yourself. You aren't in this alone. I'm here. Your friends are here. We all want the same thing, and that is to keep you safe."

Still standing behind my mum, Ayden catches my attention with his small grin as he nods in approval at my mum's words. Over my mum's other shoulder, I see Jared doing the same thing and Simon shooting me a *"duh"* look.

"I'm sorry." I return my gaze to my mum. "I'm still trying to get used to accepting help. There's a big part of me that feels the need to do all of this on my own, so no one else gets hurt."

"You're like that because you've had to be. I'm sorry for that, too." My mum pulls me into a hug, and the room fills with the sniffles of someone crying.

All eyes turn to Simon, who is sobbing, tears streaming down his face.

"This is so beautiful. I love you guys."

The air rushes out of both my mum and me as Simon lunges for us and joins our hug.

"Come on, fellas, bring it in." Simon, still crying, waves his arms one at a time so that he doesn't completely break his hug, and with a round of chuckles, Garrett, Shaun, Jared and Ayden step up to join the hug surrounding us in love.

It's the most awkwardly ridiculous hug ever, and I love it. It's missing Marcus, though. I wish he was here, too, because I hate the thought of him missing out. I have a feeling we'll have another awkward opportunity or ten just like this one in the future.

Shaun, always the Casanova, takes it upon himself to fill my mum in on the details of the night, leaving out the part about following Mike to Tasha's, and he leads her to the kitchen to make hot chocolate.

"Should I be worried about Shaun hitting on my mum?" I ask whoever is listening, and the guys chuckle as they flop back on the couches.

"He's just turning on the charm. He won't take it as far as hitting on your mum.... I don't think." Simon's brows draw together as he thinks about it.

"You're not very reassuring, Hastings." I hiss past my laugh.

"I know. I'm not even convincing myself." Simon's worried tone causes the other guys to chuckle. "Should someone go save Lexi's mum?"

"I will." Jared smiles, standing from the couch. "She's always loved me." Deliberately brushing past me, Jared shoots me a wink as he walks by to rescue my mum in the kitchen.

"Well, who's going to save your mum from Jared, then?" Simon chuckles, and I shoot a confused frown his way before he adds, "If he can't have one West woman, maybe he'll go after the other."

My brows shoot up at Simon's frankness, and Garrett turns in his seat on the couch and punches Simon in the arm.

"Shut the fuck up, dickhead."

"Ouch! That hurt, man!" Simon whines, rubbing his upper arm where I'm sure there's already a bruise forming. Garrett's punch wasn't soft.

"Good. You need to learn to keep your thoughts to yourself sometimes, Hastings." Garrett hisses at him, and my eyes dart to Ayden.

I'm expecting him to look pissed off at the very obvious statement from Simon about Jared's feelings for me, yet all I see is adoring eyes taking me in.

"Come here," Ayden mouths, and without hesitation, I move across the room to go to my man. I take his hand when he reaches out to me and let him guide me onto his lap again, moving up close to straddle him and melt into his embrace.

"I have to tell you something." His words are quiet, whispered into my ear, and although what I can hear of his tone isn't alarming, the words alone cause me to still. When I try to pull back to look at his face, Ayden holds me in place, pressed against his chest, my head in the crook of his neck.

"I told Jason about Mike going to Tasha's house."

What?!

Again, I try to pull away from him, but he keeps me in place, his arms locked around me so I can't move.

"Ayden!" I growl in my girly tone that I'm sure would only scare a mouse.

"Before you say anything, please listen first. If you're still pissed afterwards, I'll let you punch me."

"In the nuts?" I ask in a sweet voice that doesn't match my anger right now, and Ayden chuckles.

"No. You love my nuts, remember? You can punch my face."

"But I love your face," I say into the crook of his neck, and an idea has me moving to place my lips against the skin there. "I'm just going to bite you instead."

I latch my teeth on to his neck, and he goes rigid under me as I sink them in a little.

"You don't play fair, Lexi." He hisses, and I dig my teeth a little deeper, causing him to suck in a breath.

"Okay. Okay. I told him about Mike, off the record. It's not official yet. He's going to do his own looking into things on the side," Ayden sucks in as my teeth clamp tighter at that news, "but he can only give us a day before it needs to be reported."

Not liking this at all, I sink my teeth deeper, and his hands fly to my hips as he rolls them under me, making me aware of the very hard bulge between our bodies.

"I've been dying to bury myself inside you all day, Lexi. If you don't want me to fuck you in front of the others, then you need to stop turning me on."

I can't help myself. I release the lock I have on his neck and run my tongue over the dented skin that my teeth leave behind.

Ayden's quiet moan is cut off by Shaun's voice.

"Incoming."

In one swift movement, Ayden lifts me off his lap, placing me down on the couch next to him before catching a cushion Garrett tosses to him, placing it over his lap. The next moment Jared walks in the room carrying a tray of hot chocolates with my mum by his side, chatting away to him.

I glance between Shaun's, Garrett's and Simon's smirking faces and then to Ayden's as he holds the cushion over his lap as if his life depends on it.

Finally, my brain catches up, realising that Shaun saved me from an awkward situation with my mum, had she walked in to see me grinding on Ayden's lap, and Garrett saved Ayden the embarrassment of my mum witnessing his hard-on.

A laugh bubbles up, and I slap my hand over my mouth, trying to contain it.

"Are you okay, Lexi?" my mum asks as she hands Garrett a mug filled with steaming hot chocolate goodness.

I nod with my hand still over my mouth. I'm fairly certain if I move it, I'm going to lose my self-control, which is made even worse when my mum comes to sit next to Ayden on the couch as she passes him a mug.

"Hot chocolate, Six?" Jared asks, coming to stand in front of me, holding out the mug, gaining my attention.

Since I'm pretty sure if I try to speak I will have some form of verbal vomit that will clue my mum into my boyfriend's hard dick under the cushion, I keep my mouth clamped shut and pull my hand away to take the mug, giving Jared a warm smile of thanks.

We spend the next thirty minutes chatting away with my mum over hot chocolates. Some of the conversation is about Mike trying to break in, and the rest is about the footy grand final coming up this weekend. It's a pretty big deal in Fox Pines. Probably because there's not much else to do in this town. Everyone will be there to cheer on the side, and afterwards, Fox Pines will party until the sun comes up.

When yawns are all my mum can manage, she eventually returns to her room, and it's nearly 4am by the time the guys make more beds up in the living room, and I'm snuggling up to Ayden on the floor.

Sleep comes easily for everyone except me. I'm left a restless ball of energy as my mind returns to the fact that my brother is screwing Tasha. The thought is enough to make me lose my hot chocolate, so I try hard to push it to the back of my mind with little success.

Does Abbey know about Tasha and Mike? Surely, she would tell me if she did. Right?

What about Sophie, Allison and Amanda? Do they know what Tasha is up to?

I'd like to think Abbey or the other girls would tell me, but I don't know them anymore, especially Abbey. She's a different person from the blonde, braided-haired angel I grew up with. For all I know, she's probably been part of this plan to destroy me from the beginning, and if that's the case, then I'd better drink a cup of concrete because I'm going to make it my mission to ensure that anyone who helps Mike, will pay for their part in all of this.

If Abbey is one of those people, then she'd better learn how to run.

Or punch.

Probably both.

Eighteen

T he next morning, Ayden ducks out early to drop
Jared and Simon back to their places, and he
returns an hour later dressed and ready for school,
armed with Maccas for breaky. His jaw immediately
drops when he sees me dressed in my school uniform,
and I smile, snatching the bag of McDonald's from his
grip, trying to appear nonchalant, as I give him my back
and make my way to the kitchen.

"No way." Ayden's voice trails behind me.

"Hey, don't look at me like that. I tried talking her into
staying home." Shaun confesses as I pass by him, sitting
at the table, his eyes locked on Ayden behind me.

"You didn't try very hard. She's dressed for school."
Ayden scolds before grabbing my hand from behind
and spinning me around to face him. "What's going on,
Lex? I thought we agreed you would wait and go back
to school next term."

"*No*," I draw the short word out, raising my brows
and tugging my hand from his grip, even though I really
want to feel his hand in mine again. "You threw your
ideas around, and all I agreed to was taking one day

at a time. So, that's what I'm doing." I shrug and smile. "And today, I want to go to school."

"Good morning Ayden," my mum says, drawing Ayden's attention away from me as she rounds the kitchen bench to make herself a coffee.

"Uh, hi, Mrs West. Did you know about this?" Ayden gestures to me, and I roll my eyes before turning back to the bench to dig out a hash brown from the paper bag.

"I found out about ten minutes ago. I wasn't keen on the idea, but Lexi made a good case for her to return today." My mum flips on the kettle and focuses on her task.

Shoving the hash brown in my mouth, I take a seat at the table next to Garrett, whose blue-grey eyes are trained on his phone like he's avoiding Ayden's wrath.

"What case did you make?" Ayden turns back to me, scowling.

"You know you aren't very attractive when you act like a chauvinistic pig and try to tell me what to do, Ayden." I'm not trying to be a bitch. Really, I'm not. But the brat in me knows how to push Ayden's buttons, and it's kinda fun.

Also, I don't like being told what to do, and he knows it. Sure, he might get pissed at me, and we may even fight over this, but the makeup sex will be fucking epic.

Ayden's face drops, and he sighs before taking the few steps to get to my side and drops into a squat next to my chair. I focus on munching my hash brown, pretending I don't care, but the moment his hand reaches for mine and lifts it like it's a delicate crystal, I cave. My eyes find his, and they hold such raw concern that twists his handsome face that I'm helpless not to feel like shit for being a bitch.

"Lex," he whispers, and my eyes go glassy.

"I don't want to fall behind too much at school, Ayden. And I also need to be around people. I need to do something normal."

Ayden's lips thin. "Don't lie to me, Lex," he whispers, so my mum doesn't hear. "This is about Mike and Tasha."

"So? What if it is? I need to go back to school and see how she reacts. I need to find out more information. Maybe Allison or even Abbey know more about what's going on between Tasha and Mike," I whisper, hoping Ayden will understand. When he continues to frown at me, I speak a little louder. "I'll be safe at school. There's more security now, and I won't go anywhere without you or one of the guys, I promise."

"What about the toilets? Because I can totally take toilet duty. I'm a regular in the girls' bathroom." Shaun, our Spanish Casanova, shares, causing Ayden's face to turn red in frustration. Normally, Ayden would bite back at comments like this, but he doesn't. He just ignores Shaun.

"Lex, I don't think it's a good idea. Jason called before. The incident they were at last night was a house fire. An ice lab. They were planning on busting it later this week. They also had a tip that Mike was staying at the house, and while he was nowhere to be found last night, they found some belongings that they believe are Mike's in a small back room in the house. They've also had a sighting of your dad in a white car and have a watch alert for it. Mike's not your only threat, Lex. You will be safer if you stay home."

I'm a little stunned by the sighting of my dad. I didn't think he had the balls to be lurking around Fox Pines and risk being caught. Maybe he's been helping Mike stay hidden. Are they working together to get to me? To my mum? I can't let that happen. I can't let my mum get hurt again. Not by either of them.

"Did I hear you correctly, Ayden?" my mum asks, coming to stand behind me where I can't see her face. I don't need to see it to know she's worried. I can hear it in her tone. "Maxwell has been spotted in town?"

Glancing up at my mum, Ayden nods. "Yes. I believe Officer Zimora is going to pop around later this morning to fill you in. I only knew because I called him this morning, and he filled me in." Ayden flicks a glance at me, and I raise a single brow at him.

Why was he talking to Jason again? He already went against my wishes last night by telling Jason about Mike going to Tasha's. And yes, it was probably the right thing to do, but why is he going against me? He keeps asking me to trust him and let him help, but then when I do, he goes and does what he wants, anyway.

"Right. Well, I guess I'd better get dressed if I'm to expect visitors." My mum mumbles, and I glance over my shoulder to see her brows drawn together before she forgets about her coffee and goes back to her bedroom.

"Why were you talking to Jason again?" I snap, returning my gaze to Ayden, who has the audacity to hold back a grin tugging at his lips.

"I wanted to know if he had found out anything else about your brother."

"Not my brother." I snap again, my mood darkening as I try to stand, but Ayden grips my thighs, holding me in place as he studies my face.

"What's pissed you off?" Ayden asks, his blue eyes intense as they take me in.

"Dude, if you don't know, then you're fucking clueless." Shaun chuckles, and Ayden glares at him over his shoulder.

"Bossi has a point, man. You did the same thing last night," Garrett adds, and Ayden frowns at him.

"What did I do?"

I push Ayden's hands off my thighs, gaining his attention again. "This. You held me in place to control me."

"And in return, you bit me, which I'm pretty sure you enjoyed if I remember correctly." Ayden smirks, and I roll my eyes.

"I'm pretty sure you did, too, if your boner was anything to go by." Garrett teases, instantly lightening the mood, and I can't help but smile.

"I guess I should thank you for the cushion." Ayden chuckles, and Garrett shrugs.

"I was trying to save Ruth from getting an eyeful."

Ayden grins and shakes his head, probably trying to rid himself of that image in his head before he returns his ocean blues to me.

"I'm sorry for being a controlling prick. I guess I'm just trying to get my message across before you have a chance to...." Ayden stalls and his eyes widen as he thinks of the best thing to say. Oh man, he's digging his own grave here, and I want to laugh, but I hold back.

"Go ape shit?" Shaun adds.

"Dick punch him?" Garrett joins in.

"Are you arseholes saying I'm a hothead?" I ask playfully, already knowing that I am.

"Well, you are a hot something." Shaun purrs, and a growl rumbles in the back of Ayden's throat.

"You have a temper, Lexi. Sometimes I think it rivals mine." Garrett teases, and I poke my tongue out at him.

"I'm still trying to figure out how to handle you without being a bossy prick." Ayden takes my hand again, stroking his thumb over the back of it.

"I'm sorry that I have to be handled," I whisper, shame seeping in through my pores as my self-doubt rears its ugly head.

"Hey." Ayden moves closer and lifts my chin to peer into my eyes. "Don't think of that as a bad thing. I love your feistiness, Lex. The fire and passion you have is part of what draws me to you. I don't want you to change that, and I don't mean to be controlling. I'll get it right one day if I don't fuck up and push you away before then."

My eyes prickle with hot tears that I force back. "Shit, Ayden. You're not doing anything wrong. It's me. I'm a touchy bitch right now." I shake my head, and he cups my face.

"You're not a bitch, Lex." Ayden's eyes bore into mine right before he claims my lips, and I ignore the annoyed groans of Shaun and Garrett as I sink into Ayden's kiss.

If they don't like it, they can go into a different room.

Pulling back, Ayden's blue eyes dance between mine, and I realise that if he asks me to stay home at this very moment, I'll probably agree. That's the power he has over my heart. I can't let him know that right now, though.

"Ayden, please. I need to go to school and show my face. I need Tasha to see that I'm okay and I'm not hiding. I need her to go back to Mike and tell him I'm back at school. Maybe it will force him to come out of hiding and make it easier to get caught."

"I'm just so terrified of him getting his hands on you again, Lex." Ayden's truthful words slice at my heart. I don't want Mike to get his hands on me again either, but I need this all to end.

"I'll be safe at school. It's probably safer there than here. At least at school, there are security guards and teachers and all the students. Staying home, all I have is a security system and the cops doing occasional drive-bys. I'm better off being closer to you and the others."

Ayden sighs and drops his hands from my face to rest on my thighs again as he lowers his head in thought.

"Will you let one of the guys go into the girls' bathroom with you? We don't know what Tasha might try to do." Ayden pleads, looking back up at me.

Since Tasha is exactly who I want to see, I kinda hope I run into her in the girls' bathroom. Since I know about her and Mike now, maybe I can somehow push her into spilling her secrets. It's a long shot, I know, but I have to do something.

When I witnessed Mike walk into her house, holding her hand on the video footage Shaun took, more pieces of the puzzle fell into place.

Tasha's vendetta isn't about popularity. It's about Mike. It also explains how Mike had Rhys' number when he sent that message to my friends. Tasha could easily get her hands on anyone's number at Fox Pines Catholic.

"Fine. I'm happy to have a chaperone when I go to the girls' bathroom." My words cave in Ayden's dimple as his smile broadens.

I wonder if we have time to go upstairs for some Lexi time? I could really do with his hands on me right now and feel the love he has for me.

My mum takes that moment to walk back into the kitchen, seeking the coffee she made and left behind before. Ayden ignores her, though. His eyes dilating as they remain focused on mine.

"Lexi?" Ayden's growl is low and drawn out. "What are you thinking about?"

My brows shoot up as my face heats, remembering that Ayden can read me too well. Sometimes I swear he can hear my thoughts. Usually only the dirty ones, but then I feel the heat in my cheeks and know my body has sold me out once again.

Traitor.

Shaking my head at Ayden's question, I shrug and try to look away, but his hand curls around my knee and slides it up my thigh, stopping at the hem of my tartan school skirt. My eyes fall shut at the contact, and the next moment I feel his breath on my ear.

"What were you thinking about, Lexi?" The gravel of Ayden's voice makes me moan, and then I freeze, realising what I just did when I hear Shaun's voice.

"Mrs West. I think that's gone cold. Let's make you a fresh cuppa."

My eyes fly open, and my skin turns to fire, knowing I moaned not only in front of Shaun and Garrett, but my mum as well.

"It's okay, beautiful. Shaun is covering for you." Ayden's voice brushes over my ear before his lips caress my cheek.

"Look at the time. We should get going if we don't want to be late." Garrett speaks up this time, his chair scraping the tiled floor as he stands.

"Yeah, yeah. In a minute." Shaun calls over his shoulder as he chats away with my mum before I hear her giggle.

"Please tell me Shaun isn't hitting on my mum again?" I whisper, and Ayden chuckles.

"Sorry, beautiful, I can't do that. He totally is." Ayden slips his hand from my leg and I instantly miss the contact.

It's a form of torture having to walk out of the house without having some one-on-one time with Ayden. I feel almost desperate to have his lips on my skin, but I remind myself of what happened last night with Mike, and my brain slowly rises out of the gutter and prepares for war.

As I expected, all eyes are on me when I walk through the school grounds with Ayden and the guys. I can hear Rhys coming from a mile away when she spots me, running across the quad, squealing like a pig getting slaughtered. She's hilarious and doesn't care about the attention she gains or the turned-up noses of girls who think they are better than her.

They aren't, and one day they are going to realise it.

The others break off to head to class, as per Ayden's insistence, but he sticks by my side, heading to see the principal with me.

Cynthia Rogan is surprised to see me, but she doesn't send me home. Instead, she welcomes me back with a big smile and does a good job at not staring at my bruises. Of course, she has a stipulation. Daily visits with Mr Matthews, which I expected anyway.

Homeroom is over by the time we finish with Principal Rogan, so Ayden walks me to my locker to meet up with Marcus and Jared, since I have English with them first today. As luck would have it, Tasha and her merry bitches, minus Abbey, are near my locker bay. When we walk past, I work hard to hold in my grin when they do a double-take at seeing me back at school.

Yeah bitches, you can't keep me down!

"I see they let the trash back in." Tasha's words are familiar, but what isn't familiar is the remark she gets from a year twelve girl as she passes by.

"What's wrong, Tasha? Did you see your reflection in the mirror? Because that's the only trash in this school." The girl's friends start laughing as they glare at Tasha passing her by, but they smile warmly and say hi when they get to me.

What the hell just happened?

With a huff, Tasha turns her back on us to talk in hushed whispers with Allison, Sophie and Amanda.

Jared chuckles next to me and bumps my shoulder. "It looks like people finally see her for what she really is."

Smiling up at Jared, I take in his genuinely happy face. I know he's been struggling lately, so it's nice to see him a little more relaxed.

"It was a given," I say and glance back at their group, wondering where Abbey is.

Maybe she's sick.

Before I know what I'm doing, I close my locker and walk up to Tasha's group, feeling a little smug when their eyes widen and they shift nervously.

They aren't the only ones. I hear the uneasy muttering of Marcus and Ayden behind me.

"Where's Abbey?" I ask, and three sets of eyes dart to Tasha, their pathetic leader.

"Where Abbey is, is none of *your* business. She doesn't want to be friends with *you*, Lexi. Stop embarrassing yourself." Tasha hisses, poking her pale face out as she speaks.

"You'd know all about that, wouldn't you, Tasha? It seems like a lot of people aren't interested in being friends with you anymore." My voice is calm as I say the words I know will set Tasha off. She is way too predictable.

Stepping up to me, her chest butting against mine as her breath passes over my face, Tasha hisses, "I can't believe they let someone like you back in the school. Not only do you do sick things to try to lure your brother, but you attack a poor innocent child as well and blame your brother for it. Just wait until my parents kick up a stink about this."

I know what she's doing. She's trying to get me to snap, just like she did last week when I let the anger control me. The thing is, I'm not the same person I was last week. I may still have anger, but I'm in control of it now.

"You know, it really is sad how misinformed you are, Tasha. It must be tough to be the only one that believes your bullshit."

Tasha's face turns red, and I shoot her a grin before turning my back on her and walking away.

It's hard to do, and not because I want to shove my fist in her face, but because I want to ask her what the fuck she's doing letting my brother into her house.

I know asking that won't get me any answers, though. No, I need to figure out a different way of finding out what's going on with Tasha and Mike. I don't want her to know that I know yet.

English with Miss Dice is good. She's sincerely happy to see me, and for the first time in weeks, I'm able to concentrate on the class even though I'm flanked by Marcus and Jared, who bicker like an old married couple right through the lesson.

My second class of the day is Maths, also with Miss Dice, and also with the guy that turns me into mush. It's a lot harder to concentrate with Ayden sitting next to me, his hand on my thigh hinting at the promise of what could be if we were alone.

During class, while people are working in groups to problem solve, Allison approaches us from the front of the room, looking nervous. Her normally caramel skin has turned pale. I keep my eyes on her, making sure my face is straight and not showing the scowl that wants to leap out and say hello.

"Abbey stopped hanging around us at the end of last week. Apparently, Daniel wants her all to himself." Allison shrugs. "Hopefully, hanging around with him will be the lesser of two evils."

I frown. "Why do you say that?"

"Well, Tasha and Daniel are both arseholes to Abbey. I just hope he's less of an arsehole than Tasha is to her." Allison shrugs again.

"Why are you telling me this?" I'm confused. Only last week, Allison was defending Tasha.

"I guess I'm just over all the harassment. I can't even remember why I agreed to go along with Tasha's plans to destroy your reputation in the first place. It's fucked up, really. I know it will never make up for my part in all this, but I'm sorry. You didn't deserve any of it."

I'm pretty shocked at Allison's admission and apology. I could make her feel bad and remind her of everything she stood by and watched, but I won't. That has never been who I am, and I won't let my misfortunes change that about me now.

Miss Dice's eyes are on us from the front of the room. She knows what these girls have done to me, and I don't doubt that she would step in to defend me if I needed it. She need not worry now, though. The tables seem to have turned.

"I appreciate you saying that, Allison. Maybe one day I'll be able to forget it all."

"No, you won't. This isn't the sort of stuff you forget about. I have to live with that, Lexi. I'll never forgive myself. And as for Abbey." Allison swallows and glances behind her before continuing quietly, "There's some sort of fucked up shit going on with her family, I think. She wouldn't tell me what was going on, but I know Tasha knows. She's been holding something against Abbey to get her to turn on you. I don't know what it is, but I thought you should know. Abbey never wanted to be a part of Tasha's vendetta."

I feign surprise because it's a secret that Abbey spoke to me. I don't want to make things harder for her, but this whole thing with Daniel wanting Abbey all to himself is concerning. I highly doubt that he's changed his tune and is happy about Abbey's parents demanding their engagement.

Miss Dice takes that moment to approach us, and Allison clamps her mouth shut, spinning on her heel, and returns to her group at the front of the room. I smile at Miss Dice when she shoots me a look of curiosity, but she doesn't ask me to explain what just happened. Instead, she keeps walking around the room.

"How do you feel about her apology?" Ayden asks in a hushed tone, giving my leg a little squeeze under the table.

Shrugging, I draw in a steadying breath as I watch Allison. "Part of me is relieved because hopefully, it means I don't have to watch my back around her, and the other part of me wants to push her around and trip her over again when we have PE."

"Push her around and trip her over again? When did that happen?" Leaning forward on the table, Ayden catches my attention out of the corner of my eye, and I drag my eyes away from Allison.

"The day you came back to school. Right after I came face to face with you at Mr M's office." I smile and shrug as his brows lift. "I was feeling a little frustrated at the time, and Allison copped it."

When Ayden's face falls, so does mine.

"Seeing me made you so angry that you struck out at someone else?"

I rear back a little. "You make me sound like a psycho. I didn't punch on with her or anything. I just came at her hard on the court."

The ocean eyes that I've become so addicted to, study me for a few moments, dancing between my own as Ayden contemplates a response.

It scares me. The way his chest rises and falls. The way a flicker of anger sparks in his eyes. The way those lips that I love to kiss twitch ever so slightly.

Am I losing him? Is he only now realising how fucked up I really am?

Maybe he's realising that I'm too much work.

Heat burns the back of my eyes, and I flick them away from his intensity. I can't bear to have him look at me like that any longer. I need to get out of this room. Get away from him so I can clear my head and refocus on why I'm really at school today.

As if sensing my need to flee, Ayden's warm hand links with mine before he tugs me a little closer. I can't look at him, so I keep my eyes glued to the work I've barely tried to do sitting on the table in front of me.

Don't cry, Lexi. Don't show any weakness.

"Lex?" Warmth flutters over my ear when he speaks. "I'm so fucking sorry that I made you so angry when you saw I'd come back. You didn't need my shit after everything you had already been through."

Pulling away from him a little, I turn to see his expression. It looks broken. In pain. Pleading. I shake my head, and a pesky tear pops free.

"You're not angry at me? For being.... being...." I can't finish my sentence, and I don't need to because Ayden is already shaking his head.

"I'm angry at myself, beautiful. Not you. Never you."

I wish we weren't sitting in our Maths class right now surrounded by gossipy bitches and rumour-spreading dickheads. I wish I could conjure up a bubble that only we could be in, so no one can witness our private moment.

When another tear pops free from my other eye, he reaches up and cups my face, swiping at the trail it left behind with his thumb.

"Ah, guys, perhaps this isn't the right time and place." Miss Dice's voice is like a bucket of ice water being thrown over us, and we spring apart. The moment my eyes meet hers, she frowns and then turns to pull up a chair in front of our table.

"Has something happened?" she asks quietly, using her pinky to push her glasses back up when they slip forward a little.

I feel like such an idiot. Why can't things be simpler? Why can't my emotions just stay dormant until I get home?

"No. Sorry," I practically whisper. "Things are just so complicated right now. My worries never seem to stop."

It's an honest admission which I feel Miss Dice deserves, especially when I'm a sook in the middle of her class.

"Totally my fault, Miss Dice," Ayden speaks up then, gaining her attention. "I asked a question which led to a confronting answer. I've upset Lex unnecessarily."

I shake my head, glancing at him. "No, it's fine, Ayden. It's just my emotions. You know that."

His face softens. "I know I made you want to run off just now."

"May I suggest something?" Miss Dice's voice breaks my eye-lock with Ayden. I forgot she was there. "Perhaps you should see Mr Matthews together. Maybe it will be easier to talk through your worries together."

Glancing back at Ayden, his lip cocks up in a panty-melting smirk, and he shrugs one shoulder.

"I'd be happy to do that, Lex. You know I'd do anything for you." Once again, Ayden reminds me that he carries the heart of an angel inside his chest, and I totally believe that he would, in fact, do anything for me.

Nineteen

The monster in me is about ready to burst free when I witness the way Daniel leads Abbey around the school at recess. His hand may be holding hers, and to anyone that isn't looking for signs that there's trouble in paradise, they look like a couple walking hand in hand. But to me, I see the way his hand squeezes hers as they walk, especially when Abbey seems disinterested in whatever Daniel is saying to his group of friends. Each squeeze causes her eyes to squint a little as she tries to hide the pain.

"What are we looking at?" Rhys whispers in my ear.

We're walking through the school to go to our usual spot, but I stop when we pass by the courtyard, where I used to sit with Abbey and the guys.

"Any chance you'd be comfortable hanging in the courtyard today?" I ask Rhys, not taking my eyes off Abbey as she tries to pry her hand out of Daniel's without causing a scene.

"You mean where the popular kids go?" Rhys asks, and I nod. "Fuck yeah. Are we gonna stir up some shit?"

I drag my eyes from the courtyard to Rhys and grin. "Absolutely."

"What are you two devising?" Marcus pops up between Rhys and me, throwing his arms over our shoulders.

"Nothing and everything." Rhys throws a touch of drama in her tone, turning to flash her white teeth to Marcus.

"That's what I'm worried about." Marcus whines, and I giggle a little.

"What are you worried about?" Ayden joins the conversation then, coming up on my other side and linking his fingers with mine.

"These two are conspiring," Marcus complains, and I roll my eyes.

"Hardly. I've decided that I want to hang out in the courtyard today."

"Really?" Marcus sounds a little shocked.

Feeling Ayden shift beside me, I glance up and meet his intense blue gaze before he looks over to the courtyard to who I'd been watching.

"Abbey." He already knows why I want to go there, so I nod and start walking.

I hear the other guys behind me asking what we are doing, and Marcus gives them the only information he knows. We are going to hang out in the courtyard today.

The table that the guys used to occupy before hunting me down to see where I was hiding every recess and lunchtime is still free. It's like the other students know it's their table and that they would come back to it at some point, so they've left it alone.

It's now our table.

Not just for the boys and not just for the popular kids. No, now the outcasts have joined in, and we are here to stay.

While Allister takes a seat on the actual seat part of the large picnic table, the other guys use the tabletop as their seats, and so do Tillie and Bell. Rhys and Dale are too full of energy to take up a seat as they chat away to each other.

Ayden climbs up onto the table to sit, pulling me to sit between him and Simon. As soon as I plant my arse, Ayden tugs me to his side, enveloping me in his spicy scent that instantly calms me.

It's a good thing, too, because I need all the calm I can get as I keep my eyes locked on Abbey and Daniel.

"Is it just me, or is that fake fucker holding Abbey's hand too tight?" Simon whispers in my ear, and I glance at him.

"It's not just you." Sighing, I turn back to witness my friend's pain, but this time she stands on her toes and whispers something in Daniel's ear.

He turns away from his friends, which only gives me a better view of his face, and I see the way his top lip curls as he looks at Abbey in disgust and says something to her. He releases her then, and she doesn't hesitate, speed walking in the opposite direction.

"Rhys." I stand from the table. "Time to go to the ladies."

As if she hasn't been goofing around the entire time and actually been watching the interaction between Abbey and Daniel, Rhys gives me a firm nod and offers me her elbow.

Before taking it, I turn to the guys. "Can you guys keep an eye on Daniel? If he tries to go anywhere, distract him."

Jared glances at me curiously, his blue eyes squinting, but gives me a nod before dragging his gaze in Daniel's direction. Garrett, Shaun and Simon all nod as well, knowing something is going on.

I can feel Tasha's eyes on me as Rhys and I walk back out of the courtyard in search of Abbey, with our constant Ayden and Marcus shadows on our heels. I had expected a tantrum from Tasha when we entered the courtyard, but everyone seemed not to care that we were there, almost like we belonged. While it's not really a big deal coming from everyone else, it is coming from Tasha. She isn't one to sit back and let the school outcasts take over her area.

When we reach the girls' bathroom, the door swings open, and Abbey freezes in the doorway, brown eyes wide, glancing between the four of us.

"We'll take it from here," I say over my shoulder to Ayden and Marcus before stepping forward in Abbey's personal space, pushing her backwards into the bathroom.

"What are you doing?" Abbey whispers as I nudge her further inside, giving Rhys enough room to pass by and check the stalls to make sure we are alone.

One by one, Rhys opens each cubicle door, and when she's done, she gives me an "all clear," followed by a salute before going to stand by the entrance door just in case the guys aren't able to stop anyone from entering from the other side.

"Are you okay?" I ask Abbey, and confusion twists her pretty face, her cute button nose scrunching.

"I guess." She replies with caution, as if me or Rhys will turn into wild animals at any moment.

"Is your hand sore?" I direct my eyes toward her hand, where she's absentmindedly rubbing it.

Dropping her gaze, she realises what she is doing and thrusts her fists down by her sides.

"Why is he hurting you?" My question must take her off guard because she frowns in confusion before her eyes widen.

"Because he's pissed that he has to marry me." She admits.

"That's not your fault, though." I hiss, and she shrugs.

"I guess it doesn't matter who's fault it is. Daniel has decided it's my fault since it was my parents who convinced his parents that marrying me was a good idea. He'll calm down eventually. He's not my biggest concern, anyway. I hear my parents talking quietly every day. They aren't sure if letting us wait until we graduate University is the best idea. They think maybe it should happen as soon as we graduate from high school."

"Shit. What the fuck is wrong with them?" I easily fall back into best friend mode, and I internally kick myself. Even though my heart wants Abbey back, and even though I will help her if she needs it, she is no longer my best friend.

"They're a different kind of crazy, Lexi. Their threats aren't idle. As much as I want them to be, I know that's not the case. If they bring the wedding forward, then I'll run and never look back."

"But," my heart hurts hearing her say that, "where will you go?"

She shrugs. "I don't know. I'm just trying to keep my head down and stay out of trouble, so I don't stir the pot too much."

I want to hug her. I can see how sad she is. How alone she feels. I've felt that sort of loneliness before, and I'd never wish that on anyone.

That's not true, though, is it?

I'd happily wish that on Mike and my dad, but I don't even think I'd wish that sort of loneliness on Tasha.

Speaking of, "What's the deal with Tasha? Rumour has it she has a boyfriend."

Of course, I haven't heard such rumours. I've witnessed it with my own eyes, but Abbey doesn't know that.

Abbey rolls her brown eyes that no longer hold the life they used to. "It's probably a rumour she started. No one cares who she spreads her legs for. But Tasha was boasting about seeing an older guy. She wouldn't say who, though. I know she spends most nights with him. It's been a thing for a couple of weeks. Some guy she hooked up with at a Redfield party she went to with her cousin a few months back. She somehow talked him into committing to her or something because he told her he was finally ready for a relationship."

Shit. Mike has actually convinced her that he likes her. It also means that Tasha most likely wasn't Mike's girlfriend when he first attacked me, but she must have been when he attacked the second time.

She's had a problem with me since the first attack. Was she really just jealous over Mike? Is she that crazy?

Even as I think it, I know it's true. That girl has lost her marbles.

The buzzing of a phone gets my attention, and Abbey scrambles to get her phone out of her pocket.

"Shit. I have to go." She hisses and turns on her heel, her white-blonde braids swinging out as she spins, but before she reaches the door, Rhys steps in front of her.

"Was that Daniel?" Rhys gestures her head to Abbey's phone, which is still clutched in her hand. When Abbey nods, Rhys adds, "You know that thing he was doing to your hand. Next time he does it, return the favour to his nuts."

The smallest grin tugs at Abbey's lips before she gives Rhys a small nod, and after a moment, Rhys steps aside to let her pass.

Abbey would actually like Rhys if they were in a position to be friends. She may be a good Catholic girl, but she is a ball of fun that Rhys would no doubt enjoy just as much.

As soon as Abbey flies out through the door, Rhys turns back to me.

"What are you thinking? Do you think we need to dig a grave to dump Daniel's body in?"

That makes me laugh. "No. But let's keep an eye on him."

Rhys nods. "And Tasha's fuck buddy? What's the interest there?"

"You don't know?" Hasn't she read the messages? Seen the video?

"Know what?" Rhys frowns, her dark brows tugging together, and she crosses her arms over her chest and cocks her hip.

"About Mike? Last night? The video message?"

"Video message? If it was to the pack group chat, then I would have missed it. Marcus removed me." Rhys drops her arms to her sides and pouts.

"What? When did that happen?"

She sighs. "After we had another one of those chats last night. He keeps telling me it's okay, that he can do casual, and even told me he would start seeing other people. He lied, Lex. He still wants me to himself, and he's made no attempt to date anyone else." She shrugs. "He was pissed when I told him I'm going on a date with someone else, and he removed me from the group. Although he doesn't seem angry today. Maybe he'll add me again."

Jesus. These two.

Why is Marcus still trying to win her over when she has told him otherwise? And why the hell is she going back to him all the time?

"You need to stop seeing Marcus altogether." I blurt, hating the way she flinches at my words.

"Excuse me? Are you telling me what to do?" Rhys looks downright pissed.

"We're best friends, right?" I ask her, and she frowns, still looking pissed.

"Well, I thought we were." She shrugs, glaring at me.

"Well, Rhys. Best friends offer advice sometimes. And my advice is that you stop going back to Marcus. It's just confusing him, and it's not fair to keep leading him on like that. You know he wants more from you than you're willing to give, so cut ties with him now and maybe give him some space to get over you."

Rhys' eyes are dark with anger, but she stays quiet as she stares at me. It looks like she wants to say something, yet no words fall from her lips.

"Rhys, I care about both of you, and I don't want to see either of you get hurt."

"So, what conversation have you had with Marcus about this? He's your so-called family, right? Have you told him to back off from me? Have you offered him the same advice, or is it just me you give your opinion to?" Rhys snaps, glaring at me with her hands snapping open and closed by her sides.

"I haven't spoken with Marcus about this because he hasn't come to me to talk about it. If he did, then yeah, I would tell him to stop seeing you, too." I reach out to place my hand on Rhys' arm, but she takes a step back, her nostrils flaring. "Rhys, come on. You said you don't want to commit to him, so I don't see the problem if you don't care that much. Isn't it better that you cut ties with him for good? I mean, unless you really do like him more than you're willing to admit?"

"You know what, Lexi? You're right. I should cut ties with him, but in order to do that, I'm going to have to stop hanging around you. It'll only take him a day or two to forget all about me anyway and resume his obsession with you." Rhys spins on her heel and pulls the door open so hard that it bounces off the wall and slams shut behind her.

What the fuck just happened?

It takes me a moment to move, so when I do, I pull the door open to find her nowhere in sight and only Ayden's blue eyes looking at me in confusion.

"What just happened?" he asks, moving towards me to cup my face, and my bottom lip starts to wobble.

"I think Rhys just broke up with me," I whisper as a tear spills over.

Ayden's eyes widen. "What?"

"We argued. About Marcus. I basically accused her of leading him on, and she got angry and…. and…."

"Lexi," Ayden whispers, pulling me to his chest. "I hate to say this, but she *was* leading him on. She's been confusing Marcus for weeks. I've told him to stop seeing her, but he won't listen."

The bell sounds then, indicating that recess is over, and I pull back to glance up, meeting Ayden's eyes.

"It's time for you to go to your appointment with Mr M," Ayden whispers before pressing his warm lips to my forehead.

"Or I could just go to the library or even class." As weird as this sounds, I'm feeling too emotional to see the school counsellor right now.

"Nice try." Ayden chuckles, and I roll my eyes at him.

"Why do you hate me?" I whine dramatically, and he wipes away my drying tears with his thumb.

"The only thing I hate about you is when you're not with me." Ayden's voice is husky, and I'd melt if it weren't for the swarms of students filling the passage to get to their lockers.

Unlike Miss Dice's suggestion, I don't ask Ayden to come in with me to speak with Mr Matthews. The things I want to say to Ayden are for our ears only. I don't even tell Mr M about what just happened with Rhys. I need time to think over that and figure out if I've royally fucked up and overstepped.

So today, I talk about Valarie.

I let my mind drift to that awful day and admit to Mr Matthews that I had actually wished at the time that Val would die, so she wouldn't have to experience what Mike had planned for her.

Letting myself think about that day is hard, and I cry for a bit after going to that dark place. In true Mr M style, he pulls out his laptop, and we watch funny cat videos again. All in all, it's a good session.

My period four class is Psychology, which is with that panty-melting guy again that stole my heart. So once again, I find it hard to concentrate on anything but where his leg brushes mine under the table, or how his elbow is resting on the back of my chair, and those magical fingers of his gently play with the stray hairs at my nape. I still have no idea what we are learning in that class. I'm going to fail it for sure, but Ayden's nearness and subtle touches help me forget briefly about all of my worries, which now includes Rhys.

At lunchtime, it quickly becomes apparent that Rhys and my new friends aren't joining us in the courtyard, and I struggle to pretend I'm okay with it. Ayden, always wanting to cheer me up, announces that we are doing something different and leads the guys and me to the music rooms, which I haven't been inside since I was in year nine.

"What are we doing here? Don't you have to be a music student to go in here?" Garrett asks while following behind as we trail inside after Ayden.

"Mostly yes, but Mr Dean found out who my dad is and kinda offered me the use of the rooms whenever I want them," Ayden says over his shoulder before pushing open a heavy door that leads into a band room. "You guys can muck around in here, but don't break anything."

Hoots ring out from the guys as they barge in, trying to snatch up their preferred instrument.

"Here, Lex," Jared calls from the back of the musty room, holding up a set of drumsticks.

My eyes widen, and an uncontrollable grin pulls my lips up before I practically run to take the sticks from

Jared. When I sit my arse in the drum throne, my eyes connect with Ayden's across the room, and his grin is as wide as mine.

He did this to make me smile, so I mouth a *thank you,* and he rewards me with one of his winks.

Fuck, I love him.

I haven't told him yet, but I will soon.

The thought makes me blush, and as usual, he spots it, a single dark brow rising as he eyes me. So naturally, I poke out my tongue and start a rudiment-based warm-up I watched on YouTube while I was bored at home yesterday.

There's nothing but noise coming from each of us as we pretend to know how to play the instruments, and I work up a sweat as my beats get faster. I'm so focused on what I'm doing that I don't realise Ayden isn't even in the room with us.

Garrett is sitting on the floor trying to tap out a song on the xylophone, while Simon and Jared have a ridiculous, awfully sounding guitar off, and Marcus and Shaun both sit at the piano trying to play chopsticks.

I can't help but smile.

I love these guys.

While they are all busy, I slip out of the room into the quiet passage and hear the faint sounds of a piano playing. My feet carry me in that direction without a second thought, and I peer through the skinny window on the door to see my guy, looking fucking edible, sitting at the old brown upright piano.

As quietly as I can, I pop the door open and slip inside, not wanting to distract him.

The rich harmonies instantly spike recognition.

Lovely by Billie Eilish.

Emotions immediately assault me, but not in a bad way. I love this song. It's hauntingly beautiful and speaks to my soul, to the part of me that has and still fights to be free of the nightmare I've been living.

When the last note is played, Ayden turns his head, noticing me for the first time, but his smile instantly drops when he sees my glassy eyes.

"Come here, beautiful."

He doesn't have to ask me twice. Four steps and I come to stand between his legs as he stays seated on the stool. We are eye level now, and his intensity drags me in like a moth to a flame. Gentle hands slide around to my back and press me forward, closing the distance at the same time as those soft lips brush over mine.

His kiss is gentle. Sweet. That is, until he pulls me even closer and demands my lips apart to deepen the kiss. My moan fills the room, and my hands lock in his hair that has grown a little longer since we first met. When our tongues clash, my body ignites like tiny sparks are dancing across my skin. There is so much love in his kiss. So much desperation and need that it almost makes me want to cry with happiness.

Slowly, almost like its torture, Ayden turns the kiss into nibbles before reluctantly pulling back to look at me.

"I'll never get enough of kissing you, Lexi West. You're an addiction I'm not willing to give up."

Naturally, I blush, but I don't take my eyes off his as the words I thought earlier dance on the tip of my tongue.

I love you.

I don't know why I can't say it to him yet, even knowing he's shared those three little words with me already, so I let him see it in my eyes.

His grin lights up his whole face before his ocean eyes flick back to my lips.

"If we don't leave this room in a few minutes, I'm not going to be able to stop myself from kissing every inch of your body."

My brows lift. "Every inch?"

He nods.

"Surely not every inch?" I pull a serious expression, and his grin broadens.

"Yes, Lexi. Every single inch."

"What? Even my toes?" I scrunch my nose up, and he chuckles that gravelly chuckle that makes heat pool between my legs.

"Yes, even your toes. I want to devour those pretty toes of yours." Ayden leans forward and nips at my chin.

I squeal and screw my face up again, trying not to give in to the giggles bubbling up.

"How about my arm pits? You have to admit you don't want to taste that."

"Fuck yes, I do, Lexi." Ayden's eyes darken and turn drunk with lust. "I want to taste every single inch of your skin. Every part, every nook and cranny."

"No." I shake my head in disbelief. "Surely not *every* nook and cranny?"

I didn't think they could, but Ayden's eyes darken even more. "Every. Single. Part." He pauses between each word just to make sure I understand that he's serious. He doesn't mean *every* part, though, right?

"But... some places aren't for tasting." My nose scrunches again, and instead of looking like he's going to agree with me, he shakes his head.

"Listen very carefully, beautiful. I want to taste every fucking part of you."

"Even... the no-go zone?" I whisper, the heat in my cheeks scolding.

With a quirk of his lip, Ayden's face softens, and he chuckles before speaking low, "especially the no-go zone."

While there's a small part of my brain that is freaking out about his admission, the rest of my brain and body skyrockets with a level of lust I've never experienced. I'm fairly sure if I don't have him inside me in the next minute, I'll self-combust.

The chime of an incoming message snaps us both out of our lust induced coma, and Ayden reaches into his blazer pocket, taking out his phone.

"Shit." Sitting back, Ayden looks from his phone to me. "It's from my dad. Ringo just called. Muz is worse."

And just like that, an Arctic tidal wave crashes over us, dousing out our fire.

Twenty

Concentrating on the last class of the day is impossible, especially knowing this was the last class I was in last week when I leapt over the table and attacked Tasha like a crazed animal. I don't even pay her any notice through the class because all I can think about is Muz and Rhys. Tillie and Dale still sit with me but are quieter than normal, and I get the feeling Rhys may have told them what happened. Maybe they won't want to be my friends anymore, either. After all, I was the outsider that came and interrupted their friendship bubble.

I force myself not to think about Rhys, but then all I can think about is Muz and what it means if he's getting worse. Is he going to die? I can't bear to think of that possibility. Muz needs to be okay. He needs to get better. He can't die because of me. My tummy rolls just thinking about him, so I try to force those thoughts to the back of my mind, along with my thoughts of Rhys.

Even though there's a security guard stationed outside my classroom, which seems to be the norm with all of my classes so far, Simon has taken it upon himself to stand with the guard, watching in on me through the window of the door instead of going to his own class. I don't know how he's getting away with it, but he has somehow convinced the uniformed man that it's okay for him to be out there with him.

I have to admit, I feel safer knowing Simon is close by. I hadn't realised how much I depended on all the guys until this moment. One day, when all of this bullshit is over with, I'll find a way to thank them all.

After school, my pack lingers on the sidelines while I work with Travis to serve our community service. We finish weeding the garden bed and move on to trimming back some of the overgrown bushes. While I trim away at each overgrown stem, Travis hacks away at the bush he's working on like he's Edward Scissorhands. Unfortunately, Edward has more skill. That poor bush is going to be nothing but a twig soon.

"You might want to take it easy on that poor bush." I giggle as Travis flicks his hands around like he's sculpting something amazing.

"Nah. I've got a knack for this shit." Travis smirks, hacking away.

"Jesus, Trav, put the sheers down and step away from the defenceless bush."

"No way. I'm a pro." Travis tips his head back in an evil laugh, and a small smile tugs at my lips as I focus on my task.

This guy. Such a funny fucker.

"Has something happened?" Travis' question draws me out of my thoughts, and my brows knit together as I glance at him.

"What?"

"Has something happened? You're not very talkative today. Besides picking on my tree sculpture, that is." Travis drops his sheers and leans against the brick wall before slipping the cigarette out that's tucked behind his ear and popping it in his mouth.

"Have you ever known me to be that talkative?"

He frowns, his sandy brows meeting in the middle. "I guess not. Even so. Something is off today. You okay?"

Leaning against the wall to face Travis, I snatch the cancer stick from his mouth and chuck it over my shoulder. "That shit will kill you." I hiss past my grin, and he scowls.

"You're a fucking pain in the arse. You know that?"

I smile proudly. "Yes. So I've been told many times."

Travis grunts and slips his lighter back into his pocket. "Any news on your *pedo* brother?"

My smile drops, and I sigh, shrugging and knowing I can't tell him the truth.

"You know, if I come across him again, I think I'll just kill him and do everyone a favour."

I almost choke on my own saliva. "What! No Trav. Don't be silly."

"Not being silly, Sexy Lexi. He deserves to die."

"I know," I whisper, and his eyes dart to mine in surprise.

"I'm pretty sure he's on the top of everyone's hit list at the moment." Travis admits. "If he comes out of hiding, someone will fuck him up."

"One can only hope." I turn from him then, needing this conversation to be over. Bending down, I grasp the cigarette I threw over my shoulder, deciding Travis deserves to slowly kill himself if he wants, and just as I stand up, I freeze when I hear Ayden yell.

"I'll fuck you up if you look at her arse like that again!"

Spinning with wide eyes, I watch Travis turn red and lift his hands in surrender, first at me and then in the direction of Ayden, all while Simon and Shaun chant, "Fuck him up! Fuck him up!"

And that's the end of me doing community service with Travis for the day because caveman Ayden drags me away despite my protests that I still have thirty more minutes to do.

I pout like a little brat for half of the walk home while Simon walks ahead, attempting to make up a rap song about Travis while Shaun tries to beatbox.

"Uh, Lex?" A nervous-looking Garrett pops up beside Ayden and me as we walk. "Can I, uh, talk to you for a minute?" His anxious blue-grey eyes dart over my head to Ayden before returning to mine, so I nod.

"Of course."

When his eyes dart back to Ayden, I realise he wants to talk to me in private, so I turn to Ayden, who is shooting Garrett a grumpy glare and raise my brows pointedly. Getting the hint, and with great reluctance,

Ayden falls back to walk with Marcus, who has been unusually quiet ever since my argument with Rhys.

"Sorry," Garrett whispers, offering me a small smile, and I give him one back. "It's Britney's birthday tomorrow, and she asked if you would come over for dinner and cake?"

"Oh." I can't hide my surprise, but quickly replace it with a smile. Britney is one of Garrett's little sisters. "Yes. I would love to."

Garrett instantly smiles, looking relieved while I feel anything but because I know Ayden will have a problem with this. He will be annoyed, but that's okay. He can be annoyed all he wants because I'm still going. Garrett is my friend and has done a lot for me, so I can make time to go to his sister's birthday dinner.

"Great. She'll be so happy." Garrett chuckles, and I grin at how his face lights up when he talks about his little sister. Then his face drops, and he's back to looking nervously over my head again.

Turning, I see Ayden has made it back to my side and is glaring daggers at Garrett, who avoids his eyes. It's weird to see Garrett like that. He's usually so alpha male, but for some reason, he's cowering.

Has Ayden said something to him?

He better not have.

When we walk through my front door five minutes later, we're engulfed by the delicious scent of cooking food.

Not just *any* food.

It's a roast. I'd know that smell anywhere. Not because it was cooked for me often as a child, but because it was a smell my mouth would water over when I visited my friends' houses over the years. The fact that my house smells like this right now has my nose in the air as it leads me to the kitchen to find my mum chatting away to Officer Reynolds as she cooks. I stop abruptly when I see the older officer sitting at the kitchen counter wearing plain clothes. What is he doing here, and why is he out of uniform?

Ayden knocks into me from behind with an *oomph* and grabs onto my shoulders to keep me upright when I nearly tumble forward, our clash gaining the attention of Officer Reynolds and my mum.

"Oh good. You're home. Burt was just keeping me company while you were at school." When my mum flashes me a fake smile, I frown and tilt my head, taking in the scene.

Burt? She's on a first-name basis with Officer Reynolds now? What is happening here?

I could almost be fooled to think that everything is normal if it weren't for my mum's forced smile.

"Has something happened?" I ask, and my mum's dark eyes flit behind me to where the guys are standing. Whatever is happening, she doesn't want to speak in front of my friends.

I'm about to turn around and ask the guys for some privacy when Marcus speaks.

"We'll get started on our homework in the living room."

I hear the quiet agreements from Shaun and Simon as the shuffling feet of the five guys exit the room, leaving Ayden and me in the kitchen.

Officer Reynolds, *or should I call him Burt now*, clears his throat as he takes us in. "Your mother had a visitor today."

"What?" I screech, my eyes flying to meet my mum's in concern. If there is a police officer sitting in my kitchen because my mum had a visitor today, then it can't be good. "Mike?" I ask.

"No. Your father." My mum's shoulders drop. It's the first time in days that I've seen any hint of the woman she was before she went to rehab. She almost looks like she wants to curl into herself and hide.

Don't give up, Mum.

I want to say those words to her, but I don't. Not with the present company.

"Max was here?" I need confirmation because even though she said it was my dad, I don't see him as my dad anymore. "He was in the house? How did he get inside the house?" My heart is racing at the idea of him being in this space again. The last time I saw him here, he was rifling through all the cupboards, trying to find the file, and Muz protected me from him, keeping his gun trained on my dad.... I mean Max, the whole time.

Muz.

Ugh! Now I'm thinking about him again. I hope he's going to be okay.

Mum nods. "Yes, he was in the house. Maxwell came looking for some of his... belongings."

"But how did he get in the house, Mum? Tell me you didn't let him in?"

"Not willingly, Lexi!" My mum hisses at my tone, which I probably deserve.

"Your father found your mother in the backyard while she was hanging the washing out. Your mother tried to stop him from getting inside, but he overpowered her," Burt explains.

"Did he hurt you?" Ayden asks my mum, concern lacing his tone as he comes to stand beside me, his fingers finding mine by our sides.

"Nothing I couldn't handle," my mum answers, jutting her chin up as she rubs at her wrist.

Frowning, I move around the kitchen counter to stand before my mum and look down at her wrist. "Show me." My voice is a whisper, and hearing it, my mum sighs and tugs up the sleeve on her sweater to reveal a dark purple bruise spanning her thin wrist. It's a familiar sight, the handprint clear, just like it was on my upper arm after I sprung my dad with his mistress.

"It doesn't hurt." My mum's voice is soft as she hides her wrist away again, and I want to call *bull shit*. I don't, though. She doesn't need my crap or anyone else's right now.

"What else did he do?" I keep my eyes trained on my mum, hoping I can read her in case she tries to sugar coat it for me.

"He shoved me around a little. He was too preoccupied with trying to locate what he came looking for. He didn't even notice when I picked up my phone and dialled triple zero. It was only when he heard car doors close outside that he realised we had company, and he took off the same way Mike did the other night. Over the back fence."

"You need to put cops near the house over the back where they keep sneaking past." Ayden hisses at Burt, who nods.

"Already on it, young man. Our drive-bys will include the street behind here." Burt sits taller on the barstool, proud of that arrangement.

"Drive-bys? They aren't doing shit." Ayden hisses, taking a step towards Burt. "You need to have officers stationed there. And outside this house, too."

"I'm sorry," Burt offers, looking at each of us. "We just don't have the resources in Fox Pines to place officers on guard, and as much as we'd like to spend our shifts just driving around *this* area, we can't. The south end keeps our officers extremely busy."

The south end of Fox Pines is well known for its less than savoury citizens. It's also where the junkie house was that caught fire, where they found some of Mike's belongings.

"Burt, it's fine. We understand." My mum gives Burt a warm smile, which he returns.

"What I'd like to know is how Max knew Mum was out in the backyard. How did he know when to spring?" I expect my question to surprise my mum, but when she stays neutral, I realise she's already thought of the same thing.

"We're looking into that as well, Lexi," Officer Reynolds responds. "There's a possibility he might be staying nearby or has someone watching the house somehow. He indicated to your mother that he knew she was in the house alone."

My eyes meet Ayden's across the small space, and I know we are thinking the same thing. Tasha would have let Mike know I was at school, and Mike would have told my dad. It still doesn't explain how Dad knew Mum was in the backyard. Maybe it was just a fluke. Perhaps he came snooping for a way in and found her.

"The important thing is that I'm okay. Burt has kept me company for the afternoon while you've been at school." My mum rolls her shoulders back in a show of confidence, and I can tell it's not forced.

Seeing her confidence return has me relieved. I'm so scared she will fall back into that helpless woman that turned to drugs to ease her pain. I know we have a long road ahead of us, so I need to know she has what it takes to handle the tough situations when they come up. I know if she can do that, then she'll get through anything else this life of ours throws at us.

I guess, in a way, I feel like knowing she can do it means I can too.

When my mum turns to the oven to peer in at the roast cooking, I understand that it's her way of ending the conversation. I can't remember the last time she cooked anything in the kitchen that takes longer than fifteen minutes to prepare, cook, and serve. Shit, if it weren't for the hint of stress in her expression, I'd think she was happy.

"I have enough food for your friends to stay for dinner, Lexi. I'll let you know when it's ready." Shooting me a smile over her shoulder, my mum begins wiping down the bench top, returning her attention to Burt, who smiles warmly at her.

O... K... This is getting awkward.

"Lex." Ayden's voice drags my critical eyes from whatever is going on between my mum and Burt, and I'm helpless not to smile at his knowing smirk. He doesn't have to say anything else to me, my body just naturally knowing I need to be close to him again, my feet moving on their own accord towards him.

Arm in arm, we wander to the front living room to find the others, where we join them for a homework session before it turns into a fight over the PlayStation controllers. The guys manage to keep my mind off Muz and Rhys most of the time. Marcus is still quiet and has been avoiding eye contact with me for the most part. I want to talk to him about Rhys, but he probably blames me for her cutting and running.

Jesus, was it even any of my business?

Probably not, but I couldn't just sit back and watch Marcus keep getting hurt.

When my mum announces that dinner is nearly ready and Burt leaves quietly, Shaun goes to the kitchen to flirt with her again, and Ayden and Marcus keep an eye on him while they set the table, so I take that opportunity to send Muz a text message.

Lexi West
Are you still harassing the nurses?

I don't know why I send him that particular message. I guess I want to interact with him, as if that simple act will reassure me he's okay.

When he doesn't reply after a few minutes of staring at my phone, willing it to chime, I slip it back into my pocket and call for Jared, Simon and Garrett to join us in the kitchen.

Dinner is divine. My mum is a good cook. Who knew?

The meal is also hilarious with the guys telling mum stories about a camping trip they went on last summer, as well as some of the pranks that take place in the boys' change rooms at footy.

I stay relatively quiet while they re-tell their experiences, and there are a few times I can't help but laugh until it hurts at their shenanigans.

I realise now that this is what having a family is really like. Dinners together, storytelling, sharing laughs, holding each other close when things are tough. I really had no idea how powerful a family unit can make me feel. It's like I can do anything because they are by my side.

A little after dinner, once the dishes are washed and put away, Marcus, Shaun and Garrett say their goodbyes, leaving Mum and me in the capable hands of Ayden, Jared and Simon for the night.

Mum bows out early and heads to bed, leaving us to watch Maze Runner in the front living room. At first, it's hard for me to concentrate on the movie because all I can think about is the fact that Muz hasn't responded to my text.

He's probably too sick to even look at his phone. I'm an idiot for sending him the message. I'm the last person he'd want to talk to since I'm the reason he's so sick.

As usual, Ayden notices that I'm struggling with something and takes it upon himself to distract me.

We are on the floor leaning against the back couch, while Jared is on the side couch, and Simon is on the floor in front of us, laying on his tummy with his head in his hands. Shifting his legs under the fleece blanket covering us, Ayden turns his head and whispers in my ear.

"I want to make you come."

My smirk spreads slowly as I turn to him with raised brows and whisper back, "That's random. Where did that idea come from?"

His eyes darken, dropping to my lips and then back to my eyes before leaning in close, his warm breath feathering across my skin.

"I can't keep my eyes off you, Lexi, and my hands," he slides his warm palm up my bare leg, "are itching to touch you. I want to feel you come undone under my fingers."

An instant flush travels up my body, and warmth pools between my legs.

Leaning back to my ear, Ayden nips at my lobe before whispering, "Fuck yes, Lexi. There's that blush. I want to watch your beautiful face as you come."

Well fuck, how can I say no to that?

I shift my legs, about to stand, when Ayden's hand tightens on my thigh, holding me back.

"No, Lex. You don't understand." Ayden draws closer, pushing his lips against my ear. "I want to make you come, right here, right now."

My breath falters, and I turn my frown to him. "In case you haven't noticed," I whisper, "Jared and Simon are here in the room with us."

That's when I see it.

His eyes.

Those beautiful, captivating ocean eyes are smouldering with heat, and I swear I see the devil dancing in them.

A moment later, a slow, wicked grin spreads across his face, and it's fucking hot and sinful, and all for me.

"You'd better be quiet then, beautiful."

An O forms from my mouth while my eyes widen at his words.

He's fucking serious right now. He wants to make me come right now in this room while Jared and Simon are only a few feet away. What...

I can't think as his fingers slide the rest of the way up my thigh to graze over the top of my pink bunny shorts, right where I ache the most. A moan travels up my throat, ready to escape, but I squeeze my throat shut and bite my lip as one part of my brain focuses on staying quiet, and the other focuses on the intense pleasure that pulses deep inside me.

It's hard, but I try to keep my eyes open, my paranoia screaming at me as I glance from Jared to Simon and to the TV. If either of them turn around, they'll see the pleasure written all over my face. I just know it.

My hips lift a little, having a mind of their own as they greedily seek more, and Ayden doesn't hold back. With skilled fingers, he rubs gentle circles over my fabric covered clit, applying the perfect amount of pressure to torture me and turn me into a withering ball of need. The friction of his pressure and the fabric barrier quickly builds into a blinding pleasure that crashes through me unexpectedly, wave after wave rolling through me as I hold my breath and shove my wrist into my mouth, clamping down until I taste blood.

I don't know if I make noise because, for a few moments, I lose my ability to hear, and my eyes dart to Jared and Simon to see that everything seems undisturbed.

"That was so fucking hot," Ayden whispers before nipping at my ear, followed by slipping his hand down the front of my pink bunny shorts. I'm about to ask him what he's doing, but my words falter as I watch the concentration on his face as he slides two fingers between my folds, spreading my wetness around before he pulls his hand free and slides the two fingers into his mouth.

I have to bite my lip again to stop myself from groaning at the sight. Especially when he slowly drags his fingers out and licks his lips before saying, "fucking delectable."

Holy shit.

Slapping a peck on my cheek, Ayden stands while all I can do is sit nearly limp in an orgasm coma and watch as he leaves the room, his very obvious and seriously hard arousal tenting his pants.

Where is he taking that? It's mine.

The thought has me moving a moment later, and I ignore Jared's curious gaze as I leave the room in search of my guy. Hearing a door click shut upstairs, I creep up the staircase in my usual creak free way, glancing at the three closed doors on the landing. My bedroom door is open, Mike's door, the new one, is closed, as are the bathroom and the toilet. Ayden could have gone into the bathroom, and if that's the case, I won't be joining him. But the toilet door was open the last time I saw it, so I decide to head there.

Butterflies dance inside me as my nerves kick in, but the horn bag in me is a determined little bitch, so I twist the doorknob, pushing it open to slip inside. A part of me knew what Ayden would be doing in here, but I don't think I was quite prepared for the sight of him holding himself up on the wall with one hand while his other hand pumps his cock with such force that I'm sure it must hurt. Even his face looks pained.

The moment I click the door shut behind me, Ayden freezes mid-pump, his blue eyes flying open, meeting mine. I can tell he's about to stop, which I really don't want, so I quickly drop to my knees in front of him and peer up at him through my dark lashes.

"Fuck," his growl is drawn out, but he's too far gone to refuse me and instead drops his hand from the wall to gently fist my blonde waves. "You should have stayed downstairs, beautiful."

I shake my head, eyeing his hard length bobbing before me, and I lick my lips. "I want you in my mouth."

"Lex." The gravel in his tone is deep and primal, and I fucking love it. I also love the way his eyes are nearly black as he presses his engorged head to my lips.

With my eyes still locked on his, I part my lips and accept him into my mouth as far as I can manage. His eyes flick from mine to where I swallow him into my mouth, and he bites his bottom lip as he slowly drags his cock back out. This time when he slides back in, I stick my tongue out, helping him sink deeper, my throat opening to accommodate him.

A muffled moan escapes me as he pulls out again, and then his return is quicker this time as he becomes a little more frenzied and builds speed.

My eyes meet his again, and I take in his expression, recognising the uncertainty. He's holding back on me again. He still thinks I'm fragile and doesn't want to do anything to upset me or trigger me. Sure, I'm fragile, just not when it comes to wanting everything he has to offer, so when he slides out again, I let his length pop free before I glare at him.

"Lex?" Dark brows draw together as his eyes dance between mine. "You want me to stop?"

"No." I shake my head. "I want you to fuck my mouth, Ayden."

This time, his brows reach his hairline.

"Stop holding back and give me all you've got. Fuck my mouth."

For a long, drawn-out moment, I think he's going to tell me to stand up and end this now, but to my surprise, his eyes darken even more, and his hand tightens in my hair.

"Open," he growls, and I obey, eagerly accepting his thrust that reaches the back of my throat, making me gag. My eyes glass over as a natural reaction, and I grab onto the back of each of his muscular thighs, pulling him closer so I can show him I'm okay and I want more.

As he does exactly what I ask of him, I find my head trapped between the wall and his pelvis as each thrust sinks him in as far as my mouth and throat will allow.

It's not long after that I feel hot liquid spurt in the back of my throat, and I pull him taut against me as he rides out his orgasm.

I feel surprisingly powerful by this whole act.

Slowly, Ayden slides himself free of my mouth, and I lick my lips, making sure I've swallowed down every drop he released as he pulls me to stand, cupping my face in his gentle hands.

"I fucking love you, Lexi West."

I can't hide my grin, and he smiles in return briefly before he turns serious.

"Are you okay? Did I hurt you?"

"I'm perfectly okay, Ayden. I loved every minute."

With hungry eyes, Ayden captures my lips in a searing kiss, moaning when he tastes himself on my tongue.

And just like that, today's worries no longer plague me and I'm happy to say we both sleep well that night.

Better than we have in days.

Twenty-One

M y mood is lighter the next morning when I arrive at school for the second last day of term. Aside from the epic orgasms Ayden and I milked from each other last night, the message from Muz this morning has made me feel better.

Muz (Bobby Musgrove)
Am I still harassing the nurses? Never!
They are harassing me, wanting to wash my dick all the time!!
You didn't really want to know about the nurse, though, did you?
Are you worried about me, pretty girl?
I'm okay. Don't you worry about me.

I thought the worst when I found out that he had gotten worse yesterday. However, he seems to have picked up again, and that's all I need to help me walk a little taller today.

The first thing I notice when we arrive at school is that Tasha is lurking around without her usual scowl directed at me. She looks in my direction, frequently, almost as if she's trying to get my attention, but there are no daggers. There are no taunts or threats. It's a little unnerving, yet at the same time, I am curious as hell about her attitude change.

After homeroom, when Tasha approaches me, a wall of my guys block her from getting close.

What does she want? Is this a new tactic to get close to me so she can unleash her bitch on me? Not knowing what she's up to sends my mind into a spiral of scenarios, and I barely concentrate on my period one Art class.

In Media, I sense Tasha's eyes on me once again, and I have a strong urge to turn to her and ask her what her problem is this time. Maybe I should ask her why she let my brother into her house.

I don't, though, because the fact that they think it's a secret may work in my favour.... I hope.

I really need to give Jason a call and see if he's found out anything.

After the fallout with Rhys yesterday and Muz getting sicker, plus the visit my dad had with my mum, I've been too distracted to see if Jason has made our discovery of Mike and Tasha official in his reports.

Trying my best to ignore Tasha, I work on my portfolio and focus on eavesdropping on Tillie's stories that she can't help but share with Dale as she works on the table next to mine. She's funny in a cute way, easily owning up to what she calls her blonde moments. I want to talk to her and ask her if Rhys is okay, but I'm a chickenshit, apparently. I keep my eyes down and my mouth shut.

At recess, we go to the courtyard again, taking up the picnic table and soaking in the warm spring sun while Ayden feeds me hot fries. Jared glares at us every now and then, while Simon and Shaun mimic us. Apparently, Shaun is *me*, and I have an incredibly high-pitched voice, while Garrett and Marcus chuckle at the idiots.

Rhys is still nowhere in sight, and my heart sinks knowing she's avoiding me. I really need to talk to her about yesterday, so I shoot her a message.

Lexi West
Can we talk?

The bubbles pop up, so I know she is reading my message and maybe responding, but then they stop, and nothing comes through.

Shit.

"Is it just me, or does Abbey look like crap today?" Jared's voice is low in my ear, and I glance up to watch Daniel stroll past our table with Abbey by his side.

Today, Daniel's hand isn't holding hers, squeezing it. Today he has a firm grip on her wrist, the squeeze so tight I can see the skin puckering.

"She looks worse than she did yesterday," I whisper, feeling my heart break a little more.

I need to figure out how to get Abbey away from that arsehole.

Suddenly, Ayden and Jared leap up from the table to stand in front of me. Confused, I try to peer around them, no longer focused on Abbey.

"I want to talk to Lexi." Tasha's voice floats to me.

"Not going to happen." Ayden hisses, and it sends a chill up my spine, which then sends heat to pool between my legs.

What the fuck is wrong with me?

"I just want to talk to her." Tasha hisses back, which definitely doesn't have the same effect on me.

What does she want? Does it have anything to do with Mike and the fact she's been fucking him? I want to find out what she wants, but I also need to be careful because it's clearly a trap. She's doing this for Mike.

"Trashy, Tashy, no one wants you here. Why don't you go find a deep hole and fall into it?" Rhys' voice is loud and strong, and my heart races as I see her for the first time since she walked out on me yesterday. Coming to stand next to Jared, she wags her dark brows in Tasha's direction before blowing her a kiss. She's such a crazy, adorable idiot. Does this mean she still loves me?

I hear a huff, and a moment later, Jared and Ayden part as they take their places on either side of me again, while Rhys walks behind Tasha barking like a dog until Tasha shoots her a glare and walks in the other direction out of the courtyard.

I don't miss how Allison, Amanda, and Sophie stay seated on the wall under the tree, not attempting to go after their so-called leader, while Abbey sits next to Daniel at the other picnic table staring at the ground.

I sigh. I don't like this. Everything is so fucked up. My ex-friends are all unhappy, and while that should bring me joy after the way they treated me, it doesn't. All of this started because of Mike. He is the reason for the divide. He has ruined Valarie's life, Muz's too, and has done unthinkable things to my mum.

As my anger builds, my heart pulses with the need to hurry and end this. Give me a knife or a gun right now, and I'll find that fucking prick and end him once and for all.

The thought should shock me because of how absolute it is, yet it doesn't.

Before Mike returned to Fox Pines, I never considered myself a violent person. Now though, there's a thirst for blood, for vengeance pumping through my veins that I'm not sure what to do with.

This is where a therapist could help me sort through these feelings before I act on them—just another thing I should probably do.

After recess, Rhys walks away without saying anything to me, and I go to my Maths class with Miss Dice feeling an ache in my heart. Trying to get any work done is a waste of time since my head is in a bubble of trying to figure out how to fix things with Rhys one minute and then revenge plotting and daydreaming about how good it would feel to watch Mike take his last breath the next minute. I've thought about ending Mike's life before, so it should come as no surprise, yet it does because now it feels like more than a thought. It feels like something I know is inevitable, and that scares me if I'm honest.

Ayden tries to get my attention numerous times during class, but it's a challenge he doesn't win. It doesn't deter him, though, and with his hand linked with mine, he walks me to my next class, Pastoral Care. I kind of wish I didn't have to go to it. I'm in this class on my own, and while I don't feel like I'm in any danger, I've become accustomed to having a friend with me. I need to suck it up, though. I can't let myself become so needy.

When the bell rings to start the class, I notice the security guard stationed outside my class again, this time with Shaun lingering next to him, chatting away. I remember then that I'm not alone. These guys never leave me alone, just like they promised.

I can't hold back the smile it brings to my face.

I owe these guys so much.

I ignore what Mrs Monaghan says as she addresses the class, and I almost jump out of my skin when my phone starts to vibrate and flash with an incoming call from Muz. Not caring about getting in trouble for using my phone or ditching class, I grab my laptop and dart out of the classroom to answer the call before I miss it.

"Hey, pretty girl. Just checking in." The excitement I felt a moment ago at seeing Muz's name flash across my screen flies out the window the moment I hear his voice.

It's huskier than it was last time.

Weaker too.

"Hey Bobby. Been enjoying those sponge baths?" I force lightness into my tone, hoping he can't hear my worry as I glance at Shaun and the security guard before turning to walk out the doors that lead to the quad.

"You know it." Muz chuckles hoarsely, which causes him to cough.

Shit, even his cough is weak.

"Do you want to hear some good news?" Pushing through the doors, I descend the steps, stopping to sit on the bottom one, glancing around to make sure no one lurks nearby before I hear the doors open behind me.

Being respectful of my privacy, Shaun leads the security guard down the steps and over to the bench seat towards the centre of the quad, giving me some space to talk on the phone.

Besides him, the security guard, and me, there's no one else out here.

"Hell yes," Muz says with a monotone voice. "What's the tea?"

"The bitch that has been having a go at me at school is secretly seeing my brother. I'm pretty sure she's helping Mike to get to me. She doesn't know I know.

So hopefully, it will work in my favour, and I'll be able to surprise Mike before he can surprise me." I keep my voice low and cup my hand over my mouth and the phone as if someone may know how to lip read.

"Wait." Muz croaks, "Hang on, pretty girl. Let's just take a step back."

"What?" I ask, confused.

"Have you told the cops?" Muz asks a question I wasn't expecting to come from him.

"No.... Well, yes.... well, it's complicated."

Muz chuckles, "Uncomplicate it, pretty girl."

If only it were that easy.

"Ayden told one of the cops who's investigating on the side, but I think he's going to make it official on the record soon."

"Good. Let that fuckwit brother of yours get thrown in jail and be someone else's bitch," Muz croaks.

"He doesn't deserve jail. He deserves death." I grind out coldly.

"Well, since death is going to be a little hard to punish him with, you'll have to get used to the idea of prison."

"You've already told me how to kill him, Bobby. All I have to do is pull it off."

"A little advice." He mutters. "Don't use my real name, and the words *pull it off* together ever again. You're making my dick hard."

"Muz!" I scold and stand from the step as if he can see me.

"As for the advice I gave you when you came to visit, yeah, I told you how to do that, but I didn't think you would actually consider really trying to k…. uh… do that to him." Muz coughs again, but this time it sounds more like an awkward distraction. Someone must be there with him. "I taught you self-defence. That's why I gave you my uh… gift."

"Is there someone there with you?" I ask, annoyed.

"Yep. Just walked in."

I sigh, still confused. "So basically, you don't think I have what it takes?"

"It's not that at all. I'm more hoping someone will get to him first, so you don't have to." His words are stronger than before, but then he pierces my little confidence bubble and starts coughing again. He really sounds like shit.

"If it comes to it, I'll do it." The whisper falls from my lips, but he hears.

"Be careful, pretty girl. A world without you in it isn't worth living in."

"Jesus Muz. You'd better be careful what you say. Someone might overhear you and mistake you for someone with a heart."

My words cause him to chuckle again before he falls silent.

"Lexi?" I still at hearing him use my name instead of *pretty girl*. "Be careful."

And then he hangs up.

I can't stop the tears that fall then. My heart feels so heavy with pain that I can barely handle feeling it pound in my chest anymore. I plonk my arse back on the bottom step and sit in silence with no intention of going back to class this period.

"Excuse me." The deep voice startles me, and I glance up to see the security guard standing before me. "Sorry. Didn't mean to scare you."

I don't say anything and search behind him to see Shaun approaching as he continues.

"Do you have a pass to be out of class?" he asks, hitching his pants a little.

This is new—security asking for passes. I guess Cynthia wasn't kidding about the security.

"Nope." I just want to be left alone. Is finding a quiet moment going to be an issue now?

"You really need a pass to be out of class, Miss West." He pulls his smartphone out.

"Really? What about Shaun? Did you ask him if he had a pass?" I whine, and he raises a brow at me, silently telling me he isn't kidding, and I sigh.

"I have my pass right here." Shaun skites waving it in front of my face, and I snatch it to see that he does, in fact, have a pass to be out of class, signed by Principal Rogan herself. How did he get this?

The security guard looks down at the screen on his phone before returning his brown eyes to me. "Miss West, you look a little upset. Perhaps you'd like to go to the counsellor? Shall I ask Principal Rogan to arrange the pass for you?"

I should probably go to see Mr M. All he'd have to do is bring out his funny cat videos, and I'd be set to forget for a while. Maybe eat some of the lollies he always has filling the bowl on his table.

As much as I know I *should* go to the counsellor, I don't want to. I just want to sit here on this step and wallow for a little while in peace.

Looking at the security guard's name tag so I can use his name to address him, I freeze when I see the name Bobby on it, before bursting into tears.

"Y-your name is Bobby?"

He frowns and nods. "Yes. Maybe I should call the counsellor."

"No," I blurt through my sobbing, automatically sinking into Shaun's side when he sits next to me and wraps his arm over my shoulder. "Please don't call Mr Matthews. I just need to have some time to myself."

"But you're very upset, Miss West. Protocol says I should contact the counsellor."

"I'm upset because your name is Bobby." More tears flow down my face, and I see through the blur that Bobby is extremely confused. "M-my friend. He's really sick in hospital, and his name is Bobby."

Bobby's brows lift, and his mouth forms an O as my words sink in.

"I just need some time to think. Please?" I beg, and after a moment of deliberating, he nods.

"Fine, but I need to let someone know where you are, or I'll lose my job."

"Okay," I say quietly. "Let the principal know I'm here with Shaun."

Bobby's face relaxes, and he nods. "Okay, good. Well, I'll just be over there if you need anything."

When I nod in agreement, Bobby lifts his phone to his ear as he walks away, checking over his shoulder every couple of paces to glance back at me.

When the security guard takes his post by the bench seat again, I drop my head in my hands and replay my brief conversation with Muz over in my head.

"Who's Bobby?" Shaun asks, rubbing his hand up and down my back to offer me comfort.

"Muz's real name is Bobby Musgrove." Tilting my head up, I take in Shaun's raised brows and watch the smile spread across his face.

"That scary fucker's name is Bobby? Ha!" Shaun laughs, which makes me grin.

"Not so scary now that you know that, is he?" I sit up, swiping at my tears.

"Nope. Not at all." Shaun tugs me close under his arm, and I accept the hug he gives.

I really need it.

We sit on the steps for the rest of period four, chatting away. Instead of thinking about my shit show of a life, I ask Shaun more about his. Besides his ability to make most girls want to give him their bodies to do as he pleases, I know little more about him. He's a vault when it comes to talking about himself, but he opens up a little about his mum, who is sick, but he doesn't tell me what her illness is, and before we know it, the lunch bell rings, and our brief time of peace is over.

After moving like a sloth and visiting my locker, Ayden and Garrett magically appear behind me, and Ayden wraps his arm around me from behind, brushing his lips across my cheek.

"I missed you." He breathes, and I instantly relax into him.

"I missed you too." I turn in his arms and let him press me against the locker, not caring about the hordes of students filling the passage.

"Muz called?" he asks, his lips thinning.

Of course, Ayden knows about the phone call. Shaun was doing more than making sure I was safe.

"He did. He didn't sound very good. His voice was weak."

Ayden nods. "He's pretty sick. I can ask my dad to check in with Ringo again if you like? Get another update."

My face drops and Ayden frowns.

"What's wrong?"

"I don't think I want to know if he's doing worse. It's killing me that he's suffering because of me."

"Hey, don't speak like that. It's not because of you. We've been over this." Brushing my hair back, Ayden strokes his thumb over my cheek, and I now regret that there are people around. I wish it were just him and me in our own little bubble where no one can see these sacred moments we share.

A familiar shriek captures my attention, and I peer around Ayden to find Daniel walking down the passage, dragging Abbey behind him by her wrist again. His grip is so tight that she cries out in pain again, and even though she asked me to stay away from her, I can't stop my reaction.

Pushing past Ayden, I launch myself at Daniel to block his path, my nostrils flaring as my anger takes over.

"Get the fuck out of my way!" Daniel hisses, and I hear Ayden hiss something behind me.

"Let her go!" I yell. "You're fucking hurting her."

Chuckling like a sick fuck, Daniel drags Abbey forward by her wrist, squeezing tightly as a whimper escapes her pale lips. "Princess, am I hurting you?"

Daniel's eyes, which I once thought held kindness, glare at me mockingly as he holds Abbey's wrist up, his knuckles white as he grips tighter.

"N-no," Abbey says through gritted teeth, still clearly in pain.

It's then that Ayden launches forward, grabbing Daniel by the scruff and slams him against the lockers. Abbey's wrist falls free, and the wind audibly expels out of Daniel on impact, his eyes fearful as he darts them to Ayden and then Abbey, who's standing off to the side.

Then she turns to me.

"Why don't you just fuck off, Lexi, and leave me alone!"

The pain those words inflict is unbearable as I look into Abbey's caramel eyes. I'm not shocked, though. She told me to keep away from her, and I've let my emotions rule me once again and reacted before thinking things through.

Ayden turns back to look at Abbey before his questioning eyes land on me as he loosens his hold on Daniel a little.

"And you too." Abbey turns her brown-eyed glare to Ayden. "I don't even fucking know you! Mind your own business and let Daniel go!"

"Abbey!" I hiss, not liking the way she speaks to Ayden, but she rolls back her shoulders and juts up her chin. Her glare slicing and final.

We've drawn a crowd of hushed whispers, and once again, my private life isn't private.

Abbey doesn't speak again. She just glares at me in a silent conversation that I can read, but don't necessarily agree with.

She doesn't mean what she said. She's just trying to protect herself because me stepping in like that has just made things worse for her.

"Ayden, let him go." My words are quiet, but Ayden hears and drops his hold before he steps back to me.

My heart breaks as Abbey links her arm with Daniel's and leads him down the passage and out into the quad while speaking to him quietly. I know why she did it, but the fact that she *has to do it* rips my heart in two.

"What the fuck just happened?" Garrett asks, coming to stand next to Ayden and me.

"I just made things worse for Abbey."

I ignore Ayden's and Garrett's protests at my comment and walk off with them trailing behind.

I wish I had more control over my emotions. Abbey is likely to pay for what I just did. Daniel will make her life even more miserable.

Maybe coming to school was a bad idea. I just seem to make things worse for everyone. I should stay away from them all.

Lunch is a blur of dark thoughts, and Ayden, always knowing me better than anyone else, slips his earbuds in my ears and plays my Heavy playlist for me. Leaning my head against his shoulder, I close my eyes and let myself fall into the music. Comatose by Skillet, Please by Staind, and Down with the Sickness by Disturbed work their magic at bringing my raging thoughts some sort of calm.

As I listen to the music, Ayden draws little swirls on my palm, and at times presses his lips to the back of my hand, reminding me I am loved.

At the end of lunch, I wait at the end of Ayden's locker bay while he grabs his books so he can walk me to my counselling appointment with Mr M before going to class. The passage is loud and busy with boisterous students, some chanting the Fox Pines Foxes footy theme song, excited for the lead up of the grand final this weekend.

While I wait, I take my phone out, opening all of my message chats in the hopes of finding a message from Rhys. I'm distracted from my phone screen when a hand holding a folded piece of paper appears in my line of sight. Glancing up, I see a security guard I haven't seen before, and I frown.

"Uh... this is for you." The scruffy, unshaven and not very well-groomed security guard mumbles, keeping his head low as his eyes dart around nervously.

Without thinking, I take the piece of paper and look down at it in confusion. When I glance back up, the security guard is gone, and I stand taller, looking around to try to see where he went.

"What's that?" Ayden appears next to me, glancing down at the paper in my hand, and I shrug, flipping it open.

It's time to play Ali!

Twenty-Two

M y heart stops as I re-read the words that can only be written by one person.

It's time to play Ali!

"What the fuck!" Ayden hisses, snatching the paper from me.

"What's wrong?" Garrett approaches us with concern, seeing my expression.

"Where did you get this?" Ayden asks, and I dart my head left and right, my blood pounding like thunder in my ears.

"A security guard gave it to me."

"What?" Ayden and Garrett ask in unison as Marcus joins us.

"What's going on?"

Ayden shows his cousin the note, and a moment later, a loud screeching alarm blares through the speakers. Everyone stops still in the passage, recognising that the alarm is going off and waiting to figure out what the alarm is for.

We have several drills each year, and never in all my time of schooling has the alarm been anything but a drill. Those drills typically happen during class time where teachers have already marked rolls, and there's some sort of order.

There is no order now.

Something is wrong.

At Fox Pines Catholic, we have different alarms for different situations. Is it a lockdown? Is it an evacuation? We wait for an announcement that usually follows, but nothing comes—only the continuous blare of the alarm.

I look up at Ayden's concerned eyes when he takes my hand, and a second later, we hear screaming.

"FIRE! FIRE!"

A chain reaction of panicked screams reaches our ears as everyone turns to the nearest exit and runs. Chaos erupts, and a stampede of students push and shove at each other as we flatten ourselves against the wall in an attempt not to get trampled.

"Can you see anything?" Marcus asks Garrett and Ayden, who are taller than he is.

I can't see shit at my five foot five height, so I latch onto Ayden's arm, watching the students barge past, knocking others over as they go.

"There's smoke down that way," Garrett confirms, pointing in the direction the screams came from, and Ayden nods.

"I see it. Let's get out of here." Ayden tightens his hold on me.

"Where's Hastings, Bossi & Crowley?" Garrett asks, and Marcus shrugs.

"I haven't seen them since they went to their lockers."

Fear prickles at the back of my neck at not knowing where the others are. Shit, where is Rhys? And Abbey?

"Come on, beautiful, let's get outside to the evacuation area. I'm sure the guys are there already." Ayden's reassuring tone helps me to shake off the panic and remember the logic.

Jared, Simon and Shaun will evacuate. They will be on the oval, and everything will be okay.

As the panicked students thin out, we make our way to the exit, Garrett helping up a year nine girl who has been trampled on. Marcus jumps in to help, and we shuffle along behind the other students as the smell of smoke drifts over from behind us.

Glancing over my shoulder, I see thick smoke further down the passage coming from the T-section that leads to the science rooms. This definitely is no drill, and the teachers certainly weren't prepared for this, which becomes apparent as we find a couple of them looking dishevelled in the quad, directing everyone to the oval.

Two teachers take over the care of the year nine girl, and we weave through the school, ignoring the concrete paths, to join the hordes of students on the oval.

As we approach, Mr Foster, the PE teacher, bellows through the megaphone to direct everyone.

"Please go to your homeroom teachers and line up in an orderly fashion!"

"I'll go to my teacher and see if Hastings is accounted for," Garrett says before he runs off towards his teacher.

"My homeroom is next to Jared's, so I'll see if I can see him. You're with Bossi, right?" Marcus asks Ayden, and he nods. "Okay. Let's check-in with each other on the group chat."

"Yeah, okay." Ayden nods again.

"We need to check if Rhys is okay, too. And Abbey," I say to Ayden and Marcus, and they nod before Marcus takes off to his teacher.

"Are you okay?" Ayden turns to face me, ignoring a teacher I don't know when she tells us to go to our teachers.

"I'll be okay once I know everyone is alright."

"The note..." Ayden's lips thin, his ocean blues swimming with worry as they study me.

"Let's just make sure everyone is okay first."

I know what he's thinking. It's the same thing I'm thinking.

The fire isn't a coincidence. One minute I'm getting handed a note by a sketchy-looking security guard, which is a message from my brother, and the next minute alarms are going off and smoke is filling the building.

Ayden cups my face and plants his lips on mine, reminding me how much he cares.

"Message the chat as soon as you've signed in with your teacher."

I nod, thinking he's about to walk off to find his teacher, but he doesn't. Instead, he links his fingers with mine and walks down the line of organised chaos until he finds Mr Bert, my homeroom teacher, and stands me right in front of the man, so he has no choice but to see that I'm here.

I briefly pay Mr Bert attention as he marks me present on the roll, and when I'm done, I see Ayden walking further down the line in search of his teacher.

I sit on the grass in a line with the other students from my homeroom as instructed and take out my phone to message the group chat.

Garrett-Cole
Hastings is here with me.

Simon-Hastings
The Hastinator is alive!

Lexi-West
Shaun? Jared?

Ayden-Mitchell
Just signed in with my teacher.
Bossi is here chatting up some girl.

Lexi-West
Of course he is.
Marcus, have you signed in?
Is Jared there with you?

There's nothing for a minute, and I start to squirm, feeling more and more anxious. In the distance, sirens grow closer, and some dickhead begins to cheer, which causes a chain reaction with more dickheads, making it impossible to hear anything else.

When my phone buzzes, I open it to find Marcus has replied.

Marcus-Grady
I've checked in.
I saw Rhys on my way. She's okay.
No sign of Jared yet, though.
Anyone else seen him?

Shit. Where are you Jar?

Simon-Hastings

Nope.

Shaun-Bossier

We haven't seen him either.

I don't wait any longer, bringing up his number on my phone and calling him. It rings and rings, and when I think it's about to go to voicemail, it picks up.

"Jared! Where are you?" I shriek, gaining the attention of other students sitting around me.

Then my ears are met with the vilest sound on this earth—Mike's chuckle.

"I told you it was time to play, Ali. I've been having a fucking amazing time with one of your boyfriends."

I bolt up to stand.

"Where is he?" I growl into my phone, my eyes darting across the sea of students to try to find Ayden, Marcus, or whoever the hell. I don't know.

"He's taking a little nap at the moment. Give him a minute. He'll wake again soon." Mike chuckles again, and I scream.

"Fuck you! Where is he!"

"Lexi?" Ayden calls from somewhere on my right.

"Now, what fun would it be if I told you where he is? I'll give you a little hint, though. If the firefighters don't make it here soon, your little boy toy is going to be overcooked."

351

The call ends, and I scream again, tears streaming down my face.

Ayden calls my name again, and Garrett joins him from the other direction, but I don't look for them. Instead, I leap over other students sitting on the ground and take off, running back towards the school buildings. Back towards the fire.

"Lexi, wait!" Ayden calls, but I don't stop. Instead, I yell over my shoulder.

"Mike has Jared!"

I push my legs so hard, gaining speed as I reach the buildings and weave down the paths, hearing feet pounding behind me. Just as I reach the doors to the wing where the fire is, strong arms wrap around me, and Ayden huffs in my ear.

"No, Lexi. I can't let you run right into danger."

"Jared is in there, where the fire is. Mike has him." I reach my hands out, trying to take hold of the doors, but they get further away as Ayden hauls me backwards.

"What... the... fuck... is... going... on?" Garrett pants as Shaun, Simon and Marcus catch up.

"I called Jared's phone," I explain as Ayden releases me, and I turn to them. "Mike answered. He has Jared, and I think he's hurting him. He said if the firefighters don't get here in time, then Jared will be overcooked."

"Fuuuck!" Marcus yells, clawing at his hair.

"We can't wait for the fire trucks, man. They still haven't arrived yet." Simon's normally humoured voice sounds frantic.

"Fuck this!" Garrett hisses, stepping forward, nearly tearing the door off the hinges.

Thick smoke plumes out, and without even thinking twice, Garrett leaps down onto the floor and crawls into the smoke-filled passage.

"Wait for me!" Marcus cries before joining Garrett.

"Fuck!" Ayden growls, his teeth clenching together and his fists clamped so tight that I fear his bones may pierce through his skin at any moment.

"I'm going in, too. Stay here with Lex." Shaun instructs before opening the door and diving into the thick smoke.

"Wait for me," Simon calls and follows in behind him.

"Ahhhh!" Ayden roars, "I'll fucking kill him if anything happens to Marcus while he's in there trying to find Jared!"

I've only ever seen Ayden this angry once. The day he told me to leave him alone after the drug episode at Muz's party. He's so worried for his cousin right now, and I want to cry harder, but I hold back. Now's not the time for tears. Now is the time to fight.

"We should go in there, too. They might need our help." I urge Ayden, and his expression turns perplexed.

"Hey, you kids need to come back to the oval!" Mr Foster's voice bellows across the quad.

"Marcus, Garrett, Shaun and Simon have gone in there to find Jared." I cry, hoping Mr Foster can hear as he continues across the quad. "I think my brother attacked him and set the fire."

"What?" Mr Foster reaches us, halting as his expression turns stunned while he contemplates what to do. A moment later, he puts his walkie-talkie up to his mouth. "We need the police and ambulance here ASAP!"

The doors fly open behind us, and Shaun stumbles out, coughing.

"The fires... are out." He huffs and then coughs again. "Need to... open windows to clear... the smoke."

"Fires? There was more than one?" Mr Foster asks, taking hold of Shaun's arm to pull him away from the door.

"Trash cans... About ten of them were on.... fire." Shaun sucks in air, his chest heaving as he does.

"What about Jared?"

I don't care about the fire. I just care about Jared and the others. They need to be okay. Please tell me they are okay.

"Haven't found him yet." Shaun puffs.

The doors fly open again, and Garrett walks out looking like some kind of demon with smoke rising off his clothes. He has some sort of mask on that he must have found in the building, and he drags it off, sucking in the fresh air outside.

"I put the fires out with the fire extinguisher. Marcus and Simon are opening all the windows."

"Jared? Where is Jared?" I'm about ready to melt down, so Ayden hugs me to him.

Garrett looks at me with a sort of lost look in his eyes. "Haven't found him yet. He wasn't near the fires."

I scream!

Where is he?

As Ayden talks with Mr Foster, who relays more information through the ancient walkie-talkie device he has, I step away from them, taking my phone out to open SnapChat when I see a notification come up from Jared.

It's a picture of someone who looks beaten to a pulp, and Mike's head is visible at the edge of the picture with a grin and his thumb up.

"No," I whisper, and Ayden steps up to me again to peer down at my phone.

"Fuck!" He hisses, and Garrett takes out his phone to open the same message.

The background of the picture looks like a boys' bathroom with a urinal, and I remember that SnapMaps might have Jared's location. Opening the map, I zoom in to find him.

"He's in the boys' toilets in the stadium!" I cry and take off running.

Ayden calls out to me, frustration clear in his tone as he gives chase to try to catch me again. I hear more feet than just his behind me as I run, and when I make it across the quad, I reef open the stadium doors and power ahead towards the change rooms.

This time when Ayden calls my name, it echoes off the walls, as do our pounding feet. Reaching the boys' change rooms, I barge in and move past the lockers, skidding to a stop as I enter the toilet section.

There...

On the floor...

Lying halfway out of the last stall...

Is someone's beaten body.

"Jared!" I cry, launching myself towards him. Skidding across the tiled floor, I come to kneel by his side as I take in the hair that is Jared's and the uniform that is Jared's and the face that doesn't resemble Jared. This face resembles a blood-covered swollen mass that has eyelashes and a nose.

"Shit! Is he breathing?" Garrett hisses from behind me, and Ayden drops to the floor on the other side of Jared and checks for his pulse.

"Get an ambulance here now!" Mr Foster yells somewhere behind me.

"He has a pulse!" Ayden calls, and I sob uncontrollably.

Chaos sounds behind me as the room fills with other teachers and the rest of my pack. All I can do is look through tear-blurred eyes at my childhood friend as he struggles to suck in air. I find his hand and gently wrap mine over it, scared if I lift it or squeeze it, that it might break.

There's no sign of Mike, but the fucker left something behind for me. Stuck to the stall door by a piece of chewing gum is another note.

One down, Ali.
How many more have to suffer for you?

Twenty-Three

Jared's mum sits on the other side of the hospital bed, holding on to Jared's hand as she sobs. I can't look at her as I sit across from her, holding his other hand, knowing he is here, severely beaten because of me.

Potent drugs are being pumped through his bloodstream to keep him comfortable while his body tries to heal. The drugs won't do anything for him after his injuries heal, though, because the real wounds can't be seen. They are invisible, and the only person who will see them is Jared. He will wake every day to those demons that will give him flashbacks and remind him of the time he nearly lost his life. All because of a blonde-haired girl who chose another guy over him, and because he was a decent, caring guy, she got him tangled up in her mess.

I can't let this happen again.

First, it was Val, and now it's Jared.

Who else has to suffer because of me?

When my phone vibrates with an incoming call, I stand quietly to go out in the corridor so I don't disturb

Jared's mum. I pass the police officer who has been stationed outside Jared's hospital room and walk down the passage a little as I glance at the number calling. It's a number I don't recognise, but I quietly answer it in case it's important.

"Hello?"

"Alexis, it's your dad. Don't hang up!"

I freeze, stunned to hear my dad's voice, and his audacity to demand that I not hang up.

"What do you want?" I hiss through my teeth, turning to face the other direction so the police officer can't see my face.

"The file Alexis. Get me the file, and all this will be over."

"All of what will be over?" I ask.

"I'll make Mike stop if you get me the file." Bile rises in my throat at his words.

What type of sick father orders his son to attack and molest his sister?

Oh yeah, the kind that forces his son to do those things to his step mum.

"You're a sick fuck! Mum told me everything, Dad. I know what you've been doing to her for years. What you made Mike do. You will *never* get your hands on the file. We will never hand it over to you. Ever!"

"Listen here, you little bitch! If you don't hand it over, I will make sure Mike fucks with every one of your friends and their families before he finishes with you! How's the Crowley boy, anyway? I heard Mike got him good."

"I hate you!" I hiss, and my dad hisses back.

"Just hand the fucking file over, and this will all end." My dad's growl is filled with hatred and disgust.

"You will never get the file. Go fuck yourself!" My voice is loud, and when I glance up, I see I've caught the attention of a nurse and the police officer.

I hang up before I can hear his response, and a moment later, my phone buzzes with another incoming call from the same number. I let it ring out and then text the number to Jason. Maybe he can locate my dad that way?

"Lex." Ayden's voice carries to me from down the hall, and I glance up to see him walking my way with Garrett.

"Where are the others?" I take the bottle of water Ayden hands me when he reaches me.

"Footy training. Coach still wanted them to come tonight. Said it would take their mind off things for a while. It's the last training session before the grand final on Saturday." Garrett answers, looking grim.

I nod in understanding and take the lid off the water, gulping it down.

"Why are you out in the hall?" Ayden asks, hooking his finger with my pinky as he steps closer.

"My dad called, still looking for the file. Fucker knows what Mike did to Jared, too." I take a few seconds to breathe through my anger. "I sent Jason the number my dad called from. If they can locate my dad that way somehow, I'm pretty fucking sure they'll find Mike with him."

Ayden sighs, pulling me to his chest, and I wrap my arms around his waist, hanging on for dear life. I feel like a part of me died inside today when I saw Jared lying on that bathroom floor. He didn't deserve what happened. Just like Val, he's being punished for being associated with me.

I want to run far from here and let Mike follow me so he isn't near my friends, my family. I'd do it too if I wasn't sure Ayden would follow me and probably get himself killed for it. As much as I want to tell them all to leave me alone so they don't get hurt, I know they won't. I know they will continue to show up and protect me as much as they can before they even consider walking away.

I love them all for that, so the least I can do is stay and face this with them.

"Um, Lex. I know it's not great timing or anything, but it's my sister's birthday today, and since you still have to eat, I thought you might want to still come over for dinner." Garrett, the tall brute that looks like he could snap a tree trunk with his glare, looks shy and unsure as he speaks, and I pull back from Ayden.

"It's probably not a good idea tonight. I should stay here with Jared," I say regretfully, but Ayden shakes his head.

"Actually, I think it's a great idea, Lex." Ayden gives my pinky a tug. "My mum said Jared has been sedated for the night, so there's nothing you can do for him tonight, and a birthday dinner might be the perfect thing to keep your mind off things for a while."

"I don't know." I hesitate, looking back towards Jared's hospital room.

Garrett's phone rings then, and he steps away to answer it, walking down the hall.

"Hey." Ayden's warm fingers stroke my hair behind my ear, which is probably a hot mess after I pulled my ponytail out earlier. It was giving me a headache. "Jared will be alright. He's tough. He'll get through this, Lex."

"He's hurt because of me." My bottom lip wobbles and I fight back tears, sick of them wetting my cheeks.

"You can't think like that. He would do anything for you. You know that. Fuck, even *I* know that. Even though I kinda hate it. He adores you, and as long as he keeps his feelings for you to himself, he and I won't have a problem."

I can't help but grin, and Ayden smiles back, running his fingers along my jaw.

"You know, I've been trying to deal with Crowley's obsession with you, and I'd like to think I'm being okay about it, but do I have to worry about Cole too? Is this birthday dinner more than a birthday dinner to him?" Using Jared's and Garrett's surnames, Ayden brushes his fingers down my neck and over my collarbone. I know what he's doing. He's trying to distract me, and fuck, it's working.

I shake my head, smirking. "Garrett is harmless. We are nothing more than family."

Ayden's eyes squint as he looks over my shoulder to where Garrett walked off to.

"Does he know that?"

"Yes, Ayden, he knows. His sisters kinda love me after I went to his house for dinner a couple of weeks ago."

His brows shoot up. "You went to his house for dinner? Were the other guys with you?"

I shake my head.

"So, it was a date?"

"What?" I screech, pulling away from him with a frown.

"You went on a date with Garrett to have dinner at his house." Ayden's eyes darken, and his face hardens.

"It was no date, Ayden. It was him trying to get my mind off stuff because he saw I was struggling. And you know what? It worked. We went to his house, and I spent more time with his sisters and mum than I did with him. I helped them with their homework. His mum taught me how to cook spaghetti, which is a fuck load more than my mum ever did. It was a nice night, and for that entire time, I barely thought about what was troubling me."

"Which was?" he asks with a frown, drawing his dark brows together.

I can't stop the tears then. They pop free like they've been sitting in wait. "You," I whisper, and Ayden's face falls. "My broken heart."

I get no more words out before his lips press to mine, and he claims me, heart and soul. My hands claw into his hair, and his hands fall to my arse before a throat clears nearby, and we're reminded that we're standing in the middle of the damn corridor in the hospital.

"Uh, my mum is on her way to get me. Will you come for dinner, Lexi?" Garrett asks from beside us, and when I look at him, I can see the smirk he's trying to hide.

Glancing back at Ayden, he smiles and nods. "You should go. It'll be good for you."

"What about you?"

"Mum finishes her shift at seven, so I'll hang around here and keep an eye on Jared until then. Call me when you're finished at Garrett's. I'll talk Mum into letting me take the car to come pick you up."

"Okay." I grin, liking the sound of that. "I just need to see Jared before I leave."

Garrett and Ayden nod at me, and I reluctantly leave Ayden's presence and slip back into Jared's room.

Nothing has changed. He's still sedated. His face is still unrecognisable. His mum is still sobbing by his bedside.

"I'm so sorry." My words are quiet, but Jared's mum, Janie, hears them, glancing up at me.

"Come here, honey." Janie trembles as she stands, and I slowly walk around the other side of Jared's bed to go to her. She could slap me, spit in my face, or punch me in the gut for what's happened to her son. After all, I am the reason he is here right now.

She doesn't, though. Instead, Janie reaches forward and pulls me into an embrace, giving me one of those mum hugs that Andrea does so well.

"This isn't your fault, Lexi. I can see the way you blame yourself, and you shouldn't. My boy will be okay.

I just know it. Negative thoughts have no place here. Okay?"

I nod into Janie's shoulder and chew the inside of my cheek, trying to hold back an ocean of tears.

When we part, I look down at Jared, then back to his mum.

"I'm going to go, but if he wakes up, can you please let me know? I don't care what time it is."

"Of course." Janie hugs me again, and then before I leave the room, I lean down to whisper in Jared's ear.

"I love you, Jar. Don't give up, okay?"

As I walk out of the hospital room, I realise that I've just told a guy I love him, and I haven't even told Ayden that yet. I don't love Jared the same way I love Ayden, though. It's an entirely different type of love, yet I know in my gut that I can't bear to live my life without either of them in it.

Ayden comes to me the moment I step out of Jared's room, and he sees my heartache. Taking my hand, he leads me down the passage in the other direction from Garrett, and gently pushes me against the wall before sighing and pressing his forehead against mine.

"I fucking love you, Lexi. Please don't forget that. I'll do anything for you."

Fucking hell. His words are simple, yet the raw honesty makes me want to climb him like a tree. Not because I'm a horny bitch, but because I need to be as close as I can to him. I feel like I might die if I let go right now. So much has happened, and I'm terrified I'm going to lose him and everyone else I love.

"Can we talk tonight? After I get back from Garrett's. I still haven't told you about my mum, and I really need to."

"Of course." Ayden's lip tugs up at one corner. "I'll miss you while you're with another man."

Rolling my eyes, I slap his shoulder, and he moans playfully.

"Oooh yeah, do it again, baby."

"Stop it." I push him off me, and his grin broadens.

"You love me." He tugs me close again, and I kiss him quickly before pushing him away.

As I stalk towards Garrett, I turn back and grin over my shoulder. "Maybe."

And then he shoots me a knowing wink.

Twenty-Four

Dinner at Garrett's is fun during the moments I'm able to take my mind off Jared. This time I don't have to help his sisters do their homework, but I do have to help them try to get a doll out of a box. It takes fucking ages with all the ties and bands that hold the doll in its packaging. Why the hell is it so hard?

Garrett's mum serves tacos for dinner, all while wearing a Mexican hat, and Garrett dotes on both his sisters, not just the birthday girl. I get the feeling he's like that all the time with them. The anger I sometimes see storming behind his eyes is never there when he's around his family.

After dinner, I agree to read the birthday girl a bedtime story. The concept is new to me since my parents never did this, but I've watched enough movies to have a general idea of how it works, so I try to change my voice for different characters and hope I'm not a boring bedtime story reader. Britney smiles and giggles through the story, and I enjoy it more than I thought I would. If I ever get the chance to have my own kids one day, I will definitely do this with them.

Waiting out on the front steps for Ayden to pick me up, Garrett sits by my side in awkward silence.

"Thanks for inviting me tonight. I had a great time." I smile up at him, and he tilts his head down, smiling back at me.

"No problem. I didn't really have a choice. Britney would have murdered me in my sleep if I didn't invite you."

I laugh, my mind picturing the nine-year-old standing over her gentle giant of a brother with a knife.

"Can I ask you a personal question?"

Garrett shifts uncomfortably on the step next to me but grunts a yes.

"Where's your dad?"

The moment I ask it, I want to take it back. It's none of my damn business. What the fuck is wrong with me?

"Prison." Garrett's voice is low, his head ducked as he studies his sock covered feet.

"Oh. I'm sorry." I feel like shit for asking now. He obviously doesn't talk about his dad for a reason, so why would he want to with me?

He shakes his head. "No need to be sorry. He belongs there, although I don't think he'll be there for much longer. Apparently, the cockhead has been well behaved. I didn't think he had it in him."

"Oh." I don't know what else to say.

Turning his blue-grey eyes to me, Garrett offers me a half-grin. "You wanna know why he's in prison?"

"Ah, no. It's okay. I don't need to know." I stumble through my words, wishing I had kept my mouth shut.

"He beat up my mum one too many times. The only reason the cops got involved the last time was because I bashed him for what he did to my mum. Neighbours called the cops when we were scrapping, and because I fucked him up bad and knocked him out, he couldn't run and hide from the cops. I spent the night in the local lock-up, but the cops let me off with a warning. One of them actually whispered congratulations for hospitalising my old man. In the end, my mum revealed the abuse, and he got locked up. It didn't help his case that he was shady with other illegal shit as well. Boosted his time right up."

By the time Garrett finishes talking, my mouth has dropped open in shock.

This explains so much. His anger issues. His protectiveness. Why he keeps to himself.

"I'm sorry you had to go through that. And your mum as well. Shit, she's like the nicest lady ever. How could anyone want to hurt her?"

Garrett shrugs just as Ayden's car pulls up. "My dad's a monumental dick. He couldn't even use the excuse of being a fucking junkie or alcoholic. It's all just him. No excuse needed. He's a fuckhead who needs to stay locked up."

"Yeah, it sounds like it." I offer Garrett a warm smile and watch as he stands, brushing the dust off his backside as he does.

"Better not keep him waiting." Garrett gestures his head towards the car idling on the road. It looks like

Ayden convinced his mum to let him pick me up in Rachel's old, beat-up car.

Standing from the step, I move in front of Garrett and reach up to hug him. He awkwardly returns it, but a moment later, all awkwardness leaves his body, and he relaxes into the embrace.

"Thank you for tonight. I had a great time."

Pulling back, Garrett smiles down at me. "Thanks for coming, Lex. Not just for the girls, but for me, too. It's nice having a friend to talk to." His eyes slide from mine to the car, still waiting for me. "Is he likely to kill me for hugging you?"

"Maybe." I giggle before walking towards the car. "See you tomorrow, Gaz."

Garrett's chuckles fade as I slip into the front of the car and shut the door. I pretend I don't see the glare Ayden is giving me, but I still address it.

"Put your caveman away, Ayden. You've got nothing to be worried about."

"You hugged him." His words make me laugh, and when I take in his serious face, my shoulders drop, and I sigh.

"You have to stop this... jealousy thing."

"I'm not jealous," he growls.

"No? What are you then?"

Ayden sighs, "Okay, whatever. Maybe I'm a little jealous."

I smirk. "You have nothing to worry about. You know that, right?"

The faint glow of the dashboard lights up his face, making his ocean eyes appear brighter.

"I guess I *do* know that, but I can't seem to control myself when it comes to you, Lex."

I grin at him, and he returns it.

"Take me home and have your way with me." I tease, but he cringes.

"Uh... Simon and Marcus are staying there tonight, too. They're with your mum now, helping her set up the new tablet she got. If we go back now, we'll probably have to wait until your mum goes to bed."

"Oh. Right. Well, I guess we should go save them from my mum." I pull the seat belt across my body and click it into place. "How was Jared when you left the hospital?"

"I think it's more like we should save your mum from Simon." Ayden chuckles. "And Jared was the same. Still sedated. His mum hasn't left his side. My mum took her a dinner tray, but she didn't touch it. His dad turned up just as I was leaving. Mum said we will know more in the next forty-eight hours. Not much else we can do until then."

"I know. I guess I'm just hoping a miracle will happen and he'll wake up and tell us he's okay."

Ayden reaches out to brush the backs of his fingers over my cheek.

"You know, as much as the jealous guy in me wants to protest, I think Jared's a fortunate guy to have you and the others in his life. He's lucky you care so much, and all of you were willing to run into a fire for him."

"We would all do that for you too, you know?" Reaching up to my cheek, I press Ayden's palm against it, tilting my head into his touch, and the corners of those kissable lips head north.

"I know you would, beautiful."

"The others would too." I draw his hand back and press my lips to his palm.

"I've been a prick to them. I'm pretty sure they'd stand around and argue for a good amount of time before deciding if they're willing to risk their lives for me."

"You're wrong. I know them. They wouldn't hesitate, Ayden. And as alpha as you've been, I can see they like you." I grin. "If you break my heart, you're going to have a problem, though."

Tipping his head back in a laugh, Ayden tugs me closer to him and leans over the console to press his smiling lips to my forehead.

"I'll never be able to show my face in this town again. It's a good thing I'm never going to hurt you again." The smile drops from his face, and he turns serious again. "Do you want to go for a drive and talk before we go back to your place? You can tell me about your mum."

My shoulders drop. I hate talking. I'd prefer just to keep it all in and hope it goes away. I know that won't happen, though. I know talking *will* help.... but this is some heavy and deep shit I have to tell him. I think I'd rather keep it buried.

"Do I have to?" I ask, screwing my nose up.

Reaching out, Ayden pushes a wayward hair off my face before cupping my cheek.

"No, Lex. You don't have to. We can go back to your place if you'd prefer. I just thought you might want to since you said so earlier."

He should sound annoyed, right? Because I've been avoiding telling him about what my mum told me, and I know how much he wants me to open up to him. There's not an ounce of annoyance in his tone, though. Just sincereness, which is why I have to tell him. He's the air I breathe, after all. He needs to know what's happened. He needs to understand the history behind all of this.

"Let's go for a drive," I say, and his eyes warm, relaxing at the sides.

"Are you sure?" His thumb strokes close to my lips, and I nod, trying to ignore the flutter his actions cause. I feel like the world could burn down around us, and all I'd be thinking about is having my fill of Ayden.

Why am I always thinking about sex with him? I swear he created a monster the day I gave him my virginity. Maybe I can tell him the stuff about my mum and then have sex afterwards? I think then about what I have to tell him, and a cold invisible slap pulls me out of my sex-crazed mind. There's nothing good about what I'm going to share with him. Tonight, sex is definitely off the cards.

While my thoughts swirl, lingering on the edges of remembering all that my mum told me, Ayden drives us through town, his eyes constantly checking to see if anyone is behind us. As the inner town streets turn into cow lined paddocks, Ayden drives to the outskirts of town, turning up the dirt roads that lead to Lake Woodall.

I haven't been out this way for years. Last time I was there, I went for a picnic with Abbey's family back when we were in sixth grade.

This side of the lake is a relatively flat landscape with small beach coves, but across the other side, cliffs rise up, and on top sits the town of Woodall Ridge. It's a timber mill town with a small primary school, but older kids have to travel into Fox Pines or Redfield for secondary schooling. I heard there's a cool spot northeast of the lake with tranquil rock pools and waterfalls. It's a known hook up and party spot for those who can get rides out there and back into town.

By the time we pull up in front of the lake, the sun has set, and there's barely any light left in the sky. Daylight savings starts next month, which excites me. The thought of long warm days and balmy nights here and there brings me hope. Hope that all this mess will be over and I'll get some time to have fun with my friends. With Ayden. Maybe since he can drive, he will take me out to the rock pools.

When the car engine shuts off, Ayden unclips his seat belt and swivels in his seat to glance at our surroundings before turning those ocean blues to me. I match his action, looking beyond the car to see if there is anyone around. Satisfied that we are alone, I slowly undo my seat belt and melt into his eyes.

"I need you to fuck me first."

The low rumble that comes from Ayden is barely audible. But I hear it.

"Why?" he asks.

"Because after I let myself think about what I need to tell you, I won't be able to bring my head back. And after you hear what I have to say, I doubt you'll feel like going there with me tonight."

Ayden's brows pull together. "I don't understand."

"You will after I tell you, which is why you need to bury yourself inside me first. I need to feel you close to me, Ayden. I don't want to wait until tomorrow, or however long it will be before we can put what I have to tell you to the back of our minds."

Ayden stares at me for the longest time. His eyes dance between mine, searching for something, and when his shoulders relax, I know he's found what he's looking for—my honesty.

"Get out of the car. I like fucking you under the stars." My face instantly flushes at his words, and my mind goes back to the rooftop of his dad's apartment building.

I don't wait for him to ask me twice, and I'm out of the car in seconds.

Striding to the back of the car, Ayden opens the boot before returning to me with a blanket. He flicks it out, laying it a little away from the car, just near where the grass meets the sandy bank.

As I walk towards the blanket, I glance around the deserted area and strip off my blazer and school shirt before toeing my school shoes off and undoing my kilt to let it pool at my feet.

Grinning at me, Ayden rights the corner of the blanket, and those piercing blue eyes roam what he can see of my body in the moonlight. As his eyes devour me, goosebumps travel across my skin. All I'm standing in is my bra, knickers, and knee-high school socks.

"I never thought those school socks could be considered sexy, but I was fucking wrong." The huskiness in Ayden's voice is a telltale sign of his arousal.

Taking a few steps to get to me, Ayden's lips hover over mine before his fingers graze my lace covered nipple and pinch. It kind of hurts yet feels good at the same time, and I arch my chest towards him, wanting more.

He chuckles over my lips before claiming them, and I tug at his shirt, needing it off so I can feel his skin against mine. He gets the hint and breaks our kiss briefly to tug his shirt over his head before his lips find mine again.

Ayden's fingers sear my skin as they graze over my sides and around my back. With skill, he finds the clasp on my bra and flicks it open before tugging it free, my warm flesh pebbling in the cool evening air.

Desperate to feel him under my touch, I run my hands up his bare chest until I find his nipples hard already, needing to be touched. I tilt my head to the side, and Ayden breaks our kiss, feathering his lips over my jaw, neck, collarbone and, finally, my breasts.

A loud moan escapes me, floating up into the night sky to blend with the sounds of crickets and frogs.

Falling to his knees before me, Ayden's lips travel down past my navel, his teeth seizing the band of my knickers, and his lust-filled eyes dart up to mine. A wicked grin spreads across his sinfully beautiful face before he drags them down my legs with his teeth.

Holy shit, why is that so hot?

On cue, I feel the rush of heat between my thighs, and I see the moment Ayden notices because his grin turns downright evil as he looks back up at me.

"Someone is begging to be licked."

I can't even stop myself. I moan and lace my fingers into his hair, urging him forward to press those fucking delectable lips against the ones between my legs. His answering growl is all the warning I get before his hands grab firmly onto each globe of my arse, and he pulls me flush against his mouth, his tongue instantly sliding between my folds.

"Yes." I cry up into the night sky and bend my legs, trying to give him better access as my pussy aches to devour his tongue. I'm fucking desperate for it, and the next thing I know, Ayden is dragging me down, my back meeting the blanket before he spreads my legs wide and goes to town.

I'm ravenous. Desperate. It's almost as if I'm possessed by an animal. An animal that is primal and wants to hold his head to me so I can grind, and ride, and fuck his beautiful face. I fight hard against the urge, though, for the only reason that I might suffocate the love of my life.

"More." I pant, although I'm not sure what I want more of. I just feel like I need him to consume me.

Ayden knows exactly how to please my needy body, though, and three fingers replace his tongue, burying deep inside me.

I cry out, arching my back, loving the feel of the sting the stretch brings, mixed with my arousal. As he starts working his fingers in and out, his tongue meets my needy bud again, and I explode.

Wave after wave, I ride the orgasm, not feeling anything but the pleasure that takes away my hearing and vision for a brief moment.

When my trembling body falls limp, Ayden slips his fingers out and demands, "look at me."

I'm helpless to deny him, and my lazy eyes pry apart to watch him lick two of his fingers like they are a delicious treat.

I feel like it should be impossible for me to feel horny again after only coming seconds ago, yet here I am, watching him lick my juices off his fingers, my pussy aching for him again.

With one finger left to lick, he looks down at it and then back at me with a mischievous fucking grin.

"Your turn."

I'm confused, but only for a moment. Moving forward, Ayden hovers his finger over my mouth.

"Open."

I obey willingly, and he slides his finger slowly into my mouth, my lips wrapping around it and my tongue gliding over the surface to lick myself off him. The sound of his moan makes my pussy clench, so I hold his hand in place and keep sucking his finger until I induce another one from him.

This moan is followed by a growl, and he drags his finger from my mouth before standing up to work his pants down. I can't take my eyes off his engorged cock when it springs free. It almost looks as if the silky skin is glowing with the way it catches the moonlight.

My ogling is short-lived when he falls to his knees and lifts my shoulder off the blanket.

"Roll over."

Again, I do as he demands, and once I'm over, he slips his hand under my tummy and lifts my hips off the ground, my knees automatically moving under my body. Warm lips feather across my shoulder, and then Ayden whispers in my ear as his hand travels down to caress my arse.

"Is tonight the night, beautiful?"

"For what?" I pant like a wanton whore.

"For me to bury myself in this hole?" Ayden's fingers move to my back entrance, and I instantly tense before his chuckles dance across my skin. "No, I guess tonight isn't the night."

"I don't think any night will be the night. I've told you before. That isn't a place for things to go in. Only to go out."

Again, he chuckles and then nips my ear. "Have you already forgotten how good it felt to have my finger in there?"

"Ayden..."

"Remember how your body loved it and exploded, sucking my finger in deeper?"

I moan as his finger grazes over that forbidden entrance.

"Just imagine how good it will feel to have two fingers." This time Ayden lifts himself off me, and I peer over my shoulder to see him tear a foil wrapper open. His heated eyes find mine in the moonlight, and I watch as he rolls the condom down his hard length.

Oh, I love watching him do that.

He knows the effect he has on me, his lips tipping up in a sinful smirk as he grips my hip with one hand and takes his hard cock in his other hand, gliding the silky head teasingly over my dripping core. I'm desperate for him to enter me and push myself back against his cock, forcing his swollen head to slip just inside.

"So greedy." I hear him chuckle again before he surges in.

My back arches, and I hold myself up on my hands, revelling in the feel of him filling me. With a hand on each side of my hips, Ayden thrusts into me over and over, gaining momentum, and I spread my legs a little wider, helping his cock plunge deeper. I push back, meeting each of his thrusts, my eyes closing as I let the moans escape me, tangling with his as they float up into the dark sky.

"Fuck, you feel so good," Ayden growls, and I think I say yes. I don't know why. Maybe I'm agreeing about how it feels? Who knows and who cares because this right here is what I needed. Him and me, all inhibitions thrown out the window, and all that is left is our animalistic need.

I barely register until it's too late, the two fingers sinking into my arse, and instead of tensing in fear, I relax into it, feeling an unexplainable pleasure.

"Fuck yes, Lex." He rasps, "Take everything I give you."

As if the sensations he's milking out of me aren't already enough, he throws that dirty talk at me that I'm utterly weak for, and I'm gone. The orgasm hits like a bolt of lightning, and a sound I've never heard myself make rips from my throat right before Ayden's shouts join in.

It feels like hours before I'm able to move or speak, but I'm sure it's only minutes.

Taking care of me as always, Ayden dresses me slowly before tending to himself, and he lifts me in his arms to carry me back to his car.

Words can't describe the love I have for Ayden. The word love isn't even powerful enough to describe what it is I feel for him.

I watch as he packs up the blanket before returning to the car and presses his lips to mine, confessing his love to me again.

Unfortunately, our happy bubble bursts when I spend the next hour telling him about my mum and what my dad and Mike have put her through since I was a baby.

Twenty-Five

Ayden and I stay out longer than we planned, talking. Speaking the words out loud about the horrific things my mum was subjected to by my dad and Mike was so hard. But Ayden was patient with me and helped me stumble through the hardest parts. His jaw ticked so much through the whole thing that I was worried he was going to dislocate it.

He doesn't know my mum well, yet he looked like he was ready to kill my dad and Mike for what they did to her. That's the thing about Ayden Mitchell. He's a good guy. He might beat himself up over his past. He may have done some shady shit once upon a time, but when it comes down to it, he has morals, and he's a decent human.

Even though it was brutal to say what happened to my mum, now that Ayden knows, it feels like a weight has been lifted off my shoulders. Each day I spend with him, and each time I share another dark secret with him, I feel us getting closer. I didn't think it was possible, but it really is.

By the time we get back to my place, my mum has already gone to bed, and Marcus and Simon are playing with Simon's Nintendo Switch in the front living room. Ayden excuses himself and goes upstairs to shower in the bathroom I still won't go in, and I creep through Mum's bedroom to use her bathroom to shower.

"Hey sweetie." My mum's voice makes me jump in the dark bedroom when I try to sneak back through.

"Hey Mum. Sorry, I didn't mean to wake you." My hair is still wrapped up on top of my head in a towel, and I'm dressed in my bunny shorts and Ayden's hoodie that I've claimed as my own, which I left in her bathroom this morning.

"You didn't wake me. I couldn't sleep." My mum sits up in her bed, flicking on her bedside lamp.

"Is something wrong?" I ask, my eyes instantly looking for signs that she's high or drunk. She doesn't look either, though.

I wonder if I will always do that. Look for signs that she's under the influence.

"No, not really. I'm a bit anxious, I guess, after what Mike did today at school. It could have been you."

My eyes well up. "I wish it had been me. Jared didn't deserve to be beaten. Mike did that just because Jared and I are friends. I'm worried about who he might come after next. What if he goes after Val again?"

"Come here." My mum gestures for me to come to her bedside, so I go to her and sit on the edge, facing her. "Val is still in the city. I don't think her mum will return to Fox Pines until Mike has been caught, so please don't worry about her."

"You spoke to Shen?"

I'm surprised Shen would talk to her.

"No. She won't take my calls, but I spoke with one of the nurses." Mum takes my hand in hers as she offers me a sympathetic smile. "As for Jared and your other friends, I believe the police are putting extra shifts on, so there will be more manpower to increase patrols in the neighbourhood. It's important you don't blame yourself, Lexi, or say such things as you wish it had been you. I know you feel responsible, but none of this is your fault, and those boys love you and would do anything for you." Sighing, my mum shakes her head. "I'm still so confused about your relationships with the boys."

"Mum, I've told you before. They are like family. My very best friends. The only relationship I have that is more than that is with Ayden."

"You love him." It's not a question. It's a statement.

I shrug one shoulder, feeling my face heat. "I guess."

"You guess. Girl, you are head over heels." My mum laughs, and my smile turns into a stupid grin.

"Shhh, he doesn't know yet."

My mum's brows shoot up. "He doesn't know that you love him yet?" When I nod, she laughs. "Oh, Lexi. Of course he does. He sees the way you look at him. You don't have to say the words for him to know how you feel. He feels exactly the same way. It's as clear as day."

I groan like an embarrassed teenager. "Mum, stop."

She just laughs harder.

I tug the towel loose and let my damp blonde waves fall free as my mum calms down, and I comb my fingers through my hair.

"So, I'm going to the grand final on Saturday with Tina, but I wanted to make sure first and foremost that you won't be alone, and secondly, if you mind me going where I might run into your school friends."

Wow. This is new.

"Uh, no, I won't be alone. You know what the guys are like. They never leave me for long." I offer her a reassuring smile. "And yeah, that's totally okay with me if you go to the footy on Saturday. I hope you have fun."

"Will you be there?" she asks, and I nod.

"At some stage, I will be, I guess. The guys will kill me if I'm not there to watch them. It depends on how things are with Jared. I guess he won't be playing now because of what's happened. He's going to be pissed about that."

My mum nods. "Yes, I'm sure Jared won't be happy about that. But the main thing is that he's going to be okay."

"I hope so."

My mum offers me a warm smile, and we say our good nights before I leave her room.

When I return to the living room, my mood has plummeted again just thinking about poor Jared, so I tell the boys I'm tired, and they turn their games off while Ayden comes to join me on our makeshift bed on the floor. I bury my head into his neck, inhaling his scent and allowing it to work its magic and calm me. He holds me close and combs his fingers through my still-damp hair, pressing his lips to the top of my head every couple of minutes. We stay that way, snuggled together in the dark silence of my house, until I eventually feel his breathing even out and let myself fall into slumber.

It's around 4am when I'm woken by a noise. I bolt upright, gasping in terror, and Ayden follows, his head darting around as he listens. Then he sighs, and his shoulders relax.

"It's just the wind," he whispers, but my heart is racing too fast, and logic like a weather event isn't registering in my brain.

"Are you sure?" I whisper back, standing from the blankets on the floor to peer around the room. The front window rattles again, and I hear the wind howl as it beats against the pane of glass.

"See, it's just the wind." Ayden stands, pulling me to his chest. "Shit, Lex, I can feel your heart pounding. It's okay, beautiful. Try to calm down for me."

"Your kisses usually calm her down," Marcus mumbles into his pillow, where he's face down on the couch.

"I think that's more of a distraction." Simon chuckles from the couch along the back wall, their banter helping to relax me a little.

Rubbing my back as he holds me to his chest, I hear Ayden's voice through his chest, where my ear is pressed. "Would it make you feel better if we do another check of the house? Maybe check the security monitors?"

I nod into his chest, and he places a kiss on top of my head before releasing his hold on me and taking my hand.

Moving silently together, we check every door and window in the house before retreating to the small security closet.

Ayden pulls me down to his knee after he takes a seat on the small chair, and together we look over the monitors to check if anyone is lurking about. There's nothing outside but swaying trees and swirling leaves as the wind gusts against the house, making the whole building rattle.

"The weather is pretty bad out there." I turn away from the monitor and shift on Ayden's knee to face him.

"It is." His eyes travel over my face, and he tucks my wayward waves behind my ear. "Is my girl okay?"

I smile warmly at my guy, loving the way he looks at me like I'm the most important thing on this earth. "I think so. Sorry for freaking out."

"Don't apologise, Lex. It's not like we aren't all expecting another visit from Mike."

I nod, but then shake my head. "I hate him so much, Ayden. He's not going to stop."

"The police are closing in, Lex. And the school has been closed early for the holidays after the incident. We will lie low tomorrow, and hopefully, he gets caught."

"When did the school closure happen? I didn't know about this." I frown, and Ayden reaches up to smooth my brows back in place with his finger.

"An email went out around 7pm."

"Oh."

"Come on. Let's get you back to bed." Ayden pecks my nose, and I scrunch it up before standing as he chuckles.

Ayden and I make our way back to the living room where Simon and Marcus are snoring, and the wind is beating against the window, with light rain hitting it as well. When a flash of light streams in through the sides of the blinds, I jump, and a moment later, a loud clap of thunder shakes the house.

I can't hold in my squeal, and I practically leap on Ayden, squeezing my eyes shut.

"Is my queen scared of thunder?" Ayden mocks, and I bite his shoulder but release it just as quickly when another rumble comes.

Chuckling, Ayden manoeuvres us to the blankets on the floor and lays down, all while I hold on to him like a monkey. Once we are under the blankets, he rolls us over so he's hovering over me, and I cover my eyes with my hands, hoping to block any flashes of light.

Warm lips press against my hands, and I sneak a peek to see those ocean blues looking down at me.

"Want me to distract you from the storm?" Ayden whispers, and I grin.

"If by distract you mean fuck, then can you please take it somewhere else?" Marcus whines, and I stiffen because I thought he was asleep.

"What's wrong, Grady? Sexually frustrated because Rhys dumped your arse?" Simon remarks before ducking under his blanket to ward off the cushion Marcus tosses at his head.

"Tell me you really want to lie here all night with a boner when you witness them fuck, Hastings?" Marcus snaps, and Simon doesn't respond. "I didn't think so."

"How about you fuckers shut your mouths?" Ayden spits at them, and they stay silent.

Good choice.

Ayden settles for hugging me close, pulling the hood up on my hoodie to help me hide from the storm and telling me how cute I am until I finally fall asleep again.

By the time the sun rises hours later, warm lips pepper kisses over my neck, dragging me from sleep and instantly sending an aching need to my core.

"Fuck, I love you." Ayden's breath flutters over my ear. "I love waking up with you next to me."

I moan when his hand skims close to the ache between my legs.

Groans fill the room, but they aren't from Ayden or me.

"Quit it, would you? I've already got a raging morning boner." Simon whines and Marcus laughs.

"Woodie is in the house." Marcus teases, and he gets a taste of his own medicine when a pillow slaps into the side of his head from Simon.

"You want me to lock you outside again, Simon? It worked last time." I snicker and it's too late when I realise my mistake.

Ayden's eyes flare wide before pinning me in place.
Whoops.

I haven't told him about the porn-watching incident.

"What are you talking about?" Ayden hisses over Marcus' laughing while Simon sits up, shaking his head with a stupid grin spread across his face.

I quickly leap up from the blankets ready to avoid *that* conversation.

"I'm going to get ready to visit Jared in the hospital." I evade Ayden's glare as I rush out of the room. "Remember how I like my coffee?" I call back to who? I don't know. I'm just trying to deflect to avoid Ayden's questions.

Since school has been cancelled, we don't have to worry about rushing off. The last day of term is always useless anyway since we usually finish at lunchtime. Half the students don't even show up because they can't be bothered, or they are leaving early to go on their holiday getaways.

Abbey's family tends to head off to their holiday cabin early to beat the rush. At least I know she'll be safe if she's away from this place where Mike could get to her. I wish I could talk to her to make sure she's alright.

The other person I wish I could speak to is Rhys. Marcus has been tight-lipped about the two of them, and Simon's comment last night was the first time anyone has brought up Marcus and Rhys not being together anymore.

I pick up my phone and send Rhys a message before I get dressed for the day.

Lexi West
Hey Rhys. Can we talk, please?

I put my phone down to focus on getting dressed and decide that all I can be bothered wearing is my white trackies and my red cropped hoodie.

Scooping my hair up in a messy bun, I wash my face before applying a little mascara. My look is a mood. And that mood is, *'Can't Be Fucked'*.

When I return to the living room, Marcus is laughing, and Simon is trying to talk himself out of something as Ayden looks at him with murder in his eyes.

"What's going on?" I ask as I start folding the blankets on the floor.

"Marcus told Ayden about the porn incident," Simon whines, not taking his eyes off Ayden.

"You mean the woodie incident?" Marcus teases, throwing his head back as he laughs.

"Ayden." I step in front of him, blocking his view of Simon, who looks like he's about to piss his pants. "It was nothing."

"Nothing?" Ayden hisses and stands before me, his height making me crane my neck back as he glares at *me* this time. "Did he, or did he not, think you were leading him outside so you could relieve him of his fucking woodie?"

My lip twitches, and I have to breathe in deep through my nose to stop myself from laughing.

"Lexi," Ayden growls, and I can't fight it anymore. I laugh and laugh, clutching my tummy, and Marcus joins in. "Lexi!" Ayden yells this time, and I suck air in, trying to stifle my giggles and bite down on my bottom lip hard.

"Relax. It was harmless."

"Harmless? Jesus, do I have to worry about him too?" Ayden points over my shoulder towards Simon, and I shake my head, still grinning.

"No, Ayden. The poor guy had a stiffy because he was watching porn. Even I'd have that problem if girls could get boners."

The room falls quiet, and Ayden's nostrils flare. His eyes darken as he studies me. "You like porn?"

"What?"

I'm confused. What's happening here?

Ayden steps forward and whispers in my ear, "We haven't tried watching porn together yet."

My brows reach my hairline, and Ayden draws back to reveal a wicked grin, caving his dimples.

"Again... what?"

How did this conversation morph into this?

Marcus, Simon and Ayden laugh, so I stalk away, trying to clear my head as the boys talk about some porn star that I have no interest in hearing about.

Opening the blind on the front window, I pull the sheers back to see what damage the storm left behind. Leaves and twigs litter the front lawn, and I'm relieved that is all we have to worry about. That is, until I notice Ayden's car parked out on the curb. Something isn't right.

Curiosity has me hooked like a moth to a flame, so I open the front door and pad down the path in my bare feet. As I get closer to the old brown car, it's easy to see that the front windscreen has been smashed in. I walk over the grass and onto the road coming around the front of the car, thinking I'll see a tree branch or something that would cause the damage.

Instead, I see some sort of axe protruding from the windscreen.

"Lexi? What are you doing?" Ayden calls from the front door, but I don't answer him because my mind is racing, trying to process what I'm seeing.

This didn't happen from the storm.

Someone did this.

I move around to the driver's door and see the window has been shattered, and there, laying on the seat, is a note that I can read from where I stand.

Playtime has just begun, Ali!
Who will be next?

My heart nearly leaps out of my throat as I take a step back from the car, hearing Ayden call out to me again, this time closer. I glance down the street past Valarie's house, then up the other way and my lungs seize up at what I see.

There, down the end of the street is my dad standing on the road in the open driver's door of a white car smirking back at me. And on the other side, mimicking him is... Mike.

All consuming rage engulfs me from head to toe and I leap towards Ayden's car bonnet and pull on the axe handle, shifting it up and down, trying to dislodge it from the windscreen.

When it finally comes free, I glance back down the road to see my dad and Mike still smirking back at me.

Motherfuckers!

I run towards them, screaming like a crazy person with the axe in my hand.

"Lexi!" Ayden calls, but I don't stop.

As I get closer to the white car and the two men who have destroyed so many lives, they casually get back in the car and close the doors. The engine is already running, and the car idles forward slowly as I close the distance.

"Lexi, no!" Ayden and Marcus yell behind me, but I don't stop until I'm close enough, and I launch the axe over my head towards the white car.

It takes off fast then, the axe clipping the rear bumper before clanging to the road as my dad and Mike get away around the corner in a screech of tyres.

I scream again and take off running towards the corner, and by the time I make it, the white car is speeding off down the road.

"I HATE YOU!" I scream, my lungs on fire from the combination of running and my rage.

"Lexi!" Ayden puffs beside me. "Are you okay?"

I look at the guy I love and bite back tears because they have no place here.

"Did you see them?" I clench my teeth as I speak, and Ayden nods, stepping towards me cautiously, as if I'll attack at any moment. "They are fucking mocking me. Mocking us!"

"They are getting more game. Marcus is on the phone to the police now, Lex."

I shake my head and laugh in disgust. "The police? If they were doing their job, then those fuckers wouldn't have gotten close to the house. To your car. If they were doing their job, then Mike wouldn't have gone unnoticed and walked into the school grounds to set a fire diversion and attacked Jared! The cops aren't doing shit, Ayden!"

His lips thin, and I know he wants to argue with me, but he holds his tongue, probably because I'm so fucking angry right now.

"Did you see your car? Did you see the note? They are toying with us. Both of them!" I yell, my fists balled at my sides wanting nothing more than to use them on my dad and brother. "They are working together, and we are just sitting ducks. You should all just leave me now, so you don't get hurt!"

"Lex, come on, don't say that. None of us are leaving you." Ayden reaches for me, but I shake my head and step back.

"Look what happened to Valarie! Look what happened to Jared! What will they do to Shaun, or Garrett, or Simon? What will they do to Marcus?"

Ayden growls low in his chest when I mention his cousin.

"What will they do to you?" I whisper and nearly lose a tear, but manage to hold it back. "Don't you see Ayden? *You* will be the one they torture the most, and when they are finally done with you all, and I'm a broken shell from the heartache, they will finish what they started with my mum and me." I scoff and shake my head. "Better for me to give them what they want instead of losing all of you in the process."

"No!" Ayden roars and lurches forward, gripping my hips, and hefts me over his shoulder like the night he carried me out of the party.

"Ayden, put me down!" I scream and punch at his back.

"No!" he roars again, his hands clamped tight onto my legs as he stalks back to my house.

"Ayden, man, you should probably put her down." Simon's worried tone barely meets my ears, and my pulse rages in my ears.

"No!" Ayden roars again, sounding more and more like the caveman I always accuse him of being.

I punch him in the back again, growling and hissing like a feral cat as I try to kick my legs, and still, he doesn't put me down.

"What's going on?" My mum's voice meets my ears as Ayden bypasses her on the front path and carries me into the house.

"Fucking put me down, Ayden!"

He doesn't answer this time, and all I can see is the floor tiles pass by before he turns and stomps up the stairs. Voices begin to argue downstairs as Ayden keeps going, and I expect him to turn towards my bedroom when he reaches the top of the stairs, but he doesn't. He goes in the other direction.

My throat closes up as fear replaces my anger when he comes to a stop in front of the bathroom door.

The upstairs bathroom where Mike did unthinkable things to me.

No!

The door opens, and I panic, clawing at Ayden's back.

"No, no, no. Please, no!" I beg, but Ayden keeps going and steps into the room.

I flail like a madwoman. I scream and bellow and cry. Then my world turns the right way up, and I find myself back in the bathroom that holds all of my nightmares.

Twenty-Six

Tears burn a path down my cheeks as I charge towards the bathroom door. I don't know why I think I can get past the wall of Ayden, but I still try, running at him like a feral animal and screaming my rage.

"LET ME OUT!" My voice bounces off the walls in the small space before my mum starts banging on the other side of the door, demanding Ayden open it.

He ignores her.

"No." His voice is quiet and doesn't match the anger contorting his face as he responds to me.

My hand rears back, and I slap his face.

His nostrils flare, and his chest heaves as he works to keep control of his anger, but fuck him. How dare he bring me into this room.

"Again." He grits out between his teeth, and I scream, this time balling my fist and punching into his chest over and over. He doesn't make a move to stop me. He stands there against the bathroom door, taking everything I dish out, and I only stop when I hear my mum crying on the other side as she screams at Ayden to open the door.

Sucking in a shuddering breath, I fall to the floor in defeat and look up at Ayden through the blur of my tears.

"Why are you doing this?" I whisper, and his face softens a little.

"Tell your mum you're okay," he demands quietly.

I don't know why he won't answer my question. It just pisses me off more.

"Why did you bring me in here?" I sob, my bottom lip quivering as I speak.

Sighing, Ayden drops to his haunches in front of me and strokes my hair back off my face where it's plastered to my cheek from my tears.

"Let your mum know you're okay first. Then we'll talk."

My eyes roam over his face, trying to understand what the fuck is going on. I've stared at this face so many times. Studied it while he sleeps. Explored it with my fingertips and my lips. I've seen this face look at me with hate, anger, fear, happiness, love, pride, and a shitload of lust. His expression right now is one I haven't seen him look at me with.

It's disappointment.

"M-mum." My attempt is nothing more than a croak, so I force more volume into my voice, "MUM!"

"Good girl," Ayden whispers, and I glare at him.

I'll give him good fucking girl.

"Lexi? Honey, are you okay?" My mum sounds scared and upset.

"I'm okay."

"What on earth is going on? Why has Ayden taken you in there?"

I lift my brows at Ayden, silently asking him the same thing, but he says nothing.

"He just wants to talk to me. Can we please have some privacy?" I call, and I don't miss the way Ayden's shoulders relax a little.

"Are you sure? This is all very unusual. He was manhandling you, Lexi." My mum's words cause Ayden to flinch, and if I weren't so fucking mad right now, I would have smiled.

"It's okay, Mum. He has my handprint across his face for that. You'll see it after when we come out."

"Oh. Well, good." My mum mutters, "I'll give you ten minutes of privacy before I grab the axe off the road and bash my way through this door."

I hear the chuckles of Simon and Marcus on the other side of the door, then the squeak of the stairs as they descend down them.

I haven't taken my eyes off Ayden. Mostly because I'm trying to block out my surroundings. I don't want to look to my right and see the shower I was forced in or over my left shoulder where Mike pleasured himself. Just thinking about it has my heart racing, and the panic rises again.

"Lex, slow your breathing." Ayden gently places his hands on either side of my face and moves to sit close in front of me.

"Why?" I whisper.

"You feel that fear, Lex?"

I glare at him, but he raises his brow expectantly, waiting for an answer.

"Of course I fucking do."

"Why would you want to feel that again?" he asks, and I frown.

"What?"

"You said, and I quote, *Better for me to give them what they want instead of losing all of you in the process*." Ayden's nostrils flare again. "Why would you give up like that? Why would you let them win? Why would you willingly give them what they want and guarantee that you will feel the fear that will be worse than what you feel from coming back into this room?"

I can't speak. Tears are flowing, and my body trembles as I try to sort through my fucked up thoughts.

Can I really put myself through that fear again, knowing what they will do to me? Knowing what I'll have to endure?

"I don't want to." A sob shudders through my chest, and I suck air in trying to get control. "B-but the alternative of something happening to you is unbearable."

"Lexi, I have robbed someone, held a gun to their head for fifty bucks so I could score some drugs. I have stolen from my parents and lied to them to get my next fix. I have stood by and let people I care about, a girl I care about, do dangerous shit just because it made her happy even though I wanted to tell her to stop. I have used my fists as weapons to punch someone I blamed for my girlfriend's death, over and over, until he nearly died. I have been in some fucked up situations, Lexi. I've wanted to die, to end it all, and I nearly did. And do you know what stopped me?"

I shake my head, hating that the guy I love has endured so much in his eighteen years.

"Fear." He brushes my tears away with his thumbs as he speaks. "If I didn't feel fear, then I wouldn't be able to protect myself. The fear reminds me that I want to live, Lexi. The fear reminds me that I need to fight. So I did, and I do. I fight against myself, against the addiction, against the pull of influences and experiences until I can see that there is more to life than the rabbit hole I've been buried in." Leaning forward, Ayden presses his lips to my forehead before pulling back to capture my eyes in his. "If you're scared, if you're feeling fear, then you don't really want to give up. Sure, there are a lot of *what ifs* that could go wrong. But what if you keep fighting to stay away from Mike and your dad? What if they are caught before they have the chance to get to you again, and *you* get that chance to start to live your life the way you want? You and your mum have just found each other. You have a whole relationship to build with her. You have some fucking amazing, loyal friends." Ayden's voice drops to whisper, "And you have me."

"Ayden," I whisper, and he shakes his head.

"Don't you dare ever give up, Lexi. Ever. No matter what happens, never stop fighting. Promise me you won't give up. Promise me you will keep fighting."

I stare into his ocean blues for the longest time, taking in his words and recognising that he's right. I don't want to give up.

"I promise I won't give up, and I won't stop fighting." My words are whispered, and Ayden's shoulders drop as relief softens his face. "I get why you brought me into this room, to remind me of the fear, but surely you could have like... just had a conversation with me about it instead of going caveman?"

Ayden grins. "I have learnt very fucking quickly that when you are in *that* sort of rage, not just anger Lexi, but rage, there is no reasoning with you." His smile falls away. "It scares me how reckless you get when you're like that. The only way to protect you from yourself when you're in that head space is to try to keep you safe. I needed to get you somewhere safe, and I kinda thought that the shock factor of bringing you into this room might help to break the wall of rage consuming you to get through to you." Ayden drags his hands through his hair, shaking his head. "I'm sorry, Lex. That was pretty fucked up."

Ayden can't hide his regret now. I can see it in his eyes and the way his confidence wavers. Reaching out, I take his hands in mine as I drag my eyes from his and turn my head to look around the room. I swallow a huge lump in my throat as my eyes rake over the shower, and I close them tight as a memory engulfs me.

"Let's get you out of this room." Ayden goes to stand, but I shake my head.

"No. I need to take this bathroom back." Dragging my eyes from the shower, I turn back to Ayden. "Will you help me?"

"I'll do anything for you, Lexi." The determination in his tone tells me he speaks the truth.

"Will you take a shower with me?" My voice is small, like a mouse trying to convince itself that it's a cat. It's not very convincing.

He nods. "If that's what you want, then yes." Ayden stands and holds out his hand, which I take before he pulls me to stand against his chest.

When I go to lift Ayden's shirt, he shakes his head and lifts my chin with the gentle touch of his finger.

"Let me take care of you, beautiful."

I'm not sure what he means by that, but he lowers his head and presses his lips against mine in a sweet and gentle kiss.

Nibbling at my lips, Ayden proceeds to undress me, going slow as he removes each item. His hands caress me softly, and I fall into a relaxed state.

Once I'm standing before him naked and goosebumps spread across my skin, Ayden quickly drags his clothes off and moves to the shower to turn it on. I force myself to watch him, to look at the tiled shower as the steam rises from the fall of water.

I can do this. I am safe. I am loved. I can do this.

I repeat this mantra over and over in my head as Ayden takes my hand and leads me into the shower. His lips thin as my body quakes with trembles that I have no control over, so I offer him the smallest of smiles, letting him know that I'm okay, that I want this.

As the hot water hits my skin, Ayden closes us in the space and turns me to face him.

"Are you okay?"

I nod and lick the drops of water from my lips.

"Can I wash your body?" he asks, and I smile and nod before watching him reach to the shelf and squirt body wash into his hands. Rubbing them together, he lays his hands on each of my shoulders and glides the soap over my skin. Ayden washes one arm and then the other before his eyes fall to my chest and his hands follow. His touch is so soft yet very sensual as he works the lather down my chest and to each of my breasts.

A moan slips past my lips, and the corner of his lip quirks up, but that's the only reaction I get from him as his hands continue to wash my body. A minute later, after the lather has made its way down my tummy to just below my navel, Ayden turns me to face the wall and washes my back, travelling to each globe of my arse and down each leg. When he stands back up, he gently tugs me back against his chiselled chest and wraps his arms around my front, his hands coming to rest just below my breasts. I close my eyes as he shifts us under the stream of water to rinse off the suds.

"I'm so in love with you, Lexi." His lips brush my ear, and I turn in his arms, wanting to tell him how I feel.

"I—"

Ayden's finger presses to my lips, and he shakes his head. "You don't need to say anything." Then he claims my lips in a kiss filled with emotion and passion and promise.

Pulling back, Ayden grins down at me. "Let's get you out to your mum before she makes good on smashing her way in here."

I giggle and nod because it's a real possibility.

Shutting off the shower, Ayden dries me off and doesn't let me dress myself. Instead, he does it for me.

It's cute and sweet and I feel so cherished.

When I go to return the favour, he playfully slaps my hands away, and all I can do is watch him cover up that masterpiece with his clothes.

After I glance around the bathroom that I never thought I'd go into ever again, Ayden and I make our way downstairs hand in hand to find the others. We find them in the kitchen area, but now Garrett, Shaun, Jason and Burt have joined us, and all eyes fall to me as we enter the room.

I'm about to ask for an update on my dad and Mike, hoping they've been caught, but my words fail as my mum steps up to us, her eyes burning with anger as she slaps Ayden across his face.

Hard.

"Don't you ever manhandle my daughter again!"

"Mum!" I screech as Ayden's hand instinctively flies to his cheek, where I'm sure a red handprint is probably forming right over the one I left behind. "He was trying to help me!"

"Well, then he'd best find a new way of helping you in future, or we are going to have a problem with each other!"

Snickers sound from across the room, and I glance over my mum's shoulder to see the guys hiding their mouths behind their hands.

"Real mature." I hiss at them, but it only makes them worse.

"Ruth." Ayden gains our attention again. "Mrs West. Please accept my apology. I was only trying to stop Lexi from doing something that might hurt her. I should never have done that, though."

"Maybe not, but I should probably thank you. Lexi has a hot temper." Mum's tone changes, and I gape at her.

"Ah, I'm standing right here, you know?"

My mum drags her eyes to me. "We'll discuss this later. We have company."

Oh sure. Slap Ayden's face in front of everyone, but let's not talk about anything else while we have witnesses.

"Now that you're all here, we'd like to talk to you," Burt says, standing from the chair he was seated at by the kitchen counter.

Turning her back on us, my mum stalks across the kitchen to take a sip of her coffee as Ayden and I move further into the room, and he pulls me down to his lap after taking a seat next to Marcus at the kitchen table.

"We'd like to ask you all to stay together in one group or split into two separate groups from now on until we can catch Maxwell and Mike West. We just don't have enough manpower to watch over each of your homes at the same time, but if you're together, we can provide more protection."

"What about Jared?" I ask, and Burt glances at me.

"We have his room on police watch and will maintain that until he can join you again," Burt answers.

"So, do we have to, like, tell you when we are going somewhere? Because the grand final is tomorrow, and some of us have to play," Shaun asks, his dark hair hidden under a cap today. I can't remember ever seeing him wear a cap.

"We'll give you the names and numbers of the officers in charge of your protection each day so you can communicate with them when you're going somewhere or if you're splitting up for whatever reason. They will park outside your house or wherever you are, so you still have your own privacy." Jason looks at each of us as he speaks, and we all nod in understanding.

"What about my mum? If I'm not here with her, who will be watching her?"

My mum smiles warmly at my question before looking at Burt when he answers.

"I have been tasked with protecting your mother. When I'm not on duty, another of my colleagues will take over."

As weird as this is to have the police protecting us like this, I know it's a good thing. My dad and Mike have been getting too close. They could very well have used that splitting axe to break through the front door. Maybe next time they will. Knowing there will be eyes on the house all the time and not just with drive-bys makes me feel so much better.

"In saying all that. Do you have plans for today?" Jason stands from his seat and hitches up his belt that holds a taser and a gun. Jesus, that's hot. I wonder if his boyfriend likes him to keep his uniform on.

"Jared." Me, Marcus and Garrett all say at the same time, and Jason nods.

"Will you be at the hospital for the entire day?" he asks.

"We'll probably go back to my house this arvo and stay the night there. It's a tradition at the end of a school term." Simon grins, and the boys nod in agreement.

It is a tradition to go to Simon's on the last night of each school term. It's usually a big party, but I guess it will be more low key this time.

After a little more discussion, Andrea and Peter swing by and deliver us their seven-seater car and take the old brown car away to get the windows repaired. With Ayden being the only one who has a license, he drives us to the hospital, where we sit quietly in

Jared's room, staring at his beaten body in the bed, still sedated and unmoving.

Jared's parents leave us to spend some time with Jared, and the moment they leave his room, I climb up on the bed and lie down next to him and carefully cuddle him. Ayden doesn't protest. He doesn't even look jealous. Is he finally understanding that these guys are not a threat? I really hope so. If he just gives them a chance, he will love them as much as I do.

Twenty-Seven

After a couple of hours of nothing but a machine beeping and quiet whispers filling the room, we reluctantly leave Jared to heal, and Ayden drives us to Simon's house, where his parents are once again away on a trip.

I feel sorry for Simon. He doesn't deserve to be ignored by his parents. Luckily, he has us, and we have him. One day, when we are older, and we no longer have to look over our shoulders anymore, I picture us all living together. Maybe not in the same house, but perhaps in the same apartment complex or something. One thing is for sure. I don't want to be far from my family.

The guys set up the balls to have a game of pool, and I sit back on Simon's couch, smiling as I watch them argue about who won the last game they played.

Dragging my eyes away from them and poor Ayden as he referees the argument, I take out my phone to see a message pop up.

Rhys George

I can't talk at the moment.

I'm in the fucking family van going on a road trip with the olds.

They sprung it on us, so YAY family time. NOT!

The twins won't stop throwing stuff over the back seat, and fucking princess Charlotte is taking up two seats because she says she needs to stretch her legs. I'm taller than her! Anyway, I'll call you if I get a chance to ditch the rents.

FYI - I still love you!

Sorry for being bitchy.

It's so good to hear from Rhys. I can feel my cheeks strain with the grin that spreads over my face. And if she's going out of town, that means there's one less person around that Mike and my dad can get to.

Lexi West

Getting out of FP sounds like a good idea to me! Try to have fun with your family, and try not to kill them!!

FYI I still love you too!

Sorry if I overstepped.

xx

"What are you smiling about?" Ayden's smooth voice draws my attention away from my phone.

"Rhys replied. She's complaining about having to go on a road trip with her family. Oh, and she still loves me."

Ayden grins. "Of course she does." He holds his hand out to me. "Come for a walk with me?"

I don't even think twice about taking his hand, and he tugs me off the couch, leading me out to Simon's backyard to the pool area. We are only three weeks into spring, so it's still too cold to go swimming, but Ayden takes a seat on the edge of the pool, tugging me down with him.

I don't even have a minute to take in the scene before Ayden leans in and kisses me slowly and deeply. It's the type of kiss where everything around us instantly vanishes as if a little sound shell has descended on us. It fills me with warmth and eases my worries as I melt into his arms while he holds me tight. When we break apart, Ayden's lips are a little swollen, and I nibble on my own, feeling the slight puff to them.

"I have something for you." Ayden grins, and when my brows shoot up, he reaches into his pocket to pull out an envelope, handing it to me.

What is this? My face reddens because I'm not used to receiving gifts, but when he gestures to open the envelope, I fumble with the seal and eventually get it open. Clasping the contents, I slip it free to find two Archer 9 concert tickets with backstage passes.

"What? Is this? Really?" I blurt, unable to make a full sentence, and Ayden tips his head back, laughing. "I thought this concert sold out in, like, fifteen minutes or something?"

"Yep, it did. But MitchWave received a heap of VIP tickets, and my dad let me have two of them. The concert is next weekend, and I thought it would be a good idea to get out of Fox Pines while your brother is still lurking around." His grin is from ear to ear.

I leap on him, peppering his face with kisses and nearly toppling us into the pool. Ayden chuckles and steers my mauling into a hot make-out session that has our hands roaming over each other with desperation.

"Lex." His voice has that husky tone to it again. He's just as affected as I am. "Stay with me tonight? Just you and me in my loft."

I've been alone with Ayden before, but for some reason, his request makes me nervous. Not nervous like I don't want to. But nervous with excitement. Each day we are getting closer and closer, and I'm so irrevocably addicted to this guy that the anticipation alone of having time together is enough to make me burst.

I nod eagerly, my smile broad, which earns me another steamy lip-lock before we pull apart and make a plan to hang out with the guys for a few more hours before sneaking off—well, not sneaking off exactly. We have to organise the police protection and tell the guys where we are going, but sneaking off sounds more fun.

A brief call to my mum, and I manage to convince her to let me stay at Ayden's tonight. She confirms Burt is going to sleep on the couch, which is something I'm not sure how to feel about, but since his presence will help to protect her, I'm not going to question it.

Since Ayden hasn't had any drinks—something I realise he doesn't really do, which I'm sure has everything to do with his previous drug addiction—he drives us back to his house where we go inside to chat with Andrea, Peter, Barb and Tony who are settling in for a night of cards.

Our police tail followed us from Simon's after we confirmed our arrangements, and they park out the front of the Grady residence, which makes me feel so much better.

Once Ayden grabs an armful of snacks, we go out to his loft and lock ourselves inside. Light fills the space, and Ayden drops the snacks on the old coffee table while I look over the loft again, feeling like it's been forever since I've been here.

It smells like Ayden in here. I don't think I'm ever going to step foot outside again.

"Will you let me fuck that tight little arse of yours, Lexi?"

I spin from peering out the loft window to shoot Ayden an overly dramatic shocked expression where he lingers behind me.

"No more arse play, Ayden." I growl, and a slow wolfish grin transforms his face.

Stepping up to me, Ayden's hands land on my hips and he tugs me to him, pulling me against his chiselled body.

"You loved it, beautiful. Stop pretending you didn't."

If his grin wasn't so fucking adorable, I might be tempted to slap him for being.... well, right, but I'm going to keep that little secret to myself. For now, anyway.

"How about *I* fuck *your* arse, and we'll see if *you* like that?" My words make him jerk back in surprise, and then the deep rumble of his laughter fills the room.

Shoving him back, I move past him but don't make it far before he envelops me from behind, pressing his warm lips to my neck.

"Baby, if you want to fuck my arse, have at it."

"What!" I screech, spinning in his arms to face him. If only I could wipe that smug grin off his face. "You would let me.... me...."

"Stick your pretty little fingers in my arse? Sure. If that's what you want to do."

"OMG, no." I squeal and try to push away again, but Ayden tightens his hold on me, his belly laugh shaking both our bodies.

"You're too easy to stir up, Lex. I'm good with keeping my arse a virgin." Ayden chuckles between sentences.

"So, you haven't done that before?"

When he shakes his head, I suddenly get the urge to want to be his first. It's weird because I don't think I have any desire to stick my finger in that place, but knowing I'd be his first has me considering it.

"Come on, beautiful, let's get you naked and withering under my body."

He doesn't have to ask me twice. I strip each item of clothing off as I move towards his bed, walking backwards, and he does the same, following me, his eyes locked on mine the whole time.

By the time the back of my legs hit his bed, we are both naked, and with nowhere else to go, Ayden closes the distance, tilting my head up with his hand at my nape to kiss me in a way that promises dirty things.

I lose myself in his searing kiss, his tongue brushing against mine and demanding more. It's almost impossible to stay standing with the way my knees weaken, and when they start to shake a little, Ayden slides his lips from mine and kisses his way to my neck.

"I want you to scream for me tonight, Lex." He nibbles at my ear before peppering those magical lips down to my shoulder as his hand slides up my side and finds the swell of my breast.

"Yes," I moan, and Ayden gently grabs my chin with his other hand and tilts my head so he can meet my eyes.

"I mean it, Lexi. No being quiet tonight. No one will bother us. Tonight, I want you to let go completely."

I nod, my tongue darting out to lick my lips. "Okay. Same goes for you, though."

He gives me that fucking grin that would melt my clothes from my skin if I were wearing any. He's like a God—a God with the Devil in him.

"Deal." He growls in a primal tone before dropping his lips to my nipple. It's already pebbled because of the slight chill in the air and the fact he turns me on so much, but the moment his tongue darts out, my nipple strains hard and ready for more.

As Ayden focuses on my nipple, he drops to his knees and pulls me flush against his bare skin, his other hand drawing gentle circles on my arse. My hands rake through his hair as I watch his mouth devour my nipple, and my core flutters with need. I drop my head back, drowning in the sensation, which I didn't realise was possible from only focusing on a nipple. But there you have it. The pink pebbled magic gems fucking love the attention, and before I know it, my pussy is clenching, desperate to be filled, and my little nub wants to grind against anything Ayden has to offer.

"You like this?" Ayden mumbles over my nipple, and all I can do is moan. Loud.

"Good girl."

Oh my god, why is that so hot? I'm helpless not to push my hips forward and seek some skin on skin for my hungry little clit, and when I do, Ayden slaps my arse.

I'm momentarily stunned before my pussy pulses, and another loud moan slips free.

"Ayden," I whisper as I try to grind against his chest again, and he slaps my globe again.

My fingers tighten in his hair, and I pull him closer as I lose my inhibitions and start grinding with desperation as his tongue flicks over and over at my needy nipple, and his hand comes down harder on my arse cheek.

I explode.

It's a short climax, but intense as I practically wrap my legs around his waist, grinding it out.

"I fucking love making you come." Ayden pulls back from my nipple, and I look down at him with lust drunk eyes.

"I'm pretty fond of it myself," I say softly, not able to find my energy.

He chuckles at my comment and loosens his hold on me, pushing me back slowly to sit on the end of his bed.

"I wanna do it again. Shift your arse forward a little."

I didn't think it'd be possible for me to be ready to go again so soon, but one look into those stormy ocean eyes, and I'm already halfway there.

"Keep your eyes on me this time, Lex. Watch me tease your pretty pussy until you come."

"You need to stop talking like that, or I'm going to come before you've even touched me again."

The shit-eating grin Ayden shoots me is full of promise, and as he uses his hands to push my knees apart, opening all of my vulnerability to him, his eyes practically devour me like I'm the most delectable dessert on this earth.

"Watch me, Lexi."

How can I not? His dark hair is tousled after my fingers latched onto the strands only minutes ago. The shade of his stubble is darker, making him look older than his eighteen years. His tanned skin glows in the light with a sheen of sweat, and his lips are dark pink and puffy from his make-out session with my nipples. His face alone is that of dark desires and nocturnal emissions. Don't even get me started on that chiselled body and his cock that is very pretty, as Rhys would say.

Those things aren't the only reason I'm helpless not to look at him, to watch him.

It's the way his eyes own me. The way he looks at me like he never wants to look at anything else again. It's the way his eyes show me how much he loves me.

So I watch him. I watch as his hand slides up the inside of my thigh and his fingers glide over my aching skin to find that magical button that likes to be turned on. My mouth drops open as I pant and then bite my lip, all while my eyes stay locked on his fingers and their exploration of me.

"I can see how wet you are." His husky tone makes my pussy throb, and I start to gyrate a little, in time with his circling fingers. "I'm not going to fill you yet."

I whimper because fuck, I need him to fill me so bad.

He smirks wickedly and circles my clit faster as I use my hands on either side of me to help push myself towards his touch.

"I want to watch your pussy throb for me, Lexi. I want to see that wetness build and seep out of you."

"Yes." I pant, grinding my pussy harder and faster as he circles.

"Then, I'm going to drink you dry."

My orgasm hits hard. Wave after wave, I scream and try to keep my eyes on him, just as he asked. Then, before I've even finished riding it out, he growls with primal need, and his lips lock on to my pussy as he starts to suck my wetness into his mouth.

Another flutter of need pulses through me, and he grabs my hips, dragging me against his face, not relenting on making good on what he said he wanted to do.

He drinks me dry.

Well, not really dry. I feel like I'm constantly wet when he's around.

I'm panting. Puffing. Moaning from the sheer pleasure he milks from me. He already knows my body so well. Knows just how to give me what I need.

I'm never going to tire of him.

When he draws back, his tongue darts out to lick me from his lips, his chin glistening with my juices. I reach forward and pull him to me, kissing him hard, before running my tongue over his stubbled chin to taste myself.

"You're so hot, Lexi West." He smirks at me. "I can't get enough of you."

I grin, cupping his face as we look into each other's eyes with our foreheads pressed together. "Good, because I need your cock inside me."

He chuckles. "So fucking greedy, aren't you?"

Pulling back, I give him a cheesy grin and nod before I go to move back further onto the bed, but Ayden stops me with two firm hands gripping my hips.

"Stay right there, beautiful."

He leans over to pick up something off the floor, and then I see the foil packet in his hand.

"No."

Ayden's ocean blues pin me in place as he frowns. "No?"

"We don't need to use condoms, Ayden. I'm on the pill, remember? I want to feel you. *All* of you."

His face flares in excitement and a wolfish grin tugs at his lips before he tosses the condom packet over his shoulder. Tugging me closer as he stands, Ayden presses me back against the bed and lifts my hips to meet his hard cock.

We both moan as his engorged head glides through my folds, and he braces himself over me with one hand as he uses the other to guide himself inside me. The stretch of my inner walls sends sweet pleasure through me, and my eyes roll in the back of my head as he sinks into me as far as he can go.

"Lexi," Ayden pants, "You feel so good. I want to stay inside you forever."

Sounds like a good idea to me. I'd tell him too if I could talk. Which I can't because he starts to rock inside me, and I'm pretty sure I forget my name.

The burning stretch of pleasured pain has me a slave to him, my body willing to serve for his pleasure. I lock my legs around him as his rocking turns to thrusts, and he has to use his other hand to help brace himself over me. His eyes travel from watching where we're joined, up my body, and to my face, locking on my lips before capturing my gaze.

"I fucking love you." His words are a rasp as he pumps, and my hands find their way down his taut back, feeling his muscles ripple as he moves. When I feel his smooth, round arse under my palms, I dig my nails in, dragging him to me harder as he thrusts.

His lips crash into mine briefly, and he swallows my moans as he rises on his arms again, slamming himself harder into me, giving us both what we need. Wild ocean eyes lock on to mine as he moves above me, and the words, *I love you*, are on my lips, but I keep them in because I don't want the first time I say it to be while we are in a sex haze.

"I want to hear you scream, Lex. Let me hear how much your body loves mine."

Ayden's words, his voice, are what sends me over the edge once again, and I'm helpless to keep my screams in. Just like under the stars last night, my body explodes in ecstasy and milks Ayden's cock as he follows me.

By the time we are done, all that's left is the sounds of our panting breaths.

My legs remain hooked at the ankles around Ayden's pelvis as he collapses on top of me, and the urge to cry hits me hard. I fight it because I don't want to be *that* girl who cries after sex.

It's a battle, though, as the emotions of the last couple of days, weeks, months threaten to shatter me.

More than anything, I want this nightmare with my dad and brother to be over. I want to move forward and look to a future with Ayden. A long, happy life filled with laughter, passion, and feeling safe.

Leaning down, Ayden nibbles on my earlobe, successfully pulling me out of my thoughts and back to him.

"I never want to leave this bed. Can we stay here forever?" He rasps, his eyes dancing with mischief.

"Yes," I whisper, and he flashes me a toothy grin.

"Good." Slowly, Ayden pulls out of me and rolls off the bed, walking across the room to his bathroom. His arse looks fucking hot as he moves, giving me another lady boner.

Down girl!

Coming back a moment later, Ayden has a face washer and a hand towel, and he perches himself at the end of the bed, his ocean eyes still lazy with lust.

"Open."

My eyes widen, and I glance down at my nakedness and my bent-up knees that are clamped tightly together.

"What?"

"Open." He grins and then pointedly looks at my closed legs.

It's the first time in a while that we haven't used a condom. I'll admit I prefer the skin on skin so much more. No barriers. Just him and me in our rawest form. Which is also the messiest form.

I know him well enough to know he is serious right now, so I do as he asks and slowly part my legs.

"Wider," he says, his eyes dark as they take in my raw flesh, glistening with his seed.

My breath hitches, but I spread my legs wider, opening myself to him fully.

Not for the first time tonight, heat flushes up my neck and onto my cheeks as he takes in every inch of my intimate skin. Then he leans forward and presses the warm face washer to me.

I still, briefly, but relax as I feel him wiping me clean. The way he takes care of me is overwhelming, and I fucking love it.

"I love you."

Ayden stills at my words, and I want to fucking kick myself in the head for saying that while he is wiping my pussy clean.

Good job, Lexi!

"What did you say?" His voice is low, his eyes piercing.

"Sorry. Bad timing." I shake my head, embarrassed, and go to move away from him.

The face washer suddenly flies over his shoulder as he grips my hips to stop me.

"No." He shakes his head. "It's never bad timing to say that, Lex. But can you repeat it so I know I heard you right?"

Slowly, so slowly, my lips quirk up in a grin.

"I love you, Ayden."

A look I've never seen Ayden wear has me stilling. His lips are doing this weird smile thing. His dimple even makes an appearance. His eyes, though, they glass over like there are tears that want to escape.

Before I can say anything, Ayden grabs my hand, tugging me up to sit, and then he crashes his lips into mine.

Twenty-Eight

Ayden drops me home early on Saturday morning so he can take his parents' car back and head to the footy to do an early canteen duty that his aunty roped him into. With the police watching my house, we figure it's safe for me to be at home with my mum until he returns to get me before the big game later. We will only be apart for a couple of hours, but I already miss him, my addiction making itself known as I suffer withdrawal from his nearness.

Last night was a night I'll never forget. I lost count of how many times Ayden tore an orgasm from me, and even in sleep, our bodies sought each other out, and we woke twice to our bodies already seeking pleasure from each other. I will forever savour my night with Ayden and the tender moments we shared.

It was a significant night. I'm not talking about the sex, although that was fucking mind-blowing. It was significant because it feels like it cemented something inside both of us.

Commitment. Permanency. Eternity.

I don't know how to explain it, but we are closer than ever, and I know for certain that the only thing that can ever tear us apart is the end of life as we know it.

My mum is buzzing with excitement when I walk in. She's half ready for her day out at the footy, and she looks great. Her brown hair is silky and straight, and she's left it down for once. She's still wearing her nightie but excitedly shows me her outfit laid out on her bed. A blue pair of jeans that I know will hug her curves and the orange and black Fox Pines Foxes jersey that she tried on the other day when Mr Matthews was here for a session.

My mum has food storage containers lining one of the bench tops, and she explains that she wants to cook a big batch of pasta to store in the fridge so we can have quick meals to eat if we want it. It's cute that she uses that as an excuse. I'm ninety-nine percent sure she's doing it so she can feed Burt. Which just makes me wonder if he has anything to do with my mum's bubbly mood this morning.

What did they get up to last night?

Did they?

Ew! No. I'm not thinking about that.

Mum flits between the island bench and the other bench lining the wall where the stove is. I can see that her concentration is practically zero. She's either distracted, thinking of a certain police officer and can't concentrate, or she's on something.

"Mum?" My voice doesn't sink in, and my mum keeps flitting about like someone hyped up on speed.

Moving around the bench, I get in her space and stop her from moving, taking her shoulders in my hands and forcing her eyes to meet mine. Her brown eyes look into mine, not ridiculously dilated, not red, not glassy, but warm and filled with happiness.

My shoulders drop in relief as I realise she's not on anything. She's not under the influence of anything but life right now. I can't help but mirror her smile.

"What's gotten into you today?" I ask, and she grins wider.

"What? I can't be happy?"

"Of course you can. I don't suppose a particular police officer has anything to do with this happy bubble you're in right now?" I drop my hands from her shoulders, and she shrugs.

"Maybe. Maybe not."

I laugh. "Whatever, Mum. You want me to cook the pasta? I get the feeling if you try to do it right now, you'll end up burning down the house."

My mum laughs. Like full on laughs and nods. "You're right. I probably will. If you can get started on it, I'll try to refocus myself and join you."

Shaking my head, my smirk from ear to ear, I laugh and start taking out the pasta pot and other things I'll need to cook with. I fill the pot with water and light the stove, before putting the pot on the stove while my mum hums away to herself, stacking and unstacking the food storage containers on the bench, not at all focused on doing anything useful.

Once the water is nearly boiling, I pour some olive oil into the frypan and light the burner to heat it. That's when we hear the doorbell. Frowning, I turn to my mum, who is matching my frown.

"It must be Tina here to pick us up for the footy. She always used to be early for everything. I'd hoped she'd dropped that habit by now. An hour early is way too early."

"It's okay, Mum. She can come in and wait for us to get ready." I smile, and she nods, shooting me a small smile before heading to the front door.

Turning back to the stove, I pour the box of spiral pasta into the boiling water and stir it, adding a little salt. I think that's how Garrett's mum taught me.

"Lexi, your friend from school is here," my mum says, and I glance over my shoulder. "Sorry, honey, I've forgotten your name, but I'll leave you two to catch up." My mum smiles kindly and disappears from my line of sight as I take in the visitor.

Tasha fucking Pritchard is standing by my kitchen table, looking smug as fuck, as my mum walks into her bedroom and closes the door. Does she really not remember that this is Tasha, or is she playing dumb and perhaps calling someone for help right now? And how the fuck did Tasha walk up to my front door without the cops knowing?

"What do you want?" I hiss, and she just keeps grinning at me. The urge to slap that grin off her face is overwhelming.

"I feel like it's been a couple of years since I've been here. Your mum doesn't update the décor, does she? " There's the Tasha I know and hate. Smart bitch has a way with words to remind you she is better than you.

"Nah, she's been too busy trying to keep Mike from raping me."

The bitch has the nerve to flinch like I've just slapped her. Then she brings out those daggers she likes to use so often. I keep my eyes on her as I turn back to the stove, stirring the pasta. As I do, I focus my eyes on the glass splashback and pick up Tasha's reflection behind me. She's darting her head around the room and shifting nervously.

"So, are you going to tell me why you're here? Surely it's not to apologise."

With her eyes trained on my back, I watch her reflection as she steps towards the back patio door. "Pfft. As if. It'll be a cold day in hell before I ever apologise to you." She reaches up, slowly and silently flips the lock on the glass door and pushes it open a fraction.

My heart thunders in my chest because I now know *why* she is here.

I don't know what to do as I see two large, shadowed figures move past the window outside in the reflection.

Fuck, Mum, please tell me you've picked up on what's going on and called for help.

Shit! Shit! Shit!

I glance over at the food I'm cooking, the boiling water, the hot frying pan that I haven't put the minced

433

meat in yet, and the sharp butcher's knife sitting on the other side of the stove.

"Just remember, other things can be used as weapons. Just take a look around you."

Muz's words come back to me, and I suddenly see all the weapons at my disposal.

"Well, what do I owe the displeasure, Tasha? Why are you here?" I ask again, trying to keep the fear out of my voice as I watch her reflection reach through the slightly open glass door and unlock the mesh security door.

The urge to pick up the butcher's knife and throw it at Tasha's head is quickly doused when I see the two male silhouettes quietly slide the door open and start to move inside behind Tasha. My heart immediately flips and thunders in my chest, knowing that it's my dad and Mike. The two biggest monsters wanted by the police are here. Probably snuck through the backyard like Mike has done so often of late.

Now, they have been let inside the house by the bitch that is out to destroy me.

I take a steadying breath, and my pounding heart starts to slow.

This is it.

I know it is, even as my blood turns to ice in my veins.

This is the day I die *or* the day they do.

One way or another, blood will be spilled today.

If I'm going to fight and try to protect myself and my mum, then I need to stay calm. I can't panic.

Slowly, I turn to face the three people who have done nothing but torment me. I get a slither of satisfaction when my dad frowns, obviously hoping to see me looking scared. He came to the wrong fucking house to see that. I will never show him my fear again.

"Tasha, I always knew you weren't quite right in the head, but the night we followed this fuckhead," I point to Mike, "and watched him walk into your house with his herpes covered lips locked with yours, I knew you were truly a fucking headcase. I bet he tells you he'd do anything for you and that he needs you to make him feel better." When she frowns, I know I'm on the right path. "Guys like Mike will manipulate people to get what they want. And silly you, Tasha, you walked right into his trap."

"Shut up!" she screams, and Mike reaches over and grabs her face, scrunching her cheeks together.

"Shut the fuck up, or you'll get us busted."

I laugh. "See how quickly he turned on you? He doesn't love you, Tasha. He's using you."

"Bitch, I'm going to fuck you up." Mike hisses, and my dad butts in.

"Alexis. Where is your mother?"

"Mum is..." I tap my finger to my lip like I'm thinking before dropping it and glaring at him, "none of your fucking business." I snap, raising my chin in defiance and watching the red fury rise over my dad's face.

"She's in her bedroom," Tasha tells him, and he nods, not taking his eyes off me.

"I'll give you one last chance, Alexis. Tell me where the file is?" My dad has never looked more menacing to me than in this moment.

Jesus, why hadn't I realised what a monster he was sooner?

"I've told you once, and I'll tell you again, *Daddy*." I shoot him a sarcastic smirk. "Go fuck yourself."

His nostrils flare, and his fists ball by his side as he glares at me from across the room.

"You had your chance, Alexis. I'm not even sorry that it's come to this. You're just like your worthless mother." My dad's lip curls as he speaks, and then he glances at his son. "She's all yours. Do the job properly this time."

I momentarily can't breathe, my lungs seizing at my dad's words. Mike laughs when he sees the fear I can no longer hide, and my dad walks towards my mum's bedroom, not interested in a conversation with me anymore.

No!

"MUM!" I scream as loud as I can, my voice ricocheting off the walls.

It doesn't halt my dad's steps, though, and when he pushes my mum's bedroom door open, I hear her scream.

Where are the fucking police?!

I glance frantically around the room, ready to run for my mum's room, but Mike moves quickly to that end of the kitchen bench, blocking my path. He's looking a little worse for wear with his dirty blond hair longer than before and in a stringy mess. His blue eyes are dull, and his cheek is covered with a dressing to cover where my teeth sunk in during our last scuffle.

What the fuck does Tasha see in him?

"Ali, Ali, Ali. You're looking good." He nods, his cruel eyes travelling the length of my body. "Good enough to eat." Mike licks his lips, not paying Tasha any attention, and I dart my gaze back to her to see her confused expression.

Is she surprised that he basically just made a sexual comment towards his sister?

Mike clucks his tongue and rearranges his junk in his jeans. "Oh yeah, Ali. We are finally going to have all of our fun today."

Shards of ice run through my veins at his words. I forgot just how crude and sick he can be. I don't know if I can do this on my own. I need help.

Shit, where's my phone?

"Mike?" Tasha looks at him in question, clearly not understanding what is really about to happen. When he glances at her, his face turns to a sneer, like he's annoyed that she interrupted him.

"What!" he snaps.

"What fun are you talking about? You said we were just going to scare her a little. Put her in her place." Tasha speaks quietly to him as she moves closer to where he stands at the end of the bench.

Is she finally seeing through those rose-coloured glasses she wears when it comes to him?

"We will definitely put her in her place, but to do that, we have to make sure she doesn't run away screaming wolf again. Now go stand at the other end of the bench, and don't let her pass." Mike grabs Tasha by the upper arm and roughly pushes her away in the other direction.

She cries out in pain, instantly covering her arm with her hand and rubbing over the area Mike grabbed. His glare stays on her, and after a tense moment of silence, Tasha does as Mike asks and goes to stand at the other end of the kitchen bench to block my path out of the room.

The sound of something crashing against the wall in my mum's room draws my attention, and I nearly let my panic control me.

What is my dad doing to her?

As much as I don't want to know, I need to get in there and stop him.

"Today is the day, Ali. You will get everything you deserve and more." Mike snaps my attention back to him, and I watch as he slowly rounds the top end of the island bench, his menacing eyes staying locked on me. "I was going to fuck with more of your friends first. Your lover boy is certainly a temptation. It would have been as sweet as candy to fuck him up and deliver his broken body to you, but since this opportunity has arisen, I'll have my fun with you first." Mike rubs over his crotch and I don't dare look to see the bulge in his jeans. "But guess what, Ali? Your friends aren't safe. Even after I finish with you, I want you to die knowing that your friends will be next. I'm going to use your boyfriend's arse as a fuck toy."

Tasha gasps behind me, but I pay her no attention and remain faced towards Mike. Tasha may be my enemy, but she's no threat. Right now, I get the feeling she's seeing the real Mike for the first time.

As Mike moves into the space I'm in, I try to control my raging heart with slow breathing and step back a little, preparing my stance for the moment I'll retaliate.

"Oh, and let's not forget Mummy dearest. Dad won't kill her. Not yet anyway. She's easy enough to control. A little heroin, and she'll be begging us to spit roast her. She'll remain ours until she's old and wrinkly and has to be put in a nursing home because she can't even remember her own name."

"I'm going to kill you." My low growl only makes him laugh, but that's okay, arsehole. Underestimate me all you want. Today, *you* are the one that's going to die.

When the arsehole in question is about four feet away, and I can see he's about to charge me, I spring into action. Turning to the side I take hold of the large pot of boiling pasta and toss the scorching contents at him. Before the last drop has even hit his skin, his howls of pain pierce the small space, and I swing the pot and slam its underside into his face. The sizzle of his skin sounds before I see how the pot's base melts into his already blistering skin.

Mike stumbles back, shrieking like an animal getting slaughtered, and I feel hands on me from behind as Tasha grabs me, screaming for Mike.

I spin in the other direction, throwing off Tasha's momentum, and lift the hot frypan from the bench and slam the edge of it into the side of her head. She stumbles, crying out, but the blow isn't hard enough to knock her out. I have no desire to truly hurt Tasha, just Mike, but if she gets in my way, she may become collateral damage.

With both of them preoccupied, I drop the frypan and take the butcher's knife before turning to bolt out the other end of the kitchen where Tasha is no longer blocking me. I don't make it far, the hood of my jumper getting snagged, pulling me back against Mike's chest.

"You fucking bitch. I'm going to make it extra painful for what you just did!"

His hand wraps around my throat from behind, and I panic. Flailing with the knife in my hand, I try to slash him, but the way he's holding me is restricting my right arm, and I can't move it properly.

My left hand flies out as I kick my feet, no longer able to touch the floor, and the containers Mum had been sorting on the counter go flying before my fingers lock on to a large pasta bowl.

I try to scream, but Mike's hand tightens around my throat, so I rear back a little and slam the bowl against his head over my shoulder. The crunch is loud as it meets Mike's hard head, the porcelain bowl shattering on impact, and it works. Mike loses his grip, so I dart forward, desperate to get away from him.

I only make it a couple of steps before a heavy weight on my back slams me down to the tiled floor. My body expels an *oomph*. The impact of the fall knocks the wind out of me, and I struggle to get my lungs to work as Mike fumbles behind me.

In horror, I watch the butcher's knife skitter across the floor, out of my grasp. It stops mere inches from where we land, and I reach out for it, but I can't move with Mike's weight on my back.

The moment I hear a zipper lowering, I freeze.

No!

Panic sets in, and I try to thrash under him, my eyes locking on to the knife just out of my reach under one of the kitchen chairs.

"Fight me all you want, Ali. It only makes me harder." Mike hisses before I hear Tasha.

"Stop, Mike! What are you doing? This is going too far!"

Mike's weight momentarily lifts off me, and the audible sound of a slap echoes before Tasha screams. I hear her fall to the tiled floor, her sobs filling the room, so I use his distraction to shuffle forward, desperate to reach the knife. I only get as close as the chair before rough hands grab my hips from behind again.

I clasp my hands around the chair legs and drag it towards me before mustering up all of my energy and reefing myself to the side. The motion throws Mike off me enough that I can twist around and slam the chair into his head. There's a sickening crack and a grunt, but it's not enough to get him all the way off me, so I reach up above my head on the floor, wriggling like a worm on crack and manage to wrap my hands around the handle of the knife.

I don't wait a second longer. I roll over and slice the razored edge across his arm and then the side of his ribs.

Mike throws himself away from me, the action sending the knife skittering across the floor again, right under the table, out of reach. Hissing in pain, Mike's head lowers as he watches bright red blood seeping into his shirt.

Leaping up, I bolt towards the front of the house, hoping to run out the front door and get the attention of the police unit parked out front.

"You fucking bitch!" The roar of Mike's voice is right behind me, and I know I won't make it to the front door in time.

Weapons. I need more weapons.

Turning at the last second, I sprint down the short passage and through the open access door to enter the garage. Reaching the far wall, I lift a two kilogram weight plate and spin to face the door, my chest rising and falling rapidly as I struggle to breathe. The moment I see Mike's shoe step over the threshold, I frisbee the weight plate in his direction and watch in satisfaction when it smashes into the side of his head, throwing him off balance.

He shrills a howl of pain, his hand flying to his head as he falls against the wall, so while he's preoccupied, I frisbee another weight plate towards him. This time my aim is off, and the throw is weaker. The damn thing wobbles as it sails through the air, only to fall short.

He shoots me a grin, his teeth covered in blood.

"Nice try bitch." And then he charges.

Panicking, I hurl a couple more weight plates his way before trying to dodge him, but I'm too slow. Mike grabs my head, fisting both hands in my hair on either side of my face, and rears back to deliver an excruciating blow with his own head, far outdoing the headbutt I gave him last time.

My world goes black and numb.

It's a place I've been to before, but this time it doesn't seem so peaceful.

I try to fight, to scream, but nothing comes.

My body feels heavy.

It's like I'm being dragged to the bottom of the deepest ocean, and buried by the crush of the water.

I know this isn't good.

I almost wish for the peaceful bliss of being knocked out cold, because being unaware is less scary.

This time, there's a haze or a fog between me and alertness.

I can still hear things happening, although I can't make sense of the sounds.

I feel myself being moved. Maybe dragged or carried. It's hard to tell with the blanket of darkness I'm suffocating in.

My body and mind slip away, and exhaustion sends me into a dark pit briefly before a chill on my back acts like a slap in the face.

Sucking in air, I will my body to work as I recognise the cold concrete floor under my back. There's a heavy weight on top of me, right before I feel something strange.

My legs feel bare. I can feel the cold concrete on my legs, as well as my back.

Are my clothes gone?

When did that happen?

Then there's a nudge at the entrance between my legs.

No!

NO!

My eyes fly open as my body tenses, and using the only weapon I have in this moment, I clamp my teeth into Mike's bare shoulder.

"FUUUCKK!" he yells, flinging himself backwards, which gives me just enough room to slide from underneath him. "You fucking whore! Stop fighting and take what you deserve!"

Before I can get completely clear of Mike, he lurches forward and digs his fingers into my bare, intimate flesh. A place I only ever want Ayden to touch, and I cry out in pain as his nails dig into the sensitive area between my legs, and uses his grip there to drag me back towards him before baring his teeth at me and latching them on to the flesh right beside my nipple.

I scream!

I hadn't even realised I was completely naked. The blow to my head must have knocked me out worse than I thought, and now I wish I hadn't woken up.

I'm going to die in this house today, at the hands of my brother. I can't match his strength. I am physically too weak.

No, Lexi! Fight! Fight until you know he's meeting his death with you!

"Mike! Stop! What are you doing?" Tasha's pleas come from the doorway. "You told me she lied! You said you would never do this!"

"Go back in the fucking kitchen and wait for me there!" Mike booms, and I hear Tasha whimper.

"No! Tasha! Get hel—"

My words are cut off when Mike's fist slams into my cheek, and my eyes roll in the back of my head from the pain. As bad as the pain is, I push it away, trying to clear my mind and calm myself as Mike yells something back at Tasha, which I can't make out because of the ringing in my ears.

I need to stay calm.

I need to find more control, because yes, I might die here today, but so help me, so will he!

I may be physically weaker, but that doesn't mean I am weak. I can use other parts of my body as weapons, just like Muz said. I just have to be calm and outsmart Mike.

My senses kick back in on time for Mike to release his hold on one of my wrists before lifting me and slamming me back to the floor, momentarily knocking the wind out of me. Using his free hand, he lines his cock up at my entrance, and as hard as it is for me to do, I lay still, letting him think he has control.

When I feel his weight slightly shift, I rear my hips up, throwing off his attempt at entering me, and thrash and scream to make this as difficult as possible for him.

I won't be taken that easily.

"Fucking take it, bitch!"

Mike's words cause bile to rise in my throat, but I lash my free hand forward and lock my fingers onto his temple before digging my thumb into his eye.

Screaming, he lurches backwards, and I follow his movement, keeping my grip on his face and adding my other hand when it becomes free of his grip, digging into his other eye socket.

Mike's rough, callused hands latch onto my wrists, trying to pry me free, but I push my whole body forward, causing him to fall backwards. With me now on top of him, I try not to think about our naked states and push harder into his eyes until I see blood slowly seep from one.

As he howls in pain, I jump up, standing over him, readying to flee, but nails dig painfully into the bare flesh of my hip and drag like blades down my thigh, taking skin and blood with them as I struggle to get away.

Using my other leg, I throw a kick to his head, the crunch a brief satisfaction which causes him to release his grip, and I bolt out of the room. When I reach the hall that leads to the front door on the right or the kitchen and upstairs on the left, I push aside the fact I am completely naked and head towards the front door.

I need to get help!

I only make it a couple of steps before I skid to a stop and gasp a couple of metres from the man I used to call my dad. His blond hair is messed up, and his blue eyes are piercing as he blocks my path to the front entrance.

"The file, Alexis? Where is it?"

"W-where's Mum?" I risk a glance over my shoulder and notice her bedroom door open, but I can't see anything else.

"She's alive. For now." His deep voice gains my attention again, and I turn my gaze back to his. "This can all end right now if you just give me the file."

"There's no file."

His bushy brows pull together as he rakes his eyes over my naked body.

"I don't have time to waste with your lies, Alexis. Where is it?"

"You mean the money in the offshore account? The one in Mum's name? The one that only has fifty dollars left in it?" I probably shouldn't be poking the bear, yet here I am. Poking away.

"You're lying. It had millions in it." He hisses, his lip curling in disgust.

"Had, being the operative word. Now, it only has fifty dollars. Is all of this worth fifty dollars, *Daddy*?" I'm a smug bitch, and I emphasise the word I used to call him when I was little for no other reason but to get under his skin.

My breath hitches as I watch his chest rise and fall in deep pants as his face reddens, and he morphs into the same monster he taught his son how to be.

Shit.

Maybe I shouldn't have poked the bear.

A low rumble reverberates from him, and I don't wait another second. I spin on my heel and run. I make it just past the passage the leads to the garage when Mike, still completely naked and still sporting a fucking hard-on, steps out to block my path back into the kitchen, to the part of the house I last saw my mum. I have no other option as I hear my dad's polished executive shoes click quickly against the tile floor behind me. There is only one path, and it's up the stairs.

The last thing I see as I turn and take the first step is Mike as he advances on me. I scream, unable to hold in my fear as the two monsters in my nightmare chase after me. I only make it halfway up before heavy feet pound the lower steps, and my hair is reefed backwards, sending me crashing back down the stairs, where I hear the loud crack of my head on the tiles below.

This time... everything goes black.

Twenty-Nine

Like a heavy weight has me buried in a deep abyss, I struggle to pull myself free, not quite strong enough to lift it. The distant, faint sounds of someone crying gradually gets louder or closer. It's hard to tell. But I focus on it because it makes the weight pulling me down less heavy.

"M-Mike, p-please stop doing t-this! Y-you said it was a-all lies. Y-you said you would n-never do those t-things to your s-sister."

Tasha's familiar voice is what my mind grabs onto, and a moment later, my memories hit me like a tidal wave.

Tasha called in to see me. She let my dad and Mike in. My dad did something to my mum, I think. I can't be sure, but I know I haven't seen or heard from her since the crashing sounds in her bedroom. Mike has been relentless. We fought against each other. Hard. He nearly raped me on the cold floor of the garage. Someone tossed me down the stairs.... and then there's... nothing.

Willing the rest of my senses to work, I can feel softness under my back. A bed? Am I on a bed? I try focusing on my body and instantly know I'm still naked and laid out like a starfish. Again. Just like the first time Mike attacked me.

Fuck. This isn't good.

To make things worse, I feel something tight around each of my ankles and my wrists, and my mouth feels full, my tongue pressing up against something that feels like cloth.

Holy shit. He's bound and gagged me.

How am I meant to get free of this?

Fuck!

I'm going to lose. He's going to rape me and then I'm going to die.

"Stop your fucking blabbing! I'm sick of hearing your voice." Mike hisses, "Go back downstairs and wait in the kitchen. Don't you fucking move from there, or your family will be next!"

My eyes fly open as I hear Tasha cry out, and I watch Mike push her backwards through the door, her head bouncing against the wall in the passage.

Tasha is a fighter, though. I know this not just because I've gone up against her, but because her eyes lock with mine, and instead of looking scared, she shows me her strength.

Me, I'm not so tough right now, and I let Tasha see the fear in my eyes. Every fucking ounce of it. This is not the time to pretend to be strong. This is the time to admit I need help. Help from an enemy of sorts, but I get the feeling she's understanding really fucking quick that Mike is the monster the news stations have told him to be.

My connection with Tasha is cut off when Mike slams my bedroom door shut, and with that simple move, my heart goes into overdrive.

Please get help, Tasha.

"Thank fuck you're awake now," Mike rumbles. "I want you to feel everything I do to you, Ali. I want that to be the last thing you experience before you take your last breath."

I try to speak to tell him to go fuck himself, but the gag muffles my speech, and he just throws his head back, laughing.

"What's wrong, Ali? Cat got your tongue?" He laughs again like it's the funniest fucking joke.

Fucking prick!

As he approaches the bed, I keep my eyes locked on to his face and not his naked body. Coming to stop at the side of the bed, Mike digs his fingernails into my shin and drags them up my leg. I bite down onto the gag to hold in my cries of pain, but a whimper escapes right before I feel the warmth of something oozing down the side of my leg.

Blood.

"Look at my cock, Ali," Mike demands, but I disobey, keeping my eyes locked on his. "It's hard for you. I'm going to enjoy splitting you in two."

I gag, and all it does is make the sicko happy.

"Fuck yeah. I'm going to shove my cock in your mouth until you vomit all over it."

I clamp my eyes shut and picture Ayden. His chiselled face. The soft whiskers that shadow his jaw. Those adorable dimples that cave in. Those ocean eyes that see into my soul. Those lips that taste me like I'm a delectable dessert. He is my happy place. My home. Mike will never take my memories of Ayden away from me.

Something brushes over my cheek, and instinctively, my eyes fly open.

I instantly regret it.

"Look how much my cock wants you, Ali. It's fucking weeping to destroy you."

I whimper again as he uses his hand to rub the tip of his vile cock over my cheek, and then he moans as he pumps it.

The sound of a door slamming somewhere in the house has Mike pausing and looking over his shoulder at the door.

"Fuck it. Your slut of a mum must be putting up a fight." Mike takes a step back from me, frowning. His face perplexed. "I guess I'd better make sure the old man has things under control so I can finish this without being interrupted." Turning, Mike gives me his bare arse as he swings my bedroom door open and walks out of my room.

Then, I panic. I struggle against the bonds around my ankles and wrists, tugging and squirming around as tears blur my vision.

I need to get free! I need to get free!

"Lexi." Tasha's hushed voice makes me still as she tiptoes into my bedroom. "Fuck. I'm so sorry. I really didn't know." Tears are streaming down her face as she stumbles forward with my butterfly knife in her hand.

How did she get her hands on my knife? She must have found it hidden under my pillow while I was unconscious.

Flipping the knife open, she leans across my naked body and starts to cut through the binding on my right wrist. A moment later, my wrist pops free, and I feel the slightest surge of hope.

Then we both freeze as we hear Mike whistling to himself as he climbs the stairs.

"Fuck," Tasha whispers, her brown eyes practically bugging out of her head.

Moving quickly, Tasha shoves the butterfly knife into my hand and then drops to the floor, where I hear her drag her body under the bed. Knowing I need to keep playing along until I find the right moment, I shove the closed knife under the arch in my back and then throw my arm back out in the position it was before the bond was cut free, hoping Mike doesn't notice.

He doesn't.

"Oh Ali, Ali, Ali. Dad's having a fucking magnificent time with your whore of a mum. He's giving it to her good." Mike tips his head back as he wraps his hand around his cock again. "I can't wait to have my turn with her when I'm done with you. Then, I need to find Tasha. The little bitch must have run off. I gotta say, I'm not sorry about that. It's going to be fun making her watch me fuck her mum and then her dad's arse."

When I hear Tasha whimper from under the bed, I try to cover it up by screaming obscenities at Mike that don't come out because of the gag in my mouth. My muffled noises just make him laugh, which is good. It means he didn't hear Tasha.

"It's time, Ali. Let's do this," Mike growls, stroking his cock faster.

Squeezing my eyes shut to block the vile view, they fly back open a moment later when I feel the bed dip at the end as he climbs up between my spread legs. His eyes don't meet mine. They are focused solely on the flesh between my thighs. I can't hold back my tears as they stream from my eyes and down each of my temples.

The feel of Mike's bare legs against mine is almost too much to bear. My stomach rolls, and I inhale quickly through my nose, hoping to calm myself. It's no use, though. My heart is out of control. I feel cold and hot all at the same time, and my body starts quivering with the fear I didn't want to show him.

He still hasn't noticed that one of my wrists is no longer bound. It takes everything I have not to react to the feel of his naked body hovering over mine, but I have to let this go a little further. I need to have him close enough and fooled enough into thinking he is winning, so that when I strike, he won't see it coming.

Getting himself into position, looming over me with one hand holding him up, he uses the other to position himself between my legs. I gag again when I feel his head sitting right at my entrance, ready to slide in. The vileness of this is too much, and I'm sure I'm about to expel my stomach contents at any moment.

"That's it, Ali. Vomit everywhere and let me fuck you in the filth." Mike pulls my gag free and then places his other hand next to my head, now that he is lined up and in position. Then he leans down and glides his tongue up the side of my face.

Just like last time, I see an opportunity and take it before he's able to penetrate me. I bare my teeth like a feral animal and sink them into his cheek, the opposite side from last time. With all the force I can muster, I clamp down so tight that the chunk of skin rips free from his face. I spit it out, gagging as he throws his head back, howling in pain as blood spills over my face.

Moving quickly before he can get far, I use my free arm to reach under my back and pull the knife out. By the time he realises what's happening, I've already flipped it open, and I plunge it into the side of his neck.

There's screaming. Wild ferocious animalistic screaming, and after a moment of watching Mike's deer in headlights moment, I realise I'm the one making the noise.

He tries to grab for the knife, but I'm not letting go of it, and to prove the point, I twist the blade embedded in his neck like it's an apple corer, blood spraying out like a small fountain.

As he struggles to reach for the knife, his putrid body weakening, I dig it deeper, my screams never stopping, not even when he topples forward towards me.

As he falls, I pull the knife out and slam it into the side of his ribs. Gurgling noises bubble out of his throat, his mouth now next to my ear. I rip the blade free again, screaming, and plunge it into his back. I keep going over and over wherever I can stab him with my one free hand until my screams turn into cries and his gargles fall silent.

"Lexi." The sound of my name gains my rattled attention, and Tasha slowly comes into view. "Fuck!" She cries and leaps forward, trying to lift Mike off me, but it is no good.

He's dead weight.

My bedroom door flies open, nearly splintering off its hinges, causing Tasha to scream and leap back in the far corner of my room. Twisting my head past Mike's, his hair pressing into my face, I see my dad's furious face, red with rage as he stands over the bed, looking down at what I've done to his son.

"What. The. Fuck. Have. You. Done!" His bellow is loud and deep, and I swear it shakes the walls of my room. I see the moment his eyes darken even more and know I'm his next target.

He takes another step forward, and I whimper under the weight of Mike, not able to hide my fear from my dad, and just as he leans forward, he stops and darts his head towards my window.

Sirens.

My dad's face contorts with indecision for a moment before I notice him chewing the inside of his cheek.

"This isn't over!" He booms and then charges out of the room.

My eyes seek Tasha in panic, and her head darts up like she's listening for something, and then she looks back to me when we both hear a door slam.

"It's okay, Lex. Help is nearly here. It's okay. You're okay," Tasha cries, coming to the side of the bed and reaching out to me before pulling her hand back to her chest. Her tears increase until she's hysterical, her eyes roaming over my naked, lifeless brother.

The fear I felt only moments ago dissipates. A strange, sad calm washes over me, and while I still cry under the weight of Mike, I make little noise.

"I'll be back in a minute. I'll check on your mum." Tasha blubbers out through her tears, and she runs out of the room, leaving me under the crushing weight of my attacker.

The thought of Tasha leaving me alone in this room with Mike scares me momentarily before I let her words sink in and remember that my mum is somewhere in this house.

I hope she's alive. I told Dad about the account, and instead of taking his anger out on me, he left me to Mike. Which means my mum probably paid for the words I said.

As the sirens get so loud they sound like they are inside my house, my body starts to quiver, and the uncontrollable urge to fall asleep assaults me. I know that's not normal, especially with how violently my body is shaking, caught under Mike's weight and bathed in his blood. It's getting harder and harder to feel anything, though. The room is quiet. There is noise somewhere else, but not in my room. I think I can hear yelling. I don't know. My teeth are chattering together, and I let my eyes close briefly, needing something. I don't know.

Noise and light suddenly fill my bedroom as someone rushes into the room with a gun raised. My adrenaline kicks in again, and I whimper, trying to flinch back and hide from this new threat.

The gun stays aimed towards where I'm being crushed, and a moment later, a hand reaches out to check Mike's pulse.

"Clear!" the female voice calls, and then the gun lowers for me to see the face of a police officer.

Tasha comes running in and around the other side of the bed as another officer enters the room. Officer Zimora.

Jason.

A sob leaps out of my throat as I witness the horror etched across his face.

"I can't lift him off her. Help her, please!" Tasha cries, and the officers leap into motion.

"Lexi. We're going to lift him off. Okay?"

I don't nod at Jason because it's hard to move. I just keep my eyes on him, needing to keep him in my sights, scared that if he disappears, the nightmare will begin all over again.

With one officer on each side of me, they slowly lift a limp, bloodied Mike off me, and the chill in the air instantly hits my naked body, making me want to curl in on myself, but the bonds securing me to the bed keep me trapped.

"Fuck." Jason's eyes are filled with sorrow when he notices my naked body bound at my ankles and wrist. When his eyes lock on to my free hand, still clutching the butterfly knife Muz gave me, he curses again.

"Shit." Jason mutters this time, his face contorting like he's suffering physical pain, and the other officer grabs his arm, drawing his attention.

"If you're too close to this, step out, and I'll call for additional assistance," the officer says, and I have the urge to tit punch her.

He's my officer. She needs to back off!

"I'm not leaving Lexi. I'm fine!" He growls, shooting her a pointed look before she drops his arm and looks back at me.

"M-m-mum?" It's a stuttered, trembling, unrecognisable voice that I force out, but the officers hear me, and Jason speaks.

"She's downstairs in her bedroom, Lexi. She's been through an ordeal, but she's okay. Officer Reynolds is with her now."

Relief sweeps over me, knowing my mum is alive. I don't know what my dad did to her, but she's a fighter, and we will get through this together.

"Lexi. An ambulance is on the way. We are going to cut these bonds free, but first, I need you to let me take the knife." The officer goes to move her hand in the direction of where I'm still clasping the knife, but I shake my head, and she stills.

Turning my head, I look at Jason with a plea in my eyes. I don't trust anyone else, but I trust him, so hopefully, he understands my silent request.

"You want me to take the knife, Lexi?"

I nod at Jason's question, and he nods back, moving his gloved hand to mine to take the knife from my grip. Slowly, I work to loosen my hold, peeling back one finger at a time until it's sitting in my open palm.

Once Jason has it, he drops it into a clear bag, and then he works quickly with the other officer in freeing me from the binds before covering my trembling body with a blanket. As soon as I'm covered, I curl into myself and cry silently, hiding my head under the blanket.

It's done.

He's gone.

I killed Mike.

He can't hurt anyone anymore.

He can't hurt Val again.

He can't hurt Muz again.

He can't hurt Jared again.

He can't hurt my mum again.

And he will never hurt me again.

I'm not sure how long I stay curled in a ball of trembling tears before an ambulance arrives. My room remains quiet with the faint sobs of Tasha and the hushed voices of Jason and the officer, so when bustling fills my room, I know something is happening.

The blanket lifts a little, and a female paramedic glances in at me.

"Lexi, I'm Justine. I'm here to help."

"Lexi!" Another voice calls from downstairs.

That voice.

I know that voice.

It's like the call of an angel.

"Lexi!" It's getting closer. Louder.

"Lexi!" He's here.

"Ayden, stay back, mate," Jason insists.

"Fuck that! Is she okay? Lexi!" Ayden is frantic.

I hate hearing the fear in his voice, so I reach up and tug the blanket back a little, peeking out through my tear blurred vision.

Ayden stands in the doorway, frozen, his mouth quivering and tears falling from his blue eyes as shock roots him in place. His eyes dart frantically around the room, taking in the scene, and then off to the side where I think Mike's dead body must lie lifeless. Then those ocean eyes find mine.

"Fuck, no! Lexi!" His pained voice rips at my heart, and he falls to his knees beside the bed.

As if my arm weighs a ton, I use everything I have in me to slowly push my hand out of the confines of the blanket, needing Ayden's touch. His eyes leave mine briefly, studying my outstretched hand that's covered in blood, with dark red grit under my nails.

A moment later, his eyes find mine again as I peek out from under the blanket covering my head and body. His warm, gentle fingers reach out and take my hand, and then as my body recognises the love of my life, everything goes black.

Thirty

My lids flutter open to the dim light of my hospital room. Fox Pines Hospital isn't as fancy as the ones in the city, but it is familiar, which is somewhat settling. The stark white walls look more grey in this light, and in front of them, lining the room, are my friends, using each other's shoulders to sleep on.

Ayden isn't with them, though. He's right next to me, sitting in a chair with his head resting on my bed as he sleeps. He usually looks so at ease when he sleeps, but not this time. Even in sleep, he looks worried, and that worry is all for me.

Everything that happened yesterday is a blur. I remember waking up in the ambulance, but I kept falling asleep, too exhausted to keep myself awake. Ayden was with me, and he has stayed with me the whole time. My mum was frantic when she arrived at the hospital in her own ambulance. I've never seen her like that before. She practically leapt off her gurney and fought off the paramedics to get to me, and when she did, she held me so tight I thought she would squeeze the life from me. She didn't care that I was covered in blood. She kept saying sorry over and over, telling me she should have fought harder to protect me, but I saw the black eye she had. I saw the fat split lip swelling her mouth. I saw the bruising around her neck that resembles handprints. My dad's handprints. If anything, I'm sorry I didn't get to her in time to stop my dad from doing that to her.

Giving my statement of what happened was hard. Officer Zimora stayed with me for support, but it was the female officer who asked all the questions. I found out her name is Officer Fredricks, and by the end of the questioning, I kind of liked her.

I didn't know what Tasha would tell the cops, but I hoped she chose the truth. She may have been under Mike's spell, but when she realised what was really going on, she did what she could to help me.

Probably the hardest part of yesterday, besides the whole incident with Mike and my dad, was the rape kit. Jason led Ayden away and sat with him in the waiting room while Officer Fredricks wheeled my mum into the examination room in a wheelchair. They each held my hand while I cried silently through the whole thing. Even though I wasn't fully raped, they wanted to collect any DNA and record any injuries. It stung when the nurse examined me down there, where Mike had grabbed and dug his nails in. The nurse relayed that there were grazes and some mild bruising. Photos were snapped, swabs were taken, under my fingernails were even scraped clean. When it was finally over, I returned to Ayden's arms, where I stayed until I fell asleep in this hospital room surrounded by the guys, minus Jared.

Tears wet my eyes as I think over everything that happened with the realisation of how close I was to never seeing my friends again—never seeing Ayden again. Never getting a chance to have a better relationship with my mum. BUT, I *am* alive. I'm here with them all still, and that is something worth celebrating. I don't want to think about what I could have lost. Instead, I'm going to focus on all I have gained. I could never have found the courage to fight like I had without each person in this room, as well as some that aren't here with me. Jared, Rhys, Andrea and Peter. Val. Even Muz.

Glancing at the side table, I see my phone sitting on top, so I slowly lean over, careful not to wake Ayden, and grab my phone to bring up Muz's number. I hit call.

"Pretty girl?" His tired voice makes me cringe, and I pull my phone back to glance at the time. 5:21am. *Oops*.

"I did it," I whisper when I put the phone back to my ear.

"Did what?"

"Mike is dead. I did it," I whisper again, glancing at Ayden and then around the room to make sure everyone is still asleep.

"What?" Muz's tone perks up. "Mike's dead?"

"Yes," I whisper again.

"And you…"

"Yes. I did it. He can't hurt anyone again," I say.

"Fuck me." Muz sounds shocked. "Are you okay? Did he hurt you?"

"I'm okay. I fared better than he did."

"Did he... do anything..." Muz dances around the word rape, and it makes me smile that this big tough gangbanger can't say it.

"He didn't get that far." I hold my hand over the phone and my mouth like it will stop anyone else from hearing.

"Okay, good." The relief is evident in his tone. "Well done, pretty girl. You're safe now."

"So are you. And Val. And my mum. And Ayden. And my friends."

Muz chuckles weakly. "I get it." He goes quiet. "Are you sure you're okay? That's a lot to deal with *and* live with."

"I'll be fine now that he's gone. Now I can move on. We all can. Well, except my dad is still roaming around, but his time will come."

"I know your dad's time will come. And soon. All that matters is that you're okay." Muz's words have never sounded more sincere.

"I will be okay. And so will you. Right?"

"Lexi." When he says my name, I know he's serious. "For what it's worth. I'm sorry for what I did to you. To Aydo. He's a decent guy. I'm glad he found you."

"Oh..." I don't know what to say. What he did was pretty fucking shitty, but he also protected me and saved me. It's hard to hate him now.

Muz chuckles down the line and then goes into a coughing fit. Shit, is he even getting better?

"I... have... to go... pretty girl."

"Okay. Speak soon."

Muz hangs up without saying anything else, and dread fills me. He's not getting better. Is that why he didn't answer my question? Why can't they fix him?

"Mike is dead. I did it?"

Ayden's hushed voice startles me, and I jump, nearly dropping my phone.

I can't speak or move with the way his eyes grow dark in anger. He snatches up my phone and holds up the screen, raising a brow.

"Muz," I explain, and his eyes widen.

"You were just talking to Muz on the phone, and you told him that Mike is dead and that *you* did it?"

Tears burn the back of my eyes, and I drag my eyes from his intense gaze to fall on my fidgeting fingers in my lap. Why is he angry?

"Did you plan this? With Muz?" Ayden hisses quietly, and the disgust in his tone cracks my heart open.

"What?" My eyes shoot to his.

"You told Muz you killed Mike. Did you plan what happened yesterday? Lure him to you somehow?"

My own anger heats my face as I sit up taller in my bed and glare at Ayden.

"Did I lure him? What the fuck, Ayden!" I hiss, trying not to speak too loudly.

"Why would you tell Muz that you killed Mike, then?" Ayden's voice lowers, but it's still demanding, and it's pissing me off.

"Because I *did* kill Mike. I stabbed him, Ayden. Over and over until he stopped moving. Shit, I think I stabbed him even after he stopped moving." My fists clench in my lap, the need to punch something overwhelming.

Ayden sits back a little and studies me for a moment, his blue eyes travelling over every inch of my face.

"You didn't kill him, Lexi. It was self-defence," Ayden whispers, his eyes softening as they take me in.

"Self-defence or not. I killed him. I used the knife Muz gave me, and I stabbed it into Mike's flesh. I felt it slice through his skin, slide past his muscles. Hell, I even remember feeling the blade hit bone. Call it self-defence all you want. At the end of the day, Mike is dead because I stabbed him."

"You can't put that on yourself, Lex. You're not a killer. Not a murderer."

"Aren't I?" I snap. "I wanted to kill him. So many times, I thought about what it would be like to take the life from his body. Maybe I didn't lure him there yesterday. Maybe I didn't plan it. But I sure as shit did it."

"You had no choice. He was trying to rape you. He would have killed you. It was either you or him, Lexi."

"Exactly. And I chose him." I cross my arms over my chest in anger. "Tell me, Ayden. What would you say if I said I *did* lure him? What would you say if I said that I *did* plan his death? His murder? Would your feelings for me change?"

I don't know why I'm pushing this, but I feel defensive over his reaction and judgement for thinking I planned Mike's death. I study Ayden's face as he studies me, quietly thinking over his answer. When his face falls a little, the urge to cry claws at me because all of a sudden, it feels like I'm losing him.

"I'm tired," I whisper, and sink down under the blankets, turning my back on Ayden. He doesn't say anything or try to stop me, and as I close my eyes, a single tear pops free. I quickly swipe it away before it gets noticed.

I always knew it was a possibility that Ayden would change his mind about me after he got to know me better. I'm a hothead, irrational, too many skeletons in my closet type of girl. Not everyone can handle the sort of screwed up I am. I guess I'd hoped our love was stronger than the vile truth that I bear. I'd been worried about Ayden losing me if Mike had killed me, but what if I lose Ayden because I killed Mike?

I can't stop the tears then. The thought is too unbearable to consider.

The covers lift off me, and the bed dips behind me before the intoxicating scent of Ayden wraps around me at the same time his warm body does. Enveloping me from behind, Ayden slips his arm over my middle and pulls me close. Then he gently strokes my hair off my face and kisses my temple before whispering in my ear.

"I will always love you, Lexi, no matter what."

"Y-you will?" I sob.

"Yes. Always." Another warm kiss presses at my temple. "My heart belongs to you. It's yours, Lexi. Forever. I'm sorry for jumping to conclusions. Honestly, I don't think it was about what happened with Mike. I think it was more that I was jealous of you and Muz. I thought that you guys had a secret that I wasn't privy to."

My tears flow freely, like a dam has burst. I kind of want to laugh at Ayden's caveman ways. When I gain my breath, I whisper back, "I don't deserve you, Ayden."

He presses yet another kiss to my temple. "None of that talk, Lex. Sleep, beautiful. You need the rest."

Once again, like he has magical powers that control my body, I sink in closer to him and fall into a deep sleep.

By the time I rouse from sleep again, Marcus, Simon, Garrett, Shaun and Ayden are smiling and hugging each other, doing that bro hug thing, patting each other's backs. It's a strange sight to wake up to, and I pull my aching body up off the pillow to get a better look.

"What are you all hugging for?" My voice is husky, and I try to clear my throat as five pairs of eyes land on me.

"Jared's awake." Simon smiles, flashing his white teeth.

My brows shoot up. Well, I think they do. It's hard to tell with the swelling on my left eye.

"He's awake?"

"Yep. And so far, there's no sign of any brain damage." Garrett offers, coming closer to my bed, his smile from ear to ear.

"You mean any *new* brain damage. He's always had something wrong with him." Shaun teases, and the guys chuckle.

"I want to see him."

Ayden nods. "I told the nurses you would want to see him, so if it's okay with you, I got my mum to organise to put you two in a room together. Crowley is cool with it."

My smile is so big that it hurts my face, but I don't care. "Thank you."

It's about an hour later when the orderly comes to move my bed into a room with Jared. The guys trail behind my bed as we move along, going down a floor into a new wing. When I get wheeled into Jared's room, I try not to flinch at how bad the bruising and swelling still is on his face. I can't help it. I start to fucking cry again, and once my bed is all set up, I shuffle my aching body to the edge of the bed to climb off.

"What are you doing, Lex?" Ayden's hands gently grab my hips just as I slide off my bed. I'm still crying when I look up at his worried gaze.

"I need to go to him," I mutter, and Ayden sighs, glancing over his shoulder at Jared.

When he returns his eyes to me, his lips thin, but he nods and helps me take the few steps over to Jared's bed. Jared still hasn't spoken, but if the look on his face is anything to go by, he is trying to hold back his emotions.

Knowing exactly what I want to do, of course, because Ayden knows what I want even before I do, he helps lift me up on Jared's bed, and I shuffle towards Jared on my knees before bursting into uncontrollable tears and leaping at him.

His arms wrap around me, and he tugs me onto his lap, where we hug each other tight. My sobbing is met with his silent tears, and we hold on to each other for dear life, saying everything we need to in the hug because there is no way we can speak right now.

We stay that way for a while. I can't be sure how long. It's only when Ayden's voice rasps next to us that we move apart a little.

"Enjoy that hug, Crowley, because it's the last time I let my girl straddle you like that."

"Ayden." I snap, but Jared chuckles.

"Fair enough, man."

I go to pull back from Jared, but his arms tighten around me.

"Tell me you're okay, Six?"

I look into his blue eyes that are red raw around the edges and nod.

"I'm okay. I killed him for you, Jar. For Val, for Muz, for my mum. He will never hurt any of you ever again."

"I would take a trillion beatings from that fucker if it meant he couldn't get to you," Jared admits, and my lip trembles again.

"He's gone now. It's time to move forward." I offer him a small smile, and he returns it.

"That's enough. Back to bed for you." Ayden lifts me off Jared, and he reluctantly lets go of me. I can't even be mad at Ayden for getting jealous because the moment he lays me back on my bed, his lips gently press to my forehead.

As the guys settle into their new space, I lay back on the bed, feeling overwhelmingly tired again and listen to them argue about which chair they are going to sleep on tonight. Honestly, these guys are amazing. They really should go home and sleep in their own beds, yet here they are, giving Jared and me the support we need.

Ayden comes to sit next to my bed and gently strokes my hair, helping me to relax. As the guys' voices fade around me, my mind flutters back to my mum and her statement to the police. She'd asked Ayden to leave for it, and it quickly became apparent why.

Dad had beaten her and raped her. Twice. He did it because every time he came towards her with a syringe filled with heroin, she fought for her life to stop him from getting that needle anywhere near her skin.

The first time she managed to get it out of his grip and throw it across the room, so he wrestled her to the floor and raped her. The second time, which was only minutes after the first, she bit him and clawed at him, and when he dropped the syringe, she got it and pushed the plunger, squirting the contents onto her carpet. That pissed him off even more, and the beating he dealt her knocked her out. When she woke, he was just finishing up with the second rape.

The police had asked about the file my dad was after, but both Mum and I said the same thing. We didn't know what he was talking about. He was still out there somewhere, probably still pining for the fucking file for the bank account details that only has fifty dollars in it.

"Ayden?" I draw his attention. He was already looking at me as he stroked my hair, but he was lost in his own thoughts. "How did you know something had happened to me?"

"Tasha. She sent out a message blast to anyone and everyone on SnapChat."

"I took a screenshot." Shaun gets up from the chair he claimed and comes to my bedside, holding up his screen.

Tasha Pritchard
HELP! LEXI NEEDS HELP!
Please send help to her house NOW!
This is not a joke. Her brother is going to kill her!!

"Wow. How many people got that message?" I ask as Shaun pulls his phone back.

"Like, everyone. People started yelling, calling out to us, to Aydo. Things went crazy after that. We all ran, and Ayden nearly killed us twice driving from the footy grounds to your place."

"You're exaggerating." Ayden hisses, but Simon speaks up.

"You ran a fucking red light, man. Then you cut in front of traffic across a busy fucking highway."

"I had it under control." Ayden shrugs, and the guys chuckle.

"The cops were already at your place when we got there. They let Ayden in, but not the rest of us." Marcus adds as he massages the back of his neck.

"Where were the cops that were parked outside my house?" My brows knit together as I think over this. The last time I saw them was when Ayden dropped me home that morning.

"Jason and Burt are looking into that. Apparently, there was an all units required call that only *that* patrol car received. They drove to the other side of town."

A chill prickles over my skin at that news. Is there a corrupt cop helping my dad and Mike? Or does my dad wield more skills than I thought and somehow knew how to send them on a wild goose chase without the other officers knowing?

"So, how did the police know to come? Did one of you call them?"

"Nah, that was Tasha as well. After she sent the text out, she called triple zero and whispered the address to them while she was under your bed," Simon explains, and I frown.

"How do you know that?"

"I sat with Tasha when she gave the cops her statement." Simon admits and my head starts working in overdrive, going over all the details again, and as a result, a splitting headache hits me fast.

It only takes Ayden half a minute to figure out why I'm groaning, and he calls for the nurse to give me something for the pain. Whatever it is, it knocks me out good, and for a short time, my brain gets a reprieve from my nightmare.

The next time I wake, it's to hear intense whispering. Or more like a hushed argument. Slowly cracking my eyes open, I pull myself up in the bed and notice that the room has emptied out of my friends. All but Ayden, Marcus and, obviously, Jared. Huddled together, their heads are drawn close, standing next to Jared's bed in a quiet argument.

"What's going on?" My voice ceases their arguing, and three sets of eyes turn to look at me grimly. When I raise my brow in question, Ayden steps forward, but not before shooting Marcus and Jared a glare.

"What's going on?" I ask again, confused by their expressions that look almost pitying.

"I'll tell her if you want?" Jared addresses Ayden, his voice raspy from not being used.

Glancing back over his shoulder, Ayden stares at Jared for a moment before turning back to me, clearing his throat and shaking his head.

"Will someone please tell me what's happening?" My words are whispered because the guys' silence is scaring me now.

"Uh... My dad called a few minutes ago," Ayden says, turning those intense blue eyes to me. "He, uh... he got a call from Ringo."

Frowning in confusion, I glance at the three guys before focusing on Ayden again, waiting for him to spit it out.

"Lexi, I'm so sorry. Muz died about half an hour ago."

No!

The whole room spins and blurs as hot tears consume my vision.

"What? H-how? I don't understand. I was just talking to him earlier." I sob.

Ayden is on the bed with me a moment later, and Jared and Marcus join us, sitting on either side at the end. I don't know how Jared got out of his own bed so quickly, but nevertheless, he's here for me.

"The damage from the bullet was too much, and his organs had been slowly shutting down. There's nothing they could do, Lex."

"But... But... He's safe from Mike now." I make zero sense, yet Ayden still shows me comfort.

"The world is safe from Mike now. Muz was around for long enough to know that," Ayden whispers as he draws my head to his chest as I cry.

The soft rumble of Ayden's, Marcus' and Jared's voices fade into white noise as the reality of the last twenty-four hours sinks in.

Mike is dead because I drove a knife over and over into him. I still remember the sound of his gargled breaths as he drowned in his own blood. I remember the weird sensation of how it felt to sink the knife into his flesh and the scrape and crunchy feeling when it hit bone.

By my hand, I took the life of another human. I killed someone. Yes, at the time, I was trying to stop him from raping me, but I still ended a life with my own hands. Am I just as much a monster as Mike was? Like my dad is?

Bile rises in my throat, and my body heats from the inside out. I push Ayden away, scurrying to get off the bed and bolt for the small bathroom off to the side just in time to reach the toilet. I retch and retch, each action sending pain to my ribs as I empty my stomach. A cold, wet face washer brushes over the back of my neck as the violent waves ease, and Ayden's scent wraps around me, grounding me.

Guttural cries fill the room, and it takes me a moment to realise they are coming from me. I tumble back from the toilet into Ayden's chest, where he draws me close, wrapping me in his arms from behind and whispering his love for me.

My mind flutters to Muz. Bobby. His real name was Bobby Musgrove. He wasn't a great person, but he saved Val and me, so in my mind, he will always be a dark angel sent to protect us, even if it was only for a short time. I hate that he died because of me, but maybe he was happy to let go once he knew the guy who put him in that hospital was dead.

My aunt is the only other person I knew well who has died—my mum's sister, who secretly helped my mum steal from my dad years ago. I never went to her funeral, though. I've never been to a funeral at all. I'd like to go to Muz's, but he's dead because of me. His family won't want me there.

As my thoughts turn dark with self-loathing, I notice little else but Ayden's presence right up until the moment a nurse asks permission to give me something to sleep, and with a nod, I accept the injection and let the chemicals in my veins send me into a dreamless sleep.

Thirty-One

When I wake the next morning, my room is already alive with my friends' banter while my mum sits in a wheelchair by the doorway murmuring with Andrea.

"Hey, beautiful. Did you sleep okay?" Ayden's smooth voice gains my attention away from our mums. His smile is warm yet doesn't reach his eyes. He's worried. I don't need to ask what he's worried about. There's a list a mile long.

Sitting up in the lumpy hospital bed, I stretch my neck from side to side, my whole body aching like I've been hit by a bus. I'm pretty sure my face fared better than the rest of my body this time. I'm almost too scared to look at my skin underneath the white hospital gown.

I nod at Ayden and offer him a small smile. "Those drugs did their job."

"I bet they did." Ayden chuckles.

"Lexi, can you help us settle a debate?" Simon asks, bounding up to my bedside like a playful puppy.

"That depends on what your debate is about." I smile and tug out the hair tie, which is doing a lousy job of holding my blonde waves back.

"You don't need to involve Lexi. You know I'm right, Hastings. Just admit it." Shaun comes up on the other side of the bed, grinning across me to Simon.

"Nuh-uh. There is no way a bass guitarist is hotter than a lead guitarist." Simon protests, Bieber-flicking his ash-blonde hair.

"Really? That's what you are debating?" I don't know why I'm surprised when it comes to these two adorable idiots.

Ayden chuckles beside me, and when I glance at him, he shoots me a wink. Jesus, I'm still not immune to him.

"I'm pretty sure Lexi just has a thing for the pianist." Garrett teases as he comes over to join the debate.

Simon throws up his arms dramatically. "There is no fucking way a pianist is hotter than lead guitar."

"Simon! Language!" Andrea hisses from the door, and we all laugh. Well, except for Simon, who goes red.

"Sorry, Mrs Mitchell." Simon offers.

I've missed this. These guys. This banter. The lightness they bring to my life. I need this. I need them.

"What about lead vocals? They are always the hottest in a band. Which is obviously me." Shaun brushes his shoulders like he is flicking off dirt.

"You aren't in a band." I remind him.

"Semantics." His white toothy grin appears. "We've had a couple of jam sessions, which means we are a band, and obviously, I am the lead vocalist."

"Bossi, in order to be a singer, you have to be able to sing." Jared joins the debate sitting up taller in his bed next to mine.

"Ever heard of auto-tune?" Shaun shoots Jared a '*duh*' face, and everyone laughs again.

"If that's the case, then any one of us can be lead vocalist," Marcus says, coming up to stand on the other side of Jared's bed.

"Have you all looked at yourselves?" Shaun points his finger to each of the guys, and they all frown, looking at each other. "None of you are cool. Nothing about you screams rock star. Leave that stuff to the professional, will ya?"

Snickers sound around my bed, and I can't rein in my wide grin. I love these guys.

"Well, I still say lead guitarist is hotter. What do you say, Lex?" Simon asks, and all eyes turn to me.

I shake my head. "You are all idiots. Everyone knows the drummer is the hottest."

More laughter fills the room, but it's short-lived when someone clears their throat behind Simon. As Simon steps aside, my mum comes into view, and she wheels up to my bed, looking nervous.

"Can I please have a word with Lexi?" she asks everyone, but keeps her brown eyes trained on me.

The guys nod and quietly slip out of the room, leaving Ayden and me with my mum and Andrea. Jared shoots my mum a smile from his bed before he inserts his earbuds, and a moment later, we hear music as he lays back.

I'm not sure if my mum wants Ayden to leave as well, but when he slides his palm against mine, linking our fingers, my mum sees it and doesn't protest.

"We aren't going back to that house, Lexi." My mum's words are firm, yet her face looks unsure. Is she expecting me to argue with that? Because hell no, I won't. I'm not sure I can walk back in there.

"Okay." I nod, and my mum's face softens in relief. "I don't think I can go back there ever again."

"Then we won't." My mum nods, offering me a sympathetic smile.

"What will we do?"

"That's where we come in." Andrea steps forward, smiling that familiar welcoming smile of hers. "If it's okay with you, Lexi, you and your mum will stay with us until your mum can arrange a new home for you to move into."

"Oh." I glance at my mum's smiling face and then at Ayden. Satisfaction flits over his expression before it's quickly replaced with a warm smile. He's happy with this arrangement. "Um, sure. If you don't mind us invading your space again?"

"Of course not, honey. You know you are always welcome in our home, and so is Ruth." Andrea directs a smile at my mum.

"It will only be for a little while. I will find us a rental until we can figure out something more permanent. But whatever we do, Lexi, I want to make sure you feel safe." The care in my mum's tone feels foreign. Not fake. Just something I'm not used to hearing from her. The way her eyes glass over as she looks at me is different as well.

A week ago, the thought of living with my mum again made me anxious, but now it feels different. Everything feels different. I understand her more now that she told me the truth about what my dad and Mike used to do to her. I still worry about the possibility that she will relapse. Give into the call of a drink or a hit. But she seems different. Stronger than I've ever known her to be. The thing is, if she does relapse, I'll be there. I'm not going to give up on her so easily. I used to think she was just some junkie mum, but like so many addicts, there's a reason why they turn to drugs.

For my mum, it was to numb the pain of what others inflicted on her. If she's ever in a dark place where she feels the need to self-medicate, I will fight for her until she is strong enough to fight on her own again.

"Mum?" The softness in my tone draws my mum's brows together. "I'd really like that."

My mum's smile spreads wide to match mine, and she reaches out to give my hand a gentle squeeze.

Andrea takes my mum back to her room so she can get sorted to leave, and Ayden helps me to the shower so I can wash and get dressed in some clothes he had his mum bring for me. When it's time to go, I feel sad to leave Jared behind, but he is being released later today with his parents, so at least he won't have to stay in here alone again.

I ask Ayden to give me a minute, and he nods, leaving me with Jared.

"Will you be alright?" I ask Jared, and he nods.

"Will you?"

I nod back and look down at my hand as he takes it in his.

"I'm sorry about Ayden. He turns into a bit of a caveman when it comes to me."

Jared grins past his swollen lip. "I'm glad he's like that with you. It shows how much he cares about you, and it reminds me that you're not mine. I need that reminder sometimes."

My lashes flutter, and my cheeks heat at his blatant comment.

"Jar."

"It's okay. I think I'm finally coming to terms with it. You're still my Six, though, right?" Jared's hand squeezes mine, and I smile.

"I'll always be your Six. You're my dearest friend."

"I thought I was your brother?" He frowns with a smirk and then shoots me a wink.

I smile. "That too."

Leaning forward, I hug Jared, and surprisingly, he's the one who breaks it first.

"You'd better go before your caveman comes in here and beats on his chest." Jared teases, and I shake my head, grinning wide as I back away and walk out the door.

After we arrive at Ayden's, Marcus shows my mum up to the lilac bedroom, and I'm offered the couch, in which Ayden advises our mums that I'll be staying in the loft with him. I was expecting a protest, but my mum and Andrea just look at each other and start laughing as if they have a private joke.

Andrea whips up burgers for lunch, and we retreat to Ayden's loft after that, only to find several bags and a couple of boxes containing my belongings.

"I guess that was what our mums were laughing at." I grin. "They already knew we'd want to be together."

I shake my head at their cheekiness, walking over to the boxes and looking inside. I don't have many things, but it's nice to see some familiar items, like the stack of photos that used to be stuck around my dresser mirror.

"It feels like they've moved me in. I hope you're okay with this." My tone reveals my nerves, and I want to kick myself for my lack of confidence. I shouldn't be nervous around Ayden.

"I'm good with that. I never want you to leave." His voice is close behind me, so I turn to peer up into those hypnotising eyes.

"You may regret saying that after I leave my clothes all over your floor, take over your bathroom with girly stuff, and stick my pictures up everywhere."

Ayden shakes his head. "Lexi, you can paint the walls pink and put one of those frilly covers on my bed, and I still wouldn't care as long as you're here with me."

"Nawww, really?" I ask teasingly, and he smiles wider.

"Really." Ayden reaches out and grazes the backs of his fingers gently down the side of my face. "I love you, Lex."

My heart flips in my chest, and my face heats. His knowing smirk tells me he can see my blush.

"I love you too," I whisper because I don't trust my voice not to come out wobbly and emotional.

His blue eyes soften as he gazes at me before they flick to my lips.

"Can I kiss you?" His question confuses me. Why would he ask that? He should know he can kiss me whenever the hell he wants.

Studying him, I realise just how nervous *he* is right now too, and then it hits me.

We haven't kissed, not romantically, since Saturday morning when he dropped me home. That was before Mike nearly succeeded in raping me. Before I killed him.

I can't believe Ayden has stuck around through all this bullshit. Over and over, I've been assaulted in some form, and we keep coming back to this moment where the poor guy is unsure if he should touch me the way lovers do.

"Please kiss me." I don't whisper this time. The confidence flows from me easily, and he grins before that delectable tongue of his flicks out to wet his lips.

We step forward to meet each other, and his lips are gentle as they brush over mine, tasting me before deepening the kiss. It feels so good to have him close. To taste his kiss. To be wrapped in his scent. I never want to be apart from him. At least not for long.

After a minute, Ayden slows the kiss before it gets too heated. Then he breaks it softly, nipping at my bottom lip before pressing his head against mine.

"We need to talk." His words are like a cold bucket of water, and I pout.

"Do we, though? We could just skip the talking and fool around."

He chuckles, pulling back, his hands rubbing up and down my arms. "No. That's exactly what we need to talk about, Lex."

"I plead the fifth," I say seriously, and he laughs, grabbing hold of my hand.

"We've been through this. Pleading the fifth isn't an Aussie thing. You watch too many movies."

As Ayden tugs me towards his couch and not his bed, where I think we would have much more fun, I pout again.

"Is there an Aussie equivalent?" I ask in all seriousness, but Ayden shakes his head.

"I don't think so. I don't really know. But what I do know is that we need to talk about what happened and what we should and shouldn't be doing."

"Nope." I shake my head. "We don't need to talk about that at all. I'm quite happy never to bring up what happened again. Let's look forward, not back."

He wants to talk about the finer details of what Mike did to me. He knows Mike got close. He knows I have grazes.

I just want to forget it ever happened.

"Lex."

"Ayden."

"Come on. You know we need to talk about this. It's serious."

"I'm aware, Ayden." I snap, and when I see the hurt in his eyes, I sigh, dropping my head forward, wishing we weren't about to have this conversation.

"Lex, we don't have to talk about the exact details, but the doctor said there was... slight penetration." Ayden's words are strangled before he bolts up from the couch and rakes his hands through his dark hair, turning away from me.

"Ayden," I whisper and stand, taking the two steps to get to him and wrap my arms around him from behind.

"I'm sorry, Lex. The thought..." Ayden shakes his head and turns in my arms to face me.

"Don't think about it, Ayden. It will only bring you pain."

I watch as he swallows the lump in his throat, his eyes dancing between mine, nerves making him look the most vulnerable I've ever seen. "The doctor said they had to do STD testing. Doesn't that mean he... he..."

My breaths come quickly as I work myself up to say the words I don't want to say. But Ayden is right. We need to talk about this because I did need to have tests taken to check for any STDs that Mike may have passed on, and since Ayden is the guy I love, and I'm intimate with, he needs to know.

"His... bit, the top bit, kinda went in a little." Hot tears spill as I say the words, humiliation engulfing me. It isn't even a proper explanation. I can't say the right words. I can't say that the head of my brother's dick penetrated me a little. I just can't say it.

Anger fills me from head to toe at the reminder. I leap back from Ayden, bending at the waist as I grip my head tight, right before I let out a guttural scream and drop to the floor.

"Fuck, Lex. I'm sorry. I shouldn't have pushed. I'm sorry." Ayden's panicked words meet my ear as he falls to the floor with me and pulls me to his chest as I scream again.

"Ayden, what's going on?" Marcus' voice floats across the loft, but I ignore it as I cry, trying to force my memories to the back of my mind.

"It's okay. I mean, she's not okay, but she..." Ayden can't even finish, and a moment later, I feel the warmth of another body as Marcus wraps both Ayden and me in his arms.

No more words are exchanged as we stay huddled together, riding out the storm of emotions. My screams turn to excruciating tears, and eventually, the river dries up, and I find myself content in the embrace of two cousins, knowing that Marcus is giving Ayden the comfort that I can't.

Even though Mike is dead, what he did is going to linger long after the town stops talking about him and forgets the time when a monster was in their midst. Like a ghost haunting me, I'll have to endure the moments that arise in the future where I'm reminded of what he did and how he made me and the others feel.

Ayden will face this problem, too. I just hope that it's not something he thinks about every time our bodies are desperate to meet in the closest way possible.

"We need to finish the conversation." I rasp, trapped between Marcus and Ayden.

They both pull back from me at the same time, looking down at me before looking at each other. As if they have a silent conversation, Marcus nods to Ayden, places a gentle kiss on the top of my head, and leaves the loft.

I suck in a breath, mentally pulling up my big girl panties, and finish the conversation, still huddled with Ayden on the floor of his loft.

"We haven't been using protection lately because I'm on the pill, and it's safe to say we are exclusive, but given what's happened, even though the chances are low, you will need to wear condoms until I'm cleared."

Tilting his head, Ayden cups my cheek and gently strokes his thumb back and forth.

"Of course, beautiful."

I shake my head. "I'm sorry. I feel like I'm damaged goods or something."

"Lexi. No. Never. I just want to be careful. And I know you've been hurt. You know.... down there." Ayden shakes his head too and bites back a grin. "When we came up here, you had that look in your eye. It's your *I want to fuck you* look, and as much as I fucking love that look, we can't do that until you're better."

"What?"

"The doctor said you need time to heal," Ayden explains, dropping his hand from my face.

"What the fuck does that doctor know?!" I hiss, and Ayden chuckles.

"Come on, Lex. I'm pretty sure he knows what he's talking about."

"Ah... no, he doesn't. The arsehole has no idea, and it's going to leave me with the girl's equivalent of blue balls, Ayden."

"Then we can have blue balls together." He smiles.

My mouth drops open, and I stare at my addiction before me.

"You know, all I'm getting out of this conversation is a challenge, which I accept."

"Oh no, you don't. You'll make it worse for both of us if you dangle that bit of candy between us." Ayden frowns in all seriousness.

I grin. "Let's see how long you can hold out on me."

He growls and grabs me by my hips, pulling me against his body where I can feel the steel of his erection.

"Lexi West, you are going to get spanked."

I flash him my teeth. "A girl can hope."

Thirty-Two

The next couple of days are pretty cruisy. I spend any alone time with Ayden, trying to coax him to fuck me. He's stronger than I thought he was, and all I've successfully been able to do is make myself sexually frustrated.

Since my dad is still on the loose, the police decided to keep us under police watch. Not that I have any faith in that now. The guys have spent most of their time with us. Even Jared made an appearance, even though his mum cried when she dropped him off.

Today, the guys are all here for a Taco Tuesday lunch. Simon's idea, but it's a brilliant one. It's about three in the afternoon when Andrea comes out to the backyard where the guys are playing some made-up game with a golf club and ball.

"You have a call." Confused, I look at the phone she is holding out and then back to her in question. "It's Ringo. He wants to have a chat."

My face drops, but she shakes her head. "It's okay, sweetie." She holds the phone closer, so I take it and reluctantly hold it to my ear.

Is he about to tell me how his brother should never have died, and it's my fault? Because if that's the case, I totally agree with him.

"Hello?" I say, my voice sounding more like a child's than a teenager's.

"Hey, Lexi. It's Ringo here. How are you feeling?"

The gruff voice of the scary-looking biker holds nothing but warmth.

"Hey Ringo. I'm doing okay, thanks. I uh... I'm sorry about Muz. I mean Bobby."

At my blubbering and tear-filled eyes, Ayden hands his golf club to Marcus and comes to sit next to me, taking my free hand.

Ringo chuckles. "He'd hate that you called him Bobby. So, we should definitely refer to him that way from now on."

A giggle escapes while tears spill from my eyes. "Okay. Sounds good." Muz would definitely hate us using his real name. If he were still here, I'd tease him about it. Get him all worked up until he nearly blew a fuse. We probably would have been great friends in the end.

"I'm calling to invite you to his funeral tomorrow. Please don't feel obligated, but he spoke of you a lot in his last days, and I know you two had been chatting. I just want you to know you are welcome to attend if that's something you would like to do." Ringo clears his throat, and then his voice comes out a little unsteady. "He wasn't the kindest of people. Started getting into trouble at a young age and probably deserved a thousand beatings, but I've never seen him fight or care for anyone but himself before. Not until you came into his life and stirred things up. He was always going to die young, Lexi. Many bullets had his name on them, but in the end, the bullet that ended it all for him was because he was actually trying to do something good. He was really proud of that, Lexi. In his own twisted way, he died thinking he was your hero. I'm glad he got to experience doing something good before he left this world."

I'm sobbing. I'm a mess with snot coming out of my nose and my tears making it impossible to see anything. Ayden pushes a tissue into my free hand, and I make use of it quickly, trying to find the right words to say.

"T-thank y-you for s-saying that," I stutter out. "H-he s-saved me m-more than o-once." I suck in a deep breath, trying to control myself. "I would be h-honoured to come to B-Bobby's funeral."

"That's great, Lexi. Thank you. I know it would have meant a lot to him. I also have something for you that he asked me to give you. I look forward to seeing you tomorrow."

Ringo and I say our goodbyes, and when I'm able to see past my tears again, I notice the guys sitting on camp chairs close by, with their concerned eyes on me. I don't know how I got so lucky to have such caring friends, but I hope they know that if they ever need the same kind of support from me, I'll be there for them, no questions.

We spend the rest of Tuesday preparing to leave for the city in the morning. Even my mum is coming, as well as the guys. They didn't know Muz like I did, but they were grateful for him, and they want to be there for me.

Just after dinner, Jason pops by to see me out of uniform. Now, he's a good-looking guy, but without that uniform, he just looks like a regular person. As much as I miss the uniform, I feel so much more comfortable around him when he just looks like a regular guy. After all, the uniform reminds me of a certain day that I keep trying to push to the back of my mind.

We take a seat at the small kitchen table in Marcus' kitchen. Ayden on one side, and my mum on the other, while Andrea pretends to wipe down the kitchen counter, over and over.

"I thought I'd swing by and see how you are recovering." Jason smiles from across the table, and Ayden squeezes my hand that's resting on his leg.

"I'm doing okay, thanks. My body is kinda used to getting beaten up, I guess. It's beginning to feel normal."

Jason frowns. "It's not normal, and you will never feel like this again."

I nod. "I hope so. I'm okay." I shrug.

"You will be advised officially, but I wanted to put your mind at ease. We are closing the case on Mike's death. We've determined that it was self-defence. With yours and Natasha's statements and the evidence at the scene, it's evident that there was a clear intent by Mike to harm you fatally."

My mum releases a breath before grabbing my other hand under the table, squeezing it.

"Natasha has admitted to harbouring a fugitive and even conspiring to get you alone, but she remains determined that she didn't know Mike's true intent."

I nod. "Yeah, I could tell after a few things Mike said to me that she was shocked. I remember hearing her begging him to stop hurting me."

Jason nods. "There are grounds to press charges against her if that's something you feel you need to do."

"No." I shake my head. "She's a bitch and all, but she really didn't know what he was really like. She believed his lies. I don't want to punish her for that."

"Okay, well, we are still working on finding your father. There's a possibility we can flush him out by using Mike's death as a lure. Even though Mike's mother has asked for his body to be returned to her in Queensland, we have had the local funeral home advertise a viewing for local friends to say their goodbyes. We will have plain-clothed police in the vicinity to keep an eye out for your dad and extra patrols near your house."

"When is that happening?" my mum asks the question I was thinking.

"Tomorrow afternoon," Jason responds, offering my mum a warm smile.

"Oh, good. We will be out of town tomorrow for Bobby Musgrove's funeral in the city." My mum's words make Jason smile and nod.

"Good. It's safer if you aren't in the area in case he shows."

As my mum and Andrea walk Jason out, I stay seated at the table, feeling a mix of emotions.

This isn't over yet. My dad is still out there. I still remember the look on his face when he realised I'd killed his son. He's not going to just want the damn file anymore. He's going to want revenge.

I can't bear to think of going through all this crap again with him. I'm so sick of looking over my shoulder or my heart nearly leaping out of my chest when I hear a noise in the dead of night. I just have to hope that he falls for the trap the police set.

Ayden and I retreat to the loft a little while later. My mum was hovering, and it was making me cagey. I know it's because she cares, but it's just a reminder that things are still unresolved.

Locking the loft door behind us, Ayden leads me to his bathroom and turns on the shower.

"A nice warm shower should help you sleep."

"You know what would help me sleep?" I ask innocently, and Ayden doesn't pick up on my fluttering lashes because he's too busy testing the temperature of the water.

"What?"

"A good hard fuck."

Ayden's head whips in my direction, and he growls, "No."

I stomp my foot just like a toddler. "Yes!"

"No, Lexi."

"Yes, Ayden."

He sighs and looks up to the ceiling, sucking in calming breaths. He should know better than that. I'm not giving up this battle.

"If you don't fuck me, then I'll fuck myself right in front of you."

"Stop it." His glare catches me off guard, the anger in his eyes not at all playful.

Shit. I wasn't expecting that. I've been on his case about this subject for the last couple of days, but maybe I've pushed too hard.

Now I feel like crying again. I'm so sick of my emotions ruling me. My shoulders drop along with my face, and Ayden's glare turns into a frown.

"Lex." Taking me by my shoulders, he pulls me to his chest, hugging me close and planting a kiss on top of my head.

"I feel fine, Ayden."

"You know what the doctor said. You need to let yourself heal. The grazes..."

When he doesn't finish his sentence, I pull back to see the tears in his eyes.

"You still find me attractive, right?"

His eyes widen, like I've just said something unthinkable. "Fuck yes. Always, Lexi."

My heart is racing so fast. It never occurred to me that maybe what happened to me might change how he looks at me.

"Hey, I fucking love you. Every single part of you. I just need to make sure you're healed, so when we do that again, you're not thinking of...."

I nod. "So, no therapeutic sex?"

He chuckles, "Not tonight."

"How about a bit of fooling around? Just a little orgasm." I give him my best puppy dog eyes and add extra sweetness to my tone.

"What the fuck am I going to do with you, Lexi West?" Humour laces his tone, and he pulls me to his chest again.

"I mean... you can fuck me. Or how about some more arse play? I'll let you go all the way."

I feel the rumble of Ayden's laughter in his chest before he pulls back and tries to cover his laugh with a straight face.

"Stop it. Not tonight. Now get your sexy arse in that shower."

"If I say no, will you spank me?" I wag my brows, and he growls before lifting me in his arms and depositing me under the stream of water, fully clothed.

I squeal, trying to push past him to get out of the water, but he is a wall of muscle that won't budge. Huffing, I glare at his smug grin and then pull the showerhead off the hook and aim it towards him. Ayden swears, trying to duck out of the water, but it's no use. Water is everywhere, including all over him, soaking his clothes.

A moment later, he turns to look at me over his shoulder.

"Now you've done it." Turning on me, he bats away the water as he steps inside the shower with me and closes the door.

Does he think this is punishment? Because watching the water drip down from his silky dark hair as he advances on me with that heated sexy as sin expression is not punishment at all.

Ayden quickly snatches the showerhead from my grasp and returns it to the holder before backing me up against the wall.

"You like to test me, don't you?"

"I don't know what you mean," I say innocently, and he shakes his head, caging me in with a hand on each side against the tiled wall.

"You know exactly what I mean."

The next second, his lips are on mine. His kiss is searing, and a moan escapes me as I tug him closer by his drenched shirt. I pull it upwards, needing it off so I can feel his skin, and he helps me by grabbing it behind his neck and pulling it off. The next few minutes are a battle in trying to get our wet clothes off, and they slap as they hit the floor as we toss each piece over the top of the shower door.

When I'm down to my knickers and move to pull them down, Ayden stops me, his hand on mine.

"Leave them," he whispers, and my eyes catch his in an intense stare-off. "Will you do that for me, Lexi? Leave them on until I get out? I-I..."

I want to argue with him, but I bite my tongue when I see the pain in his eyes. I haven't taken a moment to think about what it must have been like for him each of the times Mike attacked me.

He needs this from me, so I will give it to him. Hell, I'd give him anything he asked for, so I nod, and relief washes over his face.

"I hate that he hurt you again. That he left marks on your body." His eyes dart to my chest, where the faint bite mark still stands out on my pale skin, right next to my nipple. "If he wasn't already dead, I'd fucking kill him myself."

I fight back the tears because I want to be stronger. I don't want to shed one more tear that is related to that vile piece of shit.

"I believe you would, but thankfully, he's gone now." I reach up and cup his face, enjoying the soft feel of his stubble. "It's time for us to move on and be happy together."

"Yes. I really want that, Lexi. I want you with me. Always."

"I want that too."

Reaching up, Ayden places his hand over mine and drags it across his stubble to his mouth, where he presses his lips softly against my palm and my skin prickles with excitement.

I believe him when he says that we won't be having sex tonight, and I'm okay with that because I realise there is more to us than that act. Sex with Ayden is fucking epic, don't get me wrong, but what we have is more than that. It's these quiet moments where our eyes speak instead of words. It's the gentle way we touch each other, like we are the most precious things on this earth. Sometimes, simple moments like this say more than words ever can.

Dropping my hand, Ayden reaches behind me and takes the shampoo off the shelf. He brings it between us and lifts my hand up, squirting shampoo into my palm. When I go to move, he shakes his head, so I stay put and watch as he squirts some into his hand, too, before returning the bottle to the shelf. Then he puts his palms together before running his hands through my hair.

Understanding dawning, I do the same, running my fingers through his hair, and he moans, pushing his head into my palm like a cat. It makes me giggle, and he smiles before turning his focus to my hair.

Oh yeah. That does feel amazing. His skilled fingers work their way to my ends, my waves not visible under the weight of the water. Then he starts to massage my head. I moan this time, and he chuckles.

"It's almost as good as sex, hey?" His voice is playful, and I drag my eyes lazily open.

"Almost."

I increase my scrubbing of his head, running my nails over his scalp and loving the feel of his hair between my fingers. A few minutes later, he reaches up and slowly pulls my hands away before turning me to face the wall.

"Let me take care of you," Ayden whispers in my ear, and I can't hold back the shiver that runs up my spine.

His fingers sink through my thick blonde hair and find my scalp, and he proceeds to massage the suds in. I relax against the tiled wall and close my eyes, enjoying every touch and stroke of his fingers.

It feels like hours before he stops pleasuring my scalp, but I'm sure it was only a matter of minutes. The spray of water hits my hair, and Ayden washes the suds free using the handheld showerhead.

When he's done pampering me, I turn and do the same for him. I have more trouble controlling my wandering hands as I watch the suds tumble down over the tattoo on his shoulder blade, down his spine, and past the dimples in his lower back. When the suds run over those two perfectly round mounds of his taut arse, I have to hold myself back from biting him. I don't know where the fuck that urge came from, but clearly, I'm an animal.

Enjoying every moment of this, my hands follow the trail of the suds, washing them away until there's none left, and then I snake my hand around the front of his hips to find a very erect cock.

"Ayden," I whisper as my hand wraps around his firm length that feels like silk in my palm.

"No," he growls low as he places his hand over mine to stop me.

My heart instantly hurts from his rejection, and I slowly pull my hand away and step back from him, hating this feeling but knowing I shouldn't push it.

"I'm sorry." His voice cracks a little, and he turns to me.

I shake my head. "It's fine." I swallow the lump in my throat, trying to remind myself that his rejection isn't personal. He thinks I need time, and he obviously needs time too.

When his eyes meet mine, I can see the sorrow in them. He wants to give me what I want. I can see that. And his body wants mine. I can see that, too, by the bobbing cock that stands at attention between us. But his strong will overrides it all. He has it in his mind that we can't go further.

"I feel like you hate me for refusing you," he whispers, and I shake my head immediately.

"No way. I could never hate you. I'm just disappointed because I want to be closer to you. I know I muck around and make it all about the orgasm, but it's more than that."

He offers me a small smile. "I know what you mean."

We are both silent for a moment. The only sound is the cascading water still streaming down.

"I'll hop out and let you finish." And with that, Ayden backs out of the cubicle.

I'm thankful for the steam filling the air because it hides the tears that silently fall. It's hard to explain why I'm crying. I feel like I miss him, yet he is right here with me. Maybe I'm hormonal. Who fucking knows?

I somehow push the sadness I'm feeling to the back of my mind to finish showering before I get out. I take my time in the small white bathroom, wrapping myself in Ayden's teal green towel and using another to dry off my hair.

When I return to the bedroom, it's lit by the dull light of the bedside lamp as Ayden waits on the bed. When I approach, he shoots me one of those panty-melting winks and proceeds to dress me, sliding a clean pair of knickers up my legs and slipping one of his Nike T-shirts over my head.

"Why am I wearing your shirt?"

"You know I like you in my clothes." He smiles before planting a kiss on the tip of my nose.

Leading me to the bed, he holds the blanket up, and I slip in before he rounds the bed to slide in next to me after turning off the lamp. He immediately pulls me to his chest, and we wrap ourselves around each other, fitting like a perfect puzzle piece.

"Ayden?" I whisper into the darkened room.

"Yeah?"

"Thank you for taking care of me."

His warm lips press against my forehead before he speaks.

"I'll make you come tomorrow, beautiful. I promise."

"You'd better." I giggle before I pass out.

Thirty-Three

All eyes turn to us as we get out of the cars outside a quaint church somewhere in Melbourne's northern suburbs. I didn't really pay attention to where we were going because I spent most of my time trying to control my breathing and not cry. I'm not ready to say goodbye to Muz. I feel like our journey had just begun.

As my pack flanks Ayden and me, Andrea holds my mum's hand on one side and links arms with Peter on the other, taking the lead as we approach the rickety weatherboard building.

At first, there isn't a single familiar face looking back at us, but as we make our way up the path, a few familiar faces stand out, mainly because of the glares they are shooting at us. Candy, the blonde bimbo from the drug party Muz forced Ayden and me to attend, stands crying with the solid arm of Butch wrapped around her shoulders. Her blonde hair is a matted mess, and black mascara streams down her red cheeks as she sobs past the daggers she is throwing my way. Her clothes don't fit the typical dress code for a funeral, with her hot pink leather skirt too short and her white cropped tee too tight.

"Just ignore them," Ayden whispers down to me, pulling me closer to his side. This must be hard for him. He knows a lot of these people from his past. The person who linked them is lying in a casket somewhere in the building we are approaching.

All because of me.

My tears start then. I can't hold them back any longer, but I try to reduce their flow by blocking my mind off and thinking about something different. I focus on the firm grip Ayden has on me. The way I can feel his touch burn through the black blouse I'm wearing. The way his scent swirls around us as we walk, travelling with us in our own little bubble.

"Thank you for coming." Ringo's voice draws my attention, and I glance up to see him shaking Peter's hand. He follows that with a kiss on Andrea's cheek and a hug with my mum. I expected it to be awkward since they've only met once before when I went to see Muz in the hospital, but they don't appear awkward at all. My mum and Ringo look like old friends.

The few times I've seen Ringo, he has looked gruff and a little dishevelled. Today is different. Today his long beard looks neat and almost like it's been styled. He has replaced the old beat-up black vest he wears with a deep navy collared shirt that's tucked into clean black pants. Even his shoes shine, their tan hue matching the belt he wears. His normally mussed, longish hair is pulled up into a man bun. With his tats peeking out on his hands and travelling up his neck, dare I say he actually looks.... handsome?

When his hard eyes find mine as Ayden's parents part, my bottom lip wobbles and his lips thin. Stepping up to me, he wraps a large hand around the back of my head and pulls me to his chest.

Then I break.

I feel terrible since I should be the one comforting him. This is his little brother's funeral, after all, but as I cry silently, he holds me close, and I hear soft whimpers of others crying around us.

The pain in my chest feels unbearable. I want to make things right, but I can't. I don't have the power to bring Muz back from the dead. I'm not able to go back to that day and change what happened. I can't do anything but feel this agonising pain that I wish would stop.

"Remember what I said on the phone yesterday, Lexi? *You* are the reason he got to do something good before his time was up." Ringo's husky voice meets my ears, so soft that only those immediately around us can hear. "And remember that it would piss him off to no end if we refer to him as Bobby."

I giggle through my tears at that and pull away, using the tissue in my hand to clean myself up. "Bobby would really hate that."

Through the thick mass of his beard, I see straight white teeth appear in a smile as Ringo's eyes crease at the sides. "Bobby really would."

Reaching into his pocket, Ringo then draws out a black felt bag. It's the sort that I've seen used for jewellery sometimes. However, this bag is too big to hold something so delicate.

"Bobby asked me to give this to you. I cleaned it up since it's pretty old, but our pop gave it to him just before he died, and Bobby wanted you to have it. Something to keep with you so he can keep protecting you."

I frown, sniffling back my tears, and close my fingers around the bag when he places it in my hand. It's heavier than it looks.

"It's probably a good idea not to take it out here, but have a look inside the bag."

Ringo waits as I drag my eyes from him back to the bag and tug on the cord to pull it open. When I see what's inside, I understand why I shouldn't take it out here. It's another butterfly knife. It looks a little bigger than the one he gave me last time, which is now in an evidence bag somewhere. It also looks well used, with scratches on the metal handle.

Even in death, Muz is still looking out for me.

"Thank you," I whisper.

Peering up at Ringo, he shoots me a wink and then sucks in a deep breath.

"Let's get this over with." Then he turns and walks with purpose through the blue paint chipped doors of the church.

I slip the cord of the black felt bag over my wrist and follow behind our parents to go inside.

The funeral is hard. Even though we sit up the back of the small space packed to the rafters, crying and sniffles float up from the front during the whole hour-long service. I'm too short to see over the crowd of questionable looking mourners, but if I had to guess, the tears are coming from a mother or an aunt, or maybe a sister.

I can't help but feel guilty. Feel responsible. I know I can't control certain things, but it doesn't matter. My heart hurts, and I feel to blame. The hardest part comes when the service finishes and the pallbearers slowly make their way up the narrow aisle carrying Muz's casket. Ringo is at the front on one side, and on the other, is a gruff-looking guy I recognise as one of the guys that came to help stop Muz from hurting Ayden and I at the party that awful night a few weeks ago.

The thing that breaks my heart wide open is the tears that wet Ringo's cheeks as he walks by.

I'm a mess after that, and Andrea decides that we won't continue on to the cemetery burial. With our heads hung low, we load back into the cars, silence meeting us as we all feel the effects of our reality.

Funerals are hard for everyone. I'd be content to never go to another one again.

Today, they buried my friend.

Bobby Musgrove AKA Muz
Born 02/01/1996
Met his maker on Sunday, September 22nd
2019, aged 23 years.
Survived by his mother, Doreen, two sisters,
Alana and Millie, and brother Cameron (AKA
Ringo)
Today, my brother, you will rise from the
ashes and find your peace.

We arrive at Peter's apartment about twenty minutes later, an eerie quietness meeting us as we all drag our feet inside and remain silent as we change out of the formal clothes we wore to the funeral. Within minutes, the guys are wearing comfy sweatpants and t-shirts, while I opt for a hoodie and leggings, even though it's not that cold today. I just feel like being wrapped up in warmth.

When I walk into the living room, I catch Ayden's eyes as they follow me, a grin tugging at the corner of his mouth as he watches me. I raise a brow, and he lets his grin show, shooting me a wink before focusing on selecting a movie to watch. An afternoon watching movies with my friends is exactly what I need. What we all need.

I leave the living area and head to the kitchen, where Andrea, Peter, and my mum are throwing together some cheese platters and nibbles for us. My mum is building a good friendship with Andrea. It's not hard.

Andrea is such a lovely person, but I'm glad my mum likes her. Andrea is a good person to have in our lives.

"You coping okay, Lexi?" Peter asks, seeing me standing in the doorway. My mum and Andrea turn their eyes to me, smiling.

"Yeah. I'll be okay. Funerals are a lot." I move to stand next to my mum, who seems content dicing up a block of cheese into cubes. She looks at me and smiles warmly, but I get distracted when my phone starts buzzing in my pocket.

I hear Ayden and Marcus enter the kitchen, chatting as I glance at my phone and I freeze.

"Who's calling?" Mum asks, and I can't speak for a moment, so I clear my throat.

"It's Dad."

The room falls silent, leaving the only noise floating down the passage from our friends in the living room. I quickly glance at Mum, whose eyes are now trained on my phone, so I lay it on the bench and hit accept and then speaker. My dad's voice fills the room.

"Alexis!" he practically yells, causing the speaker on my phone to crackle.

"What?" I ask with all the attitude of a bratty teenager.

"You killed him! You fucking killed him!" His roar makes my heart skip a beat. "You murdered him! It wasn't self-defence! You will pay for this, Alexis!"

"You will stay away from her!" My mum jumps in before I can respond, and my dad goes quiet. "Your worthless sicko son got what he had coming, and if you come anywhere near Lexi, I will kill you myself!"

I've heard my mum yell before. Scream and rant on more than one occasion, but the level of venom that laces her tone is something I've never heard.

Quiet curses fall from Marcus' and Peter's lips after my mum's public death threat, but if my dad heard it, he doesn't stop to acknowledge it.

"I'll tell you what, Ruth. How about you give me the fucking file I want, and I'll leave the country? You and Alexis will never have to see me again."

A wicked laugh flows from my mum before she leans in close to the phone. "You know it's in the house, Maxwell. Why don't you come and get the fucking thing yourself?"

My mum hits end on the call, so we never get the chance to hear my dad's response. I told Dad the other day that there was no file, that the only money in the bank account was fifty dollars. Clearly, he didn't believe me. More fool him because if he ever figures out how to access that account, he won't be getting far with fifty dollars.

My mum's ragged breathing draws my attention, and her face contorts with anger and emotion, her palms flat on the bench beside her. Reaching out, I put my hand over hers, and her brown eyes find mine, her shoulders falling as she relaxes.

"I'm so sorry for that outburst. You've all had such a sad day, you didn't need to hear all that." My mum really does sound sorry, so I squeeze her hand, and she pulls me into a hug.

"I'm so sorry, Lexi." Mum starts to cry, so I hug her tighter.

I'm not sure what she's apologising for, but I feel like it's more than just the screaming match with my dad. She's been through so much. Most likely more than she's told me about.

Pulling back a minute later, I notice Ayden and Marcus have already taken over preparing the cheese platter, and Andrea and Peter are putting trays lined with finger food in the oven.

"There's no need to apologise, Ruth. I think you handled that quite fittingly." Andrea smiles, and my mum returns it. They are definitely going to be good friends.

"Mum?" My voice gains my mum's attention. "Why'd you tell Dad that the file was at the house?" I raise my brows, hoping she gets my meaning. There is no file. She told me as much. But she just told Dad it's at our house, so I'm confused.

She pulls me into another hug, which I soon realise is just a cover, so she can whisper in my ear.

"If he's lurking around the house, then the police will catch him. Officer Zimora said they have extra patrols to watch our house."

Pulling back again, I see my mum's devious smile, and my own falls into place. She's right. He won't be able to help himself. My dad will go back to Fox Pines and search our house, trying to find something that isn't there. That will give the police the perfect opportunity to catch him.

While the adults retreat to the front living area near the kitchen, Ayden closes the doors in the passage to give us more privacy, and we join our friends for a movie. I don't even get through the opening credits before I fall asleep wrapped in Ayden's arms. By the time I wake again, the movie is over, and Shaun has the guys spread out in the room, showing them how to do some sort of fitness moves.

"Hey, beautiful. Did you have a good sleep?" Ayden's voice is low as he speaks near my ear, and I glance up from his chest to lock on to those ocean eyes that own my soul.

"I did." I try to nod, but it's hard in the position I'm in. "What is Shaun doing?"

Ayden chuckles. "Showing them yoga moves, apparently."

I glance back at my friends moving in ways I have never seen done in yoga.

"Uh-yeah, they aren't yoga moves." I giggle as I watch Simon on his back with his legs in the air, trying to spread his legs apart as far as they can go.

"Spread them further. Come on, you pussies. You'll never connect to your inner self if you don't give this all you've got." Shaun growls with all seriousness, his Spanish features making him look like some sort of God as he walks around the room, examining each one of them.

"I'm pretty fucking sure my inner self is screaming at me to stop right now," Garrett growls from across the room, and I nearly lose it, another giggle leaping out of my mouth.

"Stop whining. Now grab your legs behind each knee and draw your legs to your chest." Shaun demands, and the idiots do it. "Now start moving your pelvis up and down."

The moment they all start trying to do that, I nearly slip off the couch, onto the floor in hysterics, while Ayden isn't far behind me.

"I can't fucking do this," Jared growls, and Marcus grunts in agreement.

"Oh, come on. It's just like having sex. Thrust those hips! Thrust them!"

That's it.

I've lost control to the point I can't breathe, and even though I'm pretty sure Ayden doesn't know what Shaun is really doing, he's lost control as well, tears streaming from his eyes while he clutches his middle. It reminds me of the night I went back to his loft for the first time after I found my dad with his mistress in the restaurant. I apologised to him for the pig I was about to make out of myself after he handed me a plate of food and he pissed himself laughing.

"What's so fucking funny?" Garrett asks, stopping his thrusting and dropping his feet to the floor.

Slowly, one by one, each of the guys stops their thrusting and sits up to glare at Ayden and me. It takes me a few minutes to calm down, and I can't look Shaun in the eye because each time I do, he winks at me knowingly, and I lose it again.

"Are you good?" Marcus asks as I suck in air.

I nod. "Yep. All good here."

"Then what was so funny?" Simon asks, looking genuinely confused.

A bubble of laughter leaps up my throat, and then it takes another few moments to pull myself together.

When I've composed myself again, I glance at Shaun and raise a brow. "You want to tell them, or will I?"

He grins. "Nah. You've got this." Shaun flashes me his white teeth in a cheesy smile, and I roll my eyes before turning to the others.

"They weren't yoga moves Shaun was showing you." My grin wants to spread wide, but I hold it back as much as I can.

"What? What were they then?" Simon's confusion is adorable, his hazel eyes round with an innocence he doesn't possess.

"Sex positions," I say, and all I receive is confused glares.

"Sex positions? I haven't done any sex positions like that before," Marcus declares.

"That's because you're a guy. Those positions are what you guys move us girls into as if we are made of elastic." I drag my gaze from their confused expressions to Shaun's mischievous one. "Come to think of it, how do you know what it's like for a girl to be stretched in those positions, Bossi?"

He holds his chin up with pride. "I'll never tell."

It takes a moment, but eventually, understanding dawns on everyone else, and their expressions change to annoyed. It's in that moment that cushions start flying across the room at Shaun, and he jumps behind the couch where Ayden and I are, using us as a shield. The room erupts in a full-blown cushion fight, and due to our proximity, me and Ayden choose to join Shaun's side.

This sort of lightness is exactly what I need, what we all need. It reminds me that there is a future filled with fun and love ahead of me.

My fun is short-lived when my phone vibrates and alerts me to a new message from my dad.

It is a picture.

Of Mike.

Lying dead in his casket.

Then my dad sends a text through:

You will pay for this, Alexis!

Thirty-Four

E very time I fell asleep last night, Mike's dead body lying in the casket popped into my dreams. And every time that happened, I woke up screaming. It didn't matter that Ayden was in bed with me or that Marcus and Garrett were asleep in the room as well. Co-sleeping and not being alone wasn't going to stop Mike from getting to me in my dreams.

It's a little after lunch when we arrive back in Fox Pines, our brief visit to the city over far too soon. Since the threat of Mike is now gone, the police watch over everyone has been called off, except for Mum and me. That means all the guys head home for the night to have some time to themselves for the first time in days.

I'm not going to lie. I instantly miss their presence. I know I can't expect them to be around me all the time, though. They've given up so much for me. Getting back to their lives is well overdue.

My mum gets a call from Burt, who tells her they nearly caught my dad last night when he went to the viewing at the funeral home. Somehow, he got away. Again.

At this point, I'm seriously questioning how well trained the local police are after everything that's happened.

When mum retreats to her room to have a rest, Ayden, Marcus and I settle into some lazy time in front of Marcus' TV. I don't really watch the car restoration show Marcus declared we were watching, and instead use my phone to Google different types of careers that help people. All the shit that has happened over the last six weeks really makes you think about your life. I didn't consider myself worthy of Ayden in the beginning. I didn't think he deserved to be involved with someone who has nothing but a dark future ahead of them. Ayden showed me how wrong I was. I can have the future I want, the happiness I want, and while I know I want him to be in my life, I don't know what else I want to do with it.

At school, they make us do quizzes to pinpoint our interests and what we're good at. Mine changes all the time, and I think it's because I've been so unsettled. I could never see a future because I didn't think I would have one. Now I know I will, so it's gotten me thinking. I'm still unsure what I want to do exactly, but what I do know is that I want to do something that matters. I want to help people. Women maybe? Girls who aren't strong enough to fight on their own. Who need to know that they aren't alone and that they deserve more. I'm not really sure who those people are that do something like that, so I spend a couple of hours researching while

Ayden dozes next to me, his hand never not touching my leg or arm as if he can't bear to be apart from me.

At some point, I sprawl out on the couch with Ayden and fall asleep too, and when I wake, it's to an inferno of arousal between my legs. The moment I realise fingers are rubbing gently over my fabric covered mound, my eyes fly open. I gasp with consuming need as I take in Marcus' living room, and the boy in question sound asleep in the armchair just above my head.

"I've made you wait long enough, beautiful." Ayden's husky lust-filled tone draws my attention to find him lying next to me, his eyes half-lidded and swooning with desire as his arm moves up and down with the strokes his fingers make over my aching pussy.

"Ayden. We can't. Not here."

He grins like the devil himself. I should be scared, but fuck if that grin doesn't excite me even more.

"Lexi. We can, and we will. Right here. Right now."

My head darts up to look at Marcus, who hasn't moved, and Ayden chuckles quietly in my ear before he nips it.

"But, Marcus? And our mums?"

"Our mums just left to go for a walk. We have thirty minutes, if not more." Ayden kisses my neck, and I can't even control how I stretch my head to the side to give him better access. "And Marcus is out cold. He won't wake up. It's just you and me, Lex, and it's time for me to make you come."

He cups my mound then, and I'm helpless not to rear my pelvis up trying to seek more.

"So greedy." Ayden chuckles and drags his hand up under my hoodie, taking his sweet time to circle over the top of my bra, teasing my nipples until they pebble hard.

I whimper, holding myself back because if I let myself go, I'm pretty sure I'll push Ayden down and ride his face until he passes out. It's a fucking fantastic mental image, which just makes me needier.

Releasing my nipples, Ayden brings his hand up to cup my chin, turning me towards him for a hungry kiss. I moan, not even caring that it was a little loud, and I drag Ayden closer to me, clutching onto his t-shirt.

Pulling back from me, Ayden captures my eyes with his as he bites his lower lip before grinning and sliding his body down the front of mine. My pelvis rears up again, enjoying each part of his body as it glides over me until he settles in between my legs. I'm still wearing my leggings, and Ayden makes no attempt to remove them, even when he lowers his mouth to press a sensual kiss against my fabric covered core.

My hands fly out, one clutching the back of the couch, and the other finds thin air as it flails over the edge of the couch. When Ayden starts making out with my legging clad pussy, my back arches and I close my eyes, throwing my head back as I moan loud. Over and over, he kisses, and I feel the heat of his breath seep through my leggings and panties as it hits my soaking flesh, adding to the sensations that are building deep inside me.

My free hand finds Ayden's hair, and I start thrusting to meet the motion of his passionate kisses, my mouth falling open as I pant through each increasing pleasured ache. When Ayden's hand joins his lips between my legs, and he runs his fingers up and down the centre, I lose all control and start grinding against his pressure.

A noise above my head makes me snap my eyes open to see Marcus no longer asleep but watching us with a fucking shit-eating grin, and I gasp, trying to sit up.

"No," Ayden growls, and my eyes return to his as he uses his free hand to push me back down while his other hand still rubs against my core.

"But," I protest. But Ayden slams his mouth back to the soaking fabric and goes to town.

Marcus is watching us, and I know Ayden knows because he is watching my face, and every now and then, he looks over my head. It doesn't deter him, though. He kisses my fabric covered pussy like it's an addiction he can't stop, and fuck me if I can't help but feel every one of my nerve endings ignite as my body prepares to explode.

My mind goes into a lust haze, and I thrust and grind and moan and gasp until I detonate, my back arching right off the couch as I fly into a chasm of never-ending pleasure. Rush after rush consumes me entirely until it peters off, and I drift back into an almost numbing reality.

"That was fucking beautiful," Ayden rasps, and I drag my eyes open to see him sitting between my legs, looking down at me.

"Fuckin' oath it was," Marcus adds, and I sit up in a rush, nearly head-butting Ayden.

"What the fuck, Ayden!" I spit and slap his shoulder.

He pulls back to see the mortification etched across my face, and his face softens as he lowers his eyes to meet mine as I try to duck them away.

"Hey. Come on, Lex. There was no way I was going to leave you hanging after the week you've had." Ayden draws his eyes from mine to look over my head. "As for you, dickhead, the moment you realised what was happening, you should have got up and walked away."

Marcus chuckles. "No fucking chance of that. This is *my* house, and that is *my* couch you are making *my* friend come on. If you don't want to share your sexcapades, then keep them behind closed doors."

Ayden goes to speak, but my anger has me up off the couch and glaring at Marcus.

"Did you like what you saw, Marcus? Did it get you off? You wanna watch as I make your cousin come now?" I hiss, and he grins. "What the fuck is so funny?"

"It's hard to take you seriously when your grey gym pants are soaked through." Marcus' eyes fall to my crotch.

I feel it even before I look, and my face heats in embarrassment. I growl like a feral animal and stomp my foot like a two-year-old before storming out. The arguing voices of Ayden and Marcus fade away as I swing the back door open and retreat to Ayden's loft.

Ayden isn't far behind me, and the moment he enters, I hurl a pillow at him. He ducks it, but the second one that leaves my hand slaps into his face.

"I'm not a fucking exhibitionist, Ayden!"

He holds his hands up in surrender, a sexy smirk tilting his lips, which just infuriates me more.

"Okay, got it. We tried it, and it's not for you."

"You didn't give me much of a choice, Ayden!" I hiss, and he flinches, his eyes looking to the floor as he thinks.

"I-I. You. *Shit*." Ayden rakes his hands through his hair, and his eyes widen as he looks at me. "Lexi. I'm so sorry." His voice is laced with sorrow as he takes a step towards me, his hands held up in surrender again.

His voice. The guilt on his face. It's too much. It hurts me to see him like that. Am I really blaming him for what happened? Sure, he pushed me back down, but did I fight him? Did I say no? Did I really want him to stop, even though Marcus was watching?

No.

"Shit, Ayden. It's okay."

He shakes his head again, his eyes glassing over, so I close the distance between us and take his hands in mine.

"Ayden. You did nothing wrong. I just overreacted because I was embarrassed. If I really wanted you to stop, I would have made sure you knew I wanted that." My eyes dance over his pained expression. "My reaction is just because I'm embarrassed."

"Embarrassed?" he repeats, so I nod. "Of what? Marcus watching?"

I shrug. "Maybe more because I liked that he was watching, and then afterwards, I felt embarrassed that I liked it."

"So, I didn't force you?" He sounds so young right now. I hate that I've made him feel this way.

"No. You demanded that I submit, and I did because I love you, and I love every experience we share. You definitely didn't force me, and I'm sorry for losing my shit and making you feel that way."

"So, you still love me?" he whispers, and I grin.

"I love you so fucking much, Ayden."

A hint of a grin lights his face. "Tell me you like it when I demand things of you."

"I love it. Mostly in the bedroom, though."

Then, my devil-possessed angel returns to me. "Good. Get on your knees."

Heat engulfs my entire body, and like the brat I am, I jut my chin up. "Make me."

A low rumble is all I hear before Ayden fists his hand in my hair and claims my lips. I kiss him back with as much ferocity, enjoying the slight sting on my scalp as he tugs gently on my hair, dragging me down with it as he bends and keeps his lips locked with mine. When my knees touch the carpet, Ayden nips at my bottom lip and drags it through his teeth as he pulls back, his smouldering blue gaze intense as he stands tall to loom over me.

"Slide my pants down," he rasps, and I hesitate. Not because I don't want to, but because I enjoy defying him. It's fun, and when his eyes widen with infinite lust like they are right now, my greedy pussy rejoices.

He tugs my hair, so my head pulls back, and his eyes bore into mine with the dirtiest of promises. "My pants down NOW, Lexi."

I swear, I nearly come right there on the spot from his demanding tone. I had no idea that sort of thing turned me on until he came into my life.

Taking my time because it's fun dragging out my brattiness, I reach forward and grip his sweatpants, slowly pulling them down until they pool at his ankles. His red jocks do nothing to hold him in, his hard length protruding out from the top of the waistband, a bead of pre-cum pooling at the tip. I lick my lips, and he growls.

"Jocks too, beautiful."

I flick my eyes up to his, peering at him through my dark lashes, and the devil grins back at me. I'm helpless to deny him, so I do as he asks and hook my fingers in his jocks, sliding them down his legs to rest on top of his pants.

When I look back up, my eyes are level with the eye of his cock, and my mouth waters before he uses my hair again to pull me up higher on my knees.

"Open."

Fuck, his lust-filled voice is hot. It should be illegal, and just like a wanton whore, I open my mouth as he guides his hard cock between my lips. I moan around his silky skin as he sinks in, and his other hand joins the party by fisting in my hair on the other side. My eyes dart up past my lashes to see his lips slightly parted, his expression pleasure pained as his eyes watch where his length disappears past my lips.

"Your mouth is like heaven, Lexi."

I've been told my mouth is too smart for my own good before, even that it's a little foul, but no one has told me it's heaven. I like the sound of that much more, and I store his words in my memory so I can throw them at him down the track when he has something to say about my smart mouth.

Using my head to steer, Ayden moves his hips forward and back as he slowly fucks my mouth, his eyes darting from mine, where I remain looking up at him to where we join.

"How deep can you take me, beautiful?"

Fuck, my pussy pulses at his words, and always eager to please, I stick my tongue out and relax my throat, helping him to sink in further.

"Oh fuck, Lexi." Ayden throws his head back and starts moving faster, moving harder. For once, he's giving me everything he is without holding back. This time, I don't have to ask.

My excitement builds as he thrusts into my mouth, and I glide my hand up his inner thigh until I find his taut sac and cup his balls. His moan is loud and gravelly as he bucks and drops his head forward to look back down at me.

His hips surge forward as his hands drag me towards him, and he pumps over and over, hitting the back of my throat. As hard as I try not to, I gag, unable to control my body's natural reaction. Ayden must notice because he pulls back a little, and I feel like tit punching myself for not being able to handle him.

Practice makes perfect, Lexi.

A moment later, Ayden pulls his engorged cock free of my mouth with a pop, and I instantly miss it. One of his hands releases my hair to wrap around his cock as he starts to pump, while the other hand stays fisted in my blonde waves, keeping me in place before him.

"Is my little minx thirsty?" he asks, his ocean blues piercing me from above.

"Yes," I pant, desperate for him.

"You wanna drink me?" He pumps his fist harder, his hand closing tight around his shaft. I try to keep my eyes on his, but I fail as they are drawn to watch him pump his dick over and over.

"Yes," I whisper.

"Look at me."

My eyes dart back to his, even though I desperately want to watch his cock.

"Good girl. Open your mouth for me, beautiful. I'll give you my drink."

Tipping my head back a little, I open my mouth and slip my tongue out to rest on my lower lip as he moves forward, pumping his cock faster as he moans loud.

"It's coming."

The tip of his head presses against my tongue as he angles himself, and a moment later, warm spurts of his seed fill my mouth, coating my tongue and cheek. He releases a primal growl as he watches his white cum like he's marking me, and fuck if that isn't hot as hell.

I stay kneeling before him as he pants, my mouth still open and filled to the brim.

"You want to swallow or spit, beautiful?" His eyes are a caress as they look over me, and I know I'm dragging this out for the only reason that I want to send him crazy with lust.

As he watches me, I drag my tongue back in my mouth and close my lips together, swallowing his offering.

"Fuck, you're the hottest thing to walk this earth, Lexi."

I grin up at him with mischief in my eyes, licking my lips before using my finger to wipe up the creamy trail he left on my cheek before darting my tongue out to lick it off.

"Fuck, my dick will never go down at this rate."

"Good. Now use it to fuck me."

With yet another primal growl, Ayden leans down and sweeps me up in his arms, kicking his pants off his feet before taking me to his bed. Laying me back with a hand on either side of my head, he hovers over me, his eyes drunk, his face soft.

"Are you sure? Have you... healed?"

I nod. "I need to feel you deep inside me, Ayden. I'll beg if I have to."

His dimple makes an appearance. "Why does that sound so tempting?"

I laugh. "Probably because I'll be back on my knees."

"Probably." He smiles. "You don't have to beg, but I won't give it to you hard today, Lex. Today we are going to take it nice and slow."

"And deep." I remind him, and he chuckles.

"Slow and deep, beautiful."

Rising to stand, Ayden moves to his bedside drawer and pulls out a condom. My heart sinks with the reminder of why he has to wear it. As anger prickles at me, I close my eyes and suck in deep breaths, trying to force the reminder to the back of my mind so our moment isn't ruined.

"Don't think about it, beautiful," Ayden whispers, and my eyes dart open to find him looking down at me from the end of the bed. "All that matters is you and me."

I nod, hoping to convince myself that I'm okay, as much as I want him to know it. Ayden shoots me one of his winks and then bends over to kiss a trail up my legs. His lips lightly brush over my needy nub, up my front, and stop to give my aching nipples some attention before he comes to rest over me, his lips hovering above mine as our eyes look into each other's souls.

"You and me, beautiful. I love you." His words are not a question. They are a statement, a fact. An actuality that fills me with so much love that I feel almost invincible.

"You and me, Ayden. I love you, too."

Ayden moves forward to kiss me then. My lips part, welcoming him in as his tongue seeks out mine and they entwine together. It's a soft kiss. A caress of sorts that says more than the words I love you ever can. He kisses me for so long. Minutes and minutes, tasting me, savouring me. His lips work their magic as he holds himself over me, and without even realising, my need to feel him stretch me builds and builds.

Nibbling my lips before pulling back, Ayden positions himself at my entrance, and when a vile memory flashes through my mind, I close my eyes and whisper.

"New memories."

Ayden's fingers brush my hair back from my forehead, and he places a soft kiss there.

"New memories, beautiful. You lead the way."

I open my eyes to find his filled with emotion. It's hard to witness his struggle, just as it's hard for him to witness mine. We are here together, though. Here for each other. So I know what I need to do, what I want to do.

Gliding my hands up over the side of his hips, I palm his arse and gently tug him forward. As I do, I shift my legs further apart, opening myself to him as he slowly sinks inside me. The stretching sting nearly sends me into a frenzy, but Ayden said slow and deep, so I hold my urge to start thrusting like a horny beast and let my body work with his slow rhythm. As he moves, he sinks so deep, slowly dragging himself out and then back in. It's a form of pleasured torture, and I gasp and moan, all while we keep our eyes locked on to each other. It's the most vulnerable yet loving thing I've ever experienced.

Ayden can go from dominating primal beast to seductive gentle lover so easily, and I have to say, I like both versions. I love pushing the boundaries with him when we frenzy fuck, or he fights to control me, but this intense connection of slow and deep, where we feel each minor detail, where our souls are open and exposed to each other, is on another level.

Because I can't help myself. I dig my nails into Ayden's arse cheeks, and he rolls his hips, creating a whole new sensation. He does this over and over with each slow movement, and my walls tighten, gripping him as my orgasm builds and builds. My eyes roll back in my head, and Ayden's voice is husky above me.

"Open them for me, beautiful. Keep your eyes open."

I do, of course, because I'm helpless to deny him, and I keep my eyes locked on his as our pleasured moans fill the room.

My climax hits suddenly. It's intense and long, drawn-out as Ayden keeps moving slowly, igniting all of my most sensitive spots. A few more slow, deep thrusts later, while I'm still coming, Ayden joins me, riding out his own high.

Ayden said my climax earlier was fucking beautiful, but in my opinion, what we just did is fucking beautiful.

Thirty-Five

We emerge from Ayden's loft around 7pm to find that Marcus' mum Barbara and my mum joined forces to cook us dinner while Andrea goes into work to do a late shift. The aroma of lasagne fills the main house as plates are served up, and I watch as Barb explains something about the cooking they did and realise she is actually teaching my mum how to cook it.

When we were kids, I remember my mum chatting with Barbara at the barbeques we used to go to. At some point, that stopped, and my mum isolated herself. I realise now that I'd started to do the same when Mike moved in. I still went to parties and school and tried to appear normal, but I stopped sharing my worries with Abbey. I started keeping secrets and hiding the truth. I isolated myself too. Then, because of one very insistent guy, I opened up and accepted the help he was offering, and now, even though things are still a mess, I know my mum and I have the chance to be happy.

Barb and Tony chat away to my mum at the dinner table while I sit there red-faced with my eyes trained on my plate of food as I eat in an attempt to avoid Marcus' gaze. Every time I look up, his eyes are on me, and I can't tell if he's just trying to make me feel uncomfortable on purpose as a joke or if it's something else.

When everyone is done eating, Barb instructs me, Ayden and Marcus to do the dishes while they move to the living room to watch some sappy TV show. I have the urge to feign a tummy bug, but Ayden grabs my hand, smirking because he knows what my problem is, and drags me to the kitchen.

Wanting to keep myself busy, I rush forward and start filling the sink with water, giving the guys my back.

"Sorry, Lex," Marcus says close to my ear, and I pretend not to hear him because pretending like nothing happened sounds good to me.

A hand reaches over my side and turns off the tap, but I keep piling cutlery into the water, keeping myself busy.

"Lex." Ayden speaks this time, and he reaches in front of me, gently gripping my arms that are immersed in the soapy water, and pulls them free, turning me to face them.

These two cousins, one my childhood friend and the other the love of my life, stand side by side with their arms crossed over their chests, looking more like brothers than cousins. I raise a single brow and match their stance, crossing my own arms over my chest, only to silently curse myself when the warm water coating my skin seeps through my t-shirt.

"We should talk, don't you think?" Ayden prompts, and I raise both brows at him this time.

"I *am* sorry, Lexi. I shouldn't have watched like a creepy fucker." The sincerity in Marcus' tone manages to bring my eyebrows back down.

"Why did you watch?" Ayden asks, turning his head to Marcus.

"What?" Marcus' dark eyes widen at Ayden's question, and he looks between us.

"Why did you watch? You had to know it would make Lexi uncomfortable." Ayden glares at his cousin now, and I almost feel sorry for Marcus.

"Uh... I don't know. Because I'm a guy that thinks with his dick." Marcus shrugs, and Ayden glares.

"Were you waiting for an invitation to join in?" Ayden snaps, and I gasp.

"Ayden!"

He ignores me, waiting for Marcus to answer.

"No! What the fuck, man? I woke up, kinda thought I was having some weird sex dream at first, then realised it was real. I went to move off the seat when Lexi opened her eyes and saw me. You were the one that pushed her back down, man. When she didn't kick up a big fuss, I guess I kinda assumed she wanted me to watch. Thought maybe you two were into that or something. I wasn't about to ruin Lexi's fantasy if she wanted me to watch her."

"I have no such fantasy, Marcus." I spit, dropping my hands by my sides as my fists ball.

"Yeah, well. Maybe not, but when it came down to it, you both went with it, and so did I. It didn't mean anything. Maybe you should both keep that shit behind closed doors." Marcus glares back at Ayden, who just smirks back at him.

"I guess we put you in a tough situation, hey?"

I shoot Ayden a *'really'* glare when he glances at me, but he just winks. Sometimes he's just so infuriating.

"Like I said before. I'm a guy that thinks with my dick." Marcus shrugs. "Did you hand him his balls when you went to the loft, Lexi?"

"I mean, my balls were in her hand, and my cock—"

"Ayden!" I hiss, stepping forward and slapping my hand over his mouth. "What has gotten into you?"

When I release his grinning lips, he pulls me to his chest. "I'm love drunk, baby."

I squeal and laugh as he munches on my neck, deliberately rubbing his stubble over my skin to tickle me.

"Jesus, should I leave now before you two start fucking?" Marcus asks, sounding a little mortified.

"Nah, don't leave. Lexi liked it when you watched her."

My mouth drops open, and I slap at Ayden's shoulder. "My vagina is officially closed for business to you, Ayden Mitchell!"

Marcus roars laughing as Ayden pouts like a fucking three-year-old, and I push back from him, turning my glare to Marcus with my finger in an angry point.

"And as for *you,* Marcus Grady, you will keep your mouth shut about what happened. You will *not* tell a single soul, and we will *never* speak of this again."

Marcus stops laughing abruptly when I poke my finger to his chest, and he nods, pretending to button up his lips.

"And since you arseholes are being such douchecanoes tonight, you can do these dishes without me." I storm out of the kitchen like a woman in a wild rage when, really, I'm not at all. Sure, I don't want Marcus to tell anyone about this afternoon, and sure, Ayden is being a cheeky fucker, but I'm not mad. Just embarrassed and happy to never speak of it again.

I think about joining the olds in the living room but decide to give that a miss since I'm not into those soapy shows they love so much. Instead, I head out the back door to the old garage that the loft sits on top of, feeling the need to slip the gloves on and hit the bag Ayden bought me.

Just as I walk in the door and reach for the light switch, a hand wraps over my mouth, and I'm pulled back against a hard body. I try to scream as I'm dragged into the dark garage, but the sound is muffled by the hand. Kicking my legs, I try to struggle free, unable to loosen the hold on me before I'm spun around and pushed against the far wall with a hard thump. An *oomph* falls past my lips as the wind gets knocked from me.

A tall, shadowed figure looms over me, and before he even speaks, I know it's my dad.

"This is your last chance, Alexis. Tell me where the file is?"

My chest rises and falls in ragged breaths as I look at the familiar blue eyes barely visible in the dark space of the garage.

"I've already told you what I know. There's no file. The account is practically empty."

"Bullshit! If it's empty, then where is the money?" My dad grits between his teeth, shoving his forearm into my neck when I try to step forward.

"I think Mum gave it away to charity," I lie, and he sees right through it, pressing his arm harder against my neck, starting to cut off my air.

"Why are you lying, Alexis? If you just tell me the truth, then I will leave and never look back."

"I'm not lying." I grit out past the pressure on my oesophagus. "There's really only fifty dollars in the bank account. I don't know any more than that other than there is no file. There hasn't been for years."

My dad's rumbling growl echoes in the small space, and he steps back from me, raking his hands through his dishevelled blond hair. I'd like to think he won't hurt me, but I'd be an idiot to believe that. He spent years torturing Mum. He handed me over to his sicko son. He's capable of gruesome acts, and I'd be a fool to underestimate him.

"Your mother said it was in the house, Alexis. Why would she lie to me?"

I scoff. "Ah, I'm guessing to piss you off."

His blue eyes pierce me with a murderous glare as his chest rises and falls in anger. He studies me for so long that I think he's going to turn around and walk away.

I thought wrong.

His lip curls as a snarl passes his tongue, and he leaps for me. I scream as loud as I can, darting to the side to try to dodge him, but he's on me so fast and with a force that matches, if not outdoes, Mike's. Fisting his hand into my hair, he spins me and drags me against his chest again, moving his hand back over my mouth as he marches forward towards the door. Again, I kick and flail, using one hand to claw at his hand in my hair, and my other hand fights to pry his hand from my mouth.

The cool night air hits me as he manoeuvres us into the backyard, and I try to scream louder, my eyes darting around, trying to see through the windows of Marcus' house, hoping to catch someone's attention. It's useless, though. No one sees me. No one hears me. No one knows my dad is stealing me from under their noses.

As my dad passes through the open back gate, he keeps a firm hold on me despite my attempts to dislodge him and drags me down the driveway towards the street. There's a police patrol parked out front, right? My dad can't possibly think he'll get past them.

"Hey!" A voice roars from behind us, and my dad spins with me still in his grip to face Ayden.

My eyes widen when I see his face contort as he takes in the situation, and then, before my eyes, I watch as a switch is flipped, and Ayden's face transforms into a dark, menacing beast. An animalistic growl comes from him right before he charges towards us. I rejoice when I hear my dad curse in panic, and he retreats, running backwards.

At the last moment, my dad releases his hold on me, and Ayden yells, "Duck, Lexi!"

I do as he says, ducking and falling to the ground as Ayden leaps and sails over me, his eyes trained on my dad, his fist raised in a tight ball. The crunch is loud and is followed by a thump and a thud as I scramble on the ground to get away. When I turn back, I see Ayden and my dad in an intense fight. Punches are thrown by each of them. Growls and hisses drift up into the night sky as they tumble over the concrete driveway, like a pair of lions in a melee.

"Lexi!" Marcus skids to a stop by my side and quickly pulls me up off the ground to his side.

"We have to help Ayden," I cry, even though it's clear that he's holding his own. I've seen hints of his dark side, and he's told me a little about his past, but this guy, *no*, this *man* in front of me now, fighting with the ferocity to kill, is a side of him I haven't witnessed.

"HELP!" Marcus screams at the top of his lungs. Over and over, he screams as Ayden's fists connect with my dad's face, while my dad starts to weaken, only able to get the odd one in.

Light suddenly fills the driveway as Barb and Tony come out of the house. Unfortunately, the sudden illumination distracts Ayden momentarily, which is long enough for my dad to land a blow that topples Ayden off him, falling still on the ground.

"Ayden!" I scream and try to run for him, but Marcus holds me back as my dad staggers to a stand, takes one last look at me with blood smearing his cheek and jaw, and darts into the darkened front garden just as the police round the fence line to enter the driveway.

"He went that way!" Tony yells, taking chase with the police.

I wrestle Marcus off me and dart towards Ayden, tears burning tracks down my cheeks. I land to a knee scraping stop at Ayden's side, taking his head in my hands.

"Ayden! Ayden!" It's all I can manage, and Marcus joins me on Ayden's other side, nudging him repeatedly until a low groan greets us.

"Stop fucking nudging me." Ayden's words are a low rumble before his lids flutter open, and those ocean eyes peer up at me past dark lashes.

"Ayden," I whisper, tears dripping off my lips and chin.

"I've died and gone to heaven." His lips head north in a lazy grin, and I fall apart in a messy, smiling, crying heap as I cradle his head to me.

Thirty-Six

H e got away! My dad fucking got away! The Fox Pines Police Department is useless!

Well, all except Jason and maybe Burt. For fuck's sake, he was right there. Ayden had weakened him, and still, the police couldn't catch him.

To say I'm pissed is a fucking understatement. Unfortunately for the patrol that didn't do their job properly, and the other two officers who arrived afterwards to take our statements, they heard all about it from my lips. I've had enough. It's fucking laughable how ridiculous it is that my dad was able to sneak past the patrol in the first place and come right into the backyard of the Grady property. Then they lost him when they took chase on foot.

Andrea had rushed home from work after Barb called her, and she went into nurse mode, checking over her son and making him stay seated on the couch. Ayden kept relatively quiet through all the questions and answered what he could, but I didn't miss the smirk he kept trying to hide when I gave the police a piece of my mind.

He has the shadow of a black eye forming and a fat lip, but all in all, I'd say he fared better than my dad did. If this situation weren't so serious, I'd be dragging him up to his loft right now to show him the lady boner he gave me when I witnessed the beast inside him.

After the police leave and Andrea stops doting over her son, understandably, Barb makes us all hot chocolates, and we sit around the dining table, chatting about what happened.

My mum is quiet. She's hardly spoken throughout the whole incident, and as she stares into her cup of steaming hot chocolate, I recognise the guilt she is trying to hide. I've felt that exact same guilt so many times over the past couple of months. Guilt for dragging other people into my mess. Guilt for other people getting hurt because of me.

Standing from my chair, I release Ayden's hand, which was wound tightly with mine under the table, and walk around the other side to my mum, squatting down next to her chair. She looks to the side, tilting her brown eyes down to meet mine, her brows meeting in the middle.

"Stop." Keeping my voice soft, I rest my hand on her leg.

"Stop what?"

"Stop blaming yourself. This is not your fault." My words induce my mum's tears, and her hand comes to rest over mine on her leg.

"I can't help it. If I didn't torment your father so much about the file, he would never have come here."

Offering my mum a sympathetic smile, I rise up a little closer so only she can hear. "He deserves everything he gets, Mum. How he chooses to react is on him. It's a lesson I've had to learn myself. One I'm still learning. He will never learn it, though. He will always blame everyone else for his shortcomings instead of taking responsibility for being a shitty person. This. Is. Not. Your. Fault."

My mum's eyes warm, softening at the corners as she studies my face. "I'm lucky to have you, Lexi."

"I'm lucky to have you, too." I smile, meaning each word.

For so long, I thought she was a shitty mum, but there was a reason behind everything she did. Even though the drugs changed her persona, she never stopped trying to protect me, even when I didn't realise it.

Mum's phone starts to ring with Burt's name flashing across the screen. I smile at her and nod to her phone, letting her know it's okay for her to take his call. I stand from beside her chair and make my way around the table back to Ayden, who hasn't taken his eyes off me once, when my mum's concerned voice draws my attention again. It draws everyone's attention. Her eyes widen before they dart to me, and when she ends the call, she clears her throat to speak.

"Our house is on fire."

For a few long, tense moments, we all stay silently rooted where we are before everyone leaps into action at the same time, running around frantically trying to find shoes and jackets to slip on. Within a couple of minutes, we pile into Andrea's car, and she speeds through the sleepy streets of Fox Pines to get to our house. The house that holds all of our nightmares.

Fire trucks and emergency vehicles block the mouth of our street, so we leap from the car before Andrea has even parked it, and run up the street. Ayden has my hand, running faster than me, dragging me along, which is fine with me because I'm not watching where I'm going, not when all I can see is flames rising into the dark sky from my house.

Coming to a stop on the other side of the road, we watch past the busy fire crew who are running around trying to connect hoses while some firefighters run into my burning house.

"Holy shit." I think the words, but it's Ayden who says them as we take a step back, the heat from the flames almost too much to bear.

"Fuck, Lexi. I'm sorry," Marcus says, coming to my other side.

I don't say anything. I can't. All I'm able to do is watch on as the flames build in intensity.

"Lexi." My mum's cry gains my attention, and Marcus steps out of the way so she can hug me to her side. She's upset, but as I take her in, I see a hint of happiness. Why would she be happy?

Glancing back at the engulfed house, I realise I feel a little happiness, too. I hate that fucking house. It holds nothing but toxic memories, and the fact that it's burning right now is fucking deserving, if you ask me.

A couple of firefighters come rushing out of the front door, calling to their commander that the house is all clear but is not safe to go back into and that the line needs to be moved back. I don't know what that means, but when a neighbour from up the road who is hovering on the sidelines having a sticky beak calls out, dread fills my gut.

"There's someone in there, on the second floor!"

The firefighters turn to where my neighbour is pointing, and that's when I see who it is—my dad.

"Where is it, Ruth?!" he bellows from my shattered bedroom window upstairs, and the firefighters yell for him to climb out the window, that it isn't safe to be inside.

He doesn't listen. "Where's the file, Ruth!?" He screams out into the night, sending chills up my spine.

"Mum," I cry as she moves from my side and takes a step towards the house.

"Get out of there, Max!" she screams, cupping her hands around her mouth, trying to force the words past the roaring of the flames.

My dad screams with rage like a crazy man and steps back from the window into my room and closer to the flames licking up the walls.

"Dad!" The moment the words leave my lips, the house explodes.

The force of the explosion throws us backwards. As if in slow motion, I feel the rush of heat as it passes over our falling bodies, singeing and scalding while debris rains over us and the surrounding houses.

After a dizzying moment, I prop up on my elbows next to my mum, whose face is a mixture of stunned and devastated.

"Mum," I whisper, and without taking her eyes off the inferno, she reaches out, grasping my hand.

"Lex." Ayden sits up by my side, his hands roaming over me frantically, checking for injuries. I can't look at him. All I can do is look at my mum.

"No one was meant to be in the house," she whispers, and my eyes widen before I glance at Ayden. He heard what she said, too.

"It was meant to be empty," she whispers again, and I quickly throw my arms around her and pull her to my side, pressing her cheek against mine.

"Mum," I whisper, "you need to stop talking."

"Max wasn't meant to be inside," she whispers back, and I pull away to place my hands on each side of her face, forcing her to look at me instead of the fire.

"Mum, listen to me," I growl, her brown eyes looking confused. "Are you listening?"

It takes her a moment, but I see when the fog starts to clear in her eyes, and I know she is listening. "Stop. Talking."

Understanding dawns and her hand flies to her mouth. "Oh my god." She looks around frantically to see if anyone overheard her.

"It's okay. I don't think anyone heard, but let's not talk about that here," I whisper, and she nods.

We both turn back, huddled together, watching the flames as the firefighters start to douse the inferno with water. There are emergency services officers running around everywhere, but amongst the chaos, we stay sitting in one of our neighbour's front yards, where the force of the explosion left us.

The soothing touch of Ayden rubs over my back constantly, and Barb comes up to do the same to my mum, offering her support she probably isn't used to receiving. At some stage, Simon turns up with Garrett and Shaun, and Jared comes with his parents. I guess Marcus contacted the guys. I don't know, and I don't ask. I'm just glad that they are here with me to watch the house that held my nightmares, my mum's nightmares, turn to ash, and with it, my dad.

Silent tears stream down my face as bittersweet feelings play with my emotions. The monsters, both of them, are dead. Gone. They can no longer hurt us or anyone else, yet the little girl in me, the innocent one who looked up to her dad, her hero, mourns his loss.

I remind myself that I lost him weeks ago when he revealed his true self. Maybe even long before that, when he stopped returning home. He had me fooled for so long, and now, the toxic man he was can no longer taint this world.

It's well into the early hours of the morning by the time the fire is out, and police are left to rummage through the wreck with a couple of firefighters to search for my dad's body. An ambulance is parked off to the side, and when they pull the gurney from the back, I know they got the call that a body has been found. Or whatever is left of a body.

"Mrs West?" Officer Zimora approaches us, dressed in uniform and acting formally.

Barb helps my mum up off the ground while I stay in place on the grass, looking up at them.

"I'm sorry to inform you that we have recovered a body in the fire and believe it is your husband, Maxwell West. An autopsy will confirm his DNA, but we don't believe it could be anyone else." Jason's eyes flick to mine, and even though the monster is gone, more tears spring free.

My mum doesn't speak. She just nods, still crying too.

"Why don't you go home and get some sleep? We can catch up tomorrow if you would like to go over any other details," Jason says, and my mum nods before letting Barbara lead her away.

Squatting down on his haunches, Jason addresses me. "I'm sorry, Lexi. I know this is yet another terrible thing to happen, but if you can take anything positive from this, at least it's all over now." He's not being a cop right now. He's being a friend.

"Thank you," I say through my tears, and he shoots me a sympathetic smile before standing and walking away.

"Lex." Ayden's low voice rumbles quietly next to my ear. "I think someone wants to talk to you."

Confused, I look at him, and when he turns his eyes towards the shadows across the road, I squint, trying to see what he sees. My heart rate picks up speed when I see the shadowed silhouette of a small frame that looks very much like Valarie.

"Val?" I whisper and stand up from the grassy ground.

Walking hurriedly across the road to the shadows, I come face to face with my twelve-year-old neighbour, Valarie.

"Hey Lexi. I'm really sorry about your house. And your dad. Not your brother, though. I'm not sorry he's dead." The sweet innocence that I'd become so familiar with is void in Val's tone. There is no sweetness, just a hardness that only comes from experiencing unimaginable pain.

"Can I hug you?" My lip wobbles as I speak, and when she nods, I wrap my arms around her so tight that I think I'll never be able to let go.

"I miss you," Val whispers in my ear before she returns my hug, and we stand wrapped in each other's arms, crying silently for the longest time.

When we finally pull apart, Val swipes her tears away like they scald her cheeks, and then she sucks in a deep breath, the hardness I saw before returning.

"Mum's moving us up to New South Wales to live closer to her sister. I don't want to go, but I don't get a say."

"Oh." My heart sinks. This is because of me.

"Keep your Instagram account open." She insists. "When mum stops watching me like a hawk, I'll make a fake account so I can contact you. If that's okay?" Val shifts nervously, and I smile.

"Of course it's okay. But try not to get into trouble. Your mum loves you. That's why she is overprotective."

She smirks. "You call it overprotective. I call it psycho."

I laugh before Val's next words wipe the smile off my face.

"Thank you for killing him, Lexi. He deserved to die."

It's heartbreaking to hear those words come from a twelve-year-old. I may have slayed that demon for her, but I know from experience that the demons in her head are now what will plague her for a very long time.

"He did deserve to die." I agree with Val, and she gives me a nod.

"I'd better go before mum finds me gone."

"Good idea. Talk soon, okay?" I don't want to let her go. I want to grab her and hug her for the rest of time, so when she offers me one last tiny smile before turning her back to sink back into the shadows of her front yard, I fight the urge to reach out to her, knowing that I have to let her go.

Exhaustion sends us crashing to our beds when we finally get back to the Gradys'. We don't even shower away the soot and dirt, which is a regret when we wake at lunchtime on Friday smelling like a campfire.

I shower first, and by the time I return, Ayden has stripped the bed and taken our dirty things to the washer. I wonder if he realises how fucking hot it is that he does things like cleaning and washing? He's a keeper. I'm never letting him go.

While Ayden showers, I go in search of my mum. Last night was a lot. This whole week has been a lot, and my emotions are all over the place. Surely hers are, too, especially after the odd things she said last night while we watched our house burn with my dad inside.

I find her sitting on the bed in the lilac bedroom that was mine a short time ago. She looks younger than she is with her legs crossed as she scrolls through something on her phone.

"Mum?" My words draw her attention, and when she sees me standing in the doorway, she pats the bed next to her.

"Come in. Close the door."

I do as she asks and shut the door before climbing up next to her to take a look at her phone screen when she angles it towards me.

"There are a few rental properties that are close by. I figured it would be nice for you to stay close to your friends." My mum's smile is small and unsure, so I ease her worry by beaming happily at her.

"I'd love to stay close to Ayden and Marcus. Andrea too." I shrug, and her smile widens.

"Andrea is lovely. I'm so grateful she was there for you while I got my shit together. She's been here for me, too, helping me sort through my own issues. She's also connected me with a local addiction support group. She's going to come with me for my first session tomorrow."

"Wow, Mum. That's so great."

"We're going to get through this, Lexi." Sighing, my mum drops her phone to the bed and stares at her hands for a moment. "You make me want to be a better person."

Confused, I frown at my mum's words, and she brings her eyes to mine.

"Your strength is inspiring. You are so much stronger than I have ever been. Your drive to fight for what's right is so honourable. I'm so proud of you, Lexi, and one day, when I've worked through the mess in my head and faced the things I've been ignoring, I hope you'll be proud of me, too."

All I can do is smile because I want more than anything for her to want more for herself. But my emotions are shot, and I know if I try to speak, I will cry again. I'm so sick of crying.

We use that moment to hug it out, and when we finally pull apart, I feel stronger and know we can't avoid this next conversation.

"Did you burn our house down?" My words are whispered, just in case there's anyone outside the room.

"I arranged it, yes," my mum whispers, her brown eyes looking distant. "It was just meant to be an insurance job. We both hated that house, and it holds too many evils to just sell and let someone else live in it. So, I made arrangements for it to look like an electrical fault. Your dad wasn't meant to be there, Lexi. I had no idea. I swear I didn't."

"I know you didn't, Mum," I whisper back. "But who did you arrange it with? Like, how do you even do that sort of thing?"

I see the smallest devious look pass over my mum's face before she hides it.

"I have connections."

"Criminal connections?" I ask, dumbfounded, and she nods. Then it dawns on me. "Ringo?"

She shrugs, sliding off the bed, but I don't miss the grin.

Holy shit.

My mum arranged an insurance job with Ringo.

Maybe we are more alike than I thought.

"We won't speak of this again. What's done is done. I will always carry the weight of your dad's death, but it's one I can bear knowing he can't hurt us anymore."

I nod in agreement before a tap on the bedroom door interrupts us.

"Lex. There's someone here to see you." Ayden's voice comes through the door, and I look at my mum, but she shrugs. I was hoping she might have known if we were expecting someone. Maybe it's Abbey or Rhys.

The thought has me leaping off the bed, and I open the bedroom door to find Ayden's kind eyes. His serious expression has me hesitating with a frown.

"Who's at the door?"

"It's Tasha." His eyes roam my face, trying to read me.

"Oh." I'm disappointed that it's not Abbey but curious as to why Tasha is here to see me, so I hurry downstairs to find her standing awkwardly in the small entrance of Marcus' house. When she sees me, the eyes that have so often glared daggers at me hold nothing but sorrow.

"Sorry for just dropping by. I needed to come and see you before I chickened out."

Nodding, I gesture behind me. "Do you want to come in?"

Tasha shakes her head, her tight curls bouncing as she does. "I won't stay long. I need to apologise."

"Um. Okay." I'm not sure what else to say. My typical reaction to Tasha is to want to smack the bitch off her face, but since that reaction is missing, I'm unsure what to do.

"I honestly never thought the news reports were true. He told me they were lies, and I believed him. I don't know why I didn't believe you, Lexi. You've always been a decent person, so I can only think that perhaps I believed Mike because I wanted to." I cringe when I hear his name, but Tasha continues. "Probably because I've always been jealous of you."

My brows shoot up at her admission.

"You're just so naturally pretty. People are drawn to you. Not just because you're pretty, but because you're a nice person. I enjoyed seeing you out of sorts. I liked seeing you slowly lose control and thought you deserved to know what it's like to have a shit life. For some reason, I wanted to believe you were making it all up for attention and not because the guy I had been crushing on was a fucking sicko that got off on molesting his sister."

My face heats with anger. I feel like I could smack a bitch right now.

"Imagine my surprise when people liked you more instead of thinking you a freak when all that stuff came out. Marcus and the guys stood by you stronger than

562

ever, and I fucking hated it. So when Mike came tapping on my bedroom window one night, declaring his love for me, I fell deeper into my need to make you hurt. I swear I would have never done what I did if I had thought your brother actually did those things. I will never forgive myself for what I put you through, on top of what you were already dealing with." She shakes her head. "I'm so fucking sorry, Lexi." Tears fall from Tasha's eyes, leaving a trail over her rosy cheeks.

At first, I'm not sure what to say. It's like a slap in the face to hear her admit those things, but then I remember what she did for me. She risked her life to call for help and try to cut me free. She hid under the bed, all while knowing that if Mike caught her, he'd likely kill her. In the end, she did the right thing.

"Thank you for not leaving me alone with him and for staying and risking your own life. We will never be friends, Tasha, but I'm alive and here because you cut one of my hands free and left me with the knife. If you hadn't done that, then he would have won."

Sobs make it hard for Tasha to speak, and Ayden comes to my side, holding out a box of tissues. Tasha grabs a handful muttering a *thanks* before trying to breathe through her tears and compose herself.

Ayden doesn't leave my side. Wrapping his arm around my shoulders, he tugs me close as we both look at Tasha.

"Staying there with you was the only decent thing I've ever done, Lexi. But let's be honest, if I had pulled my head out of my arse sooner, then that day would have never happened." She clears her throat, trying to hold back more tears. "Anyway, I thought you'd be happy to know that I won't be back at school next term. My parents are sending me to my aunt's farm up in the high country. They say the clean air will do me good." She huffs. "Like what the fuck am I meant to do, learn how to ride a horse or something?"

I can't hide my smirk, and she sees it, her own following.

"You're going to love knowing how miserable I'll be, aren't you?"

I shrug. "Maybe a little."

Tasha ducks her head, hiding her grin. "Well, good luck with everything, Lexi. I hope there is nothing but happiness coming your way."

Before I can respond, Tasha turns and walks back out the front door.

"Did that really just happen?" I whisper, and Ayden chuckles.

"Yep, it really did."

It's hard to imagine Tasha on a farm with cows and horses and chickens. It's actually quite funny trying to picture it.

Not long after Tasha's visit, my mum asks Ayden and me to go for a walk with her, which is kind of strange, but as we round the corner up the road, it all starts to make sense.

Two houses into the next street is a rental house with an agent waiting for us outside the cutest cottage style house, which matches the others in the area.

Standing with charm, the grey weatherboard house boasts white framed windows and trims. A brick-paved path leads through a colonial-style wired gate to a rich timber deck resting under a short veranda. Just by looking at the façade, I already know I love it, but when we head inside, my mum's eyes light up, and I know the deal is sealed.

This house holds character and warmth, with hints of modern living to complement the historic features. On the ground level, there are two living zones with high ceilings and featured mouldings, two large bedrooms, a huge bathroom, and a well thought out laundry. While upstairs in a cute attic loft is a cosy bedroom with a sitting area, small bathroom, and walk-in robe.

While Ayden and I explore the house, my mum speaks rental jargon with the agent.

"You like it, hey?" Ayden rests his chin on my shoulder, pulling my back to his chest as we look through the cute attic window to the courtyard at the back of the house.

"I do like it. I could see myself feeling at home here." I admit.

"That's good because we move in next week." My mum's voice startles us, and I spin out of Ayden's arms.

"What?"

She grins. "I just signed the paperwork. Of course, we need to go shopping to buy... well, everything, but this house is ours to rent for the next six months."

"Six months?" The thought of only staying six months annoys me.

"If we like it here, we can buy it after that. The owners want to sell it and are happy to wait." My mum's smile is genuinely happy—something I need to see her wear more often because she looks beautiful like that. "You can have this room if you want. I hate the thought of having to walk upstairs all the time."

Ayden chuckles, and I giggle before approaching my mum and throwing my arms around her neck for a long hug.

Thirty-Seven

My heart thuds with each beat of the music blasting from the hundreds of speakers to fill the stadium. The smile plastered to my face matches Ayden's as we jump up and down in the front row of the Archer 9 concert. I've never felt so much happiness and so free as I let the lyrics and music strip away my worries. Sweat rolls down my back, and my hair sticks to my neck, but I don't care. I'm having too much fun living in this moment with Ayden.

We arrived in the city earlier today, and I thought we were going to stay in Peter's apartment, but Ayden had made other arrangements.

He surprised me by pulling the rusty old car up to a five-star hotel not far from the stadium, checked us into a room he had already booked, and took me up to the twentieth floor to the most luxurious hotel room I have ever seen. It wasn't hard, given that the only hotel rooms I have ever glimpsed were at the two star Foxy Pine Motel.

I may have done a girly squeal and jumped on the huge bed like it was a trampoline. I also may have gone through every single cupboard and drawer in the suite, clapping excitedly when I found the mini bar, the plush dressing gowns, and the cute little slipper things. Finding the tray of little toiletries in the bathroom sent me over the edge with excitement, and Ayden threw me over his shoulder, taking me to the bed, where he teased me with kisses that sent us into a frenzy of sex which nearly made us late to the concert.

Wrapping up yet another of their songs I love and know every word to, Demi Archer, the lead singer, wipes sweat from her forehead with a small towel before chucking it at one of the roadies at the side of the stage.

"Are we all having fun tonight?"

The crowd roars and cheers at Demi's question, bringing a smile to her face as she nods and then speaks to one of her guitarists.

"I'm glad you're all having fun, but for a moment, I'd like to get serious." Demi's voice echoes through the stadium, and the audience cheers in agreement.

"Life isn't always easy. In fact, for some people, life can be downright cruel. Downright heavy." The audience agrees with *yeahs* and *too rights*. "And tonight, there is a young lady in the audience who has faced the most unthinkable things. Things that no girl should ever have to endure. Things no *one* should *ever* have to endure."

My heart races, and my eyes glass over at Demi's words, and I feel Ayden tug me closer, placing a kiss into my hair.

"This girl is strong! This girl is a fighter! This girl, like so many, carries a weight around that is invisible to everyone, but not to her. Not to those close to her. That's why I am dedicating this next song to her and to every girl and boy out there who *has,* and who *does* bear that burden."

The crowd roars in approval, and when I glance around, I see some people crying, just like me.

"Ayden?" I turn to him, and he smiles down at me, gesturing his head back to the stage.

"It's a Linkin Park song, but we are going to perform this song tonight in the cover version by Fame on Fire. This is Heavy!"

The band roars to life with the crowd, while tears filled with mixed emotions, but mostly happiness, stain my cheeks. Coming to the front of the stage where we stand, Demi drops to one knee and reaches her hand out to me. I take it in my shaky hand as Ayden holds me tight against him and I lean forward when Demi leans down to speak to me.

"This is for you, Lexi." I stand frozen, staring at Archer 9's lead singer as she offers me a warm smile, part of me frozen in place because this is surreal, but the other part is frozen in place because, in that short moment, she lets me see into her eyes, and I can see it. She has experienced the same sort of pain I have.

Then the vulnerability vanishes as she lifts the microphone to her lips, all while still holding my hand, and starts to sing the words of the song Ayden found for me. The song titled with one word that has defined my life so far. Heavy.

I let myself fall into the lyrics of the song as Demi eventually joins the band on stage, singing this dedication, not just to me but to so many who have suffered their own battles.

When the song finishes, I turn in Ayden's arms and look up into those familiar eyes that own me. "You did this?"

He shrugs, giving me a lopsided grin.

"I love you, Ayden Mitchell." My words turn his grin into a full-blown smile, and he leans down, taking my lips in his, showing me how he feels about me with that one simple act.

We stand entwined in each other's arms in the throes of the concert, all sound falling away as we get wrapped up in the kiss. I can't be sure how long we kiss for, but when we come up for air, the concert is exploding, and we join back in sharing the experience together.

Archer 9 teases us with a couple of encores before taking their final bow, and the concert-goers head out of the stadium speaking of their favourite songs while we are led backstage by a couple of bouncers.

My heart is in my throat with excitement and anticipation of talking with Demi and the Archer 9 crew. I used to follow Demi's YouTube videos back when I was a 'twelvie' when she used to rock out in her garage. I've admired her from afar for so long that the idea of meeting her nearly sends me packing, but then I remember how kind she was when she took my hand and how she briefly showed me her vulnerability.

Passing through some security checkpoints, Peter meets us on the other side with some other MitchWave staff wearing the logo on their shirts, and before I know it, I'm standing face to face with Demi Archer.

"How did you like the concert, Lexi?" I blink like an idiot at Demi before I'm able to speak.

"It was amazing." I smile, and Demi returns it, flashing her white teeth behind purple lips, her purple hair matching the colour. "It's an honour to meet you."

"Actually. The honour is all mine," Demi says, her face turning serious. "I hope you didn't mind me coming to see you on stage. Peter told me your story, Lexi. I'm so sorry that such awful things have happened to you. I wanted to do something for you, and after Peter spoke with Ayden, he thought you'd like to hear us sing you that song."

I nod. "I loved it. Thank you. I didn't mind at all."

"That's good." She smiles before turning serious. "I have a pretty grim past as well. I want you to know that you aren't alone. Unfortunately, there are a lot of people, not just girls, who have endured unthinkable acts by the people who should have protected them. That's why I started the Archer Network. Have you heard of it?"

"The Archer Network? Yes, isn't there something about that on our tickets?" Upon hearing me say that, Ayden pulls out a ticket and hands it to me. There, in the bottom corner, is a small logo for The Archer Network.

"Yes," Demi says, smiling at me when I look back up from the ticket. "The Archer Network is something I started a few years ago. We work closely with Child Services and local authorities to help young people who have suffered violence in their homes to have a new start. We step in when there is no family left to help them, and we offer better opportunities than what the government can offer by relocating the kids that are put on our radar. We send them to live with a family that is approved by our network, and we make sure siblings are kept together and that they receive the very best care."

"Wow. I've never heard of that before."

"It's only been up and running for a few years in Australia, and since it's privately run, most people don't know about it until we present it to them. Not everyone takes us up on our offers. As you can imagine, it's hard for someone who has been through an ordeal to trust anyone."

"This is legal?" I ask, and she smiles, nodding.

"We have a close relationship with Child Services. We work by their referral."

"That's so cool." I smile, glancing at Ayden and Peter, who are both smiling warmly.

"I thought you might like it. Ayden told me you've been thinking about helping others when you finish school."

I nod, not sure why we are having this conversation until Demi speaks again.

"If you're interested, Lexi, I'd like to offer you the opportunity to join our Archer Network team over the summer for a couple of weeks, so you can see what our program does. It might help you decide what you want to do with your future."

"Really?" I squeak.

"Lex, that would be amazing." Ayden smiles, lifting my hand in his and bringing it to his lips to press a kiss to my skin.

"It really would." I beam at Demi, and she nods, looking pleased.

"I'll get Peter to send you some paperwork. In the meantime, let's go introduce you to the rest of the band."

My head is in a spin as Ayden and I spend the next hour talking with the other band members before we part ways and make our way back to the hotel. To say I'm exhausted is an understatement.

Emotionally exhausted.

I think I need to spend a few days in this hotel room just eating, sleeping, and hopefully having sex.

Ayden retreats to the bathroom, and a moment later, I hear the bath running. I don't know if he intends to have a bath alone or not, but I'm getting in whether he likes it or not. When I stroll into the bathroom wearing my birthday suit, Ayden's brows shoot to his dark hairline as his eyes roam over my naked skin. I can feel the burn of his gaze as he looks at me, and when I reach the oversized claw bath that is filling with steaming water and bubbles floating on the surface, I don't hesitate to step in.

"Too irresistible to wait until it's finished filling?" Ayden chuckles, and I nod as I lay back in the low line of water that only covers half of my body.

"Yes." I smile lazily up at Ayden, who is perched on the bath's edge, still fully dressed. "I hope you intend on joining me in here?"

"Absolutely." He stands. "Get comfy. I'll be in soon."

I watch his back retreat and pull the door closed, leaving me to soak in the delicious heat of the water as it continues to fill. I take the moment of quiet to close my eyes and try to calm my brain. It's been going a hundred miles an hour since the concert.

A few minutes later, Ayden strolls back in wearing one of the plush robes and carrying a tray with a couple of drinks. Offering me a sinful grin and a glass of what looks like raspberry soft drink, I accept the drink and take a sip.

Vodka and raspberry.

Nice.

"What's your drink?" I ask, eyeing Ayden's glass, which looks like cola.

"Just cola." He responds, shooting me a wink.

"No whiskey or gin?"

"Nope. I try to avoid drinking if I can." Putting his glass on the bench behind the bath, Ayden unties the robe, and I keep my eyes on him as I take another sip. He should be a stripper. He's hot enough. Fucking sinful, really. But I'll kick a chick in her box if she ogles my man. So maybe he should just be *my* stripper?

"What are you thinking about?" Ayden grins at my expression, and I shrug before placing my glass on the ledge.

"That you should be a stripper. But only for me."

A belly laugh rumbles out of his throat, but I remain serious.

"You don't drink ever?" Have I seen him drink before? I can't remember if I have.

"I have an occasional beer if I think it will make people suspicious if I don't. My addiction wasn't to alcohol, but it's still a substance, so I'd rather just not have anything."

Ayden's robe falls to the floor, and my eyes instantly go to his cock. I'm used to seeing it hard and standing to attention, but even though it's not like that now, he still looks like a God.

"Lexi, if you don't stop looking at me that way, our bath session isn't going to last very long."

I shake my head. "I don't care. I want to taste you."

"Fuck." He hisses, and then, as if my words are magic, his cock starts to grow. "Stop looking at me like I'm a piece of meat." His voice is playful as he moves to cover his junk.

"Don't you dare cover that." I growl, and when he drops his hand away with a knowing smirk on his face, I continue. "You are a piece of meat, and I want it in my mouth."

Ayden curses under his breath, and I watch him lengthen, thicken, harden and stand upright.

My mouth waters.

"You're asking for trouble," he growls, and I nod.

"I am. You'd better punish me." I flick my eyes up from under my dark lashes, and he growls again.

"Sit forward and make room for me."

I do as he says, and he steps in the steaming hot water to sit behind me, shutting off the stream as I settle back against him. When I feel his erection press against my back, I squirm around, rubbing it with my back, causing friction between our bodies.

"Behave." His lips brush my ear as he wraps his arms around my front, his hands close over my shoulders, holding me still.

I pout.

"Relax against me, beautiful."

Sighing, I do as he asks and close my eyes as he brushes his fingers up and down my arms, over my neck and then down my front to my aching breasts.

"How are you feeling?" he whispers against my ear.

"Horny."

Ayden chuckles and then nips my ear. "Not what I meant. How is your body feeling? How are your emotions?"

"Again, my answer is horny. The only ache I have is between my legs, where I need your cock."

"Fuck, Lex." He hisses against my ear right before his lips find my neck. His kisses are searing, and my moan dances off the tiled walls. One of his hands slides up to work on my nipple, and the other travels south, torturously slow under the water.

My pelvis rises, greedy to close the distance sooner, and the moment his finger brushes over my bud, I nearly come then and there. My fingers dig into his legs that cage me in, while my pelvis thrusts up to meet the friction of his fingers, needing more.

"You're already so close," he whispers, and I nod.

"Yes. I'm hungry for you."

Ayden doesn't make me wait any longer, his fingers slipping down between my folds to sink into my heat. I cry out as the stretch sends desperate pleasure to my core, and I grind against Ayden's hand, watching each time his fingers disappear inside me.

"You're so fucking hot, Lexi. I want to do this with you forever."

"Yes," I cry out, grinding harder.

"Come for me, beautiful."

With another couple of thrusts of his fingers, he presses them upwards to my top wall, and with a flick of his thumb, Ayden sends me crashing over the edge in a body wracking orgasm. My screaming moans bounce off the tiled walls as he milks me over and over, prolonging my high, and by the time I come down, the bathwater is draining, and Ayden is moving me around. I'm confused, but I don't question it, probably because I've lost the ability to speak after that orgasm.

Before I realise what's happening, Ayden drags me back up onto his lap and spreads my legs open to sit on either side of his.

"Give me a sec." Ayden releases his hold on my hips before I hear the knowing sound of a condom wrapper tearing open. A few moments later, Ayden returns his hands to my hips and presses a kiss to my spine before lowering me to slowly sink down on his hard cock. The stretch is addictive. His length spearing deep, hitting me in just the right place as we start to move together. With Ayden positioned behind me in the empty tub, he snakes his hand up to grip my breast as his head rests forward over my shoulder, watching where our bodies join.

"I fucking love you." His husky tone is all sex.

"I fucking love you, too." I hiss through the pleasure-pain of each thrust as our movements make squeaking noises against the wet tub.

"God, your pussy..." Ayden doesn't finish his sentence until he thrusts again, "is like molten lava."

"Is," pant, "that," pant, "good?"

"Fuck yes." His fingers dig into my hips, probably leaving marks. I hope they leave marks. I want his mark all over me.

"Lex." He pants as he thrusts up. "Move into a squat."

Before I can question him, he lifts me off his length and helps me stand over his legs before leading me down to squat over his cock.

As I squat down, I become very aware that Ayden has an intimate close-up view of my arse. The blush that creeps up my neck is searing, but I'm too turned on to shy away, and before I know it, the tip of his head is pushing into my aching entrance again, giving me back what I'm craving.

Ayden's moan sounds almost pained as my heat takes him in, but I don't slow. I continue to squat up and down on his length as heightened pleasure builds between us, reaching new sensations.

It takes a few goes before I find a good rhythm, but once I find it, I'm gone. Our grunts, moans, pants, and slaps fill the room, and the moment Ayden begins to stroke the puckered mouth of my arse, I explode. Wave after wave rips Ayden's own pleasure from him, and my legs give out, forcing me to collapse onto his length, taking him in as deep as my body can manage.

We stay connected, trying to regain our breath for quite some time, and when we finally part, Ayden leads me on shaky legs to the shower, where we warm back up. He gently washes me, taking his time to care for each part of my body and placing a small kiss to each part when he's done. By the time we tumble into bed, the clock ticks over to Sunday, and I yawn, feeling exhaustion closing in. Laying next to me under the covers, Ayden props his head up with one hand while the other strokes lazily over my tummy.

"I have something for you," Ayden whispers, and my sleepy eyes dart to his.

"Is it another orgasm?"

He chuckles. "I will always have them for you, but this is something different."

"You seem nervous," I whisper, trying not to look smug.

"I am nervous."

"Why?"

He shrugs. "I guess what I have might be a little corny."

My heart flutters like there are a million butterflies in my chest.

"Ayden. I will love anything you have for me."

His lips tug up in one corner, his dimple making an appearance. "I hope so."

When he doesn't say anything else, I giggle. "Are you going to give it to me?"

He thinks on that for a minute and then nods, rolling over in the bed and taking something from the bedside table.

I sit up eagerly, and he sits up next to me, the sheet dropping to his waist, his chiselled abs distracting me for a moment.

"So, I know we are still new, and we have our whole lives ahead of us, but I wanted you to have something, so you know that I'm always thinking about you, always loving you, and always dreaming of our future together."

Ayden opens his palm, and I glance down to see a braided leather band with a rose gold box-like metal plate encasing an inch of the band.

Glancing back to his eyes, I see they are studying me for my reaction, so I smile, feeling overwhelmed.

"Lexi, one day, I'm going to ask you to marry me. One day, I'm going to make you my wife. One day, if you want them, I want you to have my children, but until the day I put a ring on your finger, will you wear this bracelet?"

"Yes." The word rushes from me. I don't even need to think about it. I know I want him in my life forever.

I've seen Ayden truly smile before, but it didn't even come close to the way his face lights up now. Ducking his head, he fumbles with the clasp on the band and then fastens it to my wrist when I hold it out.

I'm smiling like an idiot as I glance down at it, and then I realise that the rose gold plate is engraved on all four sides.

My breath
My heart
My purpose
My life

With a full heart, I know that whatever path we take in our future, we will stand hand in hand and face this world together.

And just like that, things no longer feel so heavy.

THE END

Do you want more Dark High School Romance filled with violent themes but extra spice from the Fox Pines gang?
Check out the next series about Lexi's new quirky best friend, Rhys George and her trials and

tribulations with her addiction,
four friends that want to share her,
and an older man that is forbidden.
Read book 1 in the Insatiable Series now.
INSATIABLE KITTEN
https://books2read.com/KittenBookOne

Kitten - Book 1

Sarah JDs Books

READING ORDER

SERIES ONE

THE HEAVY HEARTS SERIES
A DARK HIGH SCHOOL ROMANCE

HEAVY (Book 1):
https://books2read.com/HeavyHeartsBook1
DEEP (Book 2):
https://books2read.com/HeavyHeartsBook2
BURIED (Book 3):
https://books2read.com/HeavyHeartsBook3

SERIES TWO

THE INSATIABLE SERIES
A DARK REVERSE HAREM HIGH SCHOOL ROMANCE

INSATIABLE KITTEN (Book 1):
https://books2read.com/KittenBookOne
TAINED KITTEN (Book 2):
https://books2read.com/Kitten2
VICIOUS KITTEN (Book 3):
https://books2read.com/KittenBookThree

STANDALONE

SUBBING FOR SANTA
A DARK CHRISTMAS ROMANCE WITH STALKER VIBES

SUBBING FOR SANTA:
https://books2read.com/SubbingForSanta

SERIES THREE

BREAKING THE SILENCE
A DARK HIGH SCHOOL ROMANCE

SILENT HUSH (Book 1):
https://books2read.com/BTSbook1
SAVAGE SCREAM (Book 2):
https://books2read.com/BTSbook2

SERIES FOUR
THE SCANDALOUS SECRETS SERIES
A DARK TABOO/FORBIDDEN MF ROMANCE
Three book shared world dark taboo series with **B. Lybaek, Sarah JD, and TL Hodel**.
(Books can be read as standalones)
DANTES STORM (Book 1) by B/ Lybaek:
https://books2read.com/SS1zon
LILY'S ASH (Book 2) by Sarah JD:
https://books2read.com/LilysAshSSbook2
AVERY'S FALL (Book 3) by TL Hodel:
https://books2read.com/SS3zon

STAY CONNECTED

Want to find out all the Tea before everyone else?
Join my VIP readers list to hear more about Lexi and the gang, plus the other characters that join them along the way.

SIGN UP HERE!
https://sarahjaneduncan.com/newsletter/

Want to join the conversation about your fav characters?
Join my Facebook Readers Group
SARAH'S VICIOUS KITTENS

JOIN HERE!
https://www.facebook.com/groups/
sarahjaneduncanreadersgroup

For more information on books & book signing events please visit:
sarahjaneduncan.com

STALK SARAH JD HERE:

Sarah JD

Sarah JD, also known as Sarah Jane Duncan, is a dark romance author living in Australia with Mr Duncan who stole her off the market back in high school.

Sarah can be found in her writing room plotting out her next smut filled romance filled with angst, violence, and themes so dark you should probably question why you love it so much.

Sarah writes about strong females who have to fight against the odds to find their power, their voice, and their truth. Her heroines possess the strength that only comes from being a survivor, and through their trauma, battles and struggles, they learn to trust again, and find love.

There's nothing easy about their stories. They are hard, gritty, and painfully heartbreaking at times. But what doesn't kill us makes us stronger, right? And when you throw in a swoon worthy guy, or an alphahole that you just want to slap, but also fall to your knees and obey, it's the recipe for a rollercoaster ride.

So buckle up. Read the warnings. And let yourself get lost in the dark stories Sarah creates.

www.ingramcontent.com/pod-product-compliance
Lightning Source LLC
Chambersburg PA
CBHW050058120726
47904CB00004B/1133